FAVOURITE
SPY STORIES

FAVOURITE
SPY STORIES

octopus

This edition first published in Great Britain
in 1981 by
Octopus Books Limited
59 Grosvenor Street
London W1

Reprinted 1982

ISBN 0 7064 1277 X

Illustrated by Mark Thomas

Printed in Hong Kong.

CONTENTS

TAYLOR'S RUN

JOHN LE CARRÉ

TAYLOR'S RUN

A fool lies here who tried to hustle the East.

KIPLING

Snow covered the airfield.

It had come from the north, in the mist, driven by the night wind, smelling of the sea. There it would stay all Winter, threadbare on the grey earth, an icy, sharp dust; not thawing and freezing, but static like a year without seasons. The changing mist, like the smoke of war, would hang over it, swallow up now a hangar, now the radar hut, now the machines; release them piece by piece, drained of colour, black carrion on a white desert.

It was a scene of no depth, no recession and no shadows. The land was one with the sky; figures and buildings locked in the cold like bodies in an icefloe.

Beyond the airfield there was nothing; no house, no hill, no road; not even a fence, a tree; only the sky pressing on the dunes, the running fog that lifted on the muddy Baltic shore. Somewhere inland were the mountains.

A group of children in school caps had gathered at the long observation window, chattering in German. Some wore ski clothes. Taylor gazed dully past them, holding a glass in his gloved hand. A boy turned round and stared at him, blushed and whispered to the other children. They fell silent.

He looked at his watch, making a wide arc with his arm, partly to free the sleeve of his overcoat and partly because it was his style; a military man, he wished you to say, decent regiment, decent club, knocked around in the war.

Ten to four. The plane was an hour late. They would have to announce the reason soon over the loudspeaker. He wondered what they would say: delayed by fog, perhaps; delayed take-off. They probably didn't even know – and they certainly would not admit – that she was two hundred miles off course, and south of Rostock. He finished his drink, turned to get rid of the empty glass. He had to admit that some of these foreign hooches, drunk in their own country, weren't at all bad. On the spot, with a couple of hours to kill and ten degrees of frost the other side of the window, you could do a lot worse than Steinhäger. He'd make them order it at the Alias Club when he got back. Cause quite a stir.

The loudspeaker was humming; it blared suddenly, faded out and

13

began again, properly tuned. The children stared expectantly at it. First, the announcement in Finnish, then in Swedish, now in English. Northern Air Services regretted the delay to their charter flight two-nine-zero from Düsseldorf. No hint of how long, no hint of why. They probably didn't know themselves.

But Taylor knew. He wondered what would happen if he sauntered over to that pert little hostess in the glass box and told her: two-nine-zero will be a bit of time yet, my dear, she's been blown off course by heavy northerly gales over the Baltic, bearing all to Hades. The girl wouldn't believe him, of course, she'd think he was a crank. Later she'd know better. She'd realize he was something rather unusual, something rather special.

Outside it was already growing dark. Now the ground was lighter than the sky; the swept runways stood out against the snow like dykes, stained with the amber glow of marking lights. In the nearest hangars neon tubes shed a weary pallor over men and aeroplanes; the foreground beneath him sprang briefly to life as a beam from the control tower flicked across it. A fire engine had pulled away from the workshops on the left and joined the three ambulances already parked short of the centre runway. Simultaneously they switched on their blue rotating lights, and stood in line patiently flashing out their warning. The children pointed at them, chattering excitedly.

The girl's voice began again on the loudspeaker, it could only have been a few minutes since the last announcement. Once more the children stopped talking and listened. The arrival of flight two-nine-zero would be delayed at least another hour. Further information would be given as soon as it became available. There was something in the girl's voice, midway between surprise and anxiety, which seemed to communicate itself to the half-dozen people sitting at the other end of the waiting-room. An old woman said something to her husband, stood up, took her handbag and joined the group of children. For a time she peered stupidly into the twilight. Finding no comfort there, she turned to Taylor and said in English, 'What is become of the Düsseldorf plane?' Her voice had the throaty, indignant lilt of a Dutchwoman. Taylor shook his head. 'Probably the snow,' he replied. He was a brisk man; it went with his military way.

Pushing open the swing door, Taylor made his way downstairs to the reception hall. Near to the main entrance he recognized the yellow pennant of Northern Air Services. The girl at the desk was very pretty.

'What's happened to the Düsseldorf flight?' His style was confiding; they said he had a knack with little girls. She smiled and shrugged her shoulders.

'I expect it is the snow. We are often having delays in Autumn.'

'Why don't you ask the boss?' he suggested, indicating with a nod the telephone in front of her.

'They will tell it on the loudspeaker,' she said, 'as soon as they know.'

'Who's the skipper, dear?'

'Please?'

'Who's the skipper, the captain?'

'Captain Lansen.'

'Is he any good?'

The girl was shocked. 'Captain Lansen is a very experienced pilot.'

Taylor looked her over, grinned and said, 'He's a very *lucky* pilot anyway, my dear.' They said he knew a thing or two, old Taylor did. They said it at the Alias on Friday nights.

Lansen. It was odd to hear a name spoken out like that. In the outfit they simply never did it. They favoured circumlocution, cover names, anything but the original: Archie boy, our flying friend, our friend up north, the chappie who takes the snapshots; they would even use the tortuous collection of figures and letters by which he was known on paper; but never in any circumstances the name.

Lansen. Leclerc had shown him a photograph in London: a boyish thirty-five, fair and goodlooking. He'd bet those hostesses went mad about him; that's all they were, anyway, cannon-fodder for the pilots. No one else got a look in. Taylor ran his right hand quickly over the outside of his overcoat pocket just to make sure the envelope was still there. He'd never carried this sort of money before. Five thousand dollars for one flight; seventeen hundred pounds, tax free, to lose your way over the Baltic. Mind you, Lansen didn't do that every day. This was special, Leclerc had said so. He wondered what she would do if he leant across the counter and told her who he was; showed her the money in that envelope. He'd never had a girl like that, a real girl, tall and young.

He went upstairs again to the bar. The barman was getting to know him. Taylor pointed to the bottle of Steinhäger on the centre shelf and said, 'Give me another of those, d'you mind? That's it, the fellow just behind you; some of your local poison.'

'It's German,' the barman said.

He opened his wallet and took out a banknote. In the cellophane compartment there was a photograph of a girl, perhaps nine years old, wearing glasses and holding a doll. 'My daughter,' he explained to the barman, and the barman gave a watery smile.

His voice varied a lot, like the voice of a commercial traveller. His phoney drawl was more extravagant when he addressed his own class, when it was a matter of emphasizing a distinction which did not exist; or as now, when he was nervous.

He had to admit: he was windy. It was an eerie situation for a man of his experience and age, going over from routine courier work to operational stuff. This was a job for those swine in the Circus, not for his outfit at all. A different kettle of fish altogether, this was, from the ordinary run-of-the-mill stuff he was used to; stuck out on a limb, miles from nowhere. It beat him how they ever came to put an airport in a place like this. He quite liked the foreign trips as a rule: a visit to old Jimmy Gorton in Hamburg, for instance, or a night on the tiles in Madrid. It did him good to get away from Joanie. He'd done the Turkish run a couple of times, though he didn't care for wogs. But even that was a piece of cake compared to this: first-class travel and the bags on the seat beside him, a Nato pass in his pocket; a man had status, doing a job like that; good as the diplomatic boys, or nearly. But this was different, and he didn't like it.

Leclerc had said it was big, and Taylor believed him. They had got him a passport with another name. Malherbe. Pronounced Mallaby, they said. Christ alone knew who'd chosen it. Taylor couldn't even spell it; made a botch of the hotel register when he signed in that morning. The subsistence was fantastic, of course: fifteen quid a day operational expenses, no vouchers asked for. He'd heard the Circus gave seventeen. He could make a good bit on that, buy something for Joanie. She'd probably rather have the money.

He'd told her, of course: he wasn't supposed to, but Leclerc didn't know Joanie. He lit a cigarette, drew from it and held it in the palm of his hand like a sentry smoking on duty. How the hell was he supposed to push off to Scandinavia without telling his wife?

He wondered what those kids were doing, glued to the window all this time. Amazing the way they managed the foreign language. He looked at his watch again, scarcely noticing the time, touched the envelope in his pocket. Better not have another drink; he must keep a clear head. He tried to guess what Joanie was doing now. Probably having a sit-down with a gin and something. A pity she had to work all day.

He suddenly realized that everything had gone silent. The barman was standing still, listening. The old people at the table were listening too, their silly faces turned towards the observation window. Then he heard it quite distinctly, the sound of an aircraft, still far away, but approaching the airfield. He made quickly for the window, was half-way there when the loudspeaker began; after the first few words of German the children, like a flock of pigeons, fluttered away to the reception lounge. The party at the table had stood up; the women were reaching for their gloves, the men for their coats and briefcases. At last the announcer gave the English. Lansen was coming in to land.

Taylor stared into the night. There was no sign of the plane. He waited, his anxiety mounting. It's like the end of the world, he thought, the end of the bloody world out there. Supposing Lansen crashed; supposing they found the cameras. He wished someone else were handling it. Woodford, why hadn't Woodford taken it over, or sent that clever college boy Avery? The wind was stronger; he could swear it was far stronger; he could tell from the way it stirred the snow, flinging it over the runway; the way it tore at the flares; the way it made white columns on the horizon, dashing them vehemently away like a hated creation. A gust struck suddenly at the windows in front of him, making him recoil, and there followed the rattle of ice grains and the short grunt of the wooden frame. Again he looked at his watch; it had become a habit with Taylor. It seemed to help, knowing the time.

Lansen will never make it in this, never.

His heart stood still. Softly at first, then rising swiftly to a wail, he heard the klaxons, all four together, moaning out over that godforsaken airfield like the howl of starving animals. Fire . . . the plane must be on fire. He's on fire and he's going to try and land . . . he turned frantically, looking for someone who could tell him.

The barman was standing beside him, polishing a glass, looking through the window.

'What's going on?' Taylor shouted. 'Why are the sirens going?'

'They always make the sirens in bad weather,' he replied. 'It is the law.'

'Why are they letting him land?' Taylor insisted. 'Why don't they route him farther south? It's too small, this place; why don't they send him somewhere bigger?'

The barman shook his head indifferently. 'It's not so bad,' he said indicating the airfield. 'Besides, he is very late. Maybe he has no petrol.'

They saw the plane low over the airfield, her lights alternating above the flares; her spotlights scanned the runway. She was down, safely down, and they heard the roar of her throttle as she began the long taxi to the reception point.

The bar had emptied. He was alone. Taylor ordered a drink. He knew his drill: stay put in the bar, Leclerc had said, Lansen will meet you in the bar. He'll take a bit of time; got to cope with his flight documents, clear his cameras. Taylor heard the children singing downstairs, and a woman leading them. Why the hell did he have to be surrounded by kids and women? He was doing a man's job, wasn't he, with five thousand dollars in his pocket and a phoney passport?

'There are no more flights today,' the barman said. 'They have forbidden all flying now.'

Taylor nodded. 'I know. It's bloody shocking out there, shocking.'

The barman was putting away bottles. 'There was no danger,' he added soothingly. 'Captain Lansen is a very good pilot.' He hesitated, not knowing whether to put away the Steinhäger.

'Of course there wasn't any danger,' Taylor snapped. 'Who said anything about danger?'

'Another drink?' the barman said.

'No, but you have one. Go on, have one yourself.'

The barman reluctantly gave himself a drink, locked the bottle away.

'All the same, how do they do it?' Taylor asked. His voice was conciliatory, putting it right with the barman. 'They can't see a thing in weather like this, not a damn thing.' He smiled knowingly. 'You sit there in the nose and you might just as well have your eyes shut for all the good they do. I've seen it,' Taylor added, his hands loosely cupped in front of him as though he were at the controls. 'I know what I'm talking about . . . and they're the first to catch it, those boys, if something *does* go wrong.' He shook his head. 'They can keep it,' he declared. 'They're entitled to every penny they earn. Specially in a kite that size. They're held together with string, those things; string.'

The barman nodded distantly, finished his drink, washed up the empty glass, dried it and put it on the shelf under the counter. He unbuttoned his white jacket.

Taylor made no move.

'Well,' said the barman with a mirthless smile, 'we have to go home now.'

'What do you mean, *we*?' Taylor asked, opening his eyes wide and tilting back his head. 'What do you mean?' He'd take on anyone now; Lansen had landed.

'I have to close the bar.'

'Go home indeed. Give us another drink, come on. You can go home if you like. I happen to live in London.' His tone was challenging, half playful, half resentful, gathering volume. 'And since your aircraft companies are unable to *get* me to London, or any other damn place until tomorrow morning, it's a bit silly of you to tell me to go there, isn't it, old boy?' He was still smiling, but it was the short, angry smile of a nervous man losing his temper. 'And next time you accept a drink from me, chum, I'll trouble you to have the courtesy . . .'

The door opened and Lansen came in.

This wasn't the way it was supposed to happen; this wasn't the way they'd described it at all. Stay in the bar, Leclerc had said, sit at the corner table, have a drink, put your hat and coat on the other chair as if you're waiting for someone. Lansen always has a beer when he clocks in. He likes the public lounge, it's Lansen's style. There'll be people milling about, Leclerc said. It's a small place but there's always something going on at these airports. He'll look around for somewhere to sit – quite open and above board – then he'll come over and ask you if anyone's using the chair. You'll say you kept it free for a friend but the friend hadn't turned up: Lansen will ask if he can sit there. He'll order a beer, then say, 'Boy friend or girl friend?' You'll tell him not to be indelicate, and you'll both laugh a bit and get talking. Ask the two questions: height and airspeed. Research Section must know the height and airspeed. Leave the money in your overcoat pocket. He'll pick up your coat, hang his own beside it and help himself quietly, without any fuss, taking the envelope and dropping the film into your coat pocket. You finish your drinks, shake hands, and Bob's your uncle. In the morning you fly home. Leclerc had made it sound so simple.

Lansen strode across the empty room towards them, a tall, strong figure in a blue mackintosh and cap. He looked briefly at Taylor and spoke past him to the barman: 'Jens, give me a beer.' Turning to Taylor he said, 'What's yours?'

Taylor smiled thinly. 'Some of your local stuff.'

'Give him whatever he wants. A double.'

The barman briskly buttoned up his jacket, unlocked the cupboard and poured out a large Steinhäger. He gave Lansen a beer from the cooler.

'Are you from Leclerc?' Lansen inquired shortly. Anyone could have heard.

'Yes.' He added tamely, far too late, 'Leclerc and Company, London.'

Lansen picked up his beer and took it to the nearest table. His hand was shaking. They sat down.

'Then you tell me,' he said fiercely, 'which damn fool gave me those instructions?'

'I don't know.' Taylor was taken aback. 'I don't even know what your instructions were. It's not my fault. I was sent to collect the film, that's all. It's not even my job, this kind of thing. I'm on the overt side–courier.'

Lansen leant forward, his hand on Taylor's arm. Taylor could feel him trembling. 'I was on the overt side too. Until today. There were kids on that plane. Twenty-five German schoolchildren on Winter holidays. A whole load of kids.'

'Yes.' Taylor forced a smile. 'Yes, we had the reception committee in the waiting-room.'

Lansen burst out, 'What were we *looking* for, that's what I don't understand. What's so exciting about Rostock?'

'I tell you I'm nothing to do with it.' He added inconsistently: 'Leclerc said it wasn't Rostock but the area south.'

'The triangle south: Kalkstadt, Langdorn, Wolken. You don't have to tell me the area.'

Taylor looked anxiously towards the barman.

'I don't think we should talk so loud,' he said. 'That fellow's a bit anti.' He drank some Steinhäger.

Lansen made a gesture with his hand as if he were brushing something from in front of his face. 'It's finished,' he said. 'I don't want any more. It's finished. It was OK when we just stayed on course photographing whatever there was; but this is too damn much, see? Just too damn, damn much altogether.' His accent was thick and clumsy, like an impediment.

'Did you get any pictures?' Taylor asked. He must get the film and go.

Lansen shrugged, put his hand in his raincoat pocket and, to Taylor's horror, extracted a zinc container for thirty-five-millimetre film, handing it to him across the table.

'What was it?' Lansen asked again. 'What were they after in such a place? I went under the cloud, circled the whole area. I didn't see any atom bombs.'

'Something important, that's all they told me. Something big. It's got to be done, don't you see? You can't make illegal flights over an area like that.' Taylor was repeating what someone had said. 'It has to be an airline, a registered airline, or nothing. There's no other way.'

'Listen. They picked us up as soon as we got into the place. Two MIGs. Where did they come from, that's what I want to know? As soon as I saw them I turned into cloud; they followed me. I put out a signal, asking for bearings. When we came out of the cloud, there they were again. I thought they'd force me down, order me to land. I tried to jettison the camera but it was stuck. The kids were all crowding the windows, waving at the MIGs. They flew alongside for a time, then peeled off. They came close, very close. It was bloody dangerous for the kids.' He hadn't touched his beer. 'What the hell did they want?' he asked. 'Why didn't they order me down?'

'I told you: it's not my fault. This isn't my kind of work. But whatever London are looking for, they know what they're doing.' He seemed to be convincing himself; he needed to believe in London. 'They don't waste their time. Or yours, old boy. They know what they're up to.' He frowned, to indicate conviction, but Lansen might not have heard.

'They don't believe in unnecessary risks either,' Taylor said. 'You've done a good job, Lansen. We all have to do our bit . . . take risks. We all do. I did in the war, you know. You're too young to remember the war. This is the same job; we're fighting for the same thing.' He suddenly remembered the two questions. 'What height were you doing when you took the pictures?'

'It varied. We were down to six thousand feet over Kalkstadt.'

'It was Kalkstadt they wanted most,' Taylor said with appreciation. 'That's first-class, Lansen, first-class. What was your airspeed?'

'Two hundred . . . two forty. Something like this. There was nothing there, I'm telling you, nothing.' He lit a cigarette.

'It's the end now,' Lansen repeated. 'However big the target is.' He stood up. Taylor got up too; he put his right hand in his overcoat pocket. Suddenly his throat went dry: the money, where was the money?

'Try the other pocket,' Lansen suggested.

Taylor handed him the envelope. 'Will there be trouble about this? About the MIGs, I mean?'

Lansen shrugged. 'I doubt it, it hasn't happened to me before. They'll believe me once; they'll believe it was the weather. I went off course about half-way. There could have been a fault in the ground control. In the hand-over.'

'What about the navigator? What about the rest of the crew? What do they think?'

'That's my business,' said Lansen sourly. 'You can tell London it's the end.'

Taylor looked at him anxiously. 'You're just upset,' he said, 'after the tension.'

'Go to hell,' said Lansen softly. 'Go to bloody hell.' He turned away, put a coin on the counter and strode out of the bar, stuffing carelessly into his raincoat pocket the long buff envelope which contained the money.

After a moment Taylor followed him. The barman watched him push his way through the door and disappear down the stairs. A very distasteful man, he reflected; but then he never had liked the English.

Taylor thought at first that he would not take a taxi to the hotel. He could walk it in ten minutes and save a bit of subsistence. The airline girl nodded to him as he passed her on his way to the main entrance. The reception hall was done in teak; blasts of warm air rose from the floor. Taylor stepped outside. Like the thrust of a sword the cold cut through his clothes; like the numbness of an encroaching poison it spread swiftly over his naked face, feeling its way into his neck and shoulders. Changing his mind, he looked round hastily for a taxi. He was drunk. He suddenly realized: the fresh air had made him drunk. The rank was empty. An old Citroën was parked fifty yards up the road, its engine running. He's got the heater on, lucky devil, thought Taylor and hurried back through the swing doors.

'I want a cab,' he said to the girl. 'Where can I get one, d'you know?' He hoped to God he looked all right. He was made to have drunk so much. He shouldn't have accepted that drink from Lansen.

She shook her head. 'They have taken the children,' she said. 'Six in each car. That was the last flight today. We don't have many taxis in Winter.' She smiled. 'It's a very *little* airport.'

'What's that up the road, that old car? Not a cab, is it?' His voice was indistinct.

She went to the doorway and looked out. She had a careful balancing walk, artless and provocative.

'I don't see any car,' she said.

Taylor looked past her. 'There was an old Citroën. Lights on. Must have gone. I just wondered.' Christ, it went past and he'd never heard it.

'The taxis are all Volvos,' the girl remarked. 'Perhaps one will come back after he has dropped the children. Why don't you go and have a drink?'

'Bar's closed,' Taylor snapped. 'Barman's gone home.'

'Are you staying at the airport hotel?'

'The Regina, yes. I'm in a hurry, as a matter of fact.' It was easier now. 'I'm expecting a phone call from London.'

She looked doubtfully at his coat; it was of rainproof material in a pebble weave. 'You could walk,' she suggested. 'It is ten minutes, straight down the road. They can send your luggage later.'

Taylor looked at his watch, the same wide gesture. 'Luggage is already at the hotel. I arrived this morning.'

He had that kind of crumpled, worried face which is only a hair's breadth from the music halls and yet is infinitely sad; a face in which the eyes are paler than their environment, and the contours converge upon the nostrils. Aware of this, perhaps, Taylor had grown a trivial moustache, like a scrawl on a photograph, which made a muddle of his face without concealing its shortcoming. The effect was to inspire disbelief, not because he was a rogue but because he had no talent for deception. Similarly he had tricks of movement crudely copied from some lost original, such as an irritating habit which soldiers have of arching his back suddenly, as if he had discovered himself in an unseemly posture, or he would affect an agitation about the knees and elbows which feebly caricatured an association with horses. Yet the whole was dignified by pain, as if he were holding his little body stiff against a cruel wind.

'If you walk quickly,' she said, 'it takes less than ten minutes.'

Taylor hated waiting. He had a notion that people who waited were people of no substance: it was an affront to be seen waiting. He pursed his lips, shook his head, and with an ill-tempered 'Good-night, lady,' stepped abruptly into the freezing air.

Taylor had never seen such a sky. Limitless, it curved downward to the snowbound fields, its destiny broken here and there by films of mist which frosted the clustered stars and drew a line round the yellow half moon. Taylor was frightened, like a landsman frightened by the sea. He hastened his uncertain step, swaying as he went.

He had been walking about five minutes when the car caught him up. There was no footpath. He became aware of its headlights first, because the sound of its engine was deadened by the snow, and he only noticed a light ahead of him, not realizing where it came from. It traced its way languidly over the snowfields and for a time he thought it was the beacon from the airport. Then he saw his own shadow shortening on the road, the light became suddenly brighter, and he knew it must be a car. He was walking on the right, stepping briskly along the edge of the icy rubble that lined the road. He observed that the light was unusually yellow and he guessed the headlamps were masked according to the French rule. He was rather pleased with this little piece of deduction; the old brain was pretty clear after all.

He didn't look over his shoulder because he was a shy man in his way and did not want to give the impression of asking for a lift. But it did occur to him, a little late perhaps, that on the Continent they actually drove on the right, and that therefore strictly speaking he was walking on the wrong side of the road, and ought to do something about it.

The car hit him from behind, breaking his spine. For one dreadful moment Taylor described a classic posture of anguish, his head and shoulders flung violently backwards, fingers extended. He made no cry.

It was as if his entire body and soul were concentrated in this final attitude of pain, more articulate in death than any sound the living man had made. It is quite possible that the driver was unaware of what he had done; that the impact of the body on the car was not to be distinguished from a thud of loose snow against the axle.

The car carried him for a yard or two then threw him aside, dead on the empty road, a stiff, wrecked figure at the fringe of the wilderness. His trilby hat lay beside him. A sudden blast seized it, carrying it across the snow. The shreds of his pebble-weave coat fluttered in the wind, reaching vainly for the zinc capsule as it rolled gently with the camber to lodge for a moment against the frozen bank, then to continue wearily down the slope.

SHADOW OF FU MANCHU

SAX ROHMER

'Who's the redhead,' snapped Nayland Smith, 'lunching with that embassy attaché?'

'Which table?'

'Half-right. Where I'm looking.'

Harkness, who had been briefed by Washington to meet the dynamic visitor, was already experiencing nerve strain. Sir Denis Nayland Smith, ex-chief of the Criminal Investigation Department of Scotland Yard, spoke in a Bren-gun manner, thought and moved so swiftly that his society, if stimulating, was exhausting.

Turning, when about to light a cigar, Harkness presently discovered the diplomat's table. The grill was fashionable for lunch, and full. But he knew the attaché by sight. He turned back again, dropping a match in a tray.

'Don't know. Never seen her before.'

'Haven't you? *I* have!'

'Sorry, Sir Denis. Is she important?'

'A woman who looks like that is always important. Yes, I know her. But I haven't quite placed her.'

Nayland Smith refilled his coffee cup, glanced reluctantly at a briar pipe which appeared to have been rescued from a blast furnace, and then put it back in his pocket. He selected a cigarette.

'You don't think she's a Russian?' Harkness suggested.

'I know she isn't.'

Smith surveyed the crowded, panelled room. It buzzed like an aviary. Businessmen predominated. Deals of one sort or another hung in the smoke-laden air. Nearly all these men were talking about how to make money. And nearly all the women were talking about how to spend it.

But not the graceful girl with that glowing hair. He wondered what she was talking about. Her companion appeared to be absorbed, either in what she was saying or in the way she said it.

And while Nayland Smith studied many faces, Harkness studied Nayland Smith.

He had met him only once before, and the years had silvered his hair more than ever, but done nothing to disturb its crisp virility. The lean, brown face might be a trifle more lined. It was a grim face, a face which hid a secret, until Nayland Smith smiled. His smile told the secret.

He spoke suddenly.

'Strange to reflect,' he said, 'that these people, wrapped up, airtight, in their own trifling affairs, like cigarettes in cellophane, are sitting on top of a smouldering volcano.'

'You really think so?'

'I know it. Why has a certain power sent all its star agents to the United States? What are they trying to find out?'

'Secret of the atomb bomb?'

'Rot! There's no secret about it. You know that as well as I do. Once a weapon of war is given publicity, it loses its usefulness. I gain nothing by having a rock in my boxing-glove if the other fellow has one too. No. It's something else.'

'England seems to be pretty busy?'

'England has lost two cabinet ministers, mysteriously, in the past few months.' All the time Smith's glance had been straying in the direction of a certain party, and suddenly: 'Right!' he rapped. 'Thought I was. Now I'm sure! This is my lucky day.'

'Sure of what?' Harkness was startled.

'Man at the next table. Our diplomatic acquaintance and his charming friend are being covered.'

Harkness craned around again.

'You mean the sallow man?'

'Sallow? He's Burmese! They're not *all* Communists, you know.'

Harkness stared at his cigar, as if seeking to concentrate.

'You're more than several steps beyond me. No doubt your information is away ahead of mine. But, quite honestly, I don't understand.'

Nayland Smith met the glance of Harkness's frank hazel eyes, and nodded sympathetically.

'My fault. I think aloud. Bad habit. There's hardly time to explain, now. Look! They're going! Have the redhead covered. Detail another man to keep the Burmese scout in sight. Report to me, here. Suite 1236.'

The auburn-haired girl was walking towards the exit. She wore a plain suit and a simple hat. Her companion followed. As Harkness retired speedily, Nayland Smith dropped something which made it necessary for him to stoop when the attaché passed near his table.

Coming out onto Forty-sixth Street, Harkness exchanged a word with a man who was talking to a hotel porter. The man nodded and moved away.

Manhattan danced on. Well-fed males returned to their offices to consider further projects for making more dollars. Females headed for the glamorous shops on New York's Street-Called-Straight: Fifth Avenue, the great bazaar of the New World. Beauty specialists awaited them. Designers of Paris hats. Suave young ladies to display wondrous robes. Suave young gentlemen to seduce with glittering trinkets.

In certain capitals of the Old World, men and women looked, haggard-eyed, into empty shops and returned to empty larders.

Manhattan danced on.

Nayland Smith, watching a car move from the front of the hotel, closely followed by another, prayed that Manhattan's dance might not be a *danse macabre*.

When presently he stepped into a black sedan parked further along the street, in charge of a chauffeur who looked like a policeman (possibly because he was one), and had been driven a few blocks:

'Have we got a tail?' Smith snapped.

'Yes, sir,' the driver reported. 'Three cars behind us right now. Small delivery truck.'

'Stop at the next drugstore. I'll check it.'

When he got out and walked into the drugstore the following truck passed, and then pulled in higher up.

Nayland Smith came out again and resumed the journey. Two more blocks passed:

'Right behind us,' the driver reported laconically.

Smith took up a phone installed in the sedan and gave brief directions. So that long before he had reached his destination the truck was still following the sedan, but two traffic police were following the truck. He had been no more than a few minutes in the deputy commissioner's office on Centre Street before a police sergeant came in with the wanted details.

The man had been pulled up on a technical offence and invited, firmly, to produce evidence of his identity. Smith glanced over the report.

'H'm. American citizen. Born in Athens.' He looked up. 'You're checking this story that he was taking the truck to be repaired?'

'Sure. Can't find anything wrong with it. Very powerful engine for such a light outfit.'

'Would be,' said Smith drily. 'File all his contacts. He mustn't know. You have to find out who really employs him.'

He spent a long time with the deputy commissioner, and gathered much useful data. He was in New York at the request of the Federal Bureau of Investigation, and had been given almost autocratic powers by Washington. When, finally, he left, he had two names pencilled in his notebook.

They were: Michael Frobisher, and Dr Morris Craig, of the Huston Research Laboratory.

Michael Frobisher, seated in an alcove in the library of his club, was clearly ill at ease. A big-boned, fleshy man, Frobisher had a powerful physique, with a fighting jaw, heavy brows – coal-black in contrast to nearly white hair – and deep-set eyes which seemed to act independently of what Michael Frobisher happened to be doing.

There were only two other members in the library, but Frobisher's eyes, although he was apparently reading a newspaper, moved rapidly, as his glance switched from face to face in that oddly furtive manner.

Overhanging part of the room, one of the finest of its kind in the city, was a gallery giving access to more books ranged on shelves above. A club servant appeared in the gallery, moving very quietly – and Frobisher's glance shot upward like an anxious searchlight.

It was recalled to sea level by a voice.

'Hello, Frobisher! How's your wife getting along?'

Frobisher's florid face momentarily lost colour. Then, looking up from where he sat in a deep, leathern armchair, he saw that a third member had come in – Dr Pardoe.

'Hello, Pardoe!' He had himself in hand again: the deep tone was normal. 'Quite startled me.'

'So I saw.' Pardoe gave him a professional glance, and sat on the arm of a chair near Frobisher's. 'Been overdoing it a bit, haven't you?'

'Oh, I don't say that, Doctor. Certainly been kept pretty busy. Thanks for the inquiry about Stella. She's greatly improved since she began the treatment you recommended.'

'Good.' Dr Pardoe smiled – a dry smile: he was a sandy, dry man. 'I'm not sure the professor isn't a quack, but he seems to be successful with certain types of neuroses.'

'I assure you Stella is a hundred per cent improved.'

'H'm. You might try him yourself.'

'What are you talking about?' Frobisher growled. 'There's nothing the matter with me.'

'Isn't there?' The medical man looked him over coolly. 'There will be if you don't watch your diet.' Pardoe was a vegetarian. 'Why, your heart missed a beat when I spoke to you.'

Frobisher held himself tightly in hand. His wife's physician always got on his nerves. But, all the same, he wasn't standing for any nonsense.

'Let me tell you something.' His deep voice, although subdued, rumbled around the now empty library. 'This isn't nerves. It's cold feet. An organisation like the Huston Electric has got rivals. And rivals can get dangerous if they're worsted. Someone's tracking me around. Someone broke into Falling Waters one night last week. Went through my papers.

I've seen the man. I'd know him again. I was followed right here to the club today. That isn't nerves, Doctor. And it isn't eating too much red meat!'

'H'm.' Irritating habit of Pardoe's, that introductory cough. 'I don't dispute the fact of the burglary—"

'Thanks a lot. And let me remind you: Stella doesn't know, and doesn't have to know.'

'Oh, I see. Then the attempt is known only—'

'Is known to my butler, Stein, and to me. It's not an illusion. I'm still sane, if I did have a beefsteak at lunch!'

The physician raised his sandy brows.

'I don't doubt it, Frobisher. But had it occurred to you that your later impression of being followed – not an uncommon symptom – may derive from this single, concrete fact?'

Frobisher didn't reply, and Dr Pardoe, who had been looking down at the carpet, now looked suddenly at Frobisher.

His gaze was fixed upward again. He was watching the gallery. He spoke in a whisper.

'Pardoe! Look where I'm looking. Is that a club member?'

Dr Pardoe did as Frobisher requested. He saw a slight, black-clad figure in the gallery. The man had just replaced a vase on a shelf. Only the back of his head and shoulders could be seen. He moved away, his features still invisible.

'Not a member known to me, personally, Frobisher. But there are always new members, and guest members—'

But Frobisher was up, had bounded from his chair. Already, he was crossing the library.

'That's some kind of Asiatic. I saw his face!' Regardless of the rule, Silence, he shouted. 'And I'm going to have a word with him!'

Dr Pardoe shook his head, took up a medical journal which he had dropped on the chair, and made his way out.

He was already going down the steps when Michael Frobisher faced the club secretary, who had been sent for.

'May I ask,' he growled, 'since when have Chinese been admitted to membership?'

'You surprise me, Mr Frobisher.'

The secretary, a young-old man with a bald head and a Harvard accent, could be very patriarchal.

'Do I?'

'You do. Your complaint is before me. I have a note here. If you wish it to go before the committee, merely say the word. I can only assure you that not only have we no Asiatic members, honorary or otherwise, but no visitor such as you describe has been in the club. Furthermore, Mr Frobisher, I am assured by the assistant librarian, who was last in the library gallery, that no one has been up there since.'

Frobisher jumped to his feet.

'Get Dr Pardoe!' he directed. 'He was with me. Get Dr Pardoe.'

But Dr Pardoe had left the club.

The research laboratory of the Huston Electric Corporation was on the thirty-sixth, and top floor of the Huston Building. Dr Craig's office adjoined the laboratory proper, which he could enter up three steps leading to a steel door. This door was always kept locked.

Morris Craig, slight, clean-shaven, and very agile, a man in his early thirties, had discarded his coat, and worked in shirt-sleeves before a drawing desk. His dark-brown hair, which he wore rather long, was disposed to be rebellious, a forelock sometimes falling forward, so that brushing it back with his hand had become a mannerism.

He had just paused for this purpose, leaning away as if to get a long perspective of his work and at the same time fumbling for a packet of cigarettes, when the office door was thrown open and someone came in behind him.

So absorbed was Craig that he paid no attention at first, until the heavy breathing of whoever had come in prompted him to turn suddenly.

'Mr Frobisher!'

Craig, who wore glasses when drawing or reading, but not otherwise, now removed them and jumped from his stool.

'It's all right, Craig.' Frobisher raised his hand in protest. 'Sit down.'

'But if I may say so, you look uncommon fishy.'

His way of speech had a quality peculiarly English, and he had a tendency to drawl. Nothing in his manner suggested that Morris Craig was one of the most brilliant physicists Oxford University had ever turned out. He retrieved the elusive cigarettes and lighted one.

Michael Frobisher remained where he had dropped down, on a chair just inside the door. But he was regaining colour. Now he pulled a cigar from the breast pocket of his tweed jacket.

'The blasted doctors tell me I eat too much and smoke too much,' he remarked. His voice always reminded Craig of old port. 'But I wouldn't want to live if I couldn't do as I liked.'

'Practical,' said Craig, 'if harsh. May I inquire what has upset you?'

'Come to that in a minute,' growled Frobisher. 'First – what news of the big job?'

'Getting hot. I think the end's in sight.'

'Fine. I want to talk to you about it.' He snipped the end of his cigar. 'How's the new secretary making out?'

'A-1. Knows all the answers. Miss Lewis was a sad loss, but Miss Navarre is a glad find.'

'Well – she's got a Paris degree, and had two years with Professor Jennings. Suits me if she suits you.'

Craig's boyishly youthful face lighted up.

'Suits me to nine points of decimals. Works like a pack-mule. She ought to get out of town this week-end.'

'Bring her along up to Falling Waters. Few days of fresh air would do her no harm.'

'No.' Craig seemed to be hesitating. He returned to his desk. 'But I shouldn't quit this job until it's finished.'

He resumed his glasses and studied the remarkable diagram pinned to the drawing board. He seemed to be checking certain details with a mass of symbols and figures on a large ruled sheet beside the board.

'Of course,' he murmured abstractedly, 'I might easily finish at any time now.'

The wonder of the thing he was doing, a sort of awe that he, the humble student of nature's secrets, should have been granted power to do it, claimed his mind. Here were mighty forces, hitherto no more than suspected, which controlled the world. Here, written in the indelible ink of mathematics, lay a description of the means whereby those forces might be harnessed.

He forgot Frobisher.

And Frobisher, lighting his cigar, began to pace the office floor, often glancing at the absorbed figure. Suddenly Craig turned, removing his glasses.

'Are you bothered about the cost of these experiments, Mr Frobisher?'

Frobisher pulled up, staring.

'Cost? To hell with the cost! That's not worrying me. I don't know a lot about the scientific side, but I know a commercial proposition when I see one.' He dropped down into an armchair. 'What I don't know is this.' He leaned forward, his heavy brows lowered: 'Why is somebody tracking me around?'

'Tracking you around?'

'That's what I said. I'm being tailed around. I was followed to my club today. Followed here. There's somebody watching my home up in Connecticut. Who is he? What does he want?'

Morris Craig stood up and leaned back against the desk.

Behind him a deep violet sky made a back-cloth for silhouettes of buildings higher than the Huston. Some of the windows were coming to life, forming a glittering regalia, like jewels laid on velvet.

Dusk was falling over Manhattan.

'Astoundin' state of affairs,' Craig declared – but his smile was quite disarming. 'Tell me more. Anyone you suspect?'

Frobisher shook his head. 'There's plenty to suspect if news of what's going on up here has leaked out. Suppose you're dead right – and I'm backing you to be – what'll this thing mean to Huston Electric?'

'Grateful thanks of the scientific world.'

'Damn the scientific world! I'm thinking of Huston's.'

Morris Craig, his mind wandering in immeasurable space, his spirit climbing the ladder of the stars toward higher and more remote secrets of a mysterious universe, answered vaguely.

'No idea. Can't see at the moment how it could be usefully applied.'

'What are you talking about?' Michael Frobisher was quite his old roaring self again. 'This job has cost half of a million dollars already. Are you telling me we get nothing back? Are we all bughouse around here?'

A door across the office opened, and a man came in, a short, thick-set man, slightly bandy, who walked with a rolling gait as if on the deck of a ship in dirty weather. He wore overalls, spectacles, and an eye-shade. He came in without any ceremony and approached Craig. The forbidding figure of Michael Frobisher disturbed him not at all.

'Say – have you got a bit of string?' he inquired.

'I have not got a bit of string. I have a small piece of gum, or two one-cent stamps. Would they do?'

The intruder chewed thoughtfully. 'Guess not. Miss Navarre's typewriter's jammed up in there. But I got it figured a bit of string about so long' – he illustrated – 'would fix things.'

'Sorry, Sam, but I am devoid of string.'

Sam chewed awhile, and then turned away.

'Guess I'll have to go look some other place.'

As he went out:

'Listen,' Frobisher said. 'What does that moron do for his wages?'

'Sam?' Craig answered, smiling. 'Oh, sort of handyman. Mostly helps Regan and Shaw in the laboratory.'

'Be a big help to anybody, I'd say. What I'm driving at is this: We have to be mighty careful about who gets in here. There's been a bad leak. Somebody knows more than he ought to know.'

Morris Craig, slowly, was getting back to that prosaic earth on which

34

normal, flat-footed men spend their lives. It was beginning to dawn upon him that Michael Frobisher was badly frightened.

'I can't account for it. Shaw and Regan are beyond suspicion. So, I hope, am I. Miss Navarre came to us with the highest credentials. In any case, she could do little harm. But, of course, it's absurd to suspect her.'

'What about the half-wit who just went out?'

'Knows nothing about the work. Apart from which, his refs are first-class, including one from the Fire Department.'

'Looks like he'd been in a fire.' Frobisher dropped a cone of cigar ash. 'But facts are facts. Let me bring you up to date – but not a word to Mrs F. You know how nervous she is. Some guy got into Falling Waters last Tuesday night and went through my papers with a fine-tooth comb!'

'You mean it?'

Craig's drawl had vanished. His eyes were very keen.

'I mean it. Nothing was taken – not a thing. But that's not all. I'd had more than a suspicion for quite a while someone was snooping around. So I laid for him, without saying a word to Mrs F., and one night I saw him—'

'What did he look like?'

'Yellow.'

'Indian?'

'No, sir. Some kind of Oriental. Then, only today, right in my own club, I caught another Asiatic watching me! It's a fact. Dr Pardoe can confirm it. Now – what I'm asking is this: If it's what we're doing in the laboratory there that somebody's after, why am *I* followed around, and not you?'

'The answer is a discreet silence.'

'Also I'd be glad to learn who this somebody is. I could think up plenty who'd like to know. But not one of 'em would be an Asiatic.'

Morris Craig brushed his hair back with his hand.

'You're getting *me* jumpy, too,' he declared, although his eager, juvenile smile belied the words. 'This thing wants looking into.'

'It's going to be looked into,' Frobisher grimly assured him. 'When you come up to Falling Waters you'll see I'm standing for no more monkey tricks around there, anyway.' He stood up, glancing at the big clock over Craig's desk. 'I'm picking up Mrs F. at the Ritz. Don't have to be late. Expect you and Miss Navarre, lunch on Saturday.'

Mrs F., as it happened, was thoroughly enjoying herself. She lay naked, face downward, on a padded couch, whilst a white-clad nurse ran an

35

apparatus which buzzed like a giant hornet from the back of her fluffy skull right down her spine and up again. This treatment made her purr like a contented kitten. It had been preceded by a terrific mauling at the hands of another, muscular, attendant, in the course of which Mrs F. had been all but hanged, drawn, quartered and, finally, stood on her head.

An aromatic bath completed the treatment. Mrs F. was wrapped in a loose fleecy garment, stretched upon a couch in a small apartment decorated with Pompeian frescoes, and given an Egyptian cigarette and a cup of orange-scented China tea.

She lay there in delicious languor, when the draperies were drawn aside and Professor Hoffmeyer, the celebrated Viennese psychiatrist who conducted the establishment, entered gravely. She turned her head and smiled up at him.

'How do you do, Professor?'

He did not reply at once, but stood there looking at her. Even through the dark glasses he always wore, his regard never failed to make her shudder. But it was a pleasurable shudder.

Professor Hoffmeyer presented an impressive figure. His sufferings in Nazi prison camps had left indelible marks. The dark glasses protected eyes seared by merciless lights. The silk gloves which he never removed concealed hands from which the fingernails had been extracted. He stooped much, leaning upon a heavy ebony cane.

Now he advanced almost noiselessly and took Mrs Frobisher's left wrist between a delicate thumb and forefinger, slightly inclining his head.

'It is not how do *I* do, dear lady,' he said in Germanic gutturals, 'but how do *you* do.'

Mrs Frobisher looked up at the massive brow bent over her, and tried, not for the first time, to puzzle out the true colour of the scanty hair which crowned it. She almost decided that it was colourless; entirely neutral.

Professor Hoffmeyer stood upright, or as nearly upright as she had ever seen him stand, and nodded.

'You shall come to see me on Wednesday, at three o'clock. Not for the treatment, no, but for the consultation. If some other engagement you have, cancel it. At three o'clock on Wednesday.'

He bowed slightly and went out.

Professor Hoffmeyer ruled his wealthy clientèle with a rod of iron. His reputation was enormous. His fees were phenomenal.

He proceeded, now, across a luxurious central salon where other patients waited, well-preserved women, some of them apparently out of the deep-freeze. He nodded to a chosen few as he passed, and entered an office marked 'Private.' Closing the door, he pulled out a drawer in the businesslike desk – and a bookcase filled with advanced medical works, largely German, swung open bodily.

The professor went into the opening. As the bookcase swung back into place, the drawer in the desk closed again.

Professor Hoffmeyer would see no more patients today.

The room in which the professor found himself was a study. But its appointments were far from conventional. It contained some very valuable old lacquer and was richly carpeted. The lighting (it had no visible windows) was subdued, and the peculiar characteristic of the place was its silence.

Open bookcases were filled with volumes, some of them bound manuscripts, many of great age and all of great rarity. They were in many languages, including Greek, Chinese, and Arabic.

Beside a cushioned divan stood an inlaid stool equipped with several opium pipes in a rack, gum, lamp, and bodkins.

A long, carved table of time-blackened oak served as a desk. A high-backed chair was set behind it. A faded volume lay open on the table, as well as a closely written manuscript. There were several other books there, and a number of curious objects difficult to identify in the dim light.

The professor approached a painted screen placed before a recess and disappeared behind it. Not a sound broke the silence of the room until he returned.

He had removed the gloves and dark glasses, and for the black coat worn by Professor Hoffmeyer had substituted a yellow house robe. The eyes which the glasses had concealed were long, narrow, and emerald-green. The uncovered hands had pointed fingernails. This gaunt, upright, Chinese ascetic was taller by inches than Professor Hoffmeyer.

And his face might have inspired a painter seeking a model for the Fallen Angel.

This not because it was so evil but because of a majestic and remorseless power which it possessed – a power which resided in the eyes. They were not the eyes of a normal man, moved by the desires, the impulses shared in some part by us all. They were the eyes of one who has shaken off those inhibitions common to humanity, who is undisturbed by either love or hate, untouched by fear, unmoved by compassion.

Few such men occur in the long history of civilisation, and none who has not helped to change it.

The impassive figure crossed, with a silent, catlike step, to the long table, and became seated there.

One of the curious objects on the table sprang to life, as if touched by sudden moonlight. It was a crystal globe resting on a metal base. Dimly at first, the outlines of a face materialised in the crystal, and then grew clear. They became the features of an old Chinese, white-moustached, wrinkled, benign.

'You called me, Doctor?'

The voice, though distant, was clear. A crinkled smile played over the parchment face in the crystal.

'You have all the reports?'

The second voice was harsh, at points sibilant, but charged with imperious authority. It bore no resemblance to that of Professor Hoffmeyer.

'The last is timed six-fifteen. Shall I give you a summary?'

'Proceed, Huan Tsung. I am listening.'

And Huan Tsung, speaking in his quiet room above a shop in Pell Street, a room in which messages were received mysteriously, by day and by night, from all over Manhattan, closed his wise old eyes and opened the pages of an infallible memory.

This man whose ancestors had been cultured noblemen when most of ours were living in caves, spoke calmly across a system of communication as yet unheard of by Western science . . .

'Excellency will wish to know that our Burmese agent was recognised by Nayland Smith in the grillroom and followed by two F.B.I. operatives. I gave instructions that he be transferred elsewhere. He reports that he has arrived safely. His notes of the conversation at the next table are before me. They contain nothing new. Shall I relate them?'

'No. I shall interview the woman personally. Proceed.'

'Nayland Smith visited the deputy commissioner and has been alone with him more than two hours. Nature of conversation unknown. The Greek covering his movements was intercepted and questioned, but had nothing to disclose. He is clumsy, and I have had him removed.'

'You did well, Huan Tsung. Such bunglers breed danger.'

'Mai Cha, delivering Chinese vase sent by club secretary for repair, attired herself in the black garment she carries and gained a gallery above the library where Michael Frobisher talked with a medical friend. She reports that Frobisher has had sight of our agent at Falling Waters. Therefore I have transferred this agent. Mai Cha retired, successfully, with price of repairs.'

'Commend Mai Cha.'

'I have done so, Excellency. She is on headquarters duty tonight. Excellency can commend her himself.'

'The most recent movements of Frobisher, Nayland Smith, and Dr

Craig.'

'Frobisher awaits his wife at the Ritz-Carlton. Nayland Smith is covered, but no later report has reached me. Dr Craig is in his office.'

'Frobisher has made no other contacts?'

'None, Excellency. The stream flows calmly. It is the hour for repose, when the wise man reflects.'

'Wait and watch, Huan Tsung. I must think swiftly.'

'Always I watch – and it is unavoidable that I wait until I am called away.'

Moonlight in the crystal faded out, and with it the wrinkled features of the Mandarin Huan Tsung.

Complete silence claimed the dimly lighted room. The wearer of the yellow robe remained motionless for a long time. Then, he stood up and crossed to the divan, upon which he stretched his gaunt body. He struck a silver bell which hung in a frame beside the rack of opium pipes. The bell emitted a high, sweet note.

Whilst the voice of the bell still lingered, drowsily, on the air, draperies in a narrow, arched opening were drawn aside, and a Chinese girl came in.

She wore national costume. She was very graceful, and her large, dark eyes resembled the eyes of a doe. She knelt and touched the carpet with her forehead.

'You have done well, Mai Cha. I am pleased with you.'

The girl rose, but stood, head lowered and hands clasped, before the reclining figure. A flush crept over her dusky cheeks.

'Prepare the jade pipe. I seek inspiration.'

Mai Cha began quietly to light the little lamp on the stool.

Although no report had reached old Huan Tsung, nevertheless Nayland Smith had left police headquarters.

He was fully alive to the fact that every move he had made since entering New York City had been noted, that he never stirred far without a shadow.

This did not disturb him. Nayland Smith was used to it.

But he didn't wish his trackers to find out where he was going from Centre Street – until he had got there.

He favoured, in cold weather, a fur-collared topcoat of military cut, which was almost as distinctive as his briar pipe. He had a dozen or more police officers paraded for his inspection, and selected one nearly enough of his own build, clean-shaven and brown-skinned. His name was

Moreno, and he was of Italian descent.

This officer was given clear instructions, and the driver who had brought Nayland Smith to headquarters received his orders, also.

When a man wearing a light rainproof and a dark-blue felt hat (property of Detective Officer Moreno) left by a side entrance, walked along to Lafayette Street, and presently picked up a taxi, no one paid any attention to him. But, in order to make quite sure, Nayland Smith gave the address, Waldorf-Astoria, got out at that hotel, walked through to the Park Avenue entrance, and proceeded to his real destination on foot.

He was satisfied that he had no shadow.

The office was empty, as Camille Navarre came out of her room and crossed to the long desk set before the windows. One end had been equipped for business purposes. There was a leather-covered chair and beside it a dictophone. A cylinder remained on the machine, for Craig had been dictating when he was called to the laboratory. At the other end stood a draughtsman's stool and a quantity of pens, pencils, brushes, pans of coloured ink, and similar paraphernalia. They lay beside a propped-up drawing board, illuminated by a tubular lamp.

Camille placed several typed letters on the desk, and then stood there studying the unfinished diagram pinned to the board.

She possessed a quiet composure which rarely deserted her. As Craig had once remarked, she was so restful about the place. Her plain suit did not unduly stress a slim figure, and her hair was swept back flatly to a knot at the nape of her neck. She wore black-rimmed glasses, and looked in every respect the perfect secretary for a scientist.

A slight sound, the click of a lock, betrayed the fact that Craig was about to come out. Camille returned to her room.

She had just gone in when the door of the laboratory opened, and Craig walked down the three steps. A man in a white coat, holding a pair of oddly shaped goggles in his hand, stood at the top. He showed outlined against greenish light. With the opening of the door, a curious vibration had become perceptible, a thing which might be sensed, rather than heard.

'In short, Doctor,' he was saying, 'we can focus, but we can't control the volume.'

Craig spoke over his shoulder.

'When we can do both, Regan, we'll give an audition to the pundits that will turn their wool white.'

Regan, a capable-looking technician, grey-haired and having a finely shaped mathematical head, smiled as he stepped back through the doorway.

'I doubt if Mr Frobisher will want any "auditions,"' he said drily. As the door was closed, the vibrant sound ceased.

Craig stood for a moment studying the illuminated diagram as Camille had done. He lighted a cigarette, and then noticed the letters on his desk. He dropped into the chair, switching up a reading lamp, and put on his glasses.

A moment later he was afoot again, as the office door burst open and a man came in rapidly – closely followed by Sam.

'Wait a minute!' Sam was upset. 'Listen. Wait a minute!'

Craig dropped his glasses on the desk, stared, and then advanced impulsively, hand outstretched.

'Nayland Smith! By all that's holy – Nayland Smith!' They exchanged grips, smiling happily. 'Why, I thought you were in Ispahan, or Yucatán, or somewhere.'

'Nearly right the first time. But it was Teheran. Flew from there three days ago. More urgent business here.'

'Wait a minute,' Sam muttered, his eye-shade thrust right to the back of his head.

Craig turned to him.

'It's all right, Sam. This is an old friend.'

'Oh, is that so?'

'Yes – and I don't believe he has a bit of string.'

Sam stared truculently from face to face, chewing in an ominous way, and then went out.

'Sit down, Smith. This is a great, glad surprise. But why the whirlwind business? And' – staring – 'what the devil are you up to?'

Nayland Smith had walked straight across to the long windows which occupied nearly the whole of the west wall. He was examining a narrow terrace outside bordered by an ornamental parapet. He looked beyond, to where the hundred eyes of a towering building shone in the dusk. He turned.

'Anybody else got access to this floor?'

'Only the staff. Why?'

'What do you mean when you say the staff?'

'I mean the staff! Am I on the witness stand? Well, if you must know, the research staff consists of myself; Martin Shaw, my chief assistant, a Columbia graduate; John Regan, second technician, who came to me from Vickers; and Miss Navarre, my secretary. She also has scientific training. Except for Sam, the handyman, and Mr Frobisher, nobody else has access to the laboratory. Do I make myself clear to your honour?'

Nayland Smith was staring towards the steel door and tugging at the lobe of his left ear, a mannerism which denoted intense concentration, and one with which Craig was familiar.

'You don't take proper precautions,' he snapped. '*I* got in without any difficulty.'

Morris Craig became vaguely conscious of danger. He recalled vividly the nervous but repressed excitement of Michael Frobisher. He could not ignore the tension now exhibited by Nayland Smith.

'Why these precautions, Smith? What have we to be afraid of?'

Smith swung around on him. His eyes were hard.

'Listen, Craig – we've known one another since you were at Oxford. There's no need to mince words. I don't know what you're working on up here – but I'm going to ask you to tell me. I know something else, though. Unless I have made the biggest mistake of my life, one of the few first-class brains in the world today has got you spotted.'

'But, Smith you're telling me nothing—'

'Haven't time. I baited a little trap as I came up. I'm going down to spring it.'

'Spring it?'

'Exactly. Excuse me.'

Smith moved to the door.

'The elevator man will be off duty—'

'He won't. I ordered him to stand by.'

Nayland Smith went out as rapidly as he had come in.

Craig stood for a moment staring at the door which Smith had just closed. He had an awareness of some menace, impending, creeping down upon him; a storm cloud. He scratched his chin reflectively and returned to the letters. He signed them and pressed a button.

Camille Navarre entered quietly and came over to the desk. Craig took off his glasses and looked up – but Camille's eyes were fixed on the letters.

'Ah, Miss Navarre – here we are.' He returned them to her. 'And there's rather a long one, bit of a teaser, on this thing.' He pointed to the dictaphone. 'Mind removing same and listening in to my rambling rot?'

Camille stooped and took the cylinder off the machine.

'Your dictation is very clear, Dr Craig.'

She spoke with a faint accent, more of intonation than pronunciation. It was a low-pitched, caressing voice. Craig never tired of it.

'Sweet words of flattery. I sound to myself like a half-strangled parrot. The way you construe is simply wizard.'

Camille smiled. She had beautifully moulded, rather scornful lips.

'Thank you. But it isn't difficult.'

She put the cylinder in its box and turned to go.

'By the way, you have an invitation from the boss. He bids you to Falling Waters for the week-end.'

Camille paused, but didn't turn. If Craig could have seen her face, its expression might have puzzled him.

'Really?' she said. 'That *is* sweet of Mr Frobisher.'

'Can you come? I'm going, too, so I'll drive you out.'

'That would be very kind of you. Yes, I should love to come.'

She turned, now, and her smile was radiant.

'Splendid. We'll hit the trail early. No office on Saturday.'

There was happiness in Craig's tone, and in his glance. Camille dropped her eyes and moved away.

'Er—' he added, 'is the typewriter in commission again?'

'Yes.' Camille's lip twitched. 'I managed to get it right.'

'With a bit of string?'

'No.' She laughed softly. 'With a hairpin!'

As she went out Craig returned to his drawing board. But he found it hard to concentrate. He kept thinking about that funny little *moué* peculiar to Camille, part of her. Whenever she was going to smile, one corner of her upper lip seemed to curl slightly like a rose petal. And he wondered if her eyes were really so beautiful, or if the lenses magnified them.

The office door burst open, and Nayland Smith came in again like a hot wind from the desert. He had discarded the rainproof in which he had first appeared, and now carried a fur-collared coat.

'Missed him, Craig,' he rapped. 'Slipped through my fingers – the swine!'

Craig turned half around, resting one shirt-sleeved elbow on a corner of the board.

'Of course,' he said, 'if you're training for the Olympic Games, or what-have-you, let me draw your attention to the wide-open spaces of Central Park. I *work* here – or try to.'

He was silenced by the look in Nayland Smith's eyes. He stood up. 'Smith! – what is it?'

'Murder!' Nayland Smith rapped out the word like a rifle shot. 'I have just sent a man to his death, Craig!'

'What on earth do you mean?'

'No more than I say.'

It came to Morris Craig as a revelation that something had happened to crush, if only temporarily, the indomitable spirit he knew so well. He walked over and laid a hand on his friend's shoulder.

'I'm sorry, Smith. Forgive my silly levity. What's happened?'

Nayland Smith's face looked haggard, worn, as he returned Craig's earnest stare.

'I have been shadowed, Craig, ever since I reached New York. I left police headquarters a while ago, wearing a borrowed hat and topcoat. A man slightly resembling me had orders to come to the Huston Building in the car I have been using all day, wearing my own hat, and my own topcoat.'

'Well?'

'He obeyed his orders. The driver, who is above suspicion, noticed nothing whatever unusual on the way. There was no evidence to suggest that they were being followed. I had assumed that they would be – and had laid my plans accordingly. I went down to see the tracker fall into my trap—'

'Go on, Smith! For God's sake, what had happened?'

'This!'

Nayland Smith carefully removed a small, pointed object from its wrappings and laid it on the desk. Craig was about to pick it up, when:

'Don't touch it!' came sharply. 'That is, except by the feathered end. Primitive, Craig, but deadly – and silent. Get your laboratory to analyze the stuff on the tip of the dart. *Curari* is too commonplace for the man who inspired this thing.'

'Smith! I'm appalled. What are you telling me?'

'It was flicked, or perhaps blown from a tube, into Moreno's face through the open window of the car. It stuck in his chin, and he pulled it out. But when the car got here, he was quite insensible, and—'

'You mean he's dead?'

'I had him rushed straight to hospital.'

'They'll want this for analysis.'

'There was another. The first must have missed.'

Nayland Smith dropped limply into a chair, facing Craig. He pulled out his blackened briar and began to load it from an elderly pouch.

'Let's face the facts, Craig. I must make it clear to you that a mysterious Eastern epidemic is creeping West. I'm not in Manhattan for my health. I'm here to try to head it off.'

He stuffed the pouch back into his pocket and lighted his pipe.

'I'm all attention, Smith. But for heaven's sake, what devil are you up against?'

'Listen. No less than six prominent members of the Soviet Government have either died suddenly or just disappeared – within the past few months.'

'One of those purges? Very popular with dictators.'

'A purge right enough. But not carried out by Kremlin orders. Josef Stalin is being guarded as even *he* was never guarded before.'

Craig began groping behind him for the elusive packet of cigarettes.

'What's afoot, Smith? Is this anything to do with the news from London?'

'You mean the disappearance of two of the Socialist Cabinet? Undoubtedly. They have gone the same way.'

'The same way?' Craig's search was rewarded. He lighted a cigarette. '*What* way?'

Nayland Smith took the fuming pipe from between his teeth, and fixed a steady look on Craig.

'Dr Fu Manchu's way!'

'Dr Fu Manchu! But—'

The door of Camille's room opened, and Camille came out. She held some typewritten sheets in her hand. There was much shadow at that side of the office, for only the desk lights were on, so that as the two men turned and looked towards her, it was difficult to read her expression.

But she paused at sight of them, standing quite still.

'Oh, excuse me, Dr Craig! I thought you were alone.'

'It's all right,' said Craig. 'Don't—er—go, Miss Navarre. This is my friend, Sir Denis Nayland Smith. My new secretary, Smith – Miss Navarre.'

Nayland Smith stared for a moment, then bowed, and walked to the window.

'What is it, Miss Navarre?' Craig asked.

'It's only that last cylinder, Dr Craig. I wanted to make sure I had it right. I will wait until you are disengaged.'

But Nayland Smith was looking out into the jewelled darkness, and seeing nothing of a towering building which rose like a lighted teocalli against the skyline. He saw, instead, a panelled grillroom where an attractive red-haired girl sat at a table with a man. He saw the dark-faced spy lunching alone nearby.

The girl in the grillroom had not worn her hair pinned back in that prim way, nor had she worn glasses.

Nevertheless, the girl in the grillroom and Miss Navarre were one and the same!

THE
HUMAN FACTOR

GRAHAM GREENE

THE HUMAN FACTOR

Castle, ever since he had joined the firm as a young recruit more than thirty years ago, had taken his lunch in a public house behind St James's Street, not far from the office. If he had been asked why he lunched there, he would have referred to the excellent quality of the sausages; he might have preferred a different bitter from Watney's, but the quality of the sausages outweighed that. He was always prepared to account for his actions, even the most innocent, and he was always strictly on time.

So by the stroke of one he was ready to leave. Arthur Davis, his assistant, with whom he shared a room, departed for lunch punctually at twelve and returned, but often only in theory, one hour later. It was understood that, in case of an urgent telegram, Davis or himself must always be there to receive the decoding, but they both knew well that in the particular sub-division of their department nothing was ever really urgent. The difference in time between England and the various parts of Eastern and Southern Africa, with which the two of them were concerned, was usually large enough – even when in the case of Johannesburg it was little more than an hour – for no one outside the department to worry about the delay in the delivery of a message: the fate of the world, Davis used to declare, would never be decided on their continent, however many embassies China or Russia might open from Addis Ababa to Conakry or however many Cubans landed. Castle wrote a memorandum for Davis: 'If Zaire replies to No. 172 send copies to Treasury and FO.' He looked at his watch. Davis was ten minutes late.

Castle began to pack his briefcase – he put in a note of what he had to buy for his wife at the cheese shop in Jermyn Street and of a present for his son to whom he had been disagreeable that morning (two packets of Maltesers), and a book, *Clarissa Harlowe*, in which he had never read further than Chapter LXXIX of the first volume. Directly he heard a lift door close and Davis's step in the passage he left his room. His lunchtime with the sausages had been cut by eleven minutes. Unlike Davis he always punctually returned. It was one of the virtues of age.

Arthur Davis in the staid office was conspicuous by his eccentricities. He could be seen now, approaching from the other end of the long white corridor, dressed as if he had just come from a rather horsy country week-end, or perhaps from the public enclosure of a racecourse. He wore a tweed sports jacket of a greenish over-all colour, and he displayed a scarlet spotted handkerchief in the breast pocket: he might have been attached in some way to a tote. But he was like an actor who has been miscast: when he tried to live up to the costume, he usually fumbled the part. If he looked in London as though he had arrived from the country, in the country when he visited Castle he was unmistakably a tourist from the city.

'Sharp on time as usual,' Davis said with his habitual guilty grin.

'My watch is always a little fast,' Castle said, apologising for the criticism which he had not expressed. 'An anxiety complex, I suppose.'

'Smuggling out top secrets as usual?' Davis asked, making a playful pretence at seizing Castle's briefcase. His breath had a sweet smell: he was addicted to port.

'Oh, I've left all those behind for you to sell. You'll get a better price from your shady contacts.'

'Kind of you, I'm sure.'

'And then you're a bachelor. You need more money than a married man. I halve the cost of living . . .'

'Ah, but those awful leftovers,' Davis said, 'the joint remade into shepherd's pie, the dubious meatball. Is it worth it? A married man can't even afford a good port.' He went into the room they shared and rang for Cynthia. Davis had been trying to make Cynthia for two years now, but the daughter of a major-general was after bigger game. All the same Davis continued to hope; it was always safer, he explained, to have an affair inside the department – it couldn't be regarded as a security risk, but Castle knew how deeply attached to Cynthia Davis really was. He had the keen desire for monogamy and the defensive humour of a lonely man. Once Castle had visited him in a flat, which he shared with two men from the Department of the Environment, over an antique shop not far from Claridge's – very central and W1.

'You ought to come in a bit nearer,' Davis had advised Castle in the overcrowded sitting-room where magazines of different tastes – the *New Statesman*, *Penthouse* and *Nature* – littered the sofa, and where the used glasses from someone else's party had been pushed into corners for the daily woman to find.

'You know very well what they pay us,' Castle said, 'and I'm married.'

'A grave error of judgement.'

'Not for me,' Castle said, 'I like my wife.'

'And of course there's the little bastard,' Davis went on. 'I couldn't afford children and port as well.'

'I happen to like the little bastard too.'

Castle was on the point of descending the four stone steps into Piccadilly when the porter said to him, 'Brigadier Tomlinson wants to see you, sir.'

'Brigadier Tomlinson?'

'Yes. In room A.3.'

Castle had only met Brigadier Tomlinson once, many years before, more years than he cared to count, on the day that he was appointed – the day he put his name to the Official Secrets Act, when the brigadier was a very junior officer, if he had been an officer at all. All he could remember of him was a small black moustache hovering like an unidentified flying object over a field of blotting paper, which was entirely white and blank, perhaps for security reasons. The stain of his signature after he had signed the Act became the only flaw on its surface, and that leaf was almost certainly torn up and sent to the incinerator. The Dreyfus case had exposed the perils of a wastepaper basket nearly a century ago.

'Down the corridor on the left, sir,' the porter reminded him when he was about to take the wrong route.

'Come in, come in, Castle,' Brigadier Tomlinson called. His moustache was now as white as the blotting paper, and with the years he had grown a small pot-belly under a double-breasted waistcoat – only his dubious rank remained constant. Nobody knew to what regiment he had formerly belonged, if such a regiment indeed existed, for all military titles in this building were a little suspect. Ranks might just be part of the universal cover. He said, 'I don't think you know Colonel Daintry.'

'No. I don't think . . . How do you do?'

Daintry, in spite of his neat dark suit and his hatchet face, gave a more genuine out-of-doors impression than Davis ever did. If Davis at his first appearance looked as though he would be at home in a bookmakers' compound, Daintry was unmistakably at home in the expensive enclosure or on a grouse moor. Castle enjoyed making lightning sketches of his colleagues: there were times when he even put them on to paper.

'I think I knew a cousin of yours at Corpus,' Daintry said. He spoke agreeably, but he looked a little impatient; he probably had to catch a train north at King's Cross.

'Colonel Daintry,' Brigadier Tomlinson explained, 'is our new broom,' and Castle noticed the way Daintry winced at the description. 'He has taken over security from Meredith. But I'm not sure you ever met Meredith.'

'I suppose you mean my cousin Roger,' Castle said to Daintry. 'I haven't seen him for years. He got a first in Greats. I believe he's in the Treasury now.'

'I've been describing the set-up here to Colonel Daintry,' Brigadier Tomlinson prattled on, keeping strictly to his own wavelength.

'I took Law myself. A poor second,' Daintry said. 'You read History, I think?'

'Yes. A very poor third.'

'At the House?'

'Yes.'

'I've explained to Colonel Daintry,' Tomlinson said, 'that only you and Davis deal with the Top Secret cables as far as Section 6A is concerned.'

'If you can call anything Top Secret in our section. Of course, Watson sees them too.'

'Davis – he's a Reading University man, isn't he?' Daintry asked with what might have been a slight touch of disdain.

'I see you've been doing your homework.'

'As a matter of fact I've just been having a talk with Davis himself.'

'So that's why he was ten minutes too long over his lunch.'

Daintry's smile resembled the painful reopening of a wound. He had very red lips, and they parted at the corners with difficulty. He said, 'I talked to Davis about you, so now I'm talking to you about Davis. An open check. You must forgive the new broom. I have to learn the ropes,' he added, getting confused among the metaphors. 'One has to keep to the drill – in spite of the confidence we have in both of you, of course. By the way, *did* he warn you?'

'No. But why believe me? We may be in collusion.'

The wound opened again a very little way and closed tight.

'I gather that politically he's a bit on the left. Is that so?'

'He's a member of the Labour Party. I expect he told you himself.'

'Nothing wrong in that, of course,' Daintry said. 'And you . . .?'

'I have no politics. I expect Davis told you that too.'

'But you sometimes vote, I suppose?'

'I don't think I've voted once since the war. The issues nowadays so often seem – well, a bit parish pump.'

'An interesting point of view,' Daintry said with disapproval. Castle could see that telling the truth this time had been an error of judgement, yet, except on really important occasions, he always preferred the truth. The truth can be double-checked. Daintry looked at his watch. 'I won't keep you long. I have a train to catch at King's Cross.'

'A shooting week-end?'

'Yes. How did you know?'

'Intuition,' Castle said, and again he regretted his reply. It was always safer to be inconspicuous. There were times, which grew more frequent with every year, when he daydreamed of complete conformity, as a different character might have dreamt of making a dramatic century at Lord's.

'I suppose you noticed my gun-case by the door?'

'Yes,' Castle said, who hadn't seen it until then, 'that was the clue.' He was glad to see that Daintry looked reassured.

Daintry explained, 'There's nothing personal in all this, you know. Purely a routine check. There are so many rules that sometimes some of them get neglected. It's human nature. The regulation, for example, about not taking work out of the office . . .'

He looked significantly at Castle's briefcase. An officer and a gentleman would open it at once for inspection with an easy joke, but Castle was not an officer, nor had he ever classified himself as a gentleman. He wanted to see how far below the table the new broom was liable to sweep. He said, 'I'm not going home. I'm only going out to lunch.'

'You won't mind, will you . . .?' Daintry held out his hand for the briefcase. 'I asked the same of Davis,' he said.

'Davis wasn't carrying a briefcase,' Castle said, 'when I saw him.'

Daintry flushed at his mistake. He would have felt a similar shame, Castle felt sure, if he had shot a beater. 'Oh, it must have been that other chap,' Daintry said. 'I've forgotten his name.'

'Watson?' the brigadier suggested.

'Yes, Watson.'

'So you've even been checking our chief?'

'It's all part of the drill,' Daintry said.

Castle opened his briefcase. He took out a copy of the *Berkhamsted Gazette*.

'What's this?' Daintry asked.

'My local paper. I was going to read it over lunch.'

'Oh yes, of course. I'd forgotten. You live quite a long way out. Don't you find it a bit inconvenient?'

'Less than an hour by train. I need a house and a garden. I have a child, you see – and a dog. You can't keep either of them in a flat. Not with comfort.'

'I notice you are reading *Clarissa Harlowe*. Like it?'

'Yes, so far. But there are four more volumes.'

'What's this?'

'A list of things to remember.'

'To remember?'

'My shopping list,' Castle explained. He had written under the printed address of his house, 129 King's Road, 'Two Maltesers. Half pound Earl

Grey. Cheese – Wensleydale? or Double Gloucester? Yardley Pre-Shave Lotion.'

'What on earth are Maltesers?'

'A sort of chocolate. You should try them. They're delicious. In my opinion better than Kit Kats.'

Daintry said, 'Do you think they would do for my hostess? I'd like to bring her something a little out of the ordinary.' He looked at his watch. 'Perhaps I could send the porter – there's just time. Where do you buy them?'

'He can get them at an ABC in the Strand.'

'ABC?' Daintry asked.

'Aerated Bread Company.'

'Aerated bread . . . what on earth . . .? Oh well, there isn't time to go into that. Are you sure those – teasers would do?'

'Of course, tastes differ.'

'Fortnum's is only a step away.'

'You can't get them there. They are very inexpensive.'

'I don't want to seem niggardly.'

'Then go for quantity. Tell him to get three pounds of them.'

'What is the name again? Perhaps you would tell the porter as you go out.'

'Is my check over then? Am I clear?'

'Oh yes. Yes. I told you it was purely formal, Castle.'

'Good shooting.'

'Thanks a lot.'

Castle gave the porter the message. 'Three pounds did 'e say?'

'Yes.'

'Three pounds of Maltesers!'

'Yes.'

'Can I take a pantechnicon?'

The porter summoned the assistant porter who was reading a girlie magazine. He said, 'Three pounds of Maltesers for Colonel Daintry.'

'That would be a hundred and twenty packets or thereabouts,' the man said after a little calculation.

'No, no,' Castle said, 'it's not as bad as that. The weight, I think, is what he means.'

He left them making their calculations. He was fifteen minutes late at the pub and his usual corner was occupied. He ate and drank quickly and calculated that he had made up three minutes. Then he bought the Yardley's at the chemist in St James's Arcade, the Earl Grey at Jackson's, a Double Gloucester there too to save time, although he usually went to the cheese shop in Jermyn Street, but the Maltesers, which he had intended to buy at the ABC, had run out by the time he got there – the assistant told him there had been an unexpected demand, and he had to buy Kit Kats instead. He was only three minutes late when he rejoined Davis.

'You never told me they were having a check,' he said.

'I was sworn to secrecy. Did they catch you with anything?'

'Not exactly.'

'He did with me. Asked what I had in my mackintosh pocket. I'd got that report from 59800. I wanted to read it again over my lunch.'

'What did he say?'

'Oh, he let me go with a warning. He said rules were made to be kept. To think that fellow Blake (whatever did he want to escape for?) got forty years freedom from income tax, intellectual strain and responsibility, and it's we who suffer for it now.'

'Colonel Daintry wasn't very difficult,' Castle said. 'He knew a cousin of mine at Corpus. That sort of thing makes a difference.'

'A good morning's sport,' Colonel Daintry remarked half-heartedly to Lady Hargreaves as he stamped the mud off his boots before entering the house. 'The birds were going over well.' His fellow guests piled out of cars behind him, with the forced joviality of a football team trying to show their keen sporting enjoyment and not how cold and muddy they really felt.

'Drinks are waiting,' Lady Hargreaves said. 'Help yourselves. Lunch in ten minutes.'

Another car was climbing the hill through the park, a long way off. Somebody bellowed with laughter in the cold wet air, and someone cried, 'Here's Buffy at last. In time for lunch, of course.'

'And your famous steak-and-kidney pudding?' Daintry asked. 'I've heard so much about it.'

'My pie, you mean. Did you really have a good morning, Colonel?' Her voice had a faint American accent – the more aggreeable for being faint, like the tang of an expensive perfume.

'Not many pheasants,' Daintry said, 'but otherwise very fine.'

'Harry,' she called over his shoulder, 'Dicky' and then 'Where's Dodo? Is he lost?' Nobody called Daintry by his first name because nobody knew it. With a sense of loneliness he watched the graceful elongated figure of his hostess limp down the stone steps to greet 'Harry' with a kiss on both cheeks. Daintry went on alone into the dining-room where the drinks stood waiting on the buffet.

A little stout rosy man in tweeds whom he thought he had seen somewhere before was mixing himself a dry martini. He wore silver-rimmed spectacles which glinted in the sunlight. 'Add one for me,' Daintry said, 'if you are making them really dry.'

'Ten to one,' the little man said. 'A whiff of the cork, eh? Always use a scent spray myself. You are Daintry, aren't you? You've forgotten me. I'm Percival. I took your blood pressure once.'

'Oh yes. Doctor Percival. We're in the same firm more or less, aren't we?'

'That's right. C wanted us to get together quietly – no need for all that nonsense with scramblers here. I can never make mine work, can you? The trouble is, though, that I don't shoot. I only fish. This your first time here?'

'Yes. When did you arrive?'

'A bit early. Around midday. I'm a Jaguar fiend. Can't go at less than a hundred.'

Daintry looked at the table. A bottle of beer stood by every place. He didn't like beer, but for some reason beer seemed always to be regarded as suitable for a shoot. Perhaps it went with the boyishness of the occasion like ginger beer at Lord's. Daintry was not boyish. A shoot to him was an exercise of strict competitive skill – he had once been runner-up for the King's Cup. Now down the centre of the table stood small silver sweet bowls which he saw contained his Maltesers. He had been a little embarrassed the night before when he had presented almost a crate of them to Lady Hargreaves; she obviously hadn't an idea what they were or what to do with them. He felt that he had been deliberately fooled by that man Castle. He was glad to see they looked more sophisticated in silver bowls than they had done in plastic bags.

'Do you like beer?' he asked Percival.

'I like anything alcoholic,' Percival said, 'except Fernet-Branca,' and then the boys burst boisterously in – Buffy and Dodo, Harry and Dicky and all; the silver and the glasses vibrated with joviality. Daintry was glad Percival was there, for nobody seemed to know Percival's first name either.

Unfortunately he was separated from him at table. Percival had quickly finished his first bottle of beer and begun on a second. Daintry felt betrayed, for Percival seemed to be getting on with his neighbours as easily as if they had been members of the old firm too. He had begun to tell a fishing story which had made the man called Dicky laugh. Daintry was sitting between the fellow he took to be Buffy and a lean elderly man with a lawyer's face. He had introduced himself, and his surname was familiar. He was either the Attorney-General or the Solicitor-General, but Daintry couldn't remember which; his uncertainty inhibited conversation.

Buffy said suddenly, 'My God, if those are not Maltesers!'

'You know Maltesers?' Daintry asked.

'Haven't tasted one for donkey's years. Always bought them at the movies when I was a kid. Taste wonderful. There's no movie house around here surely?'

'As a matter of fact I brought them from London.'

'You go to the movies? Haven't been to one in ten years. So they still sell Maltesers?'

'You can buy them in shops too.'

'I never knew that. Where did you find them?'

'In an ABC.'

'ABC?'

Daintry repeated dubiously what Castle had said, 'Aerated Bread Company.'

'Extraordinary! What's aerated bread?'

'I don't know,' Daintry said.

'The things they do invent nowadays. I wouldn't be surprised, would you, if their loaves were made by computers?' He leant forward and took a Malteser and crackled it at his ear like a cigar.

Lady Hargreaves called down the table, 'Buffy! Not before the steak-and-kidney pie.'

'Sorry, my dear. Couldn't resist. Haven't tasted one since I was a kid.' He said to Daintry, 'Extraordinary things computers, I paid 'em a fiver once to find me a wife.'

'You aren't married?' Daintry asked, looking at the gold ring Buffy wore.

'No. Always keep that on for protection. Wasn't really serious, you know. Like to try out new gadgets. Filled up a form as long as your arm. Qualifications, interests, professions, what have you.' He took another Malteser. 'Sweet tooth,' he said. 'Always had it.'

'And did you get any applicants?'

'They sent me along a girl. Girl! Thirty-five if a day. I had to give her tea. Haven't had tea since my mum died. I said, "My dear, do you mind if we make it a whisky? I know the waiter here. He'll slip us one!" She said she didn't drink. Didn't drink!'

'The computer had slipped up?'

'She had a degree in Economics at London University. And big spectacles. Flat-chested. She said she was a good cook. I said I always

57

took my meals at White's.'

'Did you ever see her again?'

'Not to speak to, but once she waved to me from a bus as I was coming down the club steps. Embarrassing! Because I was with Dicky at the time. That's what happened when they let buses go up St James's Street. No one was safe.'

After the steak-and-kidney pie came a treacle tart and a big Stilton cheese and Sir John Hargreaves circulated the port. There was a faint feeling of unrest at the table as though the holidays had been going on too long. People began to glance through the windows at the grey sky: in a few hours the light would fail. They drank their port rapidly as if with a sense of guilt – they were not really there for idle pleasure – except Percival who wasn't concerned. He was telling another fishing story and had four empty bottles of beer beside him.

The Solicitor-General – or was it the Attorney-General? – said heavily, 'We ought to be moving. The sun's going down.' He certainly was not here for enjoyment, only for execution, and Daintry sympathised with his anxiety. Hargreaves really ought to make a move, but Hargreaves was almost asleep. After years in the Colonial Service – he had once been a young District Commissioner on what was then the Gold Coast – he had acquired the knack of snatching his siesta in the most unfavourable circumstances, even surrounded by quarrelling chiefs, who used to make more noise than Buffy.

'John,' Lady Hargreaves called down the table, 'wake up.'

He opened blue serene unshockable eyes and said, 'A cat-nap.' It was said that as a young man somewhere in Ashanti he had inadvertently eaten human flesh, but his digestion had not been impaired. According to the story he had told the Governor, 'I couldn't really complain, sir. They were doing me a great honour by inviting me to take pot luck.'

'Well, Daintry,' he said, 'I suppose it's time we got on with the massacre.'

He unrolled himself from the table and yawned. 'Your steak-and-kidney pie, dear, is *too* good.'

Daintry watched him with envy. He envied him in the first place for his position. He was one of the very few men outside the services ever to have been appointed C. No one in the firm knew why he had been chosen – all kinds of recondite influences had been surmised, for his only experience of intelligence had been gained in Africa during the war. Daintry also envied him his wife; she was so rich, so decorative, so impeccably American. An American marriage, it seemed, could not be classified as a foreign marriage: to marry a foreigner special permission had to be obtained and it was often refused, but to marry an American was perhaps to confirm the special relationship. He wondered all the same whether Lady Hargreaves had been positively vetted by M15 and been passed by the FBI.

'Tonight,' Hargreaves said, 'we'll have a chat, Daintry, won't we? You and I and Percival. When this crowd has gone home.'

Sir John Hargreaves limped round, handing out cigars, pouring out whiskies, poking the fire. 'I don't enjoy shooting much myself,' he said. 'Never used to shoot in Africa, except with a camera, but my wife likes all the old English customs. If you have land, she says, you must have birds. I'm afraid there weren't enough pheasants, Daintry.'

'I had a very good day,' Daintry said, 'all in all.'

'I wish you ran to a trout stream,' Doctor Percival said.

'Oh yes, fishing's your game, isn't it? Well, you might say we've got a bit of fishing on hand now.' He cracked a log with his poker. 'Useless,' he said, 'but I love to see the sparks fly. There seems to be a leak somewhere in Section 6.'

Percival said, 'At home or in the field?'

'I'm not sure, but I have a nasty feeling that it's here at home. In one of the African sections – 6A.'

'I've just finished going through Section 6,' Daintry said. 'Only a routine run through. So as to get to know people.'

'Yes, so they told me. That's why I asked you to come here. Enjoyed having you for the shoot too, of course. Did anything strike you?'

'Security's got a bit slack. But that's true of all other sections too. I made a rough check for example of what people take out in their briefcases at lunchtime. Nothing serious, but I was surprised at the number of briefcases . . . It's a warning, that's all, of course. But a warning might scare a nervous man. We can't very well ask them to strip.'

'They do that in the diamond fields, but I agree that in the West End stripping would seem a bit unusual.'

'Anyone really out of order?' Percival asked.

'Not seriously. Davis in 6A was carrying a report – said he wanted to read it over lunch. I warned him, of course, and made him leave it behind with Brigadier Tomlinson. I've gone through all the traces too. Vetting has been done very efficiently since the Blake case broke, but we still have a few men who were with us in the bad old days. Some of them even go back as far as Burgess and Maclean. We *could* start tracing them all over again, but it's difficult to pick up a cold scent.'

'It's possible, of course, just possible,' C said, 'that the leak came from abroad and that the evidence has been planted here. They would like to disrupt us, damage morale and hurt us with the Americans. The knowledge that there was a leak, if it became public, could be more damaging than the leak itself.'

'That's what I was thinking,' Percival said. 'Questions in Parliament. All the old names thrown up – Vassall, the Portland affair, Philby. But if they're after publicity, there's little we can do.'

'I suppose a Royal Commission would be appointed to shut the stable door,' Hargreaves said. 'But let's assume for a moment that they are really after information and not scandal. Section 6 seems a most unlikely department for that. There are no atomic secrets in Africa: guerrillas, tribal wars, mercenaries, petty dictators, crop failures, building scandals, gold beds, nothing very secret there. That's why I wonder whether the motive may be simply scandal, to prove they have penetrated the British Secret Service yet again.'

'Is it an important leak, C?' Percival asked.

'Call it a very small drip, mainly economic, but the interesting thing is that apart from economics it concerns the Chinese. Isn't it possible – the Russians are such novices in Africa – that they want to make use of our service for information on the Chinese?'

'There's precious little they can learn from us,' Percival said.

'But you know what it's always like at everybody's Centre. One thing no one can ever stand there is a blank white card.'

'Why don't we send them carbon copies, with our compliments, of what we send the Americans? There's supposed to be a *détente*, isn't there? Save everyone a lot of trouble.' Percival took a little tube from his pocket and sprayed his glasses, then wiped them with a clean white handkerchief.

'Help yourself to the whisky,' C said. 'I'm too stiff to move after that bloody shoot. Any ideas, Daintry?'

'Most of the people in Section 6 are post-Blake. If their traces are unreliable then no one is safe.'

'All the same, the source seems to be Section 6 – and probably 6A. Either at home or abroad.'

'The head of Section 6, Watson, is a relative newcomer,' Daintry said. 'He was very thoroughly vetted. Then there's Castle – he's been with us a very long time, we brought him back from Pretoria seven years ago because they needed him in 6A, and there were personal reasons too – trouble about the girl he wanted to marry. Of course, he belongs to the slack vetting days, but I'd say he was clear. Dullish man, first-class, of course, with files – it's generally the brilliant and ambitious who are dangerous. Castle is safely married, second time, his first wife's dead. There's one child, a house on mortgage in Metroland. Life insurance – payments up to date. No high living. He doesn't even run to a car. I believe he bicycles every day to the station. A third class in history at the House. Careful and scrupulous. Roger Castle in the Treasury is his cousin.'

'You think he's quite clear then?'

'He has his eccentricities, but I wouldn't say dangerous ones. For instance he suggested I bring those Maltesers to Lady Hargreaves.'

'Maltesers?'

'It's a long story. I won't bother you with it now. And then there's Davis. I don't know that I'm quite so happy about Davis, in spite of the positive vetting.'

'Pour me out another whisky, would you, Percival, there's a good chap. Every year I say it's my last shoot.'

'But those steak-and-kidney pies of your wife's are wonderful. I wouldn't miss them,' Percival said.

'I daresay we could find another excuse for them.'

'You could try putting trout in that stream . . .'

Daintry again experienced a twitch of envy; once more he felt left out. He had no life in common with his companions in the world outside the borders of security. Even as a gun he felt professional. Percival was said to collect pictures, and C? A whole social existence had been opened up for him by his rich American wife. The steak-and-kidney pie was all that Daintry was permitted to share with them outside office hours – for the first and perhaps the last time.

'Tell me more about Davis,' C said.

'Reading University. Mathematics and physics. Did some of his military service at Aldermaston. Never supported – anyway openly – the marchers. Labour Party, of course.'

'Like forty-five per cent of the population,' C said.

'Yes, yes, of course, but all the same . . . He's a bachelor. Lives alone. Spends fairly freely. Fond of vintage port. Bets on the tote. That's a classic way, of course, of explaining why you can afford . . .'

'What does he afford? Besides port.'

'Well, he has a Jaguar.'

'So have I,' Percival said. 'I suppose we mustn't ask you how the leak was discovered?'

'I wouldn't have brought you here if I couldn't tell you that. Watson knows, but no one else in Section 6. The source of information is an unusual one – A Soviet defector who remains in place.'

'Could the leak come from Section 6 abroad?' Daintry asked.

'It could, but I doubt it. It's true that one report they had seemed to come direct from Lourenço Marques. It was word for word as 69300 wrote it. Almost like a photostat of the actual report, so one might have thought that the leak was there if it weren't for a few corrections and deletions. Inaccuracies which could only have been spotted here by comparing the report with the files.'

'A secretary?' Percival suggested.

'Daintry began his check with those, didn't you? They are more heavily vetted than anyone. That leaves us Watson, Castle and Davis.'

'A thing that worries me,' Daintry said, 'is that Davis was the one who was taking a report out of the office. One from Pretoria. No apparent importance, but it did have a Chinese angle. He said he wanted to reread it over lunch. He and Castle had got to discuss it later with Watson. I checked the truth of that with Watson.'

'What do you suggest we do?' C asked.

'We could put down a maximum security check with the help of 5 and Special Branch. On everyone in Section 6. Letters, telephone calls, bug flats, watch movements.'

'If things were as simple as that, Daintry, I wouldn't have bothered you to come up here. This is only a second-class shoot, and I knew the pheasants would disappoint you.'

Hargreaves lifted his bad leg with both hands and eased it towards the fire. 'Suppose we did prove Davis to be the culprit – or Castle or Watson. What should we do then?'

'Surely that would be up to the courts,' Daintry said.

'Headlines in the papers. Another trial *in camera*. No one outside would know how small and unimportant the leaks were. Whoever he is he won't rate forty years like Blake. Perhaps he'll serve ten if the prison's secure.'

'That's not our concern surely.'

'No, Daintry, but I don't enjoy the thought of that trial one little bit. What co-operation can we expect from the Americans afterwards? And then there's our source. I told you, he's still in place. We don't want to blow him as long as he proves useful.'

'In a way,' Percival said, 'it would be better to close our eyes like a complaisant husband. Draft whoever it is to some innocuous department. Forget things.'

'And abet a crime?' Daintry protested.

'Oh, crime,' Percival said and smiled at C like a fellow conspirator. 'We are all committing crimes somewhere, aren't we? It's our job.'

'The trouble is,' C said, 'that the situation *is* a bit like a rocky marriage. In a marriage, if the lover begins to be bored by the complaisant husband, he can always provoke a scandal. He holds the strong suit. He can choose his own time. I don't want any scandal provoked.'

Daintry hated flippancy. Flippancy was like a secret code of which he didn't possess the book. He had the right to read cables and reports marked Top Secret, but flippancy like this was so secret that he hadn't a clue to its understanding. He said, 'Personally I would resign rather than cover up.' He put down his glass of whisky so hard that he chipped the crystal. Lady Hargreaves again, he thought. She must have insisted on crystal. He said, 'I'm sorry.'

'Of course you are right, Daintry,' Hargreaves said. 'Never mind the glass. Please don't think I've brought you all the way up here to persuade you to let things drop, if we have sufficient proof . . . But a trial isn't necessarily the right answer. The Russians don't usually bring things to a trial with their own people. The trial of Penkovsky gave all of us a great boost in morale, they even exaggerated his importance, just as the CIA did. I still wonder why they held it. I wish I were a chess player. Do you play chess, Daintry?'

'No, bridge is my game.'

'The Russians don't play bridge, or so I understand.'

'Is that important?'

'We are playing games, Daintry, games, all of us. It's important not to take a game too seriously or we may lose it. We have to keep flexible, but it's important, naturally, to play the same game.'

'I'm sorry, sir,' Daintry said, 'I don't understand what you are talking about.'

He was aware that he had drunk too much whisky, and he was aware that C and Percival were deliberately looking away from each other – they didn't want to humiliate him. They had heads of stone, he thought, stone.

'Shall we just have one more whisky,' C said, 'or perhaps not. It's been a long wet day. Percival . . .?'

Daintry said, 'I'd like another.'

Percival poured out the drinks. Daintry said, 'I'm sorry to be difficult, but I'd like to get things a little clearer before bed, or I won't sleep.'

'It's really very simple,' C said. 'Put on your maximum security check if you like. It may flush the bird without more trouble. He'll soon realize what's going on – if he's guilty, that is. You might think up some kind of test – the old marked fiver technique seldom fails. When we are quite certain he's our man, then it seems to me we will just have to eliminate him. No trial, no publicity. If we can get information about his contacts

63

first, so much the better, but we mustn't risk a public flight and then a press conference in Moscow. An arrest too is out of the question. Granted that he's in Section 6, there's no information he can possibly give which would do as much harm as the scandal of a court case.'

'Elimination? You mean . . .'

'I know that elimination is rather a new thing for us. More in the KGB line or the CIA's. That's why I wanted Percival here to meet you. We may need the help of his science boys. Nothing spectacular. Doctor's certificate. No inquest if it can be avoided. A suicide's only too easy, but then a suicide always means an inquest, and that might lead to a question in the House. Everyone knows now what a "department of the Foreign Office" means. "Was any question of security involved?" You know the kind of thing some back-bencher is sure to ask. And no one ever believes the official answer. Certainly not the Americans.'

'Yes,' Percival said, 'I quite understand. He should die quietly, peacefully, without pain too, poor chap. Pain sometimes shows on the face, and there may be relatives to consider. A natural death . . .'

'It's a bit difficult, I realise, with all the new antibiotics,' C said. 'Assuming for the moment that it *is* Davis, he's a man of only just over forty. In the prime of life.'

'I agree. A heart attack might just possibly be arranged. Unless . . . Does anyone know whether he drinks a lot?'

'You said something about port, didn't you, Daintry?'

'I'm not saying he's guilty,' Daintry said.

'None of us are,' C said. 'We are only taking Davis as a possible example . . . to help us examine the problem.'

'I'd like to look at his medical history,' Percival said, 'and I'd like to get to know him on some excuse. In a way he would be my patient, wouldn't he? That is to say if . . .'

'You and Daintry could arrange that somehow together. There's no great hurry. We have to be quite sure he's our man. And now – it's been a long day – too many hares and too few pheasants – sleep well. Breakfast on a tray. Eggs and bacon? Sausages? Tea or coffee?'

Percival said, 'The works, coffee, bacon, eggs and sausages, if that's all right.'

'Nine o'clock?'

'Nine o'clock.'

'And you, Daintry?'

'Just coffee and toast. Eight o'clock if you don't mind. I can never sleep late and I have a lot of work waiting.'

'You ought to relax more,' C said.

THE FATE OF
THE TRAITOR

WILLIAM LE QUEUX

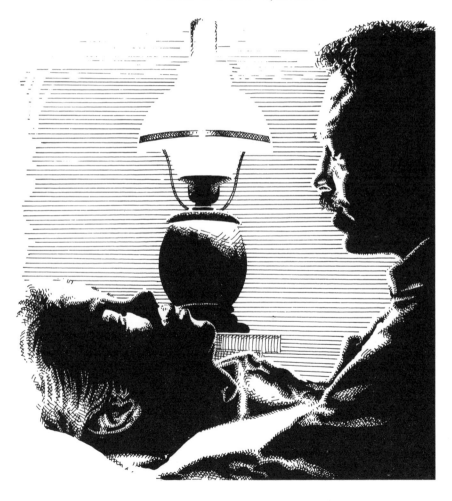

THE FATE OF THE TRAITOR

Pale yellow sunset had poured out its cold half-light upon the roofs, and gradually in the depths of the London streets everything grew grey and dim. In the clear deep blue the first star was already shining. Objects began to assume a disordered aspect, and melt away in the darkness. The city, worn out with the vanity of the day, had become calm, as if gathering strength to pass the evening in the same vanity and turmoil.

Already the lights of the street lamps in Oakleigh Gardens were springing up, forming long, straight lines, as I drew down the blind and flung myself into the inviting armchair before the cheerful fire. Taking from the table an open letter written in cipher, I read it through by the flickering firelight. It was addressed to Pétroff, and ran as follows:

'Nicolas Kassatkin, who will arrive in London on Tuesday next, is a trusted and valued member of our Circle at Novgorod. He has been twice imprisoned, first at Petropaulovsk, and secondly at Schlusselburg, whence he has escaped. We are sending him to you because we are confident that he can be of assistance. He is daring, enthusiastic, and speaks several languages. Being in possession of a private income, he will not need any financial help from the Executive. He will be the bearer of a note to you. – Signed, on behalf of the Novgorod Brothers of Freedom – SOLOMON GOLDSTEIN, ALEXANDER ROSTOVTZEFF.'

I replaced it upon the table, and leaning back in the chair, smoked reflectively.

Having called to consult the Executive on some urgent business, Pétroff had asked me to remain and welcome the newcomer. By repute I knew him as a fearless Revolutionist, who had taken an active part in several plots which had for their object the removal of corrupt officials, and had been more or less successful.

I was plunged in reverie, induced perhaps by the dim, uncertain light of the fire and the soothing properties of nicotine, when a loud ring at the hall-bell aroused me. Almost immediately afterwards I heard the voices of Pétroff, Tersinski, and Grinevitch welcoming the stranger in Russian, and a few moments later they entered and introduced him to me.

We shook hands cordially, and as Grinevitch lit the gas I saw that the stranger was a man of medium height, and about thirty years of age. His face was of a rather low type. He had deep-set, grey eyes, with a fixed stare, a large, fair moustache, prominent cheek bones, and fair, lank, unkempt hair, while his deeply-furrowed brow spoke mutely of long

67

imprisonment and infinite pain and suffering. Removing his heavy travelling-coat, he seated himself before the fire to thaw, at the same time taking a letter from his pocket and handing it to Paul Pétroff.

Presently we sat down to dinner together, and during the meal Kassatkin showed himself to be an entertaining companion and vivacious talker. I sat next him, and he told us of the progress of the revolutionary movement in Novgorod, declaring that there were unmistakable signs of general upheaval, of an awakening of the public spirit, of patriotism, and of opposition, foreshadowing a coming struggle. He was bitter in his condemnation of the dark deeds of the Tzar's officials, and expressed an opinion that if Russia could tell something approaching to the full truth about what was going on within her boundaries – the crimes committed in darkness, the malversations practised, the real state of the exchequer, the desperate tricks of the financiers – it would inflict upon the Autocracy a more severe blow than many conspiracies could strike.

'Tell us of your escape,' I said, after he had related the story of his arrest and imprisonment for carrying on propaganda among the soldiers of the Novgorod garrison.

'Ah!' he exclaimed, his face brightening. 'It has been a terrible experience, but I was driven to desperation.' Turning to Pétroff he said: 'You know the frightful horrors of Schlusselburg – the cold wet cells below the water?'

'I have, alas! much cause to remember them,' Paul answered, with a heavy sigh. 'My wife, whom I loved so well, was imprisoned there at the same time as myself. The solitary confinement and the horrors of her cell drove her hopelessly insane. She is now an inmate of the criminal asylum at Krasnoje Selo.'

'Madness is the fate of the majority of prisoners there,' said Kassatkin. 'In my case the many months of absolute silence and lack of exercise drove me into a state bordering on insanity. In order to check the imbecility that was slowly but surely taking possession of me, I used to pace my damp, dark cell and compose verses. For days, weeks, months, I had no other occupation than the composition of poems, which I afterwards committed to memory, having no writing materials. This was the only mental employment I had, and, although I grew strangely lightheaded, yet my self-imposed tasks prevented my mind becoming totally unhinged. An opportunity for escape presented itself in a most unexpected manner. A large batch of "common law" prisoners had been sent from Petersburg, and the prison being already overcrowded, I was removed from my cell and confined in a room in the fire-tower. It thus happened that I was locked up in an ordinary room, with a window looking upon the bridge. It was rather high, but it was near the waterpipe running along the wall outside, and there was a slanting roof of the lower storey which could be utilised for the descent. I could not lose such an opportunity, and, in the dead of night, I opened the window and descended upon the bridge connecting the prison with the bank, congratulating myself upon a happy escape.'

'Were you discovered?' I asked.

'Yes, almost immediately. By ill-luck a sentry noticed me and gave the alarm. It was an exciting moment as I made a dash for the forest and disappeared among the trees. Half-a-dozen soldiers pursued me, but only for a short distance, and apparently considering that they had a poor chance of capturing a fugitive in a forest, they returned to the prison for assistance. I concealed myself and waited. Presently about twenty mounted soldiers galloped past along the forest road. When they were out of sight I left my hiding-place and walked on. My position was, however, critical, therefore I returned to the Neva, as I could not lose my way beside the river. I soon came to the water's edge. By the opposite bank were some islands and something like a lake or arm of the river, near which I could see what in the fog appeared to be masts. Close beside me on the bank sat a group of fishermen, and a little way off an old man was doing something to a boat. Having two or three roubles in my pocket, I went up and asked the old man to ferry me across the river. He consented, but asked in a conversational way why I wanted to go across. Remembering the masts, I replied that I had to go on board a schooner that lay in the distance. The old man looked at me suspiciously.

'He asked who I was, and I told him that I was a working-man from Tichvin. The old man put on a very suspicious air and began a minute interrogation. I was at my wits' end, and ready to make a dash for it; but that was out of the question: the fishermen were close by and would have caught me in five minutes. I resolved to take the bull by the horns, so I told the man that I had simply made up the former story, and that, in reality, I was an escaped political prisoner seeking a hiding-place. When the old man had asked me numerous other questions, he said: "Well, I won't ferry you across myself, but I'll tell my boy to. He'll land you on the island, and you can stop there until to-morrow night. You're all right so far. Only, look here, don't you go telling anybody that you have to go to your schooner. In my young days there used to be plenty of schooners there, but for thirty years past there hasn't been one near the place."

'The old man then called a young fisherman, and told him to row me across to the island. On parting from the man who ferried me, I started to explore the place, which I found to be very marshy. The morning broke wet and cheerless, and I spent the day in a disused hut. When evening set in, it became too cold for me to spend the night shelterless, and as I was suffering severely from hunger, I wandered up and down the swampy forest looking for a village. By the time I succeeded in finding one it was quite dark. I knocked at a cottage door, but the people would not let me in. I went to a second and third cottage, but with no success. Finally I lost my temper, and addressing an obdurate householder, asked him where the *starosta* lived.

'The peasant directed me to the *starosta's* cottage, and then slammed his door. I tapped at the door of the residence indicated, and it was opened by a woman. When I asked for the official I was in search of, she replied, "I am the *starosta*. What do you want?" It appeared that she really was the *starosta*. The office was filled by all the peasants in the village in turn; and she, being an independent householder, took her turn like the men. I rattled off a wild story, how I had come for a holiday from Petersburg with some friends; how they had become intoxicated, and, for a practical joke, had returned home, leaving me alone on the island. The female *starosta* evinced the warmest sympathy with my misfortune, gave me supper, and allowed me to pass the night in her cottage.

'Next morning I hired a boat, arrived safely in Petersburg, and found my friends, who hid me for some time, while the police scoured the roads and country around Schlusselburg, and searched all the houses that appeared to them suspicious. When the excitement died down, I travelled as an ordinary passenger to the frontier, and have now arrived here.'

That evening I took Kassatkin to live with me at my chambers, and found him a pleasant, easy-going fellow, whose shrewdness proved most valuable to me in the various matters upon which I was from time to time engaged. We went about a good deal, and made many friends. I had always been considered a fair amateur actor, and was prevailed upon to join a well-known dramatic club which gave frequent performances at Kensington Town Hall.

Many of my friends belonged to the club, and I found the rehearsals a pleasant and amusing recreation, inasmuch as the people with whom I was brought into contact were useful to me in a variety of ways. They knew I was a foreigner, but believed me to be French, little suspecting that I was a Nihilist.

One evening there had been a dress-rehearsal of a new comedy which we were about to produce for copyright purposes. I was cast for the part of an affected English curate, one of the chief characters in the piece.

The rehearsal passed off satisfactorily, and it was nearly midnight

when I left the hall and started on my walk homeward. I had a good
hour's tramp through the West End before me; but, as the night was clear
and warm, I enjoyed the prospect rather than otherwise. As I walked
along Kensington Gore there was scarce a sound in the street, save the
occasional tread of a policeman, or the hurried footfall of the belated
pleasure-seeker, breaking the stillness of the night suddenly, and then
dying away in a succession of faint echoes.

Had any friend met me I should scarcely have been recognised, from
the fact that I was still in clerical attire, having dressed myself at home to
avoid trouble. I wore a long black coat of orthodox cut, black
unmentionables, a clerical collar, a soft, wide-brimmed hat, and was
effectually disguised, though I thought nothing of the circumstances at
the time, having frequently worn my stage clothes out of doors.

I had walked for perhaps half an hour in silent contemplation, when I
suddenly became aware that I had taken a wrong turning and that my
footsteps had involuntarily carried me into that patrician of Kensington
thoroughfares, Cromwell Road.

At that moment I was passing a large, handsome-looking house, the
outward appearance of which had an unmistakable air of wealth. The
other houses were in darkness, but several of the windows of this one
were brilliantly lit.

Suddenly I heard something that caused me to pause. It sounded like a
long, shrill scream.

A moment later the door was opened by a man-servant, who ran
hurriedly down the steps. As he confronted me he stopped short, and
peering into my face, said—

'Sir, would you have the kindness to step inside for a few minutes. His
lordship sent me to look for a gentleman, and it is fortunate I found one so
near.'

'A gentleman!' I exclaimed, astonished. 'But I—'

'His lordship's daughter is dying, sir, and he told me to get the first
gentleman I could find.'

The man led the way up the steps, and, dumbfounded by the sudden
manner in which I had been accosted, I followed.

He ushered me into a small but very elegantly furnished room, and
then went to find his master. Just at that moment I heard the footsteps of
two other men, who apparently entered from the street and walked down
the hall to the room adjoining the one in which I was. I had hardly time to
look about me, when the servant returned, accompanied by a strange-
looking old man. He was well dressed, but seemed out of place in the
clothes he wore. Small and thin, he had snow-white hair, sunken cheeks,

and eyes in which shone a peculiar lustre. The manner in which he advanced to greet me was strange, for he seemed to glide noiselessly across the room. His face was colourless, and would have seemed almost devoid of life had it not been for his restless, glittering eyes.

'His lordship,' explained the servant.

I bowed, and the man retired. For a moment the old gentleman's eyes shifted and roved, then he fixed my gaze with them, and said slowly, in a squeaky voice—

'I have a theory that everything may be purchased; that every man has his price. Do you agree with me?'

I was surprised. I shrank from him, and despised and hated him.

'Most things can undoubtedly be bought; but not everything,' I replied.

He smiled sadly.

'Of course, neither life nor intellect can be purchased; but the securing of any service from any person capable of performing it is merely a question of money.'

I nodded approbation of this remark, wondering what service he needed at my hands.

'I am quite at my wits' end, and I require a small service from you,' he said suddenly, as a look of blank, unutterable despair swept over his face. He looked wearied and despondent; I pitied him.

'If I can render you that service I shall be pleased,' I replied.

His face brightened; the haggard expression vanished.

'Thank you,' he said. 'It is perhaps a strange request, still I can find many men who will be only too eager to accept my offer.'

'But I am not—'

'Never mind,' he interrupted; 'allow me to explain. I am the Earl of Wansford.'

I gave vent to an ejaculation of surprise, for the Earl was a well-known figure in the diplomatic world, and until three years ago had been British Ambassador to Russia. He smiled as he noticed my astonishment, and continued—

'I have but one daughter, who, alas! is dying. The physicians say hers is a hopeless case, and I desire that her last moments shall be made happy.'

'Ah! you want me to attend at the bedside and minister words of consolation. I am sorry I cannot—'

'No,' he snarled, 'she is religious enough, and does not require you in that capacity.'

'But surely a dying person, whether prepared for the next world or not, should see a clergyman!' I said.

'True; but Muriel is insane,' he replied. 'You remember what I said a minute ago, that it is only a question of money to any man?'

'What!'

'Why, marriage.'

I was puzzled. I could not comprehend his meaning.

'But what do you want of me?' I asked.

'A trifling service. You can perform it now; but if you refuse, you will always regret.'

'Tell me what it is, and I will give my answer.'

'It is this. Some time ago – perhaps about three years – while we were living in St Petersburg, I became ill, and was obliged to go to the South of France. During my absence my daughter met a Russian for whom she conceived a violent fancy. Since I returned and brought her home to England, she has done nothing but mope and mourn for him, with the result that her intellect is impaired.'

'But will not the man marry her?' I asked, interested in the romance.

'He disappeared mysteriously, and although I have made the most strenuous efforts to trace him, he cannot be found. Of course she would marry him if she could; but her mental faculties are so weak that she would marry any one else and believe it to be him. But here's the point—'

He felt in his pocket, and producing a wallet, took from it a roll of clean crisp Bank of England notes. He counted twenty of them, each for one hundred pounds, and held them towards me.

'These are yours,' he said slowly, 'if you will consent to be my daughter's husband!'

The strange proposal caused me to gasp. Two thousand pounds! Did ever temptation stand in man's path in a more alluring guise? I had but little money of my own, and with this sum I could do many things.

Here was a dying girl whose passage to the grave would be rendered brighter by my marrying her; who would die in a few days, or weeks at most, and know no difference. Nobody need be aware of this strange midnight adventure, or the manner in which I had been bought. I hesitated.

'I give you my word that none know of her insanity except myself, and that she is upon her death-bed,' said my tempter.

Still I paused. I was wondering what could be the Earl's ulterior motive. Besides, I had no desire to enter the ranks of Benedicts.

'Come, decide. I have a clergyman ready and a licence. Some one shall make my darling's last moments happy. Is not the money enough? Well, here's another thousand. Will you accept it?'

I summoned courage, and drawing a long breath, stretched forth my hand and grasped the notes, which I thrust hastily into my pocket.

I had sold myself. I had offered myself as a sacrifice to Mammon, as others had done. My purchaser opened the door, and called softly, 'It's all right.'

'Is it?' asked the clergyman who entered. 'You are, I understand, the affianced husband of Lady Muriel?' he asked, addressing me.

'Yes,' I replied. Was it not true? Had I not three thousand pounds in my pocket as evidence of the fact?

'Come,' said the old man impatiently, as he led the way upstairs to a large bedroom on the first floor, where the light was so dim that I could hardly more than distinguish the shape of the bed and the form of some one closely covered up in it. The footman, who had accosted me in the street, entered behind us, and we took our places at the bedside.

Gradually, as my eyes grew accustomed to the semi-darkness, I could see that my future wife was lying upon her side, and with her face turned from me.

'Take her hand,' commanded the man to whom I had sold myself.

I obeyed.

'Proceed with the ceremony.'

The clergyman droned off the service by heart with the characteristic nasal intonation. Probably I faltered a little at the responses, but my dying bride never hesitated. Though her voice was low as distant music, her every word was prompt and clear.

I gave the *alias* I frequently used, Vladimir Mordvinoff, and when I uttered the name I fancied that she started.

'*Mojnoli?*' she gasped in a strange half-whisper, but she did not turn to look at me. It was evident, however, that she spoke Russian.

The ceremony concluded, we were pronounced man and wife; I was the husband of a girl who was insane, and whose face I had never looked upon!

Was ever there a stranger marriage? The thin wasted fingers that lay in my grasp were cold. A strange sense of guilt crept over me when I remembered that I had bound myself irrevocably to her, deceiving her during her last moments upon earth.

'Come,' exclaimed his lordship. 'Let us go downstairs and sign the necessary documents.'

We all descended to the library, where the register was filled up and the signatures affixed, the clergyman handing me the certificate with a murmur of congratulation. A bottle of champagne was produced, and we each drank a glass, after which I was allowed to return to the room alone to make the acquaintance of my wife.

I entered on tiptoe, almost breathlessly, and paused for a moment beside the bed, trying to speak. At first my mouth refused to utter a sound. What could I say? Suddenly the Nihilist pass-word flashed across my mind, and I uttered it. Its effect was almost magical. Struggling, she endeavoured to rise, but could only support herself upon her elbow, at the same time giving me the secret countersign.

I was anxious to see her countenance, so I turned up the gas, afterwards bending down to look upon her. It was a pretty, delicate face, but cut and swollen as if by savage blows, discoloured and disfigured, a blanched face in which were obvious signs of insanity!

When our eyes met she started, scrutinised me closely, and uttered a shrill scream of joy.

I recognised her instantly. While I was living in Petersburg several years before, she had been admitted to our Circle. She gave the name of Muriel Radford, but beyond the fact that she was English and that she apparently had plenty of money at her disposal, we knew nothing of her. At the meetings of the Circle we often met and had many a pleasant *tête-à-tête*. I had admired her and more than once was tempted to declare my love, but I refrained from doing so until too late, for suddenly, one snowy night in midwinter, I was compelled to fly from the Russian capital. Since then I had neither seen nor heard of her.

Now I had discovered her under these extraordinary circumstances.

She kissed me fondly, passionately, and I was about to explain our strange marriage, when the terrible light of insanity in her eyes caused me to hesitate. Of what use was it to speak? She did not understand.

Taking a small bunch of keys from under her lace-edged pillow, she handed them to me, saying—

'Go to that cabinet over there and unlock the second drawer. In the right-hand corner you will find a packet. Bring it here and open it.'

I did as I was commanded, and brought to the bedside a small packet of letters secured with crimson ribbon. As I untied the knot a cabinet photograph fell out upon the bed. I picked it up and looked at it.

It was a picture of myself!

'How did you obtain this?' I asked eagerly.

'I have never ceased to think of you,' she replied. 'I prevailed upon one of your friends in Petersburg to give me the picture. But there is another photograph there. Take it out and look at it.'

Searching among the papers, I found the picture she indicated.

When I turned it face upwards in the gaslight it almost fell from my grasp, for I recognised it as a portrait of my companion with whom I shared chambers.

'Do you know Kassatkin?' I asked, in astonishment.

'Yes, I do,' she said, and raising herself upon her elbow, she continued earnestly: 'Listen, Anton! You are now my husband, although I know I am dying. Nothing can save me, and I shall not live to inflict upon that cursed spy the punishment he deserves. I know—'

'Is he a spy?' I interrupted breathlessly.

'Yes. When you had left Petersburg they admitted him into the Circle, believing him to be trustworthy. Soon afterwards, however, the police arrested nearly the whole of the members, and had I not been the daughter of the British ambassador I should have been arrested also. Inquiries I afterwards made proved conclusively that Paramòn Markoff – or Nicolas Kassatkin, as he calls himself – was an officer of Secret Police; that he was admitted to the Circle by means of forged introductions, and that through his instrumentality over one hundred members of our Cause were exiled.'

'But what proof have you?' I asked excitedly, remembering how much Kassatkin knew of the conspiracy we were forming.

'The papers you hold in your hand will prove what I allege,' she replied. Then she continued wildly: 'Find the spy. Let death be his reward for ingenuity and double-dealing. Kill him! Promise me! Do not let him send to Siberia other innocent supporters of the Cause!' Clutching my hand, she added, 'Tell me that you will avenge the deaths of the men and women who fell victims to his treachery. Promise me!'

'I promise,' I replied. 'If he is a spy he shall die.'

'Ah! At last he will receive his well-merited punishment. And he had the audacity to love me!' She uttered the words feebly, sinking wearily back upon her pillow.

Her face had changed, becoming paler and more drawn. She did not move, and I stood watching, not knowing what to do. The excitement had proved too much for her. Suddenly she opened her eyes, and whispered my name. Then she gave vent to a long, deep-drawn sigh, shuddered, and lay strangely still.

I knew then that my wife had passed away!

I was kissing her pale lips and closing the glazing eyes, when the footman entered hurriedly, and whispered that I was required in the library at once. He dashed downstairs, and I followed. On going into the room a sight met my gaze which I shall never forget, for, lying stretched upon the couch was his lordship, writhing in the horrible agonies of death from poisoning. A small bottle standing upon the table and a broken champagne glass had but one tale to tell.

He had taken his own life!

The clergyman was kneeling by his side, but in a few moments the old Earl gave a final sigh, and ere I had realised it, he passed to the land that lies beyond human ken.

I learned from the doctor who attended that the Earl of Wansford had, since relinquishing his post at Petersburg, showed signs of madness. During a fit of insanity, a year before, he had struck down his daughter, inflicting such injuries that she had been an invalid ever since. Her mind, too, became unhinged. It was supposed that, seized by sudden remorse, his lordship had imbibed the fatal draught.

Morning was breaking, cold and grey, as I ascended the stairs to my chambers. Opening the door with my latch-key, I entered the sitting-room. The lamp was still burning, and there were evidences that Kassatkin had not returned.

Upon the table was a note addressed to me.

I tore it open, and read as follows:

'In the matter upon which we were engaged last week I have made an important discovery, which necessitates me leaving for the Continent to-night. Will let you know shortly where I am.'

It suddenly crossed my mind that, having ascertained the details of the plot we were preparing, he had left for Petersburg to give information to the police.

That morning I placed the papers my dead wife had given me before the Executive, and the same evening Tersinski and I, having discovered the route the spy had taken, were on our way to the Continent, following the man upon whom the sentence of our Order had been passed.

A week later the special edition of the *Pall Mall Gazette* contained the following among its general foreign news:

'Reuter's Cologne correspondent reports that a mysterious murder has created considerable sensation in Germany. Yesterday the body of a man was discovered floating in the Rhine, near Bonn, and on being taken from the water it was found that the man had been stabbed to the heart. From papers found upon him, it appears that the name of the murdered man was Nicolas Kassatkin, a Russian, who has recently been living in London.'

THE
CHAMPAGNE SPY

WOLFGANG LOTZ

THE CHAMPAGNE SPY

Israel's master spy tells his story.

'Easy boy, easy!' I drew in the reins, slowing down to a canter. Doctor, my big chestnut stallion, responded obediently to my command. I turned in the saddle and looked behind me. Waltraud was right on my heels. In these last two years she had become quite a horsewoman, riding and training for several hours each day, with a brave disregard for aching muscles, chafed skin and the occasional dislocated knee or elbow. Her favourite stallion Snowball had died six months earlier and she had now a spirited Anglo-Arab mare which she had trained herself.

'She's made a damn good job of it, too,' I thought, as Waltraud drew up beside me on Isis. We were leaving the desert behind, cantering easily along a sandy path which led through an area of densely cultivated land shaded by tall palm trees. Here, in a secluded part of the Nile Delta some ten miles from Cairo, I had leased a fair-sized farm complete with stables, paddocks, a show-ring and even a racing-track. We raised Arab horses and spent our mornings riding and training them. Apart from being a constant source of pleasure and recreation the farm was a frequent meeting place for many of our Egyptian and German friends. Some of them rode out with us, or received riding instruction; others came just to enjoy the scenery and fresh air.

'Everything all right?' I called to Waltraud who was following me now along the narrow path.

'Perfect,' came the reply, 'the gallop did us all a lot of good.'

We lengthened the reins and let the horses walk abreast of each other. They knew the way and needed no guidance. In Germany it was considered dangerous to ride stallions together with mares, but I'd found that with a little training the Arab stallions behaved themselves perfectly well in female company.

'You know, I never tire of the lovely countryside round here,' Waltraud said.

We were riding stirrup to stirrup at a slow walk and smoking – something else that wasn't done in German riding establishments. Suddenly there was a great roar, not unlike the sound of a jet plane taking off, and my stallion shied slightly. I brought Doctor under control with a word and slight pressure from my legs, looked at my watch and noted the time.

A great advantage of this particular farm was its close proximity to the experimental rocket bases situated near the kilometre 33 signpost, off the Alexandria-Cairo desert road. The rockets were fired off fairly frequently and it was important to record and report the exact times and frequency of the launchings.

'Yes,' I said to Waltraud after a pause, 'I'm glad we took the farm. It was money well spent in more ways than one.'

'It's certainly a marvellous cover,' she said. 'Look at the way they all flock here.'

'Yes, it's almost as though the Egyptian General Staff and the technical boys had nowhere else to discuss their problems.'

That was certainly the case, and it seemed that the more forthcoming we were the more they sought our hospitality. At first Waltraud had been amazed by the open way in which I went about my business. But as I'd told her, there were various kinds of spies, ranging from the nondescript, grey little man who kept very much in the background, drawing no attention to himself, to extroverts like myself who kept themselves so much in the limelight that no one suspected them for a moment. Thus no one would have dreamed (or so I hoped) that the rich and eccentric German horse breeder Lotz, strutting about the racecourse in the red and green national dress of Bavaria, sporting a six-inch high goat's beard on his hat and pronouncing his views in a loud and determined manner, was anything but what he seemed. And in Egypt, once you were taken for what you seemed you could work wonders. I had, for instance, manoeuvred General Abdel Salaam into giving me an entry permit to certain prohibited areas in the Suez Canal zone simply by saying that the fishing in the Bitter Lakes was so much better than elsewhere. It would never have occurred to him to refuse (and insult) his intimate friend who was the intimate friend of so many powerful people.

'It's funny,' I said to Waltraud, 'the Germans are convinced I can't tell an aircraft engine from a coffee grinder. And the less interest I show in it all, the more they insist on telling me. Look at the balance sheet for the last six months: two missile bases including the experimental one, precise progress reports on aircraft production in both plants, exact personal data on practically all German experts in the war factories, details of naval vessels in the Red Sea as well as of all major troop and armour movements to Sinai, not to mention economic and political information. Not a bad bag, though I say it myself.'

'Carry on like this, Obersturmbannführer,' replied Waltraud, 'and you'll get a medal.'

There was also the war in the Yemen, for through Abdo and others I had obtained precise and regular information regarding movement of troops, ships, armour and equipment to the Yemen, where Nasser's armies were fighting prolonged and not very successful battles against the Yemenite tribesmen. By now it was only too clear that he had little chance of winning the Yemen war, despite continuous bombing and the use of poisonous gas. Naturally it was important for Israel to know what forces were tied down in the Yemen and what the morale of the Egyptian troops was like.

'By the way,' Waltraud exclaimed, interrupting my thoughts, 'have you made any recommendations regarding Horst Wasser?'

'I have reported on him of course but I've not made any definite recommendations yet. I think I'll watch him a little longer. There are one or two things about him that still worry me.'

It was also part of my job to do a little 'bird-dogging' – in other words, to point out prospective candidates for recruitment as spies and informers. Naturally I never attempted to do any actual recruiting myself – that would have been fatal. I simply reported on people I thought suitable, giving an assessment of their character together with details of their work and the information they might have access to. The rest was up to the boys. If they considered it worthwhile they would approach the person in question in their own way and without my knowing anything about it.

We crossed the asphalt road near the entrance to our farm.

'Don't let Isis rush into the stable yard – hold her back,' I told Waltraud. 'Ah, here comes Abdullah to take our horses.'

Waltraud pulled a face: 'Isn't that Bauch over there in the paddock, giving his usual imitation of the Spanish Riding School?'

'Poor horse!' I replied. 'I may be a little over-sensitive where dressage work is concerned but having to watch that kind of performance quite spoils my day.'

'Well, it was you who agreed to let him stable his horse here.'

'What could I do? He knows we have plenty of room, and that I let others keep their horses here. How could I refuse him?'

Waltraud and I dismounted, put up the stirrup irons and handed the reins to Abdullah, our head groom. We fed our horses some carrots, patting their necks.

'Did you have a pleasant ride, ya saad el Pasha?' asked the old groom. Ever since I'd raised his salary by five pounds a month, he'd promoted me from 'Bey' to 'Pasha'.

'A great ride, thank you Abdullah. Tell me, has Mr Vogelsang been here this morning?'

'Yes, he's having coffee on the terrace. He says he'll be away for some days and asked if I would exercise his mare. He gave me a very generous bakshish.'

'Good for you, Abdullah,' I replied, slapping him on the shoulder. 'Now lead these two in and rub them down.'

Waltraud and I took off our spurs and went to join Vogelsang, one of the German experts, on the terrace.

'How are you, Harry?' I asked, dropping into a chair beside him. 'Abdullah tells me you're going away.'

'Yes,' he replied. 'Rusty, I'd be terribly grateful if you'd allow your groom to exercise my horse while I'm away.'

'Gladly. Are you off on leave?'

'No such luck. It's that conference in Munich. Brenner and all the others will be going too. It's a top level affair.'

'Better make sure you get a hotel reservation. I hear there's a convention in Munich. Hotels will be pretty booked up.'

'All that's taken care of, thank God. I've got my reservation. In fact the confirmation came through this morning.'

He took a slip of paper out of his pocket and showed it to me. As he did so an idea began to form at the back of my mind and I made a mental note of the hotel and the number of his room.

'By the way, Rusty,' he went on, 'where's a good place to buy a new brief-case? Mine's falling to bits. Besides, it's far too small for the plans and documents I'll have to take with me.'

'Why go to all the expense of buying a new one? I've got a brand new brief-case at home which I hardly ever use. You can borrow mine. I'll have it sent over tomorrow.'

'That's really good of you, Rusty. I'd be terribly grateful.'

So far, so good. The old miser had reacted according to form.

Lunch was waiting when we got back, and I hurried through the meal. In just half an hour I had to transmit details of the rocket launchings we'd observed that morning. I'd recently got a new transmitter, larger and more powerful than the one that had been secreted in my riding boot. This one was hidden inside a special pair of bathroom scales.

My original transmitter had proved too small and had ceased functioning properly after a few months. I'd reported this by letter, using the secret ink I'd been supplied with as an alternative means of communication, and had been told to destroy the faulty machine. This was easier said than done, for although I'd smashed the instrument into tiny pieces with a hammer, I couldn't just throw them into the dustbin –

and even throwing them into the Nile, which seemed to me the best solution, posed problems, for foreigners were always closely observed, especially when they went on foot. It was a farcical situation, and in the end Waltraud and I had had to hire a rowing boat and spend a whole day picnicking on the river, just so we could dispose of the equipment along with the remnants of our lunch!

'Ten to two,' I said to Waltraud, smiling to myself as I recalled the incident. 'I'd better go upstairs and get to work.'

My transmitting and receiving was done in our bedroom – generally in the early morning at pre-arranged times. Waltraud and I had now moved from my flat in Zamalek to a beautiful and spacious villa in the suburb of Giza. It was tastefully and expensively furnished in English style, had a large garden and was surrounded by a high fence with a thick hedge on the inside ensuring privacy. The master bedroom was on the second floor and best suited for wireless communication. Obviously it was the only room in the house where I could lock myself in without causing comment from the servants.

As I climbed the stairs the doorbell rang.

'See who it is,' I called to Waltraud, 'I can't be disturbed now.'

She ran up the stairs after me and looked out through one of the bedroom windows.

'It's Abdo and Fouad,' she said. 'The gardener is just opening the gate for them. What shall I do?'

'Go down and give them a drink, of course,' I told her. 'Tell them I'm in the shower and that I'll join them soon. This won't take long.'

I locked myself in, assembled the set and, at two o'clock sharp, went on the air. When I'd finished, I stowed away the transmitting equipment, wetted and combed my hair, and went down to the living-room where Abdo and Fouad were sipping whisky and talking to Waltraud.

'What a pleasant surprise,' I exclaimed. 'Don't you people ever do any work, or is this a holiday?'

'We're celebrating the occasion of your bi-annual shower,' countered Abdo. 'How nice and clean you look, Rusty.'

'Actually,' put in Fouad, 'we're on our way to Alex. We just dropped in to see how you both were.'

'Abdo was telling me there's been an aftermath to the swimming party we had the other night,' Waltraud said.

A couple of nights ago Abdo had visited us with his wife and their two grown-up children. Shortly before midnight Schonmann and Vogelsang had dropped in and after a drink or two suggested we all drove out to Schonmann's villa at Pyramid Gardens for a swim in his pool and a late supper. It had been a gay and carefree party.

'Did you catch cold?' I asked innocently.

'No, I didn't catch cold,' explained Abdo, 'but the State Security people got me out of bed at six in the morning.'

'You mean Fouad's men?' I asked incredulously.

'No, of course not. From a different branch. Two polite gentlemen in civilian suits who asked me what I'd been doing at Mr Schonmann's house.'

'Well if that isn't the limit! What business is it of theirs? I know Schonmann is well guarded, but you're an army general after all and . . .'

'That's precisely why, Rusty. They drew my attention to the existing regulations which state that no officer of the armed forces may have any social contacts with foreigners, foreign experts in particular, without prior permission of the State Security. It's a strict rule.'

'I thought I'd heard Nasser say that the régime stands for freedom, progress and democracy? If these are the manifestations of it . . .'

'Don't be unjust, Rusty,' Fouad interrupted hastily. 'Of course it's ridiculous to put a man like Abdo on the carpet for having a drink with Schonmann, and I told them so, but you mustn't forget we're at war. We have to protect ourselves, and even if some of the measures we adopt aren't popular, believe me they're necessary.'

'I suppose you're right,' I conceded. 'We had a lot of restrictions in Germany too, during the war. But go on, Abdo, what happened then? What did you tell them?'

'Well, I explained the situation,' he continued. 'I told them we'd met Schonmann and the other experts at your house and that we couldn't very well have left the moment they entered – anymore than we could have excluded ourselves from the party that followed, at least not without being blatantly rude.'

'Did they accept your explanation?'

'Oh yes. They said they appreciated my position at the time, but would I kindly remember the regulations in future and avoid contacts with foreigners.'

'Does that mean you must avoid us too? We're also foreigners, you know.'

He laughed. 'Good God, no! They know all about you, Rusty, and our close friendship. You were cleared years ago.' He winked at me. 'They investigated you quite thoroughly then, believe me. But they know you're in sympathy with the regime and a Jew-hater, and it's also come to their attention that some of the Germans here don't like you for it.'

'Those who don't are welcome to stay away. Have another drink.'

'Just a small one. Then we must be off. What are your plans, Rusty? Let's get together next week.'

'On the nineteenth we're going to Mersa Matrouh to pay an overdue visit to Youssef Ghorab.'

'I'd forgotten he's down there now,' said Fouad. 'Some security job, isn't it?'

'Yes. He's director of security for the Western District and acting governor.'

'What do you know, old Youssef's getting on in the world! Acting governor. That should suit the pompous old ass.'

'Now it's you who're being unjust, Fouad,' I told him. 'I'm sure he's most efficient at his job – which is more than can be said for the last governor.'

'That's why they kicked him out, and promoted him to under-secretary of state at some ministry – I forget which. The biggest fools always get the fattest part of the lamb.'

Abdo chuckled. 'Sour grapes, ya Fouad! Rusty, have you told Fouad that precious story of how you were robbed at Mersa Matrouh?'

'What story's that?' asked Fouad.

'It has to be heard to be believed,' I said. 'Last summer Waltraud and I went camping at Mersa Matrouh. Youssef put an olive grove at our disposal, as well as a servant and guard, though he couldn't understand why we preferred our tent to the comforts of the Governor's mansion. But there were others with us, and we couldn't split up the party. There was Bauch and . . .'

'Ah, Mr Gehlen's bright boy,' put in Fouad.

'Gehlen's bright boy? What do you mean?'

'What, you really didn't know, Rusty? Mr Gerhard Bauch is no less than the resident agent of German Intelligence. We've been aware of that for a long while now. He's not very bright, this countryman of yours, and we're giving him free rein. It's better than removing him and having someone else we don't know in his place. Naturally, he's under constant surveillance. But go on, Rusty, tell me your story.'

'Well, we'd been there for about a week, and then one day, when we came back from the sea, we discovered that some of our things had been stolen. Nothing very valuable, a carton of cigarettes, a bathing suit, some underwear, things like that. In the evening, when we were dining with Ghorab, I mentioned the theft. You should have seen him! My God, was he furious. He had everybody arrested within a radius of a mile and interrogations went on for three days. I tried to pacify him, telling him that the few stolen articles weren't worth all the fuss. But he would have none of it. The robbery was a personal insult. After all, we were his guests.

'Finally, we had to leave and I mentioned that we'd be staying in Alexandria overnight, though I didn't say where. Well, we'd hardly arrived in Alexandria and found a hotel when there was a telephone call for me from police headquarters. The duty officer asked me to report to General Bishbishy first thing in the morning on a very important matter.'

'You thought they wanted to arrest you, eh?'

'Well, I couldn't remember committing any major crimes, but in any case an officer came to the hotel in the morning to escort me. He didn't know what it was all about, but he did know that they'd contacted almost every hotel in town to find me, and that all police patrols in the area had the number of my car as well as descriptions of Waltraud and myself. Now, can you guess what it was all in aid of?'

'They'd found the thief?'

'Exactly! General Bishbishy told me over three cups of coffee that the thief, the former swimming champion of Mersa Matrouh, had been apprehended and that my property would be restored. He mentioned that Youssef Bey had already spoken to the judge and it was agreed that the man should get five years.'

'That's the police for you,' said Fouad. 'Imagine putting the whole police force of Alexandria on the alert for the sake of a bathing suit and a few cigarettes.'

'It's the principle, my dear boy,' mocked Abdel Salaam. 'Thou shalt not steal from the governor's guests. Not bathing suits, not brassieres . . .'

'That's enough,' said Waltraud modestly. 'You're impossible, Abdo!'

'Wait,' I said, 'it gets even better. While I was with General Bishbishy an officer came in to ask whether the search for me could now be called off. It seemed that only the General himself could countermand the order he had given, regardless of whether I had been found or not.'

Abdo was greatly amused, Fouad uncomfortable.

'Please, Rusty, don't repeat this story to anyone in Germany,' he begged me. 'The whole thing is a scandal. This could never happen in the army.'

Abdo smiled ironically, but did not voice an opinion. 'We have to leave now,' he reminded his friend.

'One for the road, fellows?' I asked them.

'Well, just a short one, Rusty. To toast our good friend Ghorab!'

As soon as they'd left, I jumped into the car and drove to Rivolis, one of

Cairo's most elegant shops. There I bought a beautiful and very expensive brief-case which I despatched to Harry Vogelsang with my compliments.

Later that evening I wrote down and coded a message for transmission the next morning. I gave the time of Vogelsang's arrival in Munich, his hotel and room number, and added that he enjoyed female company in the evenings – a diversion that would incidentally take him out of his hotel room for some length of time. I'd kept the spare key to the brief-case and this I despatched to the boys a couple of days later.

I had just finished a lengthy transmission, and as I put down the headset and switched off the wireless receiver, Waltraud called sleepily from the bed:

'Have you finished?'

'Almost,' I replied, 'I got the message all right. Reception was nice and clear today. I'll be through with de-coding in about fifteen minutes. This is a long one. Go back to sleep for a while.'

Wearily I picked up notebook, cipher key and pencil and went to work.

I looked at the sheet of paper I had used for writing, read the message again, memorized it, then stepped into the adjoining bathroom where I burned it and flushed the ashes down the toilet.

Waltraud sat up in bed when she heard me returning. 'Is it anything important, dear?' she asked.

'Yes, I'm afraid it is,' I replied. 'Very important and most urgent. Top priority in fact. It's about that rocket base in Shaloufa again.'

We had recently spent a good deal of time looking for the concealed rocket base. Headquarters knew all about it from aerial photographs. They had, however, a sneaking suspicion that it might be a dummy and therefore it was vital for me to verify it at all costs and by any means I thought suitable.

'The base is between Suez and Ismailia,' I told Waltraud. 'I shall have to go and see the damn thing for myself. It's the only way to verify it.'

'May I come too?'

'Of course, partner. We'll take some rods and disguise the whole thing as a fishing trip.'

'You know, I rather like it when you call me partner.'

'Well, isn't that what you are? You know that for me a wife must be more than a housekeeper or bed companion. She must share everything. That's why my first two marriages went on the rocks.'

'Well, you know you can count on me. Now where exactly shall we look? We've already scanned the area twice.'

From a drawer I took out some maps, selecting one of the Canal area south of Suez. I unfolded the map on my knee.

'Now let's try and work this out by elimination,' I said. 'This is the desert road running roughly north-south between Ismailia and Suez. Here is the railway line running parallel to the road. At some places they are close together, at others some distance apart. Now, the place we are looking for is supposed to be between the railway line and the road, right?'

'Yes, but we drove all along that road and back and after that you even went by train to get a view from the other side and neither of us saw anything resembling a rocket base.'

'Correct. So we can safely eliminate all those areas where the road can be seen from the railway or the other way round. You can't hide a rocket base in a mud hut or under a palm tree. It has to be an area of some size. There are three such places,' I said, pointing with my finger, 'up here, here, and there a little further down. Another thing: there has to be some sort of road leading to it.'

'I remember two roads branching off the desert highway,' said Waltraud. 'One is just a track leading to a garbage dump or something, and the other is guarded by a soldier and has a sign "No entrance and no photography."'

'Well, there are a million places like that all over Egypt, especially in the Canal Zone.'

But I remembered the place. We hadn't gone in because of the guard and also because I thought we might have been able to see the place from some other observation point. But we hadn't. As a result I decided to drive down there with Waltraud that morning, posing as ordinary tourists out for a swim in the Bitter Lakes.

Dressed in slacks, a yellow sports shirt with blue spots and a bright red peaked cap, I set off with Waltraud to do a little spying.

Suez was less than an hour's drive from Heliopolis. Just before reaching the unsightly town itself, we turned left, crossed the railway lines and went on to the desert road leading to Ismailia. Traffic was light.

Eventually I stopped the car on a lonely stretch of road to consult my map.

'Why don't I take the wheel for a bit,' said Waltraud, 'so you can take your eyes off the road and observe better.'

'Good idea.' We changed places and while she did the driving I traced our progress on the map. We passed some mud dwellings and a military camp and after that there was nothing but desert again. 'Slow down a little,' I said after we had gone on at a fast pace for some ten kilometres, 'we are almost there. Here is the track to the garbage dump. Our intersection is only two or three kilometres ahead.'

'Can we cut through the desert from here?' asked Waltraud.

'I'm looking for a suitable spot to turn off the road,' I replied, 'but it looks pretty hopeless. All deep sand – we'd get stuck in no time. Let's see what it's like a little further on.'

Try as we might, we couldn't find a stretch of desert which was firm enough to drive across. Very soon the road leading to our destination came into view, branching off to the right. There was no barrier, but a sentry box stood near the crossing.

'What do I do now?' Waltraud inquired. 'Do I go straight in?'

'No, stay on the main road,' I said, 'change into low gear and drive on slowly. I want to see what kind of a guard they have and if there is more than one.'

There was only one soldier with a military police armband leaning idly against the side of the sentry box. A revolver hung from his side in a webbing holster that had once been white. He paid no attention to us as we drove past on the main road. As soon as we were out of sight behind one of the many low hills we stopped.

'Let's turn back,' I said, 'and try again. We shall have to get in somehow. We may have to stage a breakdown and ask for help – or something of the sort.'

Waltraud made a U-turn and we went back in the opposite direction.

'Stop near the intersection and we'll have our breakdown,' I instructed her, 'we'll get out of the car and start fiddling with the engine.'

We came to a halt directly opposite the sentry box.

'Wait, don't get out,' I exclaimed, 'this is too beautiful to be true!'

The scene which met our eyes would not, perhaps, normally be described as beautiful, but at that moment it had a definite attraction for me. The soldier's belt and revolver holster were hanging from a nail on the side of his little hut. The soldier himself had withdrawn some twenty or thirty yards into the desert, where he was squatting in the sand relieving himself, his trousers dropped to the ground.

'In, quickly!' I shouted. 'Drive as fast as you can!' Waltraud slammed into gear and, spinning the steering wheel sharply to the left, took off like greased lightning. As we sped past the sentry box and a black and red signboard reading 'prohibited area' in Arabic and English, I heard a faint cry from behind us. I looked in the driving mirror, turning it slightly, and saw the sentry stumbling to his feet, his trousers held up with one hand, his other hand waving frantically. 'Don't turn your head,' I said, 'and keep going. Somebody may try and stop us at any minute and I want to get a look at that base first.'

I was literally making a forced entry into a top secret area – in broad daylight, wearing a flowered shirt, and accompanied by my wife in a speeding car. Gradually the road dropped into a valley and our soldier was no longer to be seen. A turn, a rise, another valley. 'Somebody's coming,' said Waltraud. A jeep full of soldiers was approaching from the opposite direction.

'Keep going,' I urged, 'unless they stop us.' The jeep went by, the five soldiers in it staring at us curiously.

'Take it easy now,' I said to Waltraud, 'let's find a vantage point from where we can see the base.' I glanced into the driving mirror. 'Ah-ha, the fun is starting. They've turned around and are following us.'

'What happens now,' she asked shakily, 'should I accelerate and try to lose them?'

'No point in that. It would look suspicious. Let them overtake us. But we have to prevent them from kicking us out of here before we know exactly what they keep here. They may just give us a lecture and make us drive straight back.' Then I suddenly had an idea. 'Tell you what: drive the car right into the sand! If you can get us really stuck, we may have to stay here for hours. Quick, off the road – and make it convincing!'

Waltraud increased her speed and began swerving from one side of the road to the other. 'Anything for a bit of fun!' she said between her teeth. 'Hold on to something, here she goes!'

Disregarding a bend she went straight on and landed us with a bump in the deep sand beyond the shoulder of the road.

'Keep the wheels turning,' I told her, 'it will dig us in deeper.'

'Poor little car.' She put her into first gear and raced the motor.

'Never mind the car. What we're after here is worth a thousand cars. That's enough, they are coming. Out now, and I'll start shouting at you.'

'At me?'

'Sure. Let's give them their money's worth. The stupid wife of the stupid tourist being cursed for driving in such an infernally stupid manner.'

Screaming at her and gesticulating wildly I did my best to give a convincing imitation of an infuriated husband. The jeep stopped near us, and the five soldiers, armed with sub-machine guns, jumped down and surrounded us. The Sergeant in charge addressed me in Arabic:

'What are you doing in this area? How did you get here?'

I replied in English: 'Nice of you to come and help. Come on, give me a hand!'

'Mish fahim – I don't understand. What are you doing here?'

'Do you speak English? Deutsch?'

He shook his head. 'Mish fahim.'

I opened the boot of the car and took out a small spade I always carried with me. 'Are you going to help me dig out this car?' I asked in German, gesturing with my hands to make my meaning clear. The Sergeant, in turn, motioned to us to get into the jeep. 'You are under arrest,' he said in Arabic. 'I must take you to the guardroom.'

I shrugged my shoulders and began to start digging. 'I don't know what you are talking about. All right, if you don't want to help, don't.'

The Sergeant aimed his sub-machine gun at my belly and the other soldiers followed his example. Then he pointed the barrel at the vehicle shouting at me: 'Yalla – jeep.' I shook my head and sat down on the fender of the Volkswagen.

'No jeep,' I said. 'I'm not moving from here unless it's in my own car.' He did not, of course, understand my words but their meaning was unmistakable.

'Let's take them by force,' one of the soldiers said.

'Shut up,' the Sergeant told him. 'I'm making the decisions.' He deliberated for some minutes and finally said to the driver: 'Go over to the base and report to the duty officer that we have found two foreigners within the limits of the restricted area with their car stuck in the sand. Tell the officer we cannot talk to them in their language and ask him for instructions. Hurry! Meanwhile we shall stay here and watch them.'

'What were they saying?' asked Waltraud.

'He told me we were under arrest and when I refused to get into the jeep he dispatched the driver to see an officer about it.'

She laughed. 'This is the first time I've ever been arrested.'

'This may not be as funny as you think. They are simple-minded, but they do take their security very seriously. It will be quite a job to talk ourselves out of this. We may have to get Youssef to help us and even so it won't be pleasant. It means exploiting our connections to the utmost. He will pull all kinds of strings if we get into trouble, but there are limits to what he can do, and capers like this are likely to leave an after-taste of suspicion. It can't be helped, though, the main thing is to do what we came for.'

'I think we've already done that. It's obvious this is a secret military installation of some sort.'

'Yes, but we are not positive that it is what we think it is. We shall soon

93

find out though, I hope.' I took out a packet of cigarettes and lit one for Waltraud and one for myself. The rest I offered to the soldiers who accepted them eagerly. One of them approached the car and looked inside.

'They have some nice things here,' he called out to the others. 'A camera and clothes and a carton of American cigarettes. Let's make a search.'

'You keep your hands off their property or we'll all be punished,' snapped the Sergeant. 'If they complain there will be trouble.'

'How can they complain,' retorted the initiator of the scheme, 'they will be in prison.'

We were interrupted by the return of the jeep. Next to the driver sat a Captain in khaki fatigue dress, a revolver on his hip. The soldiers came to attention as he climbed out of the jeep. 'Good morning,' he said unsmilingly in English. 'What is all this about?'

'Well, you can see for yourself, Captain,' I replied. 'We seem to have got stuck in the sand and it will take more than this little spade to get us out again. Do you think you can pull us up to the road with your jeep? I have a tow rope.'

'I'm not concerned about your car at present. What are you doing here? How did you get in here?'

'What do you mean, how did we get in? In our car obviously. We came from Cairo. As to what we are doing here – if it's any of your business – we are on our way to the Bitter Lakes for a swim. Is that a crime? Do you know that these soldiers threatened to shoot us! When I get back to Cairo I shall complain about this at police headquarters where I have many influential friends.'

He was not impressed. 'Are you Americans?' he asked.

'We are Germans and not used to this kind of treatment. We greatly resent it.'

'Why did you come here?'

'I just told you. We are going to the Bitter Lakes.'

'This is not the way to the Bitter Lakes. This is a prohibited area. There is a sign. And how did you get past the guard?'

'What guard? What sign? As a matter of fact I was asleep. My wife was driving, that's why we're stuck up to our ears in the sand now.' I expected him to be amused at this remark but if he was he did not show it.

'Show me your passports,' he demanded. I handed them over. He looked at them briefly and put them into his pocket. 'Here, give those back to me,' I protested. 'They are the only travel documents we have.'

'They will be returned to you at the proper time. What have you got in your car?'

'Nothing much. Look for yourself.' He walked over to the car and looked in.

'Ah, you have a camera! What photographs have you taken?'

'None yet. I put in a new film only this morning, just before we left.'

'Why?'

'My God, what questions you ask! Because I want to take some snapshots of our picnic, the one you are doing your best to spoil for us. Is that so extraordinary?'

He did not reply but proceeded to search our car in the most thorough manner. He took the camera from the back seat and slung it over his shoulder. Then he discovered the road map in the side pocket of the door, inspected it and stuck it into his belt. He looked under the seats, opened the boot and even the bonnet, but apparently found nothing else he deemed important.

'Have you any firearms?' he asked.

'No, we are not on safari,' I replied impatiently. 'Why should I have firearms? Look, Captain, aren't you overdoing this a little? What do you want from us? If this is the way you treat well-paying tourists in your country not many will come here, I assure you. What is this inquisition all about?'

'You will have to come with me.'

'Come with you? Where?'

'To the . . . to my camp. It is not far. The Colonel will want to see you.'

'I suppose we might as well come with you. It will give us the chance to speak to your superior. He may show more sense. But what about our car?'

'It will remain here under guard. It's evidence.'

I locked the Volkswagen carefully and helped Waltraud into the jeep, beside the driver. The Captain ushered me into the back. He ordered the soldiers to guard our car and not to touch anything and we drove off in the direction Waltraud and I had been heading for. After a few hundred yards we went through a road block manned by two military policemen, then up a steep hill, and there it was right below us. There could be no mistake – the rocket launching sites arranged in a wide circle, the storage bunkers, the administration buildings at some distance from the other installations. This was it all right. Waltraud had the sense not to turn round, but I saw the back of her neck going red with excitement.

We drew up before a heavy iron gate which was opened at a sign from the Captain, who then directed the driver to what appeared to be the main administration building. We were led along a wide passage into the right wing of the building and entered an office where a Sergeant-Major was doing some paper work at a desk. He got up and stood to attention.

'Is the Commandant in?' asked the Captain.

'Yes, effendim. Colonel Fathy is with him.'

'Ask him if he will be kind enough to see me on a matter of the greatest urgency.' The Sergeant-Major went through an adjoining door into the next room and returned after a moment. 'The Commandant will see you, effendim,' he said.

The Captain signalled us to sit down. 'Keep an eye on these two,' he ordered the Sergeant-Major. 'I hold you responsible for them until I return.'

Then he went into the next room, closing the door behind him.

'Don't talk,' I whispered to Waltraud. 'I must try and hear what they are saying.'

I heard the Captain speaking at some length but could make out only odd words like 'foreigners', 'German passports', 'most suspicious', 'searched the car', 'arrested them'.

Then suddenly I heard another voice raised in anger: 'You mean to say you brought them here?!!! You idiot!! Are you out of your mind?' There was another mumble I could not understand and then the loud voice again: 'At least you could have blindfolded them! You have the sense of a water buffalo. Next thing you will be inviting them to an inspection of the installations. All right, the harm is done now. Bring them in.'

The Captain reappeared, his face crimson. 'Come in,' he barked.

We entered a spacious office, comfortably furnished with leather armchairs, two settees and thick carpets. Behind a huge highly polished desk with four telephones on a side table, one red, one black, and two white, sat the Commandant, a full Colonel. He was about forty years old, very slim, with short-cropped dark hair and a black moustache. On the desk in front of him were our passports, my camera and the road map. To his left, on the edge of a chair, sat a somewhat younger officer in the uniform of a Lieutenant-Colonel. Both men inspected us from head to foot.

'Please sit down,' said the Commandant finally. He picked up one of the passports, then the other, turning the pages slowly. 'You are Mr and Mrs Lotz?' I replied in the affirmative. 'You are Germans. Are you tourists in our country?'

'We live in Cairo.'

'Yes, I can see from your passports that you have been here for some time. What do you do?'

'I am a horsebreeder.' His bushy eyebrows went up.

'A horsebreeder?'

'Yes. What's so strange about that?' I took out my wallet. 'Here is my visiting card with my address in Cairo, this is my identification as a steward of the racing club, and these are membership cards of the Cavalry Club, the Horsemen's Association and the Gezira Sporting Club.' I placed them all on his desk and he inspected the documents one by one.

'If you breed horses in Cairo, Mr Lotz, what are you doing here in a prohibited area?' he asked.

'Now look here, Colonel. I have been through all this with your Captain. He has already conducted an endless and mostly irrelevant investigation of our "crimes". I suggest that, in order to save a lot of questions and answers and misunderstandings, I tell you the whole story. Then everything will be cleared up.'

'Go on, Mr Lotz. I might as well tell you that you have got yourself into a most unpleasant situation. Breaking into a forbidden military area is a most serious matter.'

'I wouldn't know about that. What actually happened is this: My wife and I came down from Cairo early this morning for a swim and a picnic by the Bitter Lakes. We came on the Suez-Ismailia road. My wife was driving and . . .'

'Why was your wife driving? Isn't it more natural for the man to drive?'

'Perhaps. I hurt my knee last week and I wanted to rest it. Besides, my wife enjoys driving.'

'How did you hurt your knee, Mr Lotz?'

'Falling off a horse, getting out of the bath, does it matter?'

'Don't get excited, Mr Lotz, I'm just trying to get the facts.'

'All right, the facts are these: My wife was driving, I fell asleep and she must have taken the wrong turning. I woke up when our car got stuck in the sand. That's all I know. Then your trigger-happy soldiers came along and threatened us. Are you satisfied now, Colonel?'

'Not quite. The sentry at the intersection where our road branches off says he tried to stop you and you went through ignoring his order to stop.'

'I saw no sentry. I'm telling you I was asleep.'

'Your wife was not asleep. Why didn't she stop? There is also a written notice prohibiting entrance to unauthorized persons.'

'My wife saw nothing of the kind. Certainly no one tried to stop her. If your sentry, who was probably sleeping, is telling the truth, why didn't he telephone your office and report the matter?'

'The line to the first road block is out of order, but that is none of your

97

concern. If the man was sleeping he will be punished. As for you and your wife, Mr Lotz, I shall inform the proper authorities and a full investigation will be made.'

'But this is ridiculous, Colonel. My wife and I were looking forward to a nice outing and a swim. Why on earth should we want to come here instead, to look at a military barracks in a particularly unattractive piece of desert? Tell me that!'

'You may be spies or saboteurs for all I know. The authorities will look into it.'

'This is preposterous.' I was beginning to sweat again. 'Really, Colonel, this is going beyond a joke. Let me tell you that I am pretty well known in this country. Why don't you pick up one of your telephones and get through to General of Police Youssef Ghorab. A close personal friend of mine. He will vouch for me. Do you know who he is?'

The Commandant paused. 'Yes, I know who he is, but he has no jurisdiction over us. All the same, a recommendation from him should carry weight with the security people.'

'Security people! Colonel, you have just solved the whole problem. Do you mind if I use your phone?'

'What for?'

'To call some of the security people you have been talking about. Let's start with General Fouad Osman.'

'You know him?'

'Him and a few others.' I took out a notebook. 'Here is the number. Call him and he will confirm that I am no spy. He knows me intimately.'

He opened my passport again and leafed through it, then threw it back on to the desk. To the Lieutenant-Colonel he said in Arabic:

'A very strange affair. Do you think he is telling the truth?'

'Anna aref? How do I know?' replied the other sceptically. 'It is best not to get involved in this kind of complication. Why not hand them over to the security police and let them carry on with the investigation? That's the regular procedure.'

'If only that fool Adly hadn't brought them into the base. They won't like that. It will not look well on my record.'

'He claims he is friendly with General Osman. How would he know people like Osman and Ghorab? Perhaps he is really one of the German experts.'

The Commandant threw me an uncertain glance. 'Mr Lotz,' he asked, 'are you sure you are a horsebreeder?'

'I told you so, didn't I?' I retorted angrily. 'But since you seem to have decided to accept nothing I tell you at face value, why don't you do as I suggest and have my statements confirmed by someone whose job it is to deal with such matters!'

He thought that over for a while, finally arriving at a decision. 'All right,' he said, lifting the receiver from one of the telephones at his side, 'I will call General Osman. What was the number you said?'

I gave it to him and he ordered the call to be put through. We all waited silently for some minutes. Nearby someone was shouting at the top of his voice, trying to get a line to Cairo. I opened a fresh packet of cigarettes and, when the officers declined to smoke, lit one for Waltraud and myself.

A buzzer sounded. The Commandant answered it. 'Yes – What? – Oh, I see. – Ask him to be so kind as to call me back.' Replacing the receiver he addressed me again: 'General Osman is not at his office. It is not known when he will return.'

'That is very unfortunate,' I said, 'but we can get in touch with somebody else. Are you acquainted with Colonel Mohsen Sabri of the state security?'

'No, I've never heard of him. He has nothing to do with us. There are many officers in the different branches of state security.'

'All right, Colonel, let me speak to him and speak to him yourself, and if you are not satisfied he'll refer you to an authority you consider competent. Is that fair enough?' I consulted my notebook. 'This is the number.'

For a moment he seemed undecided then said rather impatiently: 'Very well, I don't see what harm it can do, except that I make a nuisance of myself and bother a lot of people who have more important things to do.' In an angry voice he gave Sabri's number to the operator.

The operator must still have had the line open, because the call came through almost immediately.

'Hello . . . Who is that speaking? . . . The adjutant? . . . This is Colonel Abdel Aziz Mohsen, may I speak to Colonel . . . eh . . . Sabri please . . . Hello . . .Colonel Sabri? Good morning to you. Excuse the question, Colonel, but would you be good enough to tell me what branch of the service your office belongs to . . . I see . . . I see . . . Oh yes. I will tell you why I'm asking this. I have a rather strange situation on my hands here. Are you by any chance acquainted with a German couple called Lotz? You are! You know them well? . . . What? . . . Who are they? . . . Because they are sitting right here in my office under arr . . . well, I mean I have had to detain them here temporarily. They drove into my installation this morning as if it belonged to them. I don't have to tell you what that means . . . What? . . . Yes Colonel, of course there is a guard on the base . . . Yes, outside too . . . No, no, of course

99

not. We are not at fault. Perhaps one of my junior officers was a little rash and brought them inside. No, they were not in the base, they were in the vicinity, in the prohibited area . . . Yes, I know I said that, but . . . no, I suggest we discuss this some other time. We are not to blame, I assure you. The point is, I mean my question to you is what to do with these Germans . . . Yes, certainly.' He handed the instrument to me, his face a shade paler than before. 'Colonel Sabri wishes to speak to you.' I put the receiver to my ear. 'Hello, Mohsen!' His voice at the other end was faint but clear: 'Good morning, Mr Lotz! What's this trouble you've got yourself into? What are you doing in a secret installation of the armed forces?' His voice had a slight edge to it. Was he suspicious?

'I'll tell you, Mohsen. We are here, my wife and I, because we were forcibly taken into this place by an armed escort. We were driving to the Bitter Lakes for a picnic. We took a wrong turning off the main road, it seems, and got stuck in the sand with our car. Then some soldiers came and handled us very roughly. Their officer, a Captain, does not know how to behave himself either and, after confiscating our property, forced us, practically at gunpoint, to come to these blasted barracks. Now we are being interrogated like a couple of criminals and they don't believe a word we say. I called Fouad and he wasn't in. When I get back to Cairo some people are going to hear of the hospitable treatment they afforded us. I am sorry to bother you, Mohsen . . .'

'No bother at all,' he interrupted me. His voice was more affable. 'I'm glad you called me about this. I'm sure there has been some misunderstanding. The fact remains that you entered a forbidden area. They might have accepted your explanation, but these men are a little touchy and excitable. The orders are very strict. We are on a war footing and can't take any chances, you must understand that. Anyone entering this area is to be arrested. Of course, in your case I shall see that you are cleared at once. I will also talk to Fouad, in case a report is submitted. Now, give me that Colonel again, please. My regards to Mrs Lotz and apologies for the inconvenience. I'll see both of you in Cairo. Goodbye for now.'

'Goodbye, Mohsen, and thank you. Oh, by the way, can you ask them to help us with our car? . . . O.K. fine.'

I pushed the instrument across to the Commandant who listened attentively to what Sabri was saying to him. His own contribution to the conversation consisted of monosyllabic replies of 'yes' and 'of course'. I heard cackling noises coming from the earpiece, but could not understand what was being said at the other end. The Commandant's face was a study in discomfort and embarrassment.

Once more the power that the security services wielded in Egypt was being demonstrated to me. Here was a Colonel, Commandant of an important secret missile base, who had done nothing but act according to orders, actually cringing in the most servile manner before an officer of equal rank who was in no way entitled to give him instructions of any kind. But that particular officer belonged to a branch of the secret service and could, if he wished, make life exceedingly uncomfortable for those who offended him.

'Naam, effendim, Khader effendim,' he was saying now, 'as you order. I shall attend to it immediately. The matter will be settled to your complete satisfaction. Yes, I understand . . . forgive me, I had no way of knowing . . . yes, certainly. Goodbye effendim, thank you.'

He threw the receiver on to the hook and nervously rose to his feet, at the same time creasing his features into the semblance of what he obviously considered to be an engaging smile. 'My apologies, Mr and Mrs Lotz. Colonel Sabri has explained the situation to me. I very much regret this misunderstanding, but you must realise that we have our orders. National defence secrets must be carefully protected and no unauthorised persons allowed near the sites where they are installed. It is quite clear to me now that you meant no harm – indeed, a man of your status – and that you were the victim of – a navigational error made by Madame. It could have happened to anyone. The sentry should have stopped you, but apparently he neglected his duty. He will be very severely punished.'

'There is nothing to apologise for, Colonel,' I said magnanimously. 'You acted in good faith. Through my connections with some of the leading men in the republic I know only too well how vitally important all matters pertaining to national defence are to you. In a modest way I have even been trying to help here and there. You acted quite correctly, and I shall not hesitate to say so if anybody asks me. But I do suggest you put up a barrier of some sort at the crossroads to prevent incidents of this kind.'

'Yes, yes. Colonel Sabri mentioned it also. It will be done right away. Now it is past twelve o'clock and before you go on you must give us the pleasure of your company at lunch.' He opened the door and stood aside. 'If you will be good enough to come with me. Our officers' club here at the base is small and very modest, but we will do our best to make you welcome.'

The buzzer on his desk sounded again. 'One moment please,' he said, walking across the room to take the call. 'What is it? I am going to lunch now and don't wish to be disturbed. What? . . . Yes Sir, yes Sir . . .' There was another lengthy session of 'Yes Sirs' and 'Khader Effendim' until finally he held out the instrument to me: 'General Osman on the line for you, Mr Lotz.'

'Hello – Rusty, you old devil what are you up to? Sabri just called me, told me all about your spying out our missile bases. Will you pay a bottle of champagne voluntarily as ransom or do I let you rot in prison?' His laughter boomed at me over the wire and I moved the instrument a little away from my ear.

'If it's local champagne – OK,' I responded.

'Oh no, my friend, I won't let you be a Jew! The French stuff or nothing! Seriously, Rusty, how are they treating you? Any trouble?'

'None at all. Everybody is very nice and understanding. The Commandant has kindly invited us to lunch. After that we are coming straight back to Cairo.'

'Good. Just tell me if there's anything else you want. By the way, Abdo and I and some of the other boys are throwing a stag party next Thursday. Do you think you will be able to get away for an evening? It will be most interesting.'

'I think that might be arranged.'

'Don't miss it. I'm telling you it will be very, very interesting.'

'Like the one we had in Garden City last year?'

'Better. Much better. All the trimmings. OK, I just wanted to know if you are all right. See you Thursday or perhaps before then.'

The Commandant glanced at me sideways as we were walking down the corridor. 'General Osman is very fond of you. It is indeed a pleasure to have you here as our guest, Colonel Lotz.'

'Did you call me Colonel? I was a Captain in the army, and that was ages ago.'

'Of course, Sir, if you say so I will not pry into your affairs. Yours is a secret to be proud of. The SS, they tell me, was the crème de la crème of the German Reich. I have read a great deal about it. We too will have a great Arab Reich one day. Installations like our missile base here will help to destroy Israel soon. Now you understand why we guard it so carefully. The Israelis have an excellent intelligence service. They must not learn anything about this until we strike the final blow. Now let me show you around.'

THE
BOY SPY

ALPHONSE DAUDET

THE BOY SPY

A story from the Franco-Prussian War of 1870–71.

He was called Stenne: Little Stenne. He was a boy of Paris, sickly looking and pallid, who could have been ten years old – or perhaps even fifteen. With midges like that you can never tell. His mother was dead; his father, an ex-marine, was caretaker of a garden square in the Temple quarter. The children, the nursemaids, the old ladies in deck-chairs, the poor mothers – all the people who took refuge from the traffic among those flower-bordered walks – they all knew old Papa Stenne, and adored him.

They knew that beneath the shaggy moustache there lurked a generous, almost maternal, smile – and that to provoke that smile they had only to ask the dear old fellow: 'How's your little son?' The old man was so very fond of that boy of his! He was never so happy as in the evenings, when the boy came for him after school, and the pair of them strolled along the paths, halting at every seat and bench to have a word with the regulars.

But when the Prussians besieged Paris, everything changed utterly. Papa Stenne's square was closed and taken over as an oil-store. The poor old fellow spent all his time on guard, not even able to smoke – and only getting a glimpse of his boy late at night. As for the Prussians, the old man's moustache used positively to bristle when he talked of *them*. But Little Stenne, on the other hand, didn't find all that much to grumble about in the changed conditions.

A siege! It was a great lark for the kids! No more school! No more homework! One long holiday, and the streets like a fair-ground.

The boy was out of doors playing the whole day. He used to accompany the local battalions whenever they marched off to the ramparts – preferably any battalion that had a good band, a subject on which Little Stenne was an expert. He could tell you emphatically that the band of the 98th wasn't much good, but that the 55th had a pretty good one. At other times, he would cast an eye at the reserves doing their drill, and there were always the queues to join.

With a shopping-basket on his arm, he would tag on to those long queues outside the butcher's or the baker's and there, scuffling his feet in the gutter, he would meet people and earnestly discuss the situation – for being the son of Papa Stenne his opinion was always sought. Best of all were the games of *galoche* – a game in which you had to bowl over a cork with money on it and which the Breton reservists had made popular during the siege.

Whenever Little Stenne wasn't on the ramparts or queueing at the baker's, you could be sure of finding him at some *galoche* tournament in Water-Tower Square. He didn't take part – that would have needed too much money. He just looked on, and he particularly admired one of the players, a big lad in a blue coat who invariably gambled with five-franc pieces and nothing else. When that boy ran you could hear the money jingling in his coat-pockets.

One day, as Little Stenne retrieved a coin that had rolled near the boy, the big fellow muttered to him: 'That makes you stare, eh? If you like, I'll show you where to find some more.'

At the end of the game he strolled away with Little Stenne and asked him if he'd like to go with him and sell newspapers to the Prussians, who would pay anyone thirty francs for the trouble. To begin with, Little Stenne refused indignantly – and he was so upset by the offer that he kept away from the game for several days. Terrible days they were – he couldn't eat or sleep for thinking about it all.

At night in bed he could see nothing but heaps of corks and glittering five-franc pieces. He couldn't resist the temptation. On the fourth day he went back to Water-Tower Square, spoke to the big lad again, and this time was easily persuaded.

One snowy morning the two of them started out with sacks over their shoulders and newspapers hidden in their clothes. Dawn had scarcely broken when they arrived at a place called the Pâte de Flandres on the outskirts of the city. The big boy took Little Stenne by the hand and approached the kindly looking, red-nosed French sentry.

'Here, mister,' he said in a whining tone, 'can we go on? Mother's ill and our old man's dead. My kid brother and I want to see if we can find some spuds in the fields out there.'

He started blubbering – and Little Stenne drooped his head in shame. The sentry eyed them for a moment, then glanced down the deserted, snow-covered road.

'All right, off with you,' he said, dismissing them – and straightaway they were on the road to Aubervilliers. The older boy nearly laughed himself silly.

Bewildered, as if in a dream, Little Stenne caught sight of factories that had been taken over as barracks, ramshackle barricades, towering chimneys that pierced the mist and groped into the sky. Here and there were more sentries, officers surveying the distance through telescopes, little tents wet from melted snow near half-hearted fires.

The big lad knew all the roads and short-cuts, but even so it wasn't his fault that they ran into a platoon of light infantry crouching in a trench alongside the Soissons railway. Although he told his story all over again the soldiers wouldn't let them pass. The big lad put up a show of crying again, and a sergeant, grizzled and white-haired, rather like old Papa Stenne, emerged from the level-crossing keeper's house to see what was going on.

'All right, kids,' he said, when he had listened to their story, 'stop all that noise. You can go and get your potatoes. But come in and warm yourselves first – that little fellow looks frozen!'

But it wasn't with cold that Little Stenne was shivering, it was with shame and fear. In the guardhouse, more soldiers were squatting round a miserable fire, trying to thaw out their bone-hard biscuits on the point of their bayonets. They moved over to make room for the boys, and gave them a mouthful of coffee. While they were drinking, an officer stuck his head in the door and beckoned to the Sergeant with whom he had a rapid, whispered conversation.

'Well, lads!' the Sergeant cried, rubbing his hands. 'We're going to have some fun tonight. They've got hold of the Prussian password and, if you ask me, we're going to recapture blessed old Bourget again, where we've had so many scraps in the past.'

The place echoed with cheers and exultant laughter. The soldiers began to polish their bayonets, singing and dancing as they did so, and in the midst of the tumult the boys took themselves off.

Beyond the trench lay nothing but the empty plain and in the distance a long white wall pierced with loop-holes. Pretending to be gathering potatoes, they made their way towards this wall. All the time Little Stenne kept urging the big lad to go back, but he only shrugged his shoulders and pressed on. All at once they heard the rattle of a rifle being cocked.

'Down!' said the big lad, flinging himself to the ground.

Lying there, he whistled. An answering whistle came across the snow. They crawled forward on hands and knees. In front of the wall, at ground level, a pair of yellow moustaches under a crumpled cap appeared. The big lad jumped down into the trench alongside the Prussian.

'This kid's my brother,' he said, jerking a thumb at Little Stenne.

Little Stenne was so small that the Prussian laughed at him – and had to take him in his arms to help him in.

On the other side of the breastwork there were strong earth ramparts reinforced with tree-trunks and in between them, foxholes, occupied by more yellow-moustached German soldiers in their crumpled caps.

In one corner of the fortification was a gardener's lodge, also supported with tree-trunks. On the ground floor more soldiers were playing cards or making soup on a blazing fire. The boiled cabbage and lard smelt good – very different from the poverty-stricken cooking-fire of the French infantrymen. Upstairs the officers could be heard strumming at a piano amid the popping of champagne corks.

When the two boys from Paris entered the room they were greeted with shouts of glee. They delivered their newspapers and were given drinks and encouraged to talk. All the officers looked haughty and formidable, but the big lad kept them amused with his cheeky ways and gutter slang. They roared with laughter, imitated his words, and revelled in the tittle-tattle he had brought from Paris.

Little Stenne would have liked to join in the talk, to show them he wasn't stupid either, but something held him back. Before him sat a Prussian who seemed more serious than the rest of them, and though he was pretending to read, his eyes never left Little Stenne. There was a kind of reproachful tenderness in those eyes, as if the man had a boy of his own at home and was thinking to himself: 'I'd rather be dead than see a son of mine acting like this.'

From that moment, Little Stenne felt as if a hand was pressing against his heart and preventing it from beating.

In order to get away from this pain, he gulped down his drink. Before long everything seemed to be whirling round him. He heard vaguely, to the accompaniment of laughter, his comrade mocking the French National Guard; giving an imitation of a call to arms in the Marais quarter of Paris; a night alarum on the ramparts. Eventually the big lad dropped his voice and the officers bent towards him with faces suddenly stern. The wretched youth was in the act of warning them of the infantrymen's intended attack.

At this Little Stenne leapt to his feet, angry and clear-headed: 'Not that, you great fool!' he cried. 'I won't let you . . .'

But the other simply guffawed and continued his story. Before he had completed it, all the officers were standing up. One of them ushered the boys to the door.

'Off with you, out of the camp!' he ordered them, and the officers began to talk rapidly among themselves in German. The big lad strode out, proud of himself and clinking his money. Little Stenne followed him, shamefaced, and as he passed the Prussian officer whose gaze had distressed him, he heard him saying mournfully: 'Not good, that . . . not good,' and the tears came into young Stenne's eyes.

Out on the plain the boys started to run and quickly made their way back. Their sacks were full of potatoes the Prussians had given them and they got past the infantrymen's trench without difficulty. The men were getting ready for the attack that night. Troops were coming up under cover and massing near the railway. The old Sergeant was there, busy giving orders with a keen air of anticipation. He recognised the boys as they passed and gave them a friendly grin.

That grin hurt Little Stenne deeply. For a moment he was minded to cry out in warning: 'Don't carry out the attack . . . we've given you away.' But the big lad had said to him: 'If you say anything now they'd shoot us,' and fear prevented him from acting.

At Corneneuve they entered a deserted house and divided the money. It must be admitted that once he could hear those fine five-franc pieces jingling in his pockets, Little Stenne no longer felt so bad.

But later, when he was on his own, misery swept over him. When, inside the city gates, the big lad had left him, then his pockets seemed to grow terribly heavy . . . and that hand which gripped his heart was tighter than ever. Paris was no longer the same city in his eyes. The passers-by seemed to look at him harshly as if they knew where he had been. Spy – spy – spy! He could hear the word everywhere about him, in the sound of passing wheels, in the beating of drums being played along the canal. At last he reached home. Relieved to find that his father had not yet come back, he went swiftly upstairs to their room and hid under his pillow the money that weighed so ponderously on his conscience.

Papa Stenne had never been so warm-hearted and jolly as he was that evening. News had arrived from the provinces that things had taken a turn for the better. While he ate, the old marine glanced at his musket hanging on the wall, and remarked with a laugh: 'Well, my boy, you'd go for those Prussians right enough if you were older, eh?'

Towards eight o'clock there was the sound of cannon-fire.

'Hello? That's Aubervilliers. There's fighting at Bourget,' said the old fellow, for he knew all the forts.

Little Stenne grew pale and, pretending he was very tired, took himself off to bed. But he couldn't sleep. The guns thundered on and on. He saw in his mind's eye the French infantrymen setting out under cover of darkness to surprise the Prussians – and themselves falling into an ambush. He remembered the old Sergeant who had grinned at him . . . and he could see him spreadeagled on the snow and many others with him . . . and the price of their blood was hidden there, under his very pillow. It was he, the son of Papa Stenne, ex-marine, who had betrayed them.

He was choked by tears. He heard his father moving about in the next room, opening a window. Down below in the square a call to arms rang out. A battalion of reservists was mustering urgently. Obviously a real battle was going on. The miserable boy could not contain his sobbing.

'What's it all about, then?' Papa Stenne demanded, entering the bedroom.

Little Stenne could bear it no longer. He leapt out of bed and flung himself at his father's feet. As he did so some of the money rolled to the floor.

'Hello? What's this? Have you been thieving?' the old man asked sharply, beginning to tremble.

Then, breathlessly, Little Stenne recounted how he had visited the Prussians, and what had happened there. As he uttered the words he felt his heart grow lighter. His confession made things easier to bear.

With a fearful expression Papa Stenne listened to the confession. At the end of it he bowed his head in his hands and wept silently.

'Father . . . father . . .' began the boy. But the old man repulsed him without a word and slowly gathered up the coins.

'Is this all?' was his only question.

Little Stenne nodded. The old man reached down his gun and his bandolier and put the money in his pocket. 'Ah, well,' he said, 'I am going to return it to them.'

Without speaking another word, without even a backward glance, he went down to the street to join the reservists who were setting off that night. He was never seen again.

THE
BRUCE-PARTINGTON PLANS

SIR ARTHUR CONAN DOYLE

THE BRUCE-PARTINGTON PLANS

In the third week of November, in the year 1895, a dense yellow fog settled down upon London. From the Monday to the Thursday I doubt whether it was ever possible from our windows in Baker Street to see the loom of the opposite houses. The first day Holmes had spent in cross-indexing his huge book of references. The second and third had been patiently occupied upon a subject which he had recently made his hobby – the music of the Middle Ages. But when, for the fourth time, after pushing back our chairs from breakfast we saw the greasy, heavy brown swirl still drifting past us and condensing in oily drops upon the window-panes, my comrade's impatient and active nature could endure this drab existence no longer. He paced restlessly about our sitting-room in a fever of suppressed energy, biting his nails, tapping the furniture, and chafing against inaction.

'Nothing of interest in the paper, Watson?' he said.

I was aware that by anything of interest, Holmes meant anything of criminal interest. There was the news of a revolution, of a possible war, and of an impending change of Government; but these did not come within the horizon of my companion. I could see nothing recorded in the shape of crime which was not commonplace and futile. Holmes groaned and resumed his restless meanderings.

'The London criminal is certainly a dull fellow,' said he, in the querulous voice of the sportsman whose game has failed him. 'Look out of this window, Watson. See how the figures loom up, are dimly seen, and then blend once more into the cloud-bank. The thief or the murderer could roam London on such a day as the tiger does the jungle, unseen until he pounces, and then evident only to his victim.'

'There have,' said I, 'been numerous petty thefts.'

Holmes snorted his contempt.

'This great and sombre stage is set for something more worthy than that,' said he. 'It is fortunate for this community that I am not a criminal.'

'It is, indeed!' said I, heartily.

'Suppose that I were Brooks or Woodhouse, or any of the fifty men who have good reason for taking my life, how long could I survive against my own pursuit? A summons, a bogus appointment, and all would be over. It is well they don't have days of fog in the Latin countries – the countries of assassination. By Jove! here comes something at last to break our dead monotony.'

It was the maid with a telegram. Holmes tore it open and burst out laughing.

'Well, well! What next?' said he. 'Brother Mycroft is coming round.'

'Why not?' I asked.

'Why not? It is as if you met a tram-car coming down a country lane. Mycroft has his rails and he runs on them. His Pall Mall lodgings, the Diogenes Club, Whitehall – that is his cycle. Once, and only once, he has been here. What upheaval can possibly have derailed him?'

'Does he not explain?'

Holmes handed me his brother's telegram.

'Must see you over Cadogan West. Coming at once. MYCROFT.'

'Cadogan West? I have heard the name.'

'It recalls nothing to my mind. But that Mycroft should break out in this erratic fashion! A planet might as well leave its orbit. By the way, do you know what Mycroft is?'

I had some vague recollection of an explanation at the time of the Adventure of the Greek Interpreter.

'You told me that he had some small office under the British Government.'

Holmes chuckled.

'I did not know you quite so well in those days. One has to be discreet when one talks of high matters of state. You are right in thinking that he is under the British Government. You would also be right in a sense if you said that occasionally he *is* the British Government.'

'My dear Holmes!'

'I thought I might surprise you. Mycroft draws four hundred and fifty pounds a year, remains a subordinate, has no ambitions of any kind, will receive neither honour nor title, but remains the most indispensable man in the country.'

'But how?'

'Well, his position is unique. He has made it for himself. There has never been anything like it before, nor will be again. He has the tidiest and most orderly brain, with the greatest capacity for storing facts, of any man living. The same great powers which I have turned to the detection of crime he has used for this particular business. The conclusions of every department are passed to him, and he is the central exchange, the clearing-house, which makes out the balance. All other men are specialists, but his specialism is omniscience. We will suppose that a Minister needs information as to a point which involves the Navy, India,

Canada and the bi-metallic question; he could get his separate advices from various departments upon each, but only Mycroft can focus them all, and say off-hand how each factor would affect the other. They began by using him as a short-cut, a convenience; now he has made himself an essential. In that great brain of his everything is pigeon-holed, and can be handed out in an instant. Again and again his word has decided the national policy. He lives in it. He thinks of nothing else save when, as an intellectual exercise, he unbends if I call upon him and ask him to advise me on one of my little problems. But Jupiter is descending to-day. What on earth can it mean? Who is Cadogan West, and what is he to Mycroft?'

'I have it,' I cried, and plunged among the litter of papers upon the sofa. 'Yes, yes, here he is, sure enough! Cadogan West was the young man who was found dead on the Underground on Tuesday morning.'

Holmes sat up at attention, his pipe half-way to his lips.

'This must be serious, Watson. A death which has caused my brother to alter his habits can be no ordinary one. What in the world can he have to do with it? The case was featureless as I remember it. The young man had apparently fallen out of the train and killed himself. He had not been robbed, and there was no particular reason to suspect violence. Is that not so?'

'There has been an inquest,' said I, 'and a good many fresh facts have come out. Looked at more closely, I should certainly say that it was a curious case.'

'Judging by its effect upon my brother, I should think it must be a most extraordinary one.' He snuggled down in his arm-chair. 'Now, Watson, let us have the facts.'

'The man's name was Arthur Cadogan West. He was twenty-seven years of age, unmarried, and a clerk at Woolwich Arsenal.'

'Government employ. Behold the link with brother Mycroft!'

'He left Woolwich suddenly on Monday night. Was last seen by his fiancée, Miss Violet Westbury, whom he left abruptly in the fog about 7.30 that evening. There was no quarrel between them and she can give no motive for his action. The next thing heard of him was when his dead body was discovered by a platelayer named Mason, just outside Aldgate Station on the Underground system in London.'

'When?'

'The body was found at six on the Tuesday morning. It was lying wide of the metals upon the left hand of the track as one goes eastward, at a point close to the station, where the line emerges from the tunnel in which it runs. The head was badly crushed – an injury which might well have been caused by a fall from the train. The body could only have come on the line in that way. Had it been carried down from any neighbouring street, it must have passed the station barriers, where a collector is always standing. This point seems absolutely certain.'

'Very good. The case is definite enough. The man, dead or alive, either fell or was precipitated from a train. So much is clear to me. Continue.'

'The trains which traverse the lines of rail beside which the body was found are those which run from west to east, some being purely Metropolitan, and some from Willesden and outlying junctions. It can be stated for certain that this young man, when he met his death, was travelling in this direction at some late hour of the night, but at what point he entered the train it is impossible to state.'

'His ticket, of course, would show that.'

'There was no ticket in his pockets.'

'No ticket! Dear me, Watson, this is really very singular. According to my experience it is not possible to reach the platform of a Metropolitan train without exhibiting one's ticket. Presumably, then, the young man had one. Was it taken from him in order to conceal the station from which he came? It is possible. Or did he drop it in the carriage? That also is possible. But the point is of curious interest. I understand that there was no sign of robbery?'

'Apparently not. There is a list here of his possessions. His purse contained two pounds fifteen. He had also a cheque-book on the Woolwich branch of the Capital and Counties Bank. Through this his identity was established. There were also two dress-circle tickets for the Woolwich Theatre, dated for that very evening. Also a small packet of technical papers.'

Holmes gave an exclamation of satisfaction.

'There we have it at last, Watson! British Government – Woolwich Arsenal – Technical papers – Brother Mycroft, the chain is complete. But here he comes, if I am not mistaken, to speak for himself.'

A moment later the tall and portly form of Mycroft Holmes was ushered into the room. Heavily built and massive, there was a suggestion of uncouth physical inertia in the figure, but above this unwieldy frame there was perched a head so masterful in its brow, so alert in its steel-grey, deep-set eyes, so firm in its lips, and so subtle in its play of expression, that after the first glance one forgot the gross body and remembered only the dominant mind.

At his heels came our old friend Lestrade, of Scotland Yard – thin and austere. The gravity of both their faces foretold some weighty quest. The detective shook hands without a word. Mycroft Holmes struggled out of his overcoat and subsided into an arm-chair.

'A most annoying business, Sherlock,' said he. 'I extremely dislike altering my habits, but the powers that be would take no denial. In the present state of Siam it is most awkward that I should be away from the office. But it is a real crisis. I have never seen the Prime Minister so upset. As to the Admiralty – it is buzzing like an overturned beehive. Have you read up the case?'

'We have just done so. What were the technical papers?'

'Ah, there's the point! Fortunately, it has not come out. The Press would be furious if it did. The papers which this wretched youth had in his pocket were the plans of the Bruce-Partington submarine.'

Mycroft Holmes spoke with a solemnity which showed his sense of the importance of the subject. His brother and I sat expectant.

'Surely you have heard of it? I thought everyone had heard of it.'

'Only as a name.'

'Its importance can hardly be exaggerated. It has been the most jealously guarded of all Government secrets. You may take it from me that naval warfare becomes impossible within the radius of a Bruce-Partington operation. Two years ago a very large sum was smuggled through the Estimates and was expended in acquiring a monopoly of the invention. Every effort has been made to keep the secret. The plans, which are exceedingly intricate, comprising some thirty separate patents, each essential to the working of the whole, are kept in an elaborate safe in a confidential office adjoining the Arsenal, with burglar-proof doors and windows. Under no conceivable circumstances were the plans to be taken from the office. If the Chief Constructor of the Navy desired to consult them, even he was forced to go to the Woolwich office for the purpose. And yet here we find them in the pockets of a dead junior clerk in the heart of London. From an official point of view it's simply awful.'

'But you have recovered them?'

'No, Sherlock, no! That's the pinch. We have not. Ten papers were taken from Woolwich. There were seven in the pockets of Cadogan West. The three most essential are gone – stolen, vanished. You must drop everything, Sherlock. Never mind your usual petty puzzles of the police-court. It's a vital international problem that you have to solve. Why did Cadogan West take the papers, where are the missing ones, how did he die, how came his body where it was found, how can the evil be set right? Find an answer to all these questions, and you will have done good service for your country.'

'Why do you not solve it yourself, Mycroft? You can see as far as I.'

'Possibly, Sherlock. But it is a question of getting details. Give me your details, and from an arm-chair I will return you an excellent expert opinion. But to run here and run there, to cross-question railway guards, and lie on my face with a lens to my eye – it is not my *métier*. No, you are the one man who can clear the matter up. If you have a fancy to see your name in the next honours list—'

My friend smiled and shook his head.

'I play the game for the game's own sake,' said he. 'But the problem certainly presents some points of interest, and I shall be very pleased to look into it. Some more facts, please.'

'I have jotted down the more essential ones upon this sheet of paper, together with a few addresses which you will find of service. The actual official guardian of the papers is the famous Government expert, Sir James Walter, whose decorations and sub-titles fill two lines of a book of reference. He has grown grey in the service, is a gentleman, a favoured guest in the most exalted houses, and above all a man whose patriotism is beyond suspicion. He is one of two who have a key of the safe. I may add that the papers were undoubtedly in the office during working hours on Monday, and that Sir James left for London about three o'clock taking his key with him. He was at the house of Admiral Sinclair at Barclay Square during the whole of the evening when this incident occurred.'

'Has the fact been verified?'

'Yes; his brother, Colonel Valentine Walter, has testified to his departure from Woolwich, and Admiral Sinclair to his arrival in London; so Sir James is no longer a direct factor in the problem.'

'Who was the other man with a key?'

'The senior clerk and draughtsman, Mr Sidney Johnson. He is a man of forty, married, with five children. He is a silent, morose man, but he has, on the whole, an excellent record in the public service. He is unpopular with his colleagues, but a hard worker. According to his own account, corroborated only by the word of his wife, he was at home the whole of Monday evening after office hours, and his key has never left the watch-chain upon which it hangs.'

'Tell us about Cadogan West.'

'He has been ten years in the Service, and has done good work. He has the reputation of being hot-headed and impetuous, but a straight, honest man. We have nothing against him. He was next Sidney Johnson in the office. His duties brought him into daily personal contact with the plans. No one else had the handling of them.'

'Who locked the plans up that night?'

'Mr Sidney Johnson, the senior clerk.'

'Well, it is surely perfectly clear who took them away. They are actually found upon the person of this junior clerk, Cadogan West. That seems final, does it not?'

'It does, Sherlock, and yet it leaves so much unexplained. In the first place, why did he take them?'

'I presume they were of value?'

'He could have got several thousands for them very easily.'

'Can you suggest any possible motive for taking the papers to London except to sell them?'

'No, I cannot.'

'Then we must take that as our working hypothesis. Young West took the papers. Now this could only be done by having a false key—'

'Several false keys. He had to open the building and the room.'

'He had, then, several false keys. He took the papers to London to sell the secret, intending, no doubt, to have the plans themselves back in the safe next morning before they were missed. While in London on this treasonable mission he met his end.'

'How?'

'We will suppose that he was travelling back to Woolwich when he was killed and thrown out of the compartment.'

'Aldgate, where the body was found, is considerably past the station for London Bridge, which would be his route to Woolwich.'

'Many circumstances could be imagined under which he would pass London Bridge. There was someone in the carriage, for example, with whom he was having an absorbing interview. This interview led to a violent scene, in which he lost his life. Possibly he tried to leave the carriage, fell out on the line, and so met his end. The other closed the door. There was a thick fog, and nothing could be seen.'

'No better explanation can be given with our present knowledge; and yet consider, Sherlock, how much you leave untouched. We will suppose, for argument's sake, that young Cadogan West *had* determined to convey these papers to London. He would naturally have made an appointment with the foreign agent and kept his evening clear. Instead of that he took two tickets for the theatre, escorted his fiancée half-way there, and then suddenly disappeared.'

'A blind,' said Lestrade, who had sat listening with some impatience to the conversation.

'A very singular one. That is objection No. 1. Objection No. 2: We will suppose that he reaches London and sees the foreign agent. He must bring back the papers before morning or the loss will be discovered. He took away ten. Only seven were in his pocket. What had become of the other three? He certainly would not leave them of his own free will. Then, again, where is the price of his treason? One would have expected to find a large sum of money in his pocket.'

'It seems to me perfectly clear,' said Lestrade. 'I have no doubt at all as to what occurred. He took the papers to sell them. He saw the agent. They could not agree as to price. He started home again, but the agent went with him. In the train the agent murdered him, took the more essential papers, and threw his body from the carriage. That would account for everything, would it not?'

'Why had he no ticket?'

'The ticket would have shown which station was nearest the agent's house. Therefore he took it from the murdered man's pocket.'

'Good, Lestrade, very good,' said Holmes. 'Your theory holds together. But if this is true, then the case is at an end. On the one hand the traitor is dead. On the other the plans of the Bruce-Partington submarine are presumably already on the Continent. What is there for us to do?'

'To act, Sherlock – to act!' cried Mycroft, springing to his feet. 'All my instincts are against this explanation. Use your powers! Go to the scene of the crime! See the people concerned! Leave no stone unturned! In all your career you have never had so great a chance of serving your country.'

'Well, well!' said Holmes, shrugging his shoulders. 'Come, Watson! And you, Lestrade, could you favour us with your company for an hour or two? We will begin our investigation by a visit to Aldgate Station. Good-bye, Mycroft. I shall let you have a report before evening, but I warn you in advance that you have little to expect.'

An hour later, Holmes, Lestrade and I stood upon the underground railroad at the point where it emerges from the tunnel immediately before Aldgate Station. A courteous red-faced old gentleman represented the railway company.

'This is where the young man's body lay,' said he, indicating a spot about three feet from the metals. 'It could not have fallen from above, for these, as you see, are all blank walls. Therefore, it could only have come from a train, and that train, so far as we can trace it, must have passed about midnight on Monday.'

'Have the carriages been examined for any sign of violence?'

'There are no such signs, and no ticket has been found.'

'No record of a door being found open?'

'None.'

'We have had some fresh evidence this morning,' said Lestrade. 'A passenger who passed Aldgate in an ordinary Metropolitan train about 11.40 on Monday night declares that he heard a heavy thud, as of a body striking the line, just before the train reached the station. There was dense fog, however, and nothing could be seen. He made no report of it at the time. Why, whatever is the matter with Mr Holmes?'

My friend was standing with an expression of strained intensity upon his face, staring at the railway metals where they curved out of the tunnel. Aldgate is a junction, and there was a network of points. On these his eager, questioning eyes were fixed, and I saw on his keen, alert face that tightening of the lips, that quiver of the nostrils, and concentration of the heavy tufted brows which I knew so well.

'Points,' he muttered; 'the points.'

'What of it? What do you mean?'

'I suppose there are no great number of points on a system such as this?'

'No; there are very few.'

'And a curve, too. Points, and a curve. By Jove! if it were only so.'

'What is it, Mr Holmes? Have you a clue?'

'An idea – an indication, no more. But the case certainly grows in interest. Unique, perfectly unique, and yet why not? I do not see any indications of bleeding on the line.'

'There were hardly any.'

'But I understand that there was a considerable wound.'

'The bone was crushed, but there was no great external injury.'

'And yet one would have expected some bleeding. Would it be possible for me to inspect the train which contained the passenger who heard the thud of a fall in the fog?'

'I fear not, Mr Holmes. The train has been broken up before now, and the carriages redistributed.'

'I can assure you, Mr Holmes,' said Lestrade, 'that every carriage has been carefully examined. I saw to it myself.'

It was one of my friend's most obvious weaknesses that he was impatient with less alert intelligences than his own.

'Very likely,' said he, turning away. 'As it happens, it was not the carriages which I desire to examine. Watson, we have done all we can here. We need not trouble you any further, Mr Lestrade. I think our investigations must now carry us to Woolwich.'

At London Bridge, Holmes wrote a telegram to his brother, which he handed to me before dispatching it. It ran thus:

'See some light in the darkness, but it may possibly flicker out. Meanwhile, please send by messenger, to await return at Baker Street, a complete list of all foreign spies or international agents known to be in

England, with full address.—SHERLOCK.'

'That should be helpful, Watson,' he remarked, as we took our seats in the Woolwich train. 'We certainly owe brother Mycroft a debt for having introduced us to what promises to be a really very remarkable case.'

His eager face still wore that expression of intense and high-strung energy, which showed me that some novel and suggestive circumstance had opened up a stimulating line of thought. See the foxhound with hanging ears and drooping tail as it lolls about the kennels, and compare it with the same hound as, with gleaming eyes and straining muscles, it runs upon a breast-high scent – such was the change in Holmes since the morning. He was a different man to the limp and lounging figure in the mouse-coloured dressing-gown who had prowled so restlessly only a few hours before round the fog-girt room.

'There is material here. There is scope,' said he. 'I am dull indeed not to have understood its possibilities.'

'Even now they are dark to me.'

'The end is dark to me also, but I have hold of one idea which may lead us far. The man met his death elsewhere, and his body was on the *roof* of a carriage.'

'On the roof!'

'Remarkable, is it not? But consider the facts. Is it a coincidence that it is found at the very point where the train pitches and sways as it comes round on the points? Is not that the place where an object upon the roof might be expected to fall off? The points would affect no object inside the train. Either the body fell from the roof, or a very curious coincidence has occurred. But now consider the question of the blood. Of course, there was no bleeding on the line if the body had bled elsewhere. Each fact is suggestive in itself. Together they have a cumulative force.'

'And the ticket, too!' I cried.

'Exactly. We could not explain the absence of a ticket. This would explain it. Everything fits together.'

'But suppose it were so, we are still as far as ever from unravelling the mystery of his death. Indeed, it becomes not simpler, but stranger.'

'Perhaps,' said Holmes, thoughtfully; 'perhaps.' He relapsed into a silent reverie, which lasted until the slow train drew up at last in Woolwich Station. There he called a cab and drew Mycroft's paper from his pocket.

'We have quite a little round of afternoon calls to make,' said he. 'I think that Sir James Walter claims our first attention.'

The house of the famous official was a fine villa with green lawns stretching down to the Thames. As we reached it the fog was lifting, and a thin, watery sunshine was breaking through. A butler answered our ring. 'Sir James, sir!' said he, with solemn face. 'Sir James died this morning.'

'Good heavens!' cried Holmes, in amazement. 'How did he die?'

'Perhaps you would care to step in, sir, and see his brother, Colonel Valentine?'

'Yes, we had best do so.'

We were ushered into a dim-lit drawing-room, where an instant later we were joined by a very tall, handsome, light-bearded man of fifty, the younger brother of the dead scientist. His wild eyes, stained cheeks, and unkempt hair all spoke of the sudden blow which had fallen upon the household. He was hardly articulate as he spoke of it.

'It was this horrible scandal,' said he. 'My brother, Sir James, was a man of very sensitive honour, and he could not survive such an affair. It broke his heart. He was always so proud of the efficiency of his department, and this was a crushing blow.'

'We had hoped that he might have given us some indications which would have helped us to clear the matter up.'

'I assure you that it was all a mystery to him as it is to you and to all of us. He had already put all his knowledge at the disposal of the police. Naturally, he had no doubt that Cadogan West was guilty. But all the rest was inconceivable.'

'You cannot throw any new light upon the affair?'

'I know nothing myself save what I have read or heard. I have no desire to be discourteous, but you can understand, Mr Holmes, that we are much disturbed at present, and I must ask you to hasten this interview to an end.'

'This is indeed an unexpected development,' said my friend when we had regained the cab. 'I wonder if the death was natural, or whether the poor old fellow killed himself! If the latter, may it be taken as some sign of self-reproach for duty neglected? We must leave that question to the future. Now we shall turn to the Cadogan Wests.'

A small but well-kept house in the outskirts of the town sheltered the bereaved mother. The old lady was too dazed with grief to be of any use to us, but at her side was a white-faced young lady, who introduced herself as Miss Violet Westbury, the fiancée of the dead man, and the last to see him upon that fatal night.

'I cannot explain it, Mr Holmes,' she said. 'I have not shut an eye since the tragedy, thinking, thinking, thinking, night and day, what the true meaning of it can be. Arthur was the most single-minded, chivalrous, patriotic man upon earth. He would have cut his right hand off before he would sell a State secret confided to his keeping. It is absurd, impossible, preposterous to anyone who knew him.'

'But the facts, Miss Westbury?'

'Yes, yes; I admit I cannot explain them.'

'Was he in any want of money?'

'No; his needs were very simple and his salary ample. He had saved a few hundreds, and we were to marry at the New Year.'

'No signs of any mental excitement? Come, Miss Westbury, be absolutely frank with us.'

The quick eye of my companion had noted some change in her manner. She coloured and hesitated.

'Yes,' she said, at last. 'I had a feeling that there was something on his mind.'

'For long?'

'Only for the last week or so. He was thoughtful and worried. Once I pressed him about it. He admitted that there was something, and that it was concerned with his official life. "It is too serious for me to speak about, even to you," said he. I could get nothing more.'

Holmes looked grave.

'Go on, Miss Westbury. Even if it seems to tell against him, go on. We cannot say what it may lead to.'

'Indeed I have nothing more to tell. Once or twice it seemed to me that he was on the point of telling me something. He spoke one evening of the importance of the secret, and I have some recollection that he said that no doubt foreign spies would pay a great deal to have it.'

My friend's face grew graver still.

'Anything else?'

'He said that we were slack about such matters – that it would be easy for a traitor to get the plans.'

'Was it only recently that he made such remarks?'

'Yes, quite recently.'

'Now tell us of that last evening.'

'We were to go to the theatre. The fog was so thick that a cab was useless. We walked, and our way took us close to the office. Suddenly he darted away into the fog.'

'Without a word?'

'He gave an exclamation; that was all. I waited but he never returned. Then I walked home. Next morning, after the office opened, they came to inquire. About twelve o'clock we heard the terrible news. Oh, Mr Holmes, if you could only, only save his honour! It was so much to him.'

Holmes shook his head sadly.

'Come, Watson,' said he, 'our ways lie elsewhere. Our next station must be the office from which the papers were taken.'

'It was black enough before against this young man, but our inquiries make it blacker,' he remarked, as the cab lumbered off. 'His coming marriage gives a motive for the crime. He naturally wanted money. The idea was in his head, since he spoke about it. He nearly made the girl an accomplice in the treason by telling her his plans. It is all very bad.'

'But surely, Holmes, character goes for something? Then, again, why should he leave the girl in the street and dart away to commit a felony?'

'Exactly! There are certainly objections. But it is a formidable case which they have to meet.'

Mr Sidney Johnson, the senior clerk, met us at the office, and received us with that respect which my companion's card always commanded. He was a thin, gruff, bespectacled man of middle age, his cheeks haggard, and his hands twitching from the nervous strain to which he had been subjected.

'It is bad, Mr Holmes, very bad! Have you heard of the death of the Chief?'

'We have just come from his house.'

'The place is disorganised. The Chief dead, Cadogan West dead, our papers stolen. And yet, when we closed our door on Monday evening we were as efficient an office as any in the Government service. Good God, it's dreadful to think of! That West, of all men, should have done such a thing!'

'You are sure of his guilt, then?'

'I can see no other way out of it. And yet I would have trusted him as I trust myself.'

'At what hour was the office closed on Monday?'

'At five.'

'Did you close it?'

'I am always the last man out.'

'Where were the plans?'

'In that safe. I put them there myself.'

'Is there no watchman to the building?'

'There is; but he has other departments to look after as well. He is an old soldier and a most trustworthy man. He saw nothing that evening. Of course, the fog was very thick.'

'Suppose that Cadogan West wished to make his way into the building after hours; he would need three keys, would he not, before he could reach the papers?'

'Yes, he would. The key of the outer door, the key of the office, and the key of the safe.'

'Only Sir James Walter and you had those keys?'

'I had no keys of the doors – only of the safe.'

'Was Sir James a man who was orderly in his habits?'

'Yes, I think he was. I know that so far as those three keys are concerned he kept them on the same ring. I have often seen them there.'

'And that ring went with him to London?'

'He said so.'

'And your key never left your possession?'

'Never.'

'Then West, if he is the culprit, must have had a duplicate. And yet none was found upon his body. One other point: if a clerk in this office desired to sell the plans, would it not be simpler to copy the plans for himself than to take the originals, as was actually done?'

'It would take considerable technical knowledge to copy the plans in an effective way.'

'But I suppose either Sir James, or you, or West had that technical knowledge?'

'No doubt we had, but I beg you won't try to drag me into the matter, Mr Holmes. What is the use of our speculating in this way when the original plans were actually found on West?'

'Well, it is certainly singular that he should run the risk of taking originals, if he could safely have taken copies, which would have equally served his turn.'

'Singular, no doubt – and yet he did so.'

'Every inquiry in this case reveals something inexplicable. Now there are three papers still missing. They are, as I understand, the vital ones.'

'Yes, that is so.'

'Do you mean to say that anyone holding these three papers, and without the seven others, could construct a Bruce-Partington submarine?'

'I reported to that effect to the Admiralty. But to-day I have been over the drawings again, and I am not so sure of it. The double valves with the automatic self-adjusting slots are drawn in one of the papers which have been returned. Until the foreigners had invented that for themselves they could not make the boat. Of course, they might soon get over the difficulty.'

'But the three missing drawings are the most important?'

'Undoubtedly.'

'I think, with your permission, I will now take a stroll round the premises. I do not recall any other question which I desired to ask.'

He examined the lock of the safe, the door of the room, and finally the iron shutters of the window. It was only when we were on the lawn outside that his interest was strongly excited. There was a laurel bush outside the window, and several of the branches bore signs of having been twisted or snapped. He examined them carefully with his lens, and then some dim and vague marks upon the earth beneath. Finally he asked the chief clerk to close the iron shutters, and he pointed out to me that they hardly met in the centre, and that it would be possible for anyone outside to see what was going on within the room.

'The indications are ruined by the three days' delay. They may mean something or nothing. Well, Watson, I do not think that Woolwich can help us further. It is a small crop which we have gathered. Let us see if we can do better in London.'

Yet we added one more sheaf to our harvest before we left Woolwich Station. The clerk in the ticket office was able to say with confidence that he saw Cadogan West – whom he knew well by sight – upon the Monday night, and that he went to London by the 8.15 to London Bridge. He was alone, and took a single third-class ticket. The clerk was struck at the time by his excited and nervous manner. So shaky was he that he could hardly pick up his change, and the clerk had helped him with it. A reference to the time-table showed that the 8.15 was the first train which it was possible for West to take after he had left the lady about 7.30.

'Let us reconstruct, Watson,' said Holmes, after half an hour of silence. 'I am not aware that in all our joint researches we have ever had a case which was more difficult to get at. Every fresh advance which we make only reveals a fresh ridge beyond. And yet we have surely made some appreciable progress.

'The effect of our inquiries at Woolwich has in the main been against young Cadogan West; but the indications at the window would lend themselves to a more favourable hypothesis. Let us suppose, for example, that he had been approached by some foreign agent. It might have been done under such pledges as would have prevented him from speaking of it, and yet would have affected his thoughts in the direction indicated by his remarks to his fiancée. Very good. We will now suppose that as he went to the theatre with the young lady he suddenly, in the fog, caught a glimpse of this same agent going in the direction of the office. He was an impetuous man, quick in his decisions. Everything gave way to his duty. He followed the man, reached the window, saw the abstraction of the documents, and pursued the thief. In this way we get over the objection that no one would take originals when he could make copies. This outsider had to take originals. So far it holds together.'

'What is the next step?'

'Then we come into difficulties. One would imagine that under such circumstances the first act of young Cadogan West would be to seize the villain and raise the alarm. Why did he not do so? Could it have been an official superior who took the papers? That would explain West's conduct. Or could the Chief have given West the slip in the fog, and West started at once to London to head him off from his own rooms, presuming that he knew where the rooms were? The call must have been very pressing, since he left his girl standing in the fog, and made no effort to communicate with her. Our scent runs cold here, and there is a vast gap between either hypothesis and the laying of West's body, with seven papers in his pocket, on the roof of a Metropolitan train. My instinct now is to work from the other end. If Mycroft has given us the list of addresses we may be able to pick our man, and follow two tracks instead of one.'

Surely enough, a note awaited us at Baker Street. A Government messenger had brought it post-haste. Holmes glanced at it and threw it over to me.

'There are numerous small fry, but few who would handle so big an affair. The only men worth considering are Adolph Meyer, of 13 Great George Street, Westminster; Louis La Rothière, of Campden Mansions, Notting Hill; and Hugo Oberstein, 13 Caulfield Gardens, Kensington. The latter was known to be in town on Monday, and is now reported as having left. Glad to hear you have seen some light. The Cabinet awaits your final report with the utmost anxiety. Urgent representations have arrived from the very highest quarter. The whole force of the State is at your back if you should need it.—MYCROFT.'

'I'm afraid,' said Holmes, smiling, 'that all the Queen's horses and all the Queen's men cannot avail in this matter.' He had spread out his big map of London, and leaned eagerly over it. 'Well, well,' said he presently, with an exclamation of satisfaction, 'things are turning a little in our direction at last. Why, Watson, I do honestly believe that we are going to pull it off after all.' He slapped me on the shoulder with a sudden burst of hilarity. 'I am going out now. It is only a reconnaissance. I will do nothing serious without my trusted comrade and biographer at my elbow. Do you stay here, and the odds are that you will see me again in an hour or two. If time hangs heavy get foolscap and a pen, and begin your narrative of how we saved the State.'

I felt some reflection of his elation in my own mind, for I knew well that he would not depart so far from his usual austerity of demeanour unless there was good cause for exultation. All the long November evening I waited, filled with impatience for his return. At last, shortly after nine o'clock there arrived a messenger with a note:

'Am dining at Goldini's Restaurant, Gloucester Road, Kensington. Please come at once and join me there. Bring with you a jemmy, a dark lantern, a chisel, and a revolver.—S.H.'

It was a nice equipment for a respectable citizen to carry through the dim, fog-draped streets. I stowed them all discreetly away in my overcoat, and drove straight to the address given. There sat my friend at a little round table near the door of the garish Italian restaurant.

'Have you had something to eat? Then join me in a coffee and curaçao. Try one of the proprietor's cigars. They are less poisonous than one would expect. Have you the tools?'

'They are here, in my overcoat.'

'Excellent. Let me give you a short sketch of what I have done, with some indication of what we are about to do. Now it must be evident to you, Watson, that this young man's body was *placed* on the roof of the train. That was clear from the instant that I determined the the the fact that it was from the roof, and not from a carriage, that he had fallen.'

'Could it not have been dropped from a bridge?'

'I should say it was impossible. If you examine the roofs you will find that they are slightly rounded, and there is no railing round them. Therefore, we can say for certain that young Cadogan West was placed on it.'

'How could he be placed there?'

'That was the question which we had to answer. There is only one possible way. You are aware that the Underground runs clear of tunnels at some points in the West End. I had a vague memory that as I have travelled by it I have occasionally seen windows just above my head. Now, suppose that a train halted under such a window, would there be any difficulty in laying a body upon the roof?'

'It seems most improbable.'

'We must fall back upon the old axiom that when all other contingencies fail, whatever remains, however improbable, must be the truth. Here all other contingencies *have* failed. When I found that the leading international agent, who had just left London, lived in a row of houses which abutted upon the Underground, I was so pleased that you were a little astonished at my sudden frivolity.'

'Oh, that was it, was it?'

'Yes, that was it. Mr Hugo Oberstein, of 13 Caulfield Gardens, had become my objective. I began my operations at Gloucester Road Station, where a very helpful official walked with me along the track, and allowed me to satisfy myself, not only that the back-stair windows of Caulfield Gardens open on the line, but the even more essential fact that, owing to the intersection of one of the larger railways, the Underground trains are frequently held motionless for some minutes at that very spot.'

'Splendid, Holmes! You have got it!'

'So far – so far, Watson. We advance, but the goal is afar. Well, having seen the back of Caulfield Gardens, I visited the front and satisfied myself that the bird was indeed flown. It is a considerable house, unfurnished, so far as I could judge, in the upper rooms. Oberstein lived there with a single valet, who was probably a confederate entirely in his confidence. We must bear in mind that Oberstein has gone to the Continent to dispose of his booty, but not with any idea of flight; for he had no reason to fear a warrant, and the idea of an amateur domiciliary visit would certainly never occur to him. Yet that is precisely what we are about to make.'

'Could we not get a warrant and legalize it?'

'Hardly on the evidence.'

'What can we hope to do?'

'We cannot tell what correspondence may be there.'

'I don't like it, Holmes.'

'My dear fellow, you shall keep watch in the street. I'll do the criminal part. It's not a time to stick at trifles. Think of Mycroft's note, of the Admiralty, the Cabinet, the exalted person who waits for news. We are bound to go.'

My answer was to rise from the table.

'You are right, Holmes. We are bound to go.'

He sprang up and shook me by the hand.

'I knew you would not shrink at the last,' said he, and for a moment I saw something in his eyes which was nearer to tenderness than I had ever seen. The next instant he was his masterful, practical self once more.

'It is nearly half a mile, but there is no hurry. Let us walk,' said he. 'Don't drop the instruments, I beg. Your arrest as a suspicious character would be a most unfortunate complication.'

Caulfield Gardens was one of those lines of flat-faced, pillared, and porticoed houses which are so prominent a product of the middle Victorian epoch in the West End of London. Next door there appeared to be a children's party, for the merry buzz of young voices and the clatter of a piano resounded through the night. The fog still hung about and screened us with its friendly shade. Holmes had lit his lantern and flashed it upon the massive door.

'This is a serious proposition,' said he. 'It is certainly bolted as well as locked. We would do better in the area. There is an excellent archway down yonder in case a too zealous policeman should intrude. Give me a hand, Watson, and I'll do the same for you.'

A minute later we were both in the area. Hardly had we reached the dark shadows before the step of the policeman was heard in the fog above. As its soft rhythm died away, Holmes set to work upon the lower door. I saw him stoop and strain until with a sharp crash it flew open. We sprang through into the dark passage, closing the area door behind us. Holmes led the way up the curving, uncarpeted stair. His little fan of yellow light shone upon a low window.

'Here we are, Watson – this must be the one.' He threw it open, and as he did so there was a low, harsh murmur, growing steadily into a loud roar as a train dashed past us in the darkness. Holmes swept his light along the window-sill. It was thickly coated with soot from the passing engines, but the black surface was blurred and rubbed in places.

'You can see where they rested the body. Halloa, Watson! what is this? There can be no doubt that it is a blood mark.' He was pointing to faint discolourations along the woodwork of the window. 'Here it is on the stone of the stair also. The demonstration is complete. Let us stay here until a train stops.'

We had not long to wait. The very next train roared from the tunnel as before, but slowed in the open, and then, with a creaking of brakes, pulled up immediately beneath us. It was not four feet from the window-ledge to the roof of the carriages. Holmes softly closed the window.

'So far we are justified,' said he. 'What do you think of it, Watson?'

'A masterpiece. You have never risen to a greater height.'

'I cannot agree with you there. From the moment that I conceived the idea of the body being upon the roof, which surely was not a very abstruse one, all the rest was inevitable. If it were not for the grave interests involved the affair up to this point would be insignificant. Our difficulties are still before us. But perhaps we may find something here which may help us.'

We had ascended the kitchen stair and entered the suite of rooms upon the first floor. One was a dining-room, severely furnished and containing nothing of interest. A second was a bedroom, which also drew blank. The remaining room appeared more promising, and my companion settled down to a systematic examination. It was littered with books and papers, and was evidently used as a study. Swiftly and methodically Holmes turned over the contents of drawer after drawer and cupboard after cupboard, but no gleam of success came to brighten his austere face. At the end of an hour he was no further than when he started.

'The cunning dog has covered his tracks,' said he. 'He has left nothing to incriminate him. His dangerous correspondence has been destroyed or removed. This is our last chance.'

It was a small tin cash-box which stood upon the writing-desk. Holmes prised it open with his chisel. Several rolls of paper were within, covered with figures and calculations, without any note to show to what they referred. The recurring words, 'Water pressure,' and 'Pressure to the square inch' suggested some possible relation to a submarine. Holmes tossed them all impatiently aside. There only remained an envelope with some small newspaper slips inside it. He shook them out on the table, and at once I saw by his eager face that his hopes had been raised.

'What's this, Watson? Eh? What's this? Record of a series of messages in the advertisements of a paper. *Daily Telegraph* agony column by the print and paper. Right-hand top corner of a page. No dates – but messages arrange themselves. This must be the first:

'"Hoped to hear sooner. Terms agreed to. Write fully to address given on card.—Pierrot."

'Next comes: "Too complex for description. Must have full report. Stuff awaits you when goods delivered.—Pierrot."

'Then comes: "Matter presses. Must withdraw offer unless contract completed. Make appointment by letter. Will confirm by advertisement.—Pierrot."

'Finally: "Monday night after nine. Two taps. Only ourselves. Do not be so suspicious. Payment in hard cash when goods delivered.—Pierrot."

'A fairly complete record, Watson! If we could only get at the man at the other end!' He sat lost in thought, tapping his fingers on the table. Finally he sprang to his feet.

'Well, perhaps it won't be so difficult after all. There is nothing more to be done here, Watson. I think we might drive round to the offices of the *Daily Telegraph*, and so bring a good day's work to a conclusion.'

Mycroft Holmes and Lestrade had come round by appointment after breakfast next day and Sherlock Holmes had recounted to them our proceedings of the day before. The professional shook his head over our confessed burglary.

'We can't do these things in the force, Mr Holmes,' said he. 'No wonder you get results that are beyond us. But some of these days you'll go too far, and you'll find yourself and your friend in trouble.'

'For England, home and beauty – eh, Watson? Martyrs on the altar of our country. But what do you think of it, Mycroft?'

'Excellent, Sherlock! Admirable! But what use will you make of it?'

Holmes picked up the *Daily Telegraph* which lay upon the table.

'Have you seen Pierrot's advertisement to-day?'

'What! Another one?'

'Yes, here it is: "To-night. Same hour. Same place. Two taps. Most vitally important. Your own safety at stake.—Pierrot."'

'By George!' cried Lestrade. 'If he answers that we've got him!'

'That was my idea when I put it in. I think if you could both make it convenient to come with us about eight o'clock to Caulfield Gardens we might possibly get a little nearer to a solution.'

One of the most remarkable characteristics of Sherlock Holmes was his power of throwing his brain out of action and switching all his thoughts on to lighter things whenever he had convinced himself that he could no longer work to advantage. I remember that during the whole of that memorable day he lost himself in a monograph which he had undertaken upon the Polyphonic Motets of Lassus. For my own part I had none of this power of detachment, and the day, in consequence, appeared to be interminable. The great national importance of the issue, the suspense in high quarters, the direct nature of the experiment which we were trying – all combined to work upon my nerve. It was a relief to me when at last, after a light dinner, we set out upon our expedition. Lestrade and Mycroft met us by appointment at the outside of Gloucester Road Station. The area door of Oberstein's house had been left open the night before, and it was necessary for me, as Mycroft Holmes absolutely and indignantly declined to climb the railings, to pass in and open the hall door. By nine o'clock we were all seated in the study, waiting patiently for our man.

An hour passed and yet another. When eleven struck, the measured beat of the great church clock seemed to sound the dirge of our hopes. Lestrade and Mycroft were fidgeting in their seats and looking twice a minute at their watches. Holmes sat silent and composed, his eyelids half shut, but every sense on the alert. He raised his head with a sudden jerk.

'He is coming,' said he.

There had been a furtive step past the door. Now it returned. We heard a shuffling sound outside, and then two sharp taps with the knocker. Holmes rose, motioning to us to remain seated. The gas in the hall was a mere point of light. He opened the outer door, and then as a dark figure slipped past him he closed and fastened it. 'This way!' we heard him say, and a moment later our man stood before us. Holmes had followed him closely, and as the man turned with a cry of surprise and alarm he caught him by the collar and threw him back into the room. Before our prisoner had recovered his balance the door was shut and Holmes standing with his back against it. The man glared round him, staggered, and fell senseless upon the floor. With the shock, his broad-brimmed hat flew from his head, his cravat slipped down from his lips, and there was the long light beard and the soft, handsome delicate features of Colonel Valentine Walter.

Holmes gave a whistle of surprise.

'You can write me down an ass this time, Watson,' said he. 'This was not the bird that I was looking for.'

'Who is he?' asked Mycroft eagerly.

'The younger brother of the late Sir James Walter, the head of the Submarine Department. Yes, yes; I see the fall of the cards. He is coming to. I think that you had best leave his examination to me.'

We had carried the prostrate body to the sofa. Now our prisoner sat up, looked round him with a horror-stricken face, and passed his hand over his forehead, like one who cannot believe his own senses.

'What is this?' he asked. 'I came here to visit Mr Oberstein.'

'Everything is known, Colonel Walter,' said Holmes. 'How an English gentleman could behave in such a manner is beyond my comprehension. But your whole correspondence and relations with Oberstein are within our knowledge. So also are the circumstances connected with the death of young Cadogan West. Let me advise you to gain at least the small credit for repentance and confession, since there are still some details which we can only learn from your lips.'

The man groaned and sank his face in his hands. We waited, but he was silent.

'I can assure you,' said Holmes, 'that every essential is already known. We know that you were pressed for money; that you took an impress of the keys which your brother held; and that you entered into a correspondence with Oberstein, who answered your letters through the advertisement columns of the *Daily Telegraph*. We are aware that you went down to the office in the fog on Monday night, but that you were seen and followed by young Cadogan West, who had probably some previous reason to suspect you. He saw your theft, but could not give the alarm, as it was just possible that you were taking the papers to your brother in London. Leaving all his private concerns, like the good citizen that he was, he followed you closely in the fog, and kept at your heels until you reached this very house. There he intervened, and then it was, Colonel Walter, that to treason you added the more terrible crime of murder.'

'I did not! I did not! Before God I swear that I did not!' cried our wretched prisoner.

'Tell us, then, how Cadogan West met his end before you laid him upon the roof of a railway carriage.'

'I will. I swear to you that I will. I did the rest. I confess it. It was just as you say. A Stock Exchange debt had to be paid. I needed the money badly. Oberstein offered me five thousand. It was to save myself from ruin. But as to murder, I am as innocent as you.'

'What happened then?'

'He had his suspicions before, and he followed me as you describe. I never knew it until I was at the very door. It was thick fog, and one could not see three yards. I had given two taps and Oberstein had come to the door. The young man rushed up and demanded to know what we were about to do with the papers. Oberstein had a short life-preserver. He always carried it with him. As West forced his way after us into the house Oberstein struck him on the head. The blow was a fatal one. He was dead within five minutes. There he lay in the hall, and we were at our wits' end what to do. Then Oberstein had this idea about the trains which halted under his back window. But first he examined the papers which I had brought. He said that three of them were essential, and that he must keep them. "You cannot keep them," said I. "There will be a dreadful row at Woolwich if they are not returned." "I must keep them," said he, "for they are so technical that it is impossible in the time to make copies." "Then they must all go back together to-night," said I. He thought for a little, and then cried out that he had it. "Three I will keep," said he. "The others we will stuff into the pocket of this young man. When he is found the whole business will assuredly be put to his account." I could see no other way out of it, so we did as he suggested. We waited half an hour at the window before a train stopped. It was so thick that nothing could be seen, and we had no difficulty in lowering West's body on to the train. That was the end of the matter so far as I was concerned.'

'And your brother?'

'He said nothing, but he had caught me once with his keys, and I think that he suspected. I read in his eyes that he suspected. As you know, he never held up his head again.'

There was silence in the room. It was broken by Mycroft Holmes.

'Can you not make reparation? It would ease your conscience, and possibly your punishment.'

'What reparation can I make?'

'Where is Oberstein with the papers?'

'I do not know.'

'Did he give you no address?'

'He said that letters to the Hôtel du Louvre, Paris, would eventually reach him.'

'Then reparation is still within your power,' said Sherlock Holmes.

'I will do anything I can. I owe this fellow no particular goodwill. He has been my ruin and my downfall.'

'Here are paper and pen. Sit at this desk and write to my dictation. Direct the envelope to the address given. That is right. Now the letter: 'Dear Sir,—With regard to our transaction, you will no doubt have observed by now that one essential detail is missing. I have a tracing which will make it complete. This has involved me in extra trouble, however, and I must ask you for a further advance of five hundred pounds. I will not trust it to the post, nor will I take anything but gold or notes. I would come to you abroad, but it would excite remark if I left the country at present. Therefore I shall expect to meet you in the smoking-room of the Charing Cross Hotel at noon on Saturday. Remember that only English notes, or gold, will be taken.' That will do very well. I shall be very much surprised if it does not fetch our man.'

And it did! It is a matter of history – that secret history of a nation which is often so much more intimate and interesting than its public chronicles – that Oberstein, eager to complete the coup of his lifetime, came to the lure and was safely engulfed for fifteen years in a British prison. In his trunk were found the invaluable Bruce-Partington plans, which he had put up for auction in all the naval centres of Europe.

Colonel Walter died in prison towards the end of the second year of his sentence. As to Holmes, he returned refreshed to his monograph upon the Polyphonic Motets of Lassus, which has since been printed for private circulation, and is said by experts to be the last word upon the subject. Some weeks afterwards I learned incidentally that my friend spent a day at Windsor, whence he returned with a remarkably fine emerald tie-pin. When I asked him if he had bought it, he answered that it was a present from a certain gracious lady in whose interests he had once been fortunate enough to carry out a small commission. He said no more; but I fancy that I could guess at that lady's august name, and I have little doubt that the emerald pin will for ever recall to my friend's memory the adventure of the Bruce-Partington plans.

STRANGE
CONFLICT

DENNIS WHEATLEY

STRANGE CONFLICT

The Duke de Richleau and Sir Pellinore Gwaine-Cust had gone into dinner at eight o'clock, but coffee was not served till after ten. The war had been in progress for many months and the bombing of London for some weeks. A small shower of incendiary bombs having fallen in Curzon Street, just outside the Duke's flat, had caused an interruption of the meal while they went down to lend a hand in extinguishing them, but both were by now so hardened to the blitzkrieg that after a wash they returned to the table as though nothing very out-of-the-ordinary had happened.

The Duke and his guest had much in common. Both had been blessed with an ancient name, good looks, brains and charm, which had made them outstanding figures in the European society of their day. That day was passing, but they had made the most of it and regretted nothing of their tempestuous early years when they had fought and loved to the limit of their capacity, or the quiet period that had followed, during which they had dabbled most successfully in high finance and played a hand in many of the secret moves behind the diplomatic scene. That a better world might emerge with the passing of the privileged caste that they represented they both hoped, but rather doubted, and as each was unshakably convinced that it would not do so if the Nazis were not utterly destroyed it is doubtful if Hitler had two more inveterate enemies.

These men had lived their lives, and it meant very little to them now if they lost them. They had no jobs to lose, no favours to seek, no ambition which was not already satisfied, and neither acknowledged any master except the King of England; so they said what they thought, often with brutal frankness, and used every ounce of power and prestige that they possessed, through their many contacts in high places, to force the pace of the war regardless of all considerations except that of Victory.

Although they had so much in common, they were very different in appearance. Sir Pellinore, who was considerably the older of the two, stood six feet two in his socks. He had a head of fine white hair, bright blue eyes, a great sweeping cavalry moustache, a booming voice and an abrupt, forthright way of speaking. The Duke was a slim, delicate-looking man, somewhat above middle height, with slender, fragile hands and greying hair but with no trace of weakness in his fine, distinguished face. His aquiline nose, broad forehead and grey 'devil's' eyebrows might well have replaced those of the Cavalier in the Van Dyck that gazed down from the wall opposite his chair.

It would have been utterly against the principles of either to allow the war to interfere with their custom of changing for dinner, but instead of the conventional black the Duke wore a claret-coloured vicuna smoking-suit with silk lapels and braided fastenings. This touch of colour increased his likeness to the portrait.

During dinner they had talked of the war, but when coffee was served there fell a short silence as Max, the Duke's man, produced the long Hoyo de Monterrey cigars which were his master's especial pride, and the Duke was thinking: 'Now I shall learn what old Gwaine-Cust really wanted to see me about. I'll bet a monkey that he didn't propose himself for dinner here just to discuss the general situation.'

As Max left the quiet, candle-lit room the anti-aircraft guns in Hyde Park came into action, shattering the silence. Sir Pellinore looked across, and said a little thoughtfully:

'Wonder you stay here with this damn'd racket goin' on night after night.'

De Richleau shrugged. 'I don't find the bombing particularly terrifying. Perhaps that's because London covers such a vast area. Anyhow, it's child's play compared to some of the bombardments which I have survived in other wars. I think that American journalist hit the nail on the head when he said that at this rate it would take the Nazis two thousand weeks to destroy London and he didn't think that Hitler had another forty years to live.'

'Damn' good!' guffawed Sir Pellinore. 'Damn' good! All the same, it makes things deuced uncomfortable. They've outed two of my clubs, and it's the devil's own job to get hold of one's friends on the telephone. As you've no job that ties you here I wonder you don't clear out to the country.'

'For that matter, my dear fellow, why don't you – since you're in the same category? Or has the Government had the wisdom to avail itself of your services?'

'Good Lord, no! They've no time for old fogeys like me. They're right, too. This is a young man's war. Still, it wouldn't be a good show if some of us didn't stick it when there are so many people who darned well have to.'

'Exactly,' replied the Duke smoothly. 'And that is the answer to your own question. I loathe discomfort and boredom, but no amount of either would induce me to leave London when there are such thousands of poor people who cannot afford to do so.'

There was another silence as de Richleau waited with inward amusement for Sir Pellinore to make a fresh opening, and after a moment the elderly Baronet said:

'Of course, by staying on one is able to keep in touch with things. The very fact of knowing a lot of people enables me to push the boat along here and there.'

A mocking little smile lit the Duke's grey eyes, which at times could flash with such piercing brilliance. 'Perhaps, then, you would like to tell me in which particular direction you are now contemplating pushing *my* canoe?'

'Ha!' Sir Pellinore brushed up his fine cavalry moustache. 'You're a shrewd feller – always were. I might have known you'd guess that I didn't ask myself here for the sake of your drink and cigars, superb as they are. I've hardly seen you alone for a moment, though, since the slaughter started; so d'you mind telling me what you've been up to so far? I'm damned certain you haven't been idle.'

The smile moved to de Richleau's strong, thin-lipped mouth. 'I have fought in many wars, but I am too old to become again a junior officer and far too young in temperament ever to become a Civil Servant; so, like yourself, I have not even the status of an unpaid A.R.P. Warden. In consequence, you will forgive me if I suggest that neither of us has any right to question the other.'

'You old fox! Cornered me, eh? All right. I'm close to the War Cabinet. *Why*, God knows! But some of the people there still seem to think I'm useful, although everybody knows that I've no brains. I've always had an eye for a horse or a pretty woman and an infinite capacity for vintage port; but no brains – no brains at all.'

'That,' murmured the Duke, 'accounts for the fact that after being compelled to leave the Army because of your debts, somewhere way back in the '90's, you managed to amass a fortune of a cool ten million. Am I to take it that you have been sent to see me?'

'No. But it amounts to the same thing. My powers are pretty wide. I can't get people shot, as I would like to, for criminal negligence, but I've been instrumental in getting some of our slower movers sacked, and most of my recommendations go through except where they come into direct conflict with government policy. Unofficially, too, I've been able to initiate various little matters which have given the Nazis a pain in the neck. We're all in this thing together, and when I saw you admiring the ducks in St James's Park the other day I had a hunch that you might be the very man to help us in something that at the moment is giving the Government very grave concern. *Now* will you tell me what you've been up to?'

De Richleau swivelled the old brandy in the medium-sized ballon-shaped glass that he was holding, sniffed its ethers appreciatively and replied: 'Certainly. Before Britain declared war on Germany I flew with some friends of mine to Poland.'

Sir Pellinore gave him a sharp glance. 'The fellers who accompanied you on your Russian and Spanish exploits? I remember hearing about your adventures in the Forbidden Territory and later the fantastic story of the eight million pounds in gold that the four of you got out of Spain during the Civil War. One was the son of old Channock Van Ryn, the American banker, wasn't he? I've never met the other two, but I'd like to some time.'

'Rex Van Ryn is the one of whom you're thinking; the other two are Richard Eaton and Simon Aron. All three of them were with me through the Polish Campaign. What we did there is far too long a story to tell now, but I'll give it to you some time. We got out by the skin of our teeth in a manner which was most inconvenient for certain persons; but, that, of course, was entirely their affair for trying to stop us. When we eventually arrived back in England no particular opening offered in which we could work together, so we decided to split up.'

'What happened to the others?'

'Rex, as you may know, is an ace airman, and although he's an American citizen he managed to wangle his way into the Royal Air Force. He did magnificent work in the battles of August and September and was awarded the D.F.C.; but early in October he ran into a flock of Nazis where the odds were six to one, and they got him. His left leg was badly smashed. He's well on the road to recovery now, but I'm afraid his wounds will prevent him from flying as a fighter-pilot any more.

'Simon Aron went back to his counting-house. He is a director of one of our big financial houses and he felt that he could give his best service to the country by helping the dollar position and in all the intricacies of foreign exchange that he understands so well.

'Richard Eaton is an airman, too, but he's over age for a fighter-pilot so they wouldn't take him – which made poor Richard very sick. But he has a big place down in Worcestershire, so he went in at once for intensive farming. However, he comes to London now and again to console himself for not being able to do anything more actively offensive in the war, by helping me in one or two little jobs that I've been fortunate enough to be able to take on.'

'What sort of jobs?' boomed Sir Pellinore.

'Details would only bore you but, like yourself, I have many friends and I also speak several languages with considerable fluency, so here and there I've been tipped off to keep my eyes open and I've been successful in putting a number of unpleasant people behind the bars. Incidentally, I made a secret trip to Czechoslovakia last spring and I've been in the Low Countries since the German occupation – in fact, I only got back last week. But of course I have no official position – no official position at all.'

Sir Pellinore's blue eyes twinkled. 'You certainly haven't let the grass grow under your feet. As a matter of fact, I had it through official channels that you had been making yourself pretty useful in a variety of ways, because I made inquiries before coming along to see you tonight, although I didn't press for details. What are you up to now?'

'Nothing of any great importance. Just keeping my eye on a few people who in any other country but this would have been put against a wall well over a year ago, and trying to trace various leakages of information which come from people who regard themselves as patriotic citizens but talk too much to the ladies of their acquaintance. There is nothing at all to prevent me from packing a bag and leaving for Kamchatka or Peru tomorrow morning if you feel that by so doing I could drive another nail into Hitler's coffin.'

'That's the sort of thing I like to hear,' roared Sir Pellinore. 'Wish to God some of the people in our government departments showed the same keenness to get these German swine under. But I don't think we'll have to call on you even to leave London – although one can never tell. It's the use of that fine brain of yours I want, and you mentioned the subject yourself only a moment ago when you spoke of leakage of information.'

De Richleau raised his slanting eyebrows. 'I shouldn't have thought there was any grave cause to worry about that. Even the smallest indiscretions should be jumped on, of course, but from all I've gathered very little important stuff has got through since all normal communications with the Continent was severed after the collapse of France.'

'In a way you're right.' Sir Pellinore nodded his white head. 'We ourselves were amazed in the difference that made. For example, when the first major air-attacks on this country started many of us were acutely anxious about the Air Force. We feared that by sheer weight of numbers the Germans would smash more planes on the ground than we could possibly afford to lose. As everybody knows now, we cleared all our airfields on the south and east coasts before the attack developed, so that there was nothing left for the Nazis to smash except the empty hangars and machine shops. Directly they had done that we expected them to start on our new bases, but they didn't; they kept on hammering day after day at the old ones when there was nothing left but burnt-out sheds for them to strike at; which proved quite definitely that they hadn't the faintest idea that we had ever shifted our planes at all. That's ancient history now, of course, but in all sorts of other ways the same thing has gone on in recent months, demonstrating beyond doubt that once the German agents here were cut off from the Continent their whole system of conveying information speedily to the enemy had broken down.'

'I don't understand, then, what you're worrying about.'

'The fact that it has not broken down in one particular direction. The biggest menace that we're up against at the moment is our shipping losses, and the extraordinary thing is that although the Nazis now seem to have only the vaguest idea of what is going on here in every other direction, they have our shipping arrangements absolutely taped. Naturally, every convoy that sails to or from America is sent by a different route. Sometimes they go right up into the Arctic, sometimes as far south as Madeira, and sometimes dead-straight across; but, whichever way we choose, the Nazis seem to know about it. They meet each convoy in mid-Atlantic after its escort has left it, just as though they were keeping a prearranged appointment.'

'That *is* pretty grim.'

'Yes. It's no laughing matter; and to be quite honest we're at our wits' end. The Navy is working night and day, and the Air Arm too; but the sea and sky are big places. Our Intelligence people have done their damn'dest – and they're pretty hot – whatever uninformed people may think about them – but just this one thing seems to have got them beaten.'

'Why should you imagine that I might succeed where the best brains in our Intelligence have failed?' asked the Duke mildly.

'Because I feel that our only chance now is to get an entirely fresh mind on the subject; someone who isn't fogged by knowing too much detail and having his nose too close to the charts, yet someone who has imagination and a great reservoir of general knowledge. The Nazis must be using some channel which is quite outside normal espionage methods – the sort of thing to which there is no clue but that anyone with a shrewd mind might happen on by chance. That's why, when I saw you the other day, it occurred to me that it might be a good idea to put this damnable problem up to you.'

De Richleau stared at Sir Pellinore for a moment. 'You are absolutely certain that the Nazi Intelligence are not using any normal method of communication in this thing?'

'Absolutely. The fact that all sorts of other vital information does not get through proves it.'

'Then, if they are not using normal methods, they must be using subnormal – or rather, the supernatural.'

It was Sir Pellinore's turn to stare. 'What the blazes d'you mean?' he boomed abruptly.

The Duke leant forward and gently knocked the inch-long piece of ash from his cigar into the onyx ash-tray as he said: 'That they are using what for lack of a better term is called Black Magic.'

'You're joking!' gasped Sir Pellinore.

'On the contrary,' said the Duke quietly: 'I was never more serious in my life.'

A strange expression crept into Sir Pellinore's blue eyes. He had known the Duke for many years, but never intimately; only as one of that vast army of acquaintances who drifted across his path from time to time for a brief week-end at a country-house, in the smoking-room of a West End club or during the season at fashionable resorts such as Deauville. He had often heard de Richleau spoken of as a man of dauntless courage and infinite resource, but also as a person whom normal people might well regard as eccentric. The Duke had never been seen in a bowler-hat or wielding that emblem of English respectability, an umbrella. Instead, when he walked abroad he carried a beautiful Malacca cane. In peace-time he drove about London in a huge silver Hispano with a chauffeur and footman on the box, both dressed like Cossacks and wearing tall, grey, astrakhan *papenkas*. Some people considered that the most vulgar ostentation, while to the Duke himself it was only a deplorable substitute for the sixteen outriders who had habitually preceded his forebears in more spacious days. Sir Pellinore being a broad-minded man had put these little foibles down to the Duke's foreign ancestry, but it now occurred to him that in some respects de Richleau had probably always been slightly abnormal and that, although he appeared perfectly sane, a near miss from a Nazi bomb might recently have unhinged his brain.

'Black Magic, eh?' he said with unwonted gentleness. 'Most interesting theory. Well, if you – er – get any more ideas on the subject you must let me know.'

'I shall be delighted to do so,' replied the Duke with suave courtesy. 'And now I will tell you what has just been passing through your mind. You have been thinking: "I've drawn a blank here; this fellow's no good; he's got a screw loose; probably sustained concussion in an air-raid. Pity, as I was rather hoping that he might produce some practical suggestions for the Intelligence people to work on. As it is, I must remember to tell my secretary to put him off politely if he rings up – one can't waste time with fellows who've gone nuts, while there's a war on."'

'Damme!' Sir Pellinore thumped the table with his huge fist. 'You're right, Duke; I admit it. But you must agree that no sane person could take your suggestion seriously.'

'I wouldn't go as far as that, but I would agree that anyone who has no personal knowledge of the occult is quite entitled to disbelieve in it. I assume that you've never witnessed the materialisation of an astral force or, to put it into common parlance "seen a ghost" with your own eyes?'

'Never,' said Sir Pellinore emphatically.

'D'you know anything of hypnotism?'

'Yes. As a matter of fact, I'm gifted with slight hypnotic powers myself. When I was a young man I sometimes used to amuse my friends by giving mild demonstrations, and I've often found that I can make people do minor things, such as opening up on a particular subject, merely by willing them to do so.'

'Good. Then at least we're at one on the fact that certain forces can be called into play which the average person does not understand.'

'I suppose so, within limits.'

'Why "within limits"? Surely, fifty years ago you would have considered wireless to be utterly outside such limits if somebody had endeavoured to convince you that messages and even pictures could be transferred from one end of the world to the other upon ether waves.'

'Of course,' Sir Pellinore boomed. 'But wireless is different; and as for hypnotism, that's simply the power of the human will.'

'Ah, there you have it.' The Duke sat forward suddenly. '*The will to good* and *the will to evil.* That is the whole matter in a nutshell. The human will is like a wireless set and when properly adjusted can tune in with the invisible influences which are all about us.'

'Invisible influences, eh? No, I'm sorry, Duke, I just don't believe in such things.'

'Do you believe in the miracles performed by Jesus Christ?'

'Yes. I'm old-fashioned enough to have remained an unquestioning believer in the Christian faith, although God knows I've committed enough sins in my time.'

'You also believe, then, in the miracles performed by Christ's disciples and certain of the Saints?'

'I do. But they had some special powers granted to them.'

'Exactly. *Special powers.* But I suppose you would deny that Gautama Buddha and his disciples performed miracles of a similar nature?'

'Not a bit of it. I'm sufficiently broad-minded to believe that Buddha was a sort of Indian Christ, or at least a very holy man, and no doubt he, too, had some special power granted to him.'

'Then if you admit that miracles, as you call them – although you object to the word *Magic* – have been performed by two men of different faiths, living in different countries and in periods hundreds of years apart, you can't reasonably deny that other mystics have also performed similar acts in many portions of the globe and, therefore, that there is a power existing outside us which is *not peculiar to any religion* but can be utilised if one can get into communication with it.'

Sir Pellinore laughed. 'I've never looked at it that way before, but I suppose you're right.'

De Richleau poured another portion of the old brandy into his friend's glass as Sir Pellinore went on more slowly.

'All the same, it doesn't follow that because a number of good men have been granted supernatural powers there is anything in Black Magic.'

'Then you do not believe in witchcraft?'

'Nobody does these days.'

'Really? How long d'you think it is since the last trial for witchcraft took place?'

'Two hundred years.'

'No. It was in January 1926, at Melun, near Paris.'

'God bless my soul! D'you mean that?'

'I do,' de Richleau assured him solemnly. 'The records of the court are the proof of it; so, you see, you are hardly accurate when you say that *nobody* believes in witchcraft in these days; and many, many thousands still believe in a personal Devil.'

'Central European peasants, perhaps, but not educated people.'

'Yet every thinking man must admit that there is such a thing as the power of Evil.'

'Why?'

'My dear fellow, all qualities have their opposites, like love and hate, pleasure and pain, generosity and avarice. How could we recognise the goodness of Jesus Christ, Lao-Tze, Ashoka, Marcus Aurelius, Francis of Assisi, and thousands of others, if it were not for the evil lives of Herod, Cesare Borgia, Rasputin, Landru and the rest?'

'That's true.'

'Then, if an intensive cultivation of Good can beget strange powers, is there any reason why an intensive cultivation of Evil should not beget them also?'

'That sounds feasible.'

'I hope I'm not boring you; but just on the off-chance that there might be something in my suggestion that the Nazis are using occult forces to get information out of this country, I think it is really important that you should understand the theory of the occult, since you appear to know so

149

little about it.'

'Go ahead, go ahead.' Sir Pellinore waved a large hand. 'Mind you, I don't say that I'm prepared to take for granted everything you may tell me, but you certainly won't bore me.'

De Richleau sat forward. 'Very well; I'll try and expound to you the simple rudiments of the Old Wisdom which has come down to us through the ages. You will have heard of the Persian myth of Ormuzd and Ahriman, the eternal powers of Light and Darkness, said to be co-equal and warring without cessation for the good or ill of mankind. All ancient Sun and Nature worship – Festivals of Spring and so on – were only an outward expression of that myth, for Light typifies Health and Wisdom, Growth and Life, while Darkness means Disease and Ignorance, Decay and Death.

'In its highest sense Light symbolises the growth of the spirit towards that perfection in which it becomes Light itself. But the road to perfection is long and arduous, too much to hope for in one short human life; hence the widespread belief in Reincarnation: that we are born again and again until we begin to transcend the pleasures of the flesh. This doctrine is so old that no man can trace its origin, yet it is the inner core of Truth common to all religions at their inception. Consider the teaching of Jesus Christ with that in mind and you will be amazed that you have not realised before the true purport of His message. Did He not say that the Kingdom of God was within us? And when he walked upon the waters he declared: "These things that I do ye shall do also, and greater things than these shall ye do, for I go unto my Father which is in Heaven"; meaning most certainly that he was nearing perfection but that others had the same power within each one of them to do likewise.'

De Richleau paused for a moment, then went on more slowly: 'Unfortunately the hours of the night are still equal to the hours of the day, so the power of Darkness is no less active than when the world was young, and no sooner does a fresh Master appear to reveal the Light than Ignorance, Greed and Lust for Power cloud the minds of his followers. The message becomes distorted and the simplicity of the Truth submerged and forgotten in the pomp of ceremonies and the meticulous performance of rituals which have lost their meaning. Yet the real Truth is never entirely lost, and through the centuries new Masters are continually arising either to proclaim it or, if the time is not propitious, to pass it on in secret to the chosen few.

'Apollonius of Tyana learned it in the East. The so-called heretics whom we know as the Albigenses preached it in the twelfth century throughout Southern France until they were exterminated. Christian

Rosenkreutz had it in the Middle Ages; it was the innermost secret of the Order of the Templars, who were suppressed because of it by the Church of Rome; the alchemists, too, searched for and practised it. Only the ignorant take literally their struggle to find the Elixir of Life. Behind such phrases, designed to protect them from the persecution of their enemies, they sought Eternal Life, and their efforts to transmute base-metals into gold were only symbolical of their sublimation of matter into Light. And still today, while the bombing of London goes on about us, there are mystics and adepts who are seeking the Way to Perfection in many corners of the earth.'

'You honestly believe that?' remarked Sir Pellinore with mild scepticism.

'I do.' De Richleau's answer held no trace of doubt.

'Granted that there are such mystics who follow this particular Faith which is outside all organised religions, I still don't see where Black Magic comes in.'

'Let's not talk of Black Magic, which is associated with the preposterous in our day, but of the Order of the Left-Hand Path. That, too, has its adepts, and just as the Reincarnationists scattered all over the world are the preservers of the Way of Light, the Way of Darkness is perpetuated in the horrible Voodoo cult which had its origin in Madagascar and has held Africa, the Dark Continent, in its grip for centuries and spread with the slave trade to the West Indies.'

A stick of bombs crumped dully in the distance and Sir Pellinore smiled. 'It's a pretty long cry from the mumbo-jumbo stuff practised by the Negroes of the Caribbean to the machinations of this damn'd feller Hitler.'

'Not so far as you might suppose. Most of the black man's Magic is crude stuff but that does not affect the fact that certain of these Voodoo priests have cultivated the power of Evil to a very high degree. Among whites, though, it is generally the wealthy and intellectual, who are avaricious for greater riches or power, to whom it appeals. In the Paris of Louis XIV, long after the Middle Ages were forgotten, the Black Art was particularly rampant. The poisoner, La Voisin, was proved to have procured over fifteen hundred children for the infamous Abbé Guibourg to sacrifice at Black Masses. He used to cut their throats, drain the blood into a chalice and then pour it over the naked body of the inquirer which lay stretched upon the altar. I speak of actual history, and you can read the records of the trial that followed, in which two hundred and forty-six men and women were indicted for these hellish practices.'

'Come, come; that's all a very long time ago.'

'If you need more modern evidence of its continuance there is the well-authenticated case of Prince Borghese. He let his Venetian *palazzo* on a long lease, expiring as late as 1895. The tenants had not realised that the lease had run out until he notified them of his intention to resume possession. They protested, but Borghese's agents forced an entry. What d'you think they found?'

'Lord knows.'

'That the principal salon had been redecorated at enormous cost and converted into a Satanic Temple. The walls were hung from ceiling to floor with heavy curtains of scarlet-and-black silk damask to exclude the light. At the further end, dominating the whole room, there was stretched a large tapestry upon which was woven a colossal figure of Lucifer. Beneath it an altar had been built and amply furnished with the whole liturgy of Hell; black candles, vessels, rituals – nothing was lacking. Cushioned *priedieus* and luxurious chairs of crimson-and-gold were set in order for the assistants and the chamber was lit with electricity fantastically arranged so that it should glare through an enormous human eye.

'If that's not enough I can give you even more modern instances of Satanic temples here in London; not so luxuriously furnished, perhaps, but having all the essentials for performing Black Masses. There was one in Earl's Court after the 1914–1918 War, there was another in St John's Wood as recently as 1935, which I myself had occasion to visit, and less than three years ago there was one in Dover Street, where a woman was flogged to death during one of the ceremonies.'

De Richleau hammered the table with his clenched fist. 'These are facts that I'm giving you – things I can prove by eye-witnesses still living. Despite our electricity, our aeroplanes, our modern scepticism, the Power of Darkness is still a living force, worshipped by depraved human beings for their unholy ends in the great cities of Europe and America to this very day.'

Sir Pellinore shrugged his broad shoulders. 'I'm quite prepared to take your word for all this, and, of course, I have myself heard from time to time that such things go on, even to an occasional murder the motive for which remains undiscovered by the police. But, quite honestly, I feel that you're putting an entirely wrong interpretation upon the facts. Such parties are simply an excuse for certain wealthy and very decadent people, of which a certain number exist in every great city, to indulge in deliberately planned orgies where they can give themselves up to the most revolting sexual practices. Such circles are, in fact, very exclusive vice-clubs, generally run by clever crooks who make an exceedingly good thing out of them. I don't for one moment doubt that you're right about the trimmings, but in my view the ceremonial part of it is simply a mental stimulant which serves to get these people into the right frame of mind for the abominable licence in which they intend to indulge later the same night when they've got their clothes off. I don't believe that these so-called Satanists could harm a rabbit by exercising supernatural powers in the manner that you suggest.'

'That is a pity', replied the Duke; 'because this is no question of my endeavouring to convince you that I am right for the mere pleasure of triumphing in a purely academic argument. You came to me this evening with a problem which it is vital that we should solve if we are to get the better of the Nazis. I put up what I consider to be a possible solution to that problem. If you brush it aside as nonsense, yet it later proves that I am right, entirely through your reluctance to accept what may sound a fantastic solution we shall be in a fair way to lose the war, or at least it will be prolonged to a point where grave hardship will be inflicted upon our entire people. Either my theory is a possible one, or it is not. If it *is* possible, we can take steps to counter the menace. Therefore, whether you like it or not, you have laid it upon me as a national duty to convince you that Magic is an actual scientific force and may, therefore, be employed by our enemies.'

Sir Pellinore nodded gravely. 'I appreciate your point, Duke, and there can be no question whatever about the sincerity of your own belief or the honesty of your intentions, but if we sat here until the middle of next week you would never succeed in convincing me that anyone could use occult forces in a similar manner to that in which they could operate a wireless.'

'Oh, yes, I shall,' replied the Duke, and his grey eyes bored into Sir Pellinore's with a strange, hard light. 'You force me, in the interests of the nation, to do something that I do not like; but I know sufficient about this business to call certain supernatural forces to my aid, and when you leave this flat tonight you will never again be able to say that you do not believe in Magic.'

Sir Pellinore looked a little startled, then his hearty laugh rang out. 'Not proposing to turn me into a donkey or anything, are you?'

'No,' de Richleau smiled. 'I rather doubt if my powers extend that far, but I might cause you to lose your memory for the best part of a week.'

'The devil! That would be deuced inconvenient.'

'Don't worry; I have no intention of doing so. I'm happy to say that I have never allowed myself to be tempted into practising anything but White Magic.'

'White Magic – White Magic,' repeated Sir Pellinore suspiciously. 'But that's only conjuring-tricks, isn't it?'

'Not at all.' The Duke's voice was a trifle acid. 'It only differs from Black Magic in that it is a ceremony performed without intent to bring harm to anyone or any personal gain to the practitioner. I propose to use such powers as I possess to bring it about that a certain wish which you have expressed tonight shall be granted. Let's go into the other room, shall we?'

Distinctly mystified and vaguely uneasy at this unusual proposal for his after-dinner entertainment, Sir Pellinore passed with the Duke into that room in the Curzon Street flat which was so memorable for those who had been privileged to visit it; not so much on account of its size and decorations as for the unique collection of rare and beautiful objects which it contained – a Tibetan Buddha seated upon the Lotus, bronze figurines from Ancient Greece, delicately chased rapiers of Toledo steel and Moorish pistols inlaid with turquoise and gold, ikons from Holy Russia set with semi-precious stones, and curiously carved ivories from the East – each a memento of some strange adventure which de Richleau had undertaken as a soldier of fortune or traveller in little-known lands. The walls were lined shoulder-high with richly bound books and the spaces above them were decorated with priceless historical documents, old colour-prints and maps.

Having settled his guest in a comfortable chair before the glowing fire, the Duke went over to a great carved-ivory chest, which he unlocked with a long, spindle-like key. On the front of it being lowered one hundred and one drawers were disclosed – deep and shallow, large and small. From one of the larger drawers he took a battered old iron tray, twenty-one inches long and seven inches broad, which had certain curious markings engraved upon it, and this he placed on top of the chest; from another drawer he took an incense burner and some cones of incense which he inserted in the burner then lit with a white taper.

When the incense was well alight he left the chest and went over to a handsome table-desk, where he sat down and, picking up a pen, drew a sheet of notepaper towards him. Having covered both sides of the sheet with neat writing he folded it, placed it in an envelope and, turning, handed it to Sir Pellinore, as he said:

'Slip that in your pocket. When the time is ripe I shall ask you to open it, and if my ceremony is successful it will prove to you that there has been no element of coincidence about this business.'

De Richleau next took from the ivory chest four little bronze bowls, each supported by three winged legs obviously fashioned after a portion of the male body. To the contents of one he applied the lighted taper, upon which the matter in it began to burn with a steady blue flame. Another of the bowls already had some dark substance in it, while the remaining two were empty. Taking one of them, he walked over to a tray of drinks that stood on a side-table and half-filled it from a bottle of Malvern water. As he replaced the bowl in a line with the three others he glanced across at the Baronet, who was watching him with faintly cynical disapproval, and remarked:

'Here we have the four Elements, Air, Earth, Fire, and Water, all of which are necessary to the performance of any magical ceremony.'

The cones of incense were now giving off spirals of blue smoke which scented the air of the quiet room with a strong, musky perfume, and as the Duke selected three small pay-envelopes from a number of others, each marked with a name, that were arranged alphabetically in one of the drawers, he added:

'This doubtless seems a lot of tomfoolery to you, yet there is a sound reason for everything in these little-understood but very ancient practices. For example, the incense will prevent our noses being offended by the – to some – unpleasant odour of the things which I am about to dissolve by fire.'

'What are they?' Sir Pellinore inquired.

The Duke opened one of the little envelopes, tapped its contents into the palm of his hand and held it out. 'They are, as you see, the parings of human nails.'

'Good God!' Sir Pellinore turned away quickly. He was not at all happy about this business as his life-long disbelief in the occult had suddenly become tinged with a vague fear now that all against his wish he was being brought in direct contact with it. The fact that he had won a V.C. in the Boer War, and had performed many acts of bravery since, was not the least comfort to him. Bullets and bombs he understood; but not erudite gentlemen who proposed to bring about abnormal happenings by burning small portions of the human body.

De Richleau read his thoughts and smiled. Returning to the ivory chest, he took from it a silvery powder of which he made three little heaps on the old iron tray, and upon each heap he put a few pieces of the nail parings. He then made a sign which was neither that of the Cross nor the touching of the forehead that Mohammedans make when they mention the Prophet, lit one of the little heaps of powder and in a ringing voice, which startled Sir Pellinore, pronounced an incantation of eleven words from a long-dead language.

The powder flared up in a dazzling flame, the nail-parings were consumed in a little puff of acrid smoke and de Richleau repeated the sign which was neither that of the Cross nor the touching of the forehead that Mohammedans make when they mention the Prophet.

Twice more the Duke went through the same motions and the same words; then he put out the flame which was burning in one bowl, emptied the water from another, snuffed out the incense in the burner, and, putting all his impedimenta back into the ivory chest, relocked it with the spindle-like key.

'There,' he said, in the same inconsequent tone that he might have used had he just finished demonstrating a new type of carpet-sweeper. 'It will be a little time before the logical results of the enchantment which I have effected will become apparent, so what about a drink? Brandy, Chartreuse, or a glass of wine – which do you prefer?'

'Brandy-and-soda, thanks,' replied Sir Pellinore, distinctly relieved that the queer antics of his friend were over.

As he brought the drink and sat down before the fire the Duke smiled genially. 'I'm so sorry to have made you uncomfortable – a great failing in any host towards his guest – but you brought it on yourself, you know.'

'Good Lord, yes! You have every possible right to prove your own statement if you can, and I'm delighted for you to do so; although I must confess that this business gave me a rather creepy feeling – sort of thing I haven't experienced for years. D'you honestly believe, though, that the *Fuehrer* monkeys about with incense and bowls of this and that, and bits of human nail, as you have done tonight?'

'I haven't the least doubt that he does; everything that is known about him indicates it. Witness his love of high places, the fact that he shuts himself up in that secret room of his at Berchtesgaden, sometimes for as much as twelve hours at a stretch, when nobody is allowed to disturb him however urgent their business; his so-called fits, and, above all, his way of life: no women, no alcohol and a vegetarian diet.'

'What on earth's that got to do with it?'

'To attain occult power it is generally essential to forgo all joys of the flesh, often even to the point of carrying out prolonged fasts, so as to purify the body. You will recall that all the holy men who performed miracles were famed for their asceticism, and it is just as necessary to deny oneself every sort of self-indulgence if one wishes to practise the Black Art as for any other form of occultism.'

'That doesn't fit in with your own performance this evening. We enjoyed a darned good dinner and plenty of fine liquor before you set to

156

work.'

'True. But then, as I told you, I only proposed to perform quite a small magic. I couldn't have attempted anything really difficult without having first got myself back into training.'

Sir Pellinore nodded. 'All the same, I find it impossible to believe that a man in Hitler's position would be able to give the time to a whole series of these – er – ceremonies day after day, week after week, to discover the route by which each of our convoys is sailing, when he must have such a mass of important things to attend to.'

'I shouldn't think so either. Doubtless there are many people round him to whom he could delegate such routine work, while reserving himself for special occasions on which he seeks power to bring about far greater Evils.'

'God bless my soul! Are you suggesting that all the Nazis are tarred with the same brush?'

'Not all of them, but a considerable number, I don't suppose it has ever occurred to you to wonder why they chose a left-handed Swastika as their symbol?'

'I've always thought that it was on account of their pro-Aryan policy. The Swastika is Aryan in origin, isn't it?'

'Yes. Long before the Cross was ever heard of the Swastika was the Aryan symbol for Light, and its history is so ancient that no man can trace it; but that was a right-handed Swastika, whereas the Nazi badge is left-handed and, being the direct opposite, was the symbol for Darkness.'

Sir Pellinore frowned. 'All this is absolutely new to me, and I find it very difficult to accept your theory.'

De Richleau laughed. 'If you had time to go into the whole matter you'd soon find that it's much more than a theory. D'you know anything about astrology?'

'Not a thing; though a feller did my horoscope once and I must confess he made a remarkably good job of it. That's many years ago now, but practically everything he predicted about me has since come true.'

'It always does if the astrologer really knows his job, is provided with accurate data and spends enough time on it. The sort of horoscope that people get for half a guinea is rarely much good, because astrology is a little-understood but very exact science and it takes many hours of intricate calculation to work out the influence which each celestial body will have upon a child at the hour of birth. Even hard work and a sound knowledge of the science are not alone sufficient, as the astrologer must have had years of practice in assessing the manner in which the influence of one heavenly body will increase or detract from the influence of all the others that are above the horizon at the natal hour. But the labourer is worthy of his hire, and to pay ten or twenty guineas to have the job done by a man who really understands his stuff is worth it a hundredfold. One can make a really good horoscope the key to one's life by using the warnings it contains to remould tendencies and thus guard against many ills.'

'Really?' Sir Pellinore looked a little surprised. 'I was under the impression that these astrologer gentry all believed that what the stars foretold *must* come to pass. That's why I've never regarded my horoscope as anything but a curiosity. Nothing would induce me to believe that we're not the masters of our own fate.'

'We are,' the Duke replied mildly; 'but our paths are circumscribed. The Great Planners give to each child at its birth circumstances together with certain strengths and weaknesses of character which are exactly suited to it and are, in fact, the outcome of the sum of all its previous existence. On broad lines, the life of that child is laid out, because its parents and environment will automatically have a great influence upon its future and it is pre-ordained that from time to time during its life other persons will come into its orbit, exercising great influence for good or ill upon it. Temptations will be put in its path, but also chances for it to achieve advancement. These things are decreed by the Overseers in accordance with the vast plan into which everything fits perfectly; and that is why character, tendencies and periods of special stress or opportunity can be predicted from the stars prevailing at any birth. But free will remains, and that is why, although future events can be foreseen in a life with a great degree of probability, they cannot be foretold with absolute certainty; because the person concerned may suddenly evince some hidden weakness or great strength and thus depart from the apparent destiny.'

'Then a horoscope is by no means final?'

'Certainly not; yet it can be an invaluable guide to one's own shortcomings and potentialities, and the fact that we frequently go off the predestined track in one direction or another does not necessarily mean that we leave it for good. Surely you've noticed how people often fail in some direction through their own folly yet achieve their aims a little later by some quite unexpected avenue; and again, how, through what appear to be entirely fortuitous circumstances, a man's life is often completely changed so that his whole future is given an entirely different direction. That is not chance, because there is no such thing; it is merely that, having been faced with a certain test, and having reacted with unexpected strength or weakness to it, he is swung back, by powers over which he has no control, on to the path where other trials or opportunities have been laid out in advance for him.'

The anti-aircraft fire flared up again so that the glasses on the side-table jingled, then two bombs whined over the house and exploded somewhere behind it in the direction of Piccadilly. The whole place shuddered and the menacing hum of the enemy planes could be heard clearly overhead.

For a few moments they sat silent, then when the din had faded, Sir Pellinore said: 'Damn that house-painter feller! There soon won't be a window left in any of the clubs. But what were you going to say about him and astrology?'

'Simply that his every major move so far – with one exception – has been made at a time when his stars were in the ascendant. His march into the Rhine, his *Anschluss* with Austria, the rape of Czechoslovakia and a score of smaller but nevertheless important acts in his career all took place upon dates when the stars were particularly propitious to him. I don't ask you to accept my word for that – go to any reputable astrologer and he will substantiate what I say – but, to my mind, that is conclusive proof that Hitler either practises astrology himself or employs a first-class astrologer and definitely chooses the dates for each big move he makes in accordance with occult forces ruling at those times.'

'What was the exception?'

'September the 2nd, 1939. Evil persons can use occult forces for their own ends, but only within limits. The all-seeing powers of Light are ever watchful, and inevitably a time comes when they trap the Black occultist through his own acts. They trapped Hitler over Poland. I am sure he never thought for one moment that Great Britain would go to war on account of his marching into Danzig; therefore when he consulted the stars as to a propitious date for that adventure he was thinking only in terms of Poland. He chose a date upon which Poland's stars were bad and his stars were good; but he forgot or neglected to take into account the stars of Great Britain and her Empire on that date and the day following. We all know what happened to Poland; but the same thing has not happened to Britain yet – and will never happen. In the map of the heavens for September the 3rd, 1939, you will find that Britain's stars are more powerful than Hitler's. He thought that he was only going to launch a short, devastating attack on Poland on the 2nd, whereas, actually, he precipitated a second World War; and that is where this servant of Darkness has at last been trapped by the powers of Light.'

'Just supposing – *supposing*, mind – that you were right about this thing, how d'you think Hitler's people would go to work in passing on information by occult means?'

'Whoever secures the information about the sailings must either be capable of maintaining continuity of thought while awake and asleep or pass the information on to somebody else who can do that.'

'What the deuce are you talking about?'

De Richleau smiled as he took his friend's glass over to the side-table and refilled it. 'To explain what I mean I shall have to take you a little further along the path of the Old Wisdom. Since you're a Christian you already subscribe to the belief that when you die your spirit lives on and that what we call Death is really Life Eternal?'

'Certainly.'

'But there is much more to it than that. As I remarked some time ago, the basis of every great religion, without exception, is the belief in Reincarnation and that at intervals which vary considerably each one of us is born into the world again in a fresh body in order that we may gain further experience and a greater command over ourselves. Those periods are rather like short terms at school, since in them we are compelled to learn, whether we will or no, and we rarely manage to achieve happiness for any considerable length of time. The periods when we are free of a body, which are much longer, are the holidays in which we gain strength for new trials, enjoy the companionship of all the dear friends that we have made on our long journey through innumerable past lives and live in a far higher and more blissful state than is ever possible on Earth. That is the real Eternal Life; yet each time that we are born again in the flesh we do not entirely lose touch with that other spiritual plane where we live our true lives and know real happiness. Whenever we sleep our spirit leaves its body and is free to refortify itself for the trials of the morrow by visiting the astral sphere to meet and talk with others many of whose bodies are also sleeping on Earth.

'Some people dream a lot, others very little – or so they say; but what they actually mean is that they are incapable of remembering their dreams when they wake. The fact is that we all dream – or, if you prefer, leave our bodies – from the very moment we fall asleep. A dream, therefore, is really no more than a confused memory of our activities while the body is sleeping. By writing down everything one can remember of one's dreams, immediately upon waking, it is perfectly possible gradually to train oneself to recall what one's spirit did when it was absent from the body. It needs considerable strength of will to rouse oneself at once and the process of establishing a really clear memory requires a very great patience; but you may take my word for it that it can be done. If you doubt me, I could easily produce at least half a dozen other people living in England at the present time who have trained themselves to a degree in which they can recall, without the least difficulty, their nightly journeyings. And, of course, the spirit needs no training to remember what it has done in the body during the daytime. That's what I mean by continuity of thought when waking and sleeping.'

'I seldom dream,' announced Sir Pellinore, 'and if ever I do it's just an absurd, confused muddle.'

'That is the case with most people, but the explanation is quite simple. When you're out of your body, time, as we know it, ceases to exist, so in a single night you may journey great distances, meet many people and do an extraordinary variety of things. Therefore, when you awake, if you have any memory at all, it is only of the high spots in your night's adventures.'

'But they don't make sense. One thing doesn't even lead to another.'

'Of course not. But tell me about your normal waking life. Starting from Monday morning, what have you done this week?'

'Well, now, let me see. On Monday I had a meeting with Beaverbrook – very interesting. On Tuesday I lunched with the Admiral responsible for arranging our convoy routes – no, that was Wednesday – it was Tuesday I damn'd-near ricked my ankle – slid down the Duke of York's Steps. That morning, too, I had a letter from my nephew – hadn't heard from the young devil for months – he's with the Coldstream, in the Middle East. Wednesday I lost an important paper, got in a hell of a stew; quite unnecessary, as I had it in the lining of my hat-band all the time, but it gave me a devilish bad half-hour. Yesterday I met you and . . .'

'That's quite enough to illustrate my point,' interrupted the Duke. 'If those three days had been compressed into a one-night dream you would probably have wakened up with a muddled impression that you were walking in an aircraft factory with Lord Beaverbrook when you suddenly fell and nearly ricked your ankle, to pick yourself up and find that he had disappeared and that you were out with the Admiral on the cold waters of the Atlantic where we are losing so much of our shipping; then that you had the awful impression that you had lost something of the greatest importance, although you couldn't think what it was, and that you were hunting for it with your soldier-nephew in the sands of Libya, in an interval from chasing the Italians. That is what is called telescoping. None of these things would have had the least apparent connection any more than the events in real life which you gave to me; but it's quite natural that memory either of real life or of dream activities leaps to the matters which have made great impressions upon the mind. Things of less importance very soon become submerged in the general stream of the subconscious, and I'm willing to bet you a tenner that you could not now recall accurately what you ate at each meal during those three days, however hard you tried. It's just the same with the memory of a dream, except that by training one can bring oneself to fill in gaps and follow the whole sequence.'

'Yes; I get your line of argument. But how would this help a German spy to convey information to the enemy?'

'Once one is able to remember one's dreams clearly, the next step is to learn how to direct them, since that, too, can be done by practice. One can go to sleep having made up one's mind that one wishes to meet a certain friend on the astral and be quite certain of doing so. Such a state is not easy of achievement, but it is possible to anybody who has sufficient determination to go through the dreary training without losing heart, and it is no matter of education or secret ritual but simply a case of having enough will-power to force oneself into swift wakefulness each morning and concentrating one's entire strength of mind upon endeavouring to recall every possible detail about one's dreams. Once that has been successfully accomplished, one has only to go to sleep thinking of the person whom one wishes to meet on the astral plane, then one wakes in the morning with the full consciousness of having done so. It is a tragic fact that countless couples who have been separated by the war *do* meet each other every night in their spirit bodies, but, through never having trained themselves, by the time they are fully awake the next morning barely one out of ten thousand is conscious of the meeting. However, you will readily appreciate that if lovers can meet on the astral while the bodies they inhabit in the daytime are sleeping thousands of miles apart, there is nothing to prevent enemy agents also doing so.'

'God bless my soul!' Sir Pellinore suddenly sat forward. 'Are you suggesting that if a German agent in England had certain information he could go to sleep, report in a dream to some damn'd Gestapo feller who was asleep in Germany, and that if the Gestapo feller was a dream-rememberer he could wake up with the information in his head the following morning?'

'Exactly,' said the Duke quietly.

'But, man alive, that'd be a terrible thing! It's too frightful to contemplate. No, no; I don't want to be rude or anything of that kind, and I'm quite sure you're not deliberately trying to make a fool of me, but honestly, my dear feller, I just don't believe it.'

De Richleau shrugged. 'There are plenty of people in London who will support my contention; and if I am not greatly mistaken, here comes one of them.'

As he was speaking there had been a soft rap on the door and his manservant, Max, now appeared, to murmur: 'Excellency, Mr Simon Aron has called and wishes to know if you will receive him.'

'Ask him to come in, Max,' the Duke replied, and turned to Sir Pellinore with a smile. 'This is one of my old friends of whom we were speaking earlier in the evening.'

Max had thrown the door open and Simon stood upon the threshold, smiling a little diffidently. He was a thin, slightly built man of middle height, with black hair, a rather receding chin, a great beak of a nose and dark, restless, intelligent eyes. As he came forward the Duke introduced him to Sir Pellinore and the two shook hands.

'Delighted to meet you,' boomed Sir Pellinore. 'At one time or another I've heard quite a lot about you as one of the people who accompanied de Richleau on some of his famous exploits.'

Simon wriggled his bird-like head in a little nervous gesture and smiled. ''Fraid I can't claim much credit for that. The others did all the exciting stuff; I don't – er – really care much about adventures.' He glanced swiftly at the Duke, and went on: 'I do hope I'm not interrupting. Just thought I'd look in – make certain that you hadn't been bombed.'

'Thank you, Simon. That was most kind of you, but I didn't know that you were given to wandering about London at night while the blitzkrieg is in progress?'

'Ner.' Simon stooped his head towards his hand to cover a somewhat sheepish grin, as he uttered the curious negative that he sometimes used. 'As a matter of fact, I'm not – much too careful of myself; but it occurred to me about half an hour ago that I hadn't seen you for a week, so when I'd finished my rubber at bridge I jumped into a taxi and came along.'

'Good! Help yourself to a drink.' De Richleau motioned towards the side-table and, as Simon picked up the brandy decanter, went on: 'We were talking about occult matters and debating whether it was possible for a German agent in Britain to transmit intelligence to a colleague in Germany by a conversation on the astral plane while both of them were sleeping. What do you think?'

Simon jerked his head in assent. 'Um – I should say that it was perfectly possible.'

Sir Pellinore looked at him a little suspiciously. 'I take it, sir, that you're a believer in all this occult stuff?'

'Um,' Simon nodded again. 'If it hadn't been for the Duke I might have lost something more precious than my reason through monkeying with the occult some years ago.'

De Richleau smiled. 'Naturally you'll consider that Aron is pre-judiced, but whatever beliefs he may hold about the occult, his record shows him to have an extraordinarily astute – in fact, I might say brilliant – brain, and I personally vouch for his integrity. You can speak in front of him with perfect confidence that nothing you say will go outside these four walls, and I think it would be an excellent idea if you put up to him the proposition that you put up to me just after dinner.'

'Very well,' Sir Pellinore agreed, and he gave Simon a brief outline of the grave position regarding Britain's shipping losses.

When he had done, Simon proceeded to embroider the subject in a quick spate of words during which he quoted accurate figures and cases in which convoys had suffered severely.

'Wait a moment, young feller,' Sir Pellinore exclaimed. 'How d'you know all this? It's supposed to be highly secret.'

Simon grinned. 'Of course. And I wouldn't dream of mentioning figures to an outsider, but it's partly my job to know these things. Got to, because they affect the markets and, er – the Government aren't the only people who have an Intelligence Service, you know. It's never occurred to me before, but the transmission of information by occult means is definitely possible. Shouldn't be a bit surprised if that's the explanation of the leakage. Anyhow, I think the Duke's idea ought to be investigated.'

Sir Pellinore glanced at the Duke. 'How would you set about such an investigation?'

'I should need to be put in touch with all the people at the Admiralty who are in the secret as to the route each convoy is to take. Then I should go out at night to cover them when they leave their bodies in sleep, to see if I could find the person who is communicating with the enemy.'

'Are you seriously suggesting that your spirit could shadow theirs on the – er – astral plane?'

'That's the idea. I see no other way in which one could attempt to solve such a mystery. It would be a long job, too, if there are many people in the secret.'

'And damnably dangerous,' added Simon.

'Why?' Sir Pellinore inquired.

'Because whoever is giving the information away might find out what I was up to,' replied the Duke, 'and would then stick at nothing to stop me.'

'How?'

'When a spirit goes out from a body that is asleep, as long as life continues in the body the spirit is attached to it by a tenuously thin cord of silver light which is capable of stretching to any distance. The cord acts as a telephone wire, and that is how, if sudden danger threatens the body, it is able to recall the spirit to animate it. But if that silver cord is once severed the body dies – in fact, that is what has actually happened when people are said to have died in their sleep. If my intentions are discovered the Powers of Darkness will do their damn'dest to break the silver cord that links my spirit with my body, so that I can never get back to it and report the result of my investigations to you.'

The elderly Baronet had considerable difficulty in keeping open disbelief out of his voice as he grunted: 'So even the spirits go in for murder, eh?'

'Certainly. The eternal fight between Good and Evil rages just as fiercely on the astral plane as it does here; only the weapons used are much more terrible, and if one comes into conflict with one of the entities of the Outer Circle one's soul may sustain grievous harm which is infinitely worse than the mere loss of a body.'

Sir Pellinore glanced at the clock and stood up. 'Well,' he said, with his genial bluffness, 'it's been a most interesting evening – thoroughly enjoyed myself – but I must be getting along.'

'No, no,' said the Duke. 'I can see that you still think I'm talking nonsense, but in fairness to me you must await the outcome of my magical experiment.'

'What have you been up to?' Simon inquired with sudden interest, but the others ignored him, as Sir Pellinore replied:

'Of course I will, if you wish, but honestly, my dear fellow, I don't think anything you could do would really convince me. All this business about silver cords, spirits committing murder, and even one's immortal soul not being safe in God's keeping, is a bit too much for a man of my age to swallow.'

At that moment there was another knock on the door and Max stood there again. 'Excellency, Mr Rex Van Ryn and Mr Richard Eaton are here and wish to know if you will receive them.'

'Certainly,' said the Duke. 'Ask them to come in.'

Rex, tall, broad-shouldered, in the uniform of an R.A.F. flight-lieutenant but leaning heavily on a stick, was the first to enter, and Sir Pellinore greeted him with hearty congratulations on his D.F.C. Richard, much slighter in build, followed him and was duly introduced.

'Well, well,' laughed Sir Pellinore to his host, 'it seems that you're holding quite a reception tonight, and the four famous companions are now reunited.'

A broad smile lit Rex's ugly attractive face as he said to the Duke: 'Richard and I had just negotiated a spot of dinner together round the corner, at the Dorchester, when we had a hunch, almost simultaneously, that after we'd finished our magnum it'd be a great idea to drop along and take a brandy off you.'

De Richleau turned to Sir Pellinore. 'The note that I gave you – would you produce it now?'

Sir Pellinore fished in his pocket, brought out the envelope, ripped it open and read what the Duke had written half an hour before. It ran as follows:

'You will bear witness that since writing this note I have not left your presence, used the telephone, or communicated in any way with my servants. You expressed the wish, just after dinner, to meet my friends, Simon Aron, Rex Van Ryn, and Richard Eaton.

'If they are not in London the ceremony that I propose to perform will not be successful, because they will not have time to reach here before you go home, but if, as I believe, they are, it is virtually certain that at least one of them will put in an appearance here before midnight.

'If any or all of them turn up I shall see to it that they testify, without prompting, that they have not called upon me by arrangement but have done so purely owing to a sudden idea that they would like to see me which came into their minds. That idea is no matter of mere chance but because *through a magical ceremony I have conveyed to them my will that they shall appear here.*

'If the ceremony is successful I trust that this will convince you that the Nazis may use magic for infinitely more nefarious purposes and that it is *our* duty to conduct an investigation in this matter with the least possible delay.'

Sir Pellinore lowered the note and glanced round the little circle. His blue eyes held a queer, puzzled look, as he exclaimed:

'By God, I'd never have believed it! You win, Duke, I've got to admit that. Mind you, that's not to say I'm prepared to swallow all the extraordinary things you've said this evening. Still, in a case like this we can't afford to neglect *any* avenue. Our Atlantic Life-line is our one weak spot and it may be – yes, it may be that in those slender hands of yours lies the Victory or Defeat of Britain.'

THE
SECRET AGENT

JOSEPH CONRAD

THE SECRET AGENT
================

Such was the house, the household, and the business Mr Verloc left behind him on his way westward at the hour of half past ten in the morning. It was unusually early for him; his whole person exhaled the charm of almost dewy freshness; he wore his blue cloth overcoat unbuttoned; his boots were shiny; his cheeks, freshly shaven, had a sort of gloss; and even his heavy-lidded eyes, refreshed by a night of peaceful slumber, sent out glances of comparative alertness. Through the park railings these glances beheld men and women riding in the Row, couples cantering past harmoniously, others advancing sedately at a walk, loitering groups of three or four, solitary horsemen looking unsociable, and solitary women followed at a long distance by a groom with a cockade to his hat and a leather belt over his tight-fitting coat. Carriages went bowling by, mostly two-horse broughams, with here and there a victoria with the skin of some wild beast inside and a woman's face and hat emerging above the folded hood. And a peculiarly London sun – against which nothing could be said except that it looked bloodshot – glorified all this by its state. It hung at a moderate elevation above Hyde Park Corner with an air of punctual and benign vigilance. The very pavement under Mr Verloc's feet had an old-gold tinge in that diffused light, in which neither wall, nor tree, nor beast, nor man cast a shadow. Mr Verloc was going westward through a town without shadows in an atmosphere of powdered old gold. There were red, coppery gleams on the roofs of houses, on the corners of walls, on the panels of carriages, on the very coats of the horses, and on the broad back of Mr Verloc's overcoat, where they produced a dull effect of rustiness. But Mr Verloc was not in the least conscious of having got rusty. He surveyed through the park railings the evidences of the town's opulence and luxury with an approving eye. All these people had to be protected. Protection is the first necessity of opulence and luxury. They had to be protected; and their horses, carriages, houses, servants had to be protected; and the source of their wealth had to be protected in the heart of the city and the heart of the country; the whole social order favourable to their hygienic idleness had to be protected against the shallow enviousness of unhygienic labour. It had to – and Mr Verloc would have rubbed his hands with satisfaction had he not been constitutionally averse from every superfluous exertion. His idleness was not hygienic, but it suited him very well. He was in a manner devoted to it with a sort of inert fanaticism, or perhaps rather

169

with a fanatical inertness. Born of industrious parents for a life of toil, he had embraced indolence from an impulse as profound as inexplicable and as imperious as the impulse which directs a man's preference for one particular woman in a given thousand. He was too lazy even for a mere demagogue, for a workman orator, for a leader of labour. It was too much trouble. He required a more perfect form of ease; or it might have been that he was the victim of a philosophical unbelief in the effectiveness of every human effort. Such a form of indolence requires, implies, a certain amount of intelligence. Mr Verloc was not devoid of intelligence – and at the notion of a menaced social order he would perhaps have winked to himself if there had not been an effort to make in that sign of scepticism. His big, prominent eyes were not well adapted to winking. They were rather of the sort that closes solemnly in slumber with majestic effect.

Undemonstrative and burly in a fat-pig style, Mr Verloc, without either rubbing his hands with satisfaction or winking sceptically at his thoughts, proceeded on his way. He trod the pavement heavily with his shiny boots, and his general get-up was that of a well-to-do mechanic in business for himself. He might have been anything from a picture-frame maker to a locksmith; an employer of labour in a small way. But there was also about him an indescribable air which no mechanic could have acquired in the practice of his handicraft however dishonestly exercised: the air common to men who live on the vices, the follies, or the baser fears of mankind; the air of moral nihilism common to keepers of gambling hells and disorderly houses; to private detectives and inquiry agents; to drink sellers and, I should say, to the sellers of invigorating electric belts and to the inventors of patent medicines. But of the last I am not sure, not having carried my investigations so far into the depths. For all I know, the expression of these last may be perfectly diabolic. I shouldn't be surprised. What I want to affirm is that Mr Verloc's expression was by no means diabolic.

Before reaching Knightsbridge, Mr Verloc took a turn to the left out of the busy main thoroughfare, uproarious with the traffic of swaying omnibuses and trotting vans, in the almost silent, swift flow of hansoms. Under his hat, worn with a slight backward tilt, his hair had been carefully brushed into respectful sleekness; for his business was with an embassy. And Mr Verloc, steady like a rock – a soft kind of rock – marched now along a street which could with every propriety be described as private. In its breadth, emptiness, and extent it had the majesty of inorganic nature, of matter that never dies. The only reminder of mortality was a doctor's brougham arrested in august solitude close to the kerbstone. The polished knockers of the doors gleamed as far as the eye could reach, the clean windows shone with a dark opaque lustre. And all was still. But a milk cart rattled noisily across the distant perspective; a butcher boy, driving with the noble recklessness of a charioteer at Olympic Games, dashed round the corner sitting high above a pair of red wheels. A guilty-looking cat issuing from under the stones ran for a while in front of Mr Verloc, then dived into another basement; and a thick police constable, looking a stranger to every emotion, as if he, too, were part of inorganic nature, surging apparently out of a lamp-post, took not the slightest notice of Mr Verloc. With a turn to the left Mr Verloc pursued his way along a narrow street by the side of a yellow wall which, for some inscrutable reason, had No. 1 Chesham Square written on it in black letters. Chesham Square was at least sixty yards away, and Mr Verloc, cosmopolitan enough not to be deceived by London's topographical mysteries, held on steadily, without a sign of surprise or indignation. At last, with a business-like persistency, he reached the Square, and made diagonally for the number 10. This belonged to an imposing carriage gate in a high, clean wall between two houses, of which one rationally enough bore the number 9 and the other was numbered 37; but the fact that this last belonged to Porthill Street, a street well known in the neighbourhood, was proclaimed by an inscription placed above the ground-floor windows by whatever highly effecient authority is charged with the duty of keeping track of London's strayed houses. Why powers are not asked of Parliament (a short Act would do) for compelling those edifices to return where they belong is one of the mysteries of municipal administration. Mr Verloc did not trouble his head about it, his mission in life being the protection of the social mechanism, not its perfectionment or even its criticism.

It was so early that the porter of the Embassy issued hurriedly out of his lodge still struggling with the left sleeve of his livery coat. His waistcoat was red, and he wore knee-breeches, but his aspect was flustered. Mr Verloc, aware of the rush on his flank, drove it off by simply holding out an envelope stamped with the arms of the Embassy, and passed on. He produced the same talisman also to the footman who opened the door, and stood back to let him enter the hall.

A clear fire burned in a tall fireplace, and an elderly man standing with his back to it, in evening dress and with a chain round his neck, glanced up from the newspaper he was holding spread out in both hands before his calm and severe face. He didn't move; but another lackey, in brown trousers and clawhammer coat edged with thin yellow cord, approaching Mr Verloc listened to the murmur of his name, and turning on his heel in silence, began to walk, without looking back once. Mr Verloc, thus led along a ground-floor passage to the left of the great carpeted staircase, was suddenly motioned to enter a quite small room furnished with a heavy writing-table and a few chairs. The servant shut the door, and Mr Verloc remained alone. He did not take a seat. With his hat and stick held in one hand he glanced about, passing his other podgy hand over his uncovered sleek head.

Another door opened noiselessly, and Mr Verloc immobilizing his glance in that direction saw at first only black clothes. The bald top of a head, and a drooping dark grey whisker on each side of a pair of wrinkled hands. The person who had entered was holding a batch of papers before his eyes and walked up to the table with a rather mincing step, turning the papers over the while. Privy Councillor Wurmt, Chancelier d'Ambassade, was rather shortsighted. The meritorious official, laying the papers on the table, disclosed a face of pasty complexion and of melancholy ugliness surrounded by a lot of fine, long, dark grey hairs, barred heavily by thick and bushy eyebrows. He put on a black-framed pince-nez upon a blunt and shapeless nose, and seemed struck by Mr Verloc's appearance. Under the enormous eyebrows his weak eyes blinked pathetically through the glasses.

He made no sign of greeting; neither did Mr Verloc who certainly knew his place; but a subtle change about the general outlines of his shoulders and back suggested a slight bending of Mr Verloc's spine under the vast surface of his overcoat. The effect was of unobtrusive deference.

'I have here some of your reports,' said the bureaucrat in an unexpectedly soft and weary voice, and pressing the tip of his forefinger on the papers with force. He paused; and Mr Verloc, who had recognized his own handwriting very well, waited in an almost breathless silence. 'We are not very satisfied with the attitude of the police here', the other continued, with every appearance of mental fatigue.

The shoulders of Mr Verloc, without actually moving, suggested a shrug. And for the first time since he left his home that morning his lips opened.

'Every country has its police,' he said, philosophically. But as the official of the Embassy went on blinking at him steadily he felt constrained to add: 'Allow me to observe that I have no means of action upon the police here.'

'What is desired,' said the man of papers, 'is the occurrence of something definite which should stimulate their vigilance. That is within your province – is it not so?'

Mr Verloc made no answer except by a sigh, which escaped him involuntarily, for instantly he tried to give his face a cheerful expression.

The official blinked doubtfully, as if affected by the dim light of the room. He repeated vaguely:

'The vigilance of the police – and the severity of the magistrates. The general leniency of the judicial procedure here, and the utter absence of all repressive measures, are a scandal to Europe. What is wished for just now is the accentuation of the unrest – of the fermentation which undoubtedly exists—'

'Undoubtedly, undoubtedly,' broke in Mr Verloc in a deep, deferential bass of an oratorical quality, so utterly different from the tone in which he had spoken before that his interlocutor remained profoundly surprised. 'It exists to a dangerous degree. My reports for the last twelve months make it sufficiently clear.'

'Your reports for the last twelve months,' State Councillor Wurmt began in his gentle and dispassionate tone, 'have been read by me. I failed to discover why you wrote them at all.'

A sad silence reigned for a time. Mr Verloc seemed to have swallowed his tongue, and the other gazed at the papers on the table fixedly. At last he gave them a slight push.

'The state of affairs you expose there is assumed to exist as the first condition of your employment. What is required at present is not writing, but the bringing to light of a distinct, significant fact – I would almost say of an alarming fact.'

'I need not say that all my endeavours shall be directed to that end,' Mr Verloc said, with convinced modulations in his conversational husky tone. But the sense of being blinked at watchfully behind the blind glitter of these eyeglasses on the other side of the table disconcerted him. He stopped short with a gesture of absolute devotion. The useful hardworking, if obscure member of the Embassy had an air of being impressed by some newly born thought.

'You are very corpulent,' he said.

This observation, really of a psychological nature, and advanced with the modest hesitation of an officeman more familiar with ink and paper than with the requirements of active life, stung Mr Verloc in the manner of a rude personal remark. He stepped back a pace.

'Eh? What were you pleased to say?' he exclaimed, with husky resentment.

The Chancelier d'Ambassade, entrusted with the conduct of this interview seemed to find it too much for him.

'I think,' he said, 'that you had better see Mr Vladimir. Yes, decidedly I think you ought to see Mr Vladimir. Be good enough to wait here,' he added, and went out with mincing steps.

At once Mr Verloc passed his hand over his hair. A slight perspiration had broken out of his forehead. He let the air escape from his pursed-up lips like a man blowing at a spoonful of hot soup. But when the servant in brown appeared at the door silently, Mr Verloc had not moved an inch from the place he had occupied throughout the interview. He had remained motionless as if feeling himself surrounded by pitfalls.

He walked along a passage lighted by a lonely gas-jet, then up a flight of winding stairs, and through a glazed and cheerful corridor on the first floor. The footman threw open a door, and stood aside. The feet of Mr Verloc felt a thick carpet. The room was large, with three windows; and a young man with a shaven, big face, sitting in a roomy armchair before a vast mahogany writing-table, said in French to the Chancelier d'Ambassade, who was going out with the papers in his hand:

'You are quite right, *mon cher*. He's fat – the animal.'

Mr Vladimir, First Secretary, had a drawing-room reputation as an agreeable and entertaining man. He was something of a favourite in society. His wit consisted in discovering droll connexions between incongruous ideas; and when talking in that strain he sat well forward on his seat, with his left hand raised, as if exhibiting his funny demonst-rations between the thumb and forefinger, while his round and clean-shaven face wore an expression of merry perplexity.

But there was no trace of merriment or perplexity in the way he looked at Mr Verloc. Lying far back in the deep armchair, with squarely spread elbows, and throwing one leg over a thick knee, he had with his smooth and rosy countenance the air of a preternaturally thriving baby that will not stand nonsense from anybody.

'You understand French, I suppose?' he said.

Mr Verloc stated huskily that he did. His whole vast bulk had a forward inclination. He stood on the carpet in the middle of the room, clutching his hat and stick in one hand; the other hung lifelessly by his side. He muttered unobtrusively somewhere deep down in his throat something about having done his military service in the French artillery. At once, with contemptuous perversity, Mr Vladimir changed the language, and began to speak idiomatic English without the slightest trace of a foreign accent.

'Ah! Yes. Of course. Let's see. How much did you get for obtaining the design of the improved breech-block of their new field-gun?'

'Five years' rigorous confinement in a fortress,' Mr Verloc answered, unexpectedly, but without any sign of feeling.

'You got off easily,' was Mr Vladimir's comment. 'And anyhow, it served you right for letting yourself get caught. What made you go in for that sort of thing – eh?'

Mr Verloc's husky conversational voice was heard speaking of youth, of a fatal infatuation for an unworthy——

'Aha! *Cherchez la femme,*' Mr Vladimir deigned to interrupt, unbending, but without affability; there was, on the contrary, a touch of grimness in his condescension. 'How long have you been employed by the Embassy here?' he asked.

'Ever since the time of the late Baron Stott-Wartenheim,' Mr Verloc answered in the subdued tones, and protruding his lips sadly, in sign of sorrow for the deceased diplomat. The First Secretary observed this play of physiognomy steadily.

'Ah! ever since. . . . Well! What have you got to say for yourself? he asked, sharply.

Mr Verloc answered with some surprise that he was not aware of having anything special to say. He had been summoned by a letter – And he plunged his hand busily into the side pocket of his overcoat, but before the mocking, cynical watchfulness of Mr Vladimir, concluded to leave it there.

'Bah!' said the latter. 'What do you mean by getting out of condition like this? You haven't got even the physique of your profession. You – a member of a starving proletariat – never! You – a desperate socialist or anarchist – which is it?'

'Anarchist,' stated Mr Verloc in a deadened tone.

'Bosh!' went on Mr Vladimir, without raising his voice. 'You startled old Wurmt himself. You wouldn't deceive an idiot. They all are that by-the-by, but you seem to me simply impossible. So you began your connexion with us by stealing the French gun designs. And you got yourself caught. That must have been very disagreeable to our Government. You don't seem to be very smart.'

Mr Verloc tried to exculpate himself huskily.

'As I've had occasion to observe before, a fatal infatuation for an unworthy——'

Mr Vladimir raised a large, white, plump hand.

'Ah, yes. The unlucky attachment – of your youth. She got hold of the money, and then sold you to the police – eh?'

The doleful change in Mr Verloc's physiognomy, the momentary drooping of his whole person, confessed that such was the regrettable case. Mr Vladimir's hand clasped the ankle reposing on his knee. The sock was of dark blue silk.

'You see, that was not very clever of you. Perhaps you are too susceptible'

Mr Verloc intimated in a throaty, veiled murmur that he was no longer young.

'Oh! That's a failing which age does not cure,' Mr Vladimir remarked, with sinister familiarity. 'But no! You are too fat for that. You could not have come to look like this if you had been at all susceptible. I'll tell you what I think is the matter: you are a lazy fellow. How long have you been drawing pay from this Embassy?'

'Eleven years,' was the answer, after a moment of sulky hesitation. 'I've been charged with several missions to London while His Excellency Baron Stott-Wartenheim was still Ambassador in Paris. Then by his Excellency's instructions I settled down in London. I am English.'

'You are! Are you? Eh?'

'A natural-born British subject,' Mr Verloc said, stolidly. 'But my father was French, and so—'

'Never mind explaining,' interrupted the other. 'I daresay you could have been legally a Marshal of France and a Member of Parliament in England – and then, indeed, you would have been of some use to our Embassy.'

This flight of fancy provoked something like a faint smile on Mr Verloc's face. Mr Vladimir retained an imperturbable gravity.

'But, as I've said, you are a lazy fellow; you don't use your opportunities. In the time of Baron Stott-Wartenheim we had a lot of soft-headed people running this Embassy. They caused fellows of your sort to form a false conception of the nature of a secret fund. It is my business to correct this misapprehension by telling you what the secret service is not. It is not a philanthropic institution. I've had you called here on purpose to tell you this.'

Mr Vladimir observed the forced expression of bewilderment on Verloc's face, and smiled sarcastically.

'I see that you understand me perfectly. I daresay you are intelligent enough for your work. What we want now is activity – activity.'

On repeating this last word Mr Vladimir laid a long white forefinger on the edge of the desk. Every trace of huskiness disappeared from Verloc's voice. The nape of his gross neck became crimson above the velvet collar of his overcoat. His lips quivered before they came widely open.

'If you'll only be good enough to look up my record,' he boomed out in his great, clear, oratorical bass, 'you'll see I gave a warning only three months ago on the occasion of the Grand Duke Romuald's visit to Paris, which was telegraphed from here to the French police, and—'

'Tut, tut!' broke out Mr Vladimir, with a frowning grimace. 'The French police had no use for warning. Don't roar like this. What the devil do you mean?'

With a note of proud humility Mr Verloc apologised for forgetting himself. His voice, famous for years at open-air meetings and at workmen's assemblies in large halls, had contributed, he said, to his reputation of a good and trustworthy comrade. It was, therefore, a part of his usefulness. It had inspired confidence in his principles. 'I was always put up to speak by the leaders at a critical moment,' Mr Verloc declared, with obvious satisfaction. There was no uproar above which he could not make himself heard, he added; and suddenly he made a demonstration.

'Allow me,' he said. With lowered forehead, without looking up, swiftly and ponderously, he crossed the room to one of the french windows. As if giving way to an uncontrollable impulse, he opened it a little. Mr Vladimir jumped up amazed from the depths of the armchair, looked over his shoulder; and below, across the courtyard of the Embassy, well beyond the open gate, could be seen the broad back of a policeman watching idly the gorgeous perambulator of a wealthy baby being wheeled in state across the Square.

'Constable!' said Mr Verloc, with no more effort than if he were whispering; and Mr Vladimir burst into a laugh on seeing the policeman spin round as if prodded by a sharp instrument. Mr Verloc shut the window quietly, and returned to the middle of the room.

'With a voice like that,' he said, putting on the husky conversational pedal, 'I was naturally trusted. And I knew what to say, too.'

Mr Vladimir, arranging his cravat, observed him in a glass over the mantelpiece.

'I daresay you have the social revolutionary jargon by heart well enough,' he said, contemptuously. '*Vox et.* . . . You haven't even studied Latin – have you?'

'No,' growled Mr Verloc. 'You did not expect me to know it. I belong to the million. Who knows Latin? Only a few hundred imbeciles who aren't fit to take care of themselves.'

For some thirty seconds longer Mr Vladimir studied in the mirror the fleshy profile, the gross bulk, of the man behind him. And at the same time he had the advantage of seeing his own face, clean-shaved and round, rosy about the gills, and with the thin, sensitive lips formed exactly for the utterance of those delicate witticisms which had made him such a favourite in the very highest society. Then he turned, and advanced into the room with such determination that the very ends of his quaintly old-fashioned bow necktie seemed to bristle with unspeakable menaces. The movement was so swift and fierce that Mr Verloc, casting an oblique glance, quailed inwardly. 'Aha! You dare be impudent,' Mr

Vladimir began, with an amazingly guttural intonation not only utterly un-English, but absolutely un-European, and startling even to Mr Verloc's experience of cosmopolitan slums. 'You dare! Well, I am going to speak plain English to you. Voice won't do. We have no use for your voice. We don't want a voice. We want facts – startling facts – damn you,' he added, with a sort of ferocious discretion, right into Mr Verloc's face.

'Don't you try to come over me with your Hyperborean manners,' Mr Verloc defended himself, huskily, looking at the carpet. At this his interlocutor, smiling mockingly above the bristling bow of his necktie, switched the conversation into French.

'You give yourself for an *agent provocateur*. The proper business of an *agent provocateur* is to provoke. As far as I can judge from your record kept here, you have done nothing to earn your money for the last three years.'

'Nothing!' exclaimed Verloc, stirring not a limb, and not raising his eyes, but with the note of sincere feeling in his tone. 'I have several times prevented what might have been—'

'There is a proverb in this country which says prevention is better than cure,' interrupted Mr Vladimir, throwing himself into the armchair. 'It is stupid in a general way. There is no end to prevention. But it is characteristic. Thy dislike finality in this country. Don't you be too English. And in this particular instance, don't be absurd. The evil is already here. We don't want prevention – we want cure.'

He paused, turned to the desk, and turning over some papers lying there, spoke in a changed, business-like tone, without looking at Mr Verloc.

'You know, of course, of the International Conference assembled in Milan?'

Mr Verloc intimated hoarsely that he was in the habit of reading the daily papers. To a further question his answer was that, of course, he understood what he read. At this Mr Vladimir, smiling faintly at the documents he was still scanning one after another, murmured 'As long as it is not written in Latin, I suppose.'

'Or Chinese,' added Mr Verloc, stolidly.

'H'm. Some of your revolutionary friends' effusions are written in a *charabia* every bit as incomprehensible as Chinese –' Mr Vladimir let fall disdainfully a grey sheet of printed matter. 'What are all these leaflets headed F.P., with a hammer, pen, and torch crossed? What does it mean, this F.P.?' Mr Verloc approached the imposing writing-table.

'The Future of the Proletariat. It's society,' he explained, standing ponderously by the side of the armchair, 'not anarchist in principle, but open to all shades of revolutionary opinion.'

'Are you in it?'

'One of the Vice-Presidents,' Mr Verloc breathed out heavily; and the First Secretary of the Embassy raised his head to look at him.

'Then you ought to be ashamed of yourself,' he said, incisively, 'Isn't your society capable of anything else but printing this prophetic bosh in blunt type on this filthy paper – eh? Why don't you do something? Look here. I've this matter in hand now, and I tell you plainly that you will have to earn your money. The good old Stott-Wartenheim times are over. No work, no pay.'

Mr Verloc felt a queer sensation of faintness in his stout legs. He stepped back one pace, and blew his nose loudly.

He was, in truth, startled and alarmed. The rusty London sunshine struggling clear of the London mist shed a lukewarm brightness into the First Secretary's private room: and in the silence Mr Verloc heard against a window-pane the faint buzzing of a fly – his first fly of the year – heralding better than any number of swallows the approach of spring. The useless fussing of that tiny energetic organism affected unpleasantly this big man threatened in his indolence.

In the pause Mr Vladimir formulated in his mind a series of disparaging remarks concerning Mr Verloc's face and figure. The fellow was unexpectedly vulgar, heavy, and impudently unintelligent. He looked uncommonly like a master plumber come to present his bill. The First Secretary of the Embassy, from his occasional excursions into the field of American humour, had formed a special notion of that class of mechanic as the embodiment of fraudulent laziness and incompetency.

This was then the famous and trusty secret agent, so secret that he was never designated otherwise but by the symbol Δ in the late Baron Stott-Wartenheim's official, semi-official, and confidential correspondence; the celebrated agent Δ whose warnings had the power to change the schemes and the dates of royal, imperial, grand-ducal journeys, and sometimes cause them to be put off altogether! This fellow! And Mr Vladimir indulged mentally in an enormous and derisive fit of merriment, partly at his own astonishment, which he judged naïve, but mostly at the expense of the universally regretted Baron Stott-Wartenheim. His late Ex-cellency, whom the august favour of his Imperial master had imposed as Ambassador upon several reluctant Ministers of Foreign Affairs, had enjoyed in his life-time a fame for an owlish, pessimistic gullibility. His Excellency had the social revolution on the brain. He imagined himself to be a diplomatist set apart by a special dispensation to watch the end of diplomacy, and pretty nearly the end of the world, in a horrid, democratic upheaval. His prophetic and doleful dispatches had been for years the joke of Foreign Offices. He was said to have exclaimed on his deathbed (visited by his Imperial friend and master): 'Unhappy Europe! Thou shalt perish by the moral insanity of thy children!' He was fated to be the victim of the first humbugging rascal that came along, thought Mr Vladimir, smiling vaguely at Mr Verloc.

'You ought to venerate the memory of Baron Stott-Wartenheim,' he exclaimed, suddenly.

The lowered physiognomy of Mr Verloc expressed a sombre and weary annoyance.

'Permit me to observe to you,' he said, 'that I came here because I was summoned by a peremptory letter. I have been here only twice before in the last eleven years, and certainly never at eleven in the morning. It isn't very wise to call me up like this. There is just a chance of being seen. And that would be no joke for me.'

'Mr Vladimir shrugged his shoulders.

'It would destroy my usefulness,' continued the other hotly.

'That's your affair,' murmured Mr Vladimir, with soft brutality. 'When you cease to be useful you shall cease to be employed. Yes. Right off. Cut short. You shall—' Mr Vladimir, frowning, paused, at a loss for a sufficiently idiomatic expression, and instantly brightened up, with a grin of beautifully white teeth. 'You shall be chucked,' he brought out, ferociously.

Once more Mr Verloc had to react with all the force of his will against that sensation of faintness running down one's legs which once upon a time had inspired some poor devil with the felicitous expression: 'My heart went down into my boots.' Mr Verloc, aware of the sensation, raised his head bravely.

Mr Vladimir bore the look of heavy inquiry with perfect serenity.

'What we want is to administer a tonic to the Conference in Milan,' he said, airily. 'Its deliberations upon international action for the suppression of political crime don't seem to get anywhere. England lags. This country is absurd with its sentimental regard for individual liberty. It's intolerable to think that all your friends have got only to come over to—'

'In that way I have them all under my eye,' Mr Verloc interrupted, huskily.

'It would be much more to the point to have them all under lock and key. England must be brought into line. The imbecile bourgeoisie of this country makes themselves the accomplices of the very people whose aim is to drive them out of their houses to starve in ditches. And they have the political power still, if they only had the sense to use it for their

preservation. I suppose you agree that the middle classes are stupid?'
Mr Verloc agreed hoarsely.

'They are.'

'They have no imagination. They are blinded by an idiotic vanity.
What they want just now is a jolly good scare. This is the psychological
moment to set your friends to work. I have had you called here to develop
to you my idea.'

And Mr Vladimir developed his idea from on high, with scorn and
condescension, displaying at the same time an amount of ignorance as to
the real aims, thoughts, and methods of the revolutionary world which
filled the silent Mr Verloc with inward consternation. He confounded
causes with effects more than was excusable; the most distinguished
propagandists with impulsive bomb throwers; assumed organization
where in the nature of things it could not exist; spoke of the social
revolutionary party one moment as of a perfectly disciplined army, where
the words of chiefs was supreme, and at another as if it had been the
loosest association of desperate brigands that ever camped in a mountain
gorge. Once Mr Verloc had opened his mouth for a protest, but the
raising of a shapely, large white hand arrested him. Very soon he became
too appalled to even try to protest. He listened in a stillness of dread
which resembled the immobility of profound attention.

'A series of outrages,' Mr Vladimir continued, calmly, 'executed here
in this country; not only planned here – that would not do – they would
not mind. your friends could set half the Continent on fire without
influencing the public opinion here in favour of a universal repressive
legislation. They will not look outside their backyard here.'

Mr Verloc cleared his throat, but his heart failed him, and he said
nothing.

'These outrages need not be especially sanguinary,' Mr Vladimir went
on, as if delivering a scientific lecture, 'but they must be sufficiently
startling – effective. Let them be directed against buildings, for instance.
What is the fetish of the hour that all the bourgeoisie recognize – eh, Mr
Verloc?'

Mr Verloc opened his hands and shrugged his shoulders slightly.

'You are too lazy to think,' was Mr Vladimir's comment upon that
gesture. 'Pay attention to what I say. The fetish of today is neither royalty
nor religion. Therefore the palace and the church should be left alone.
You understand what I mean, Mr Verloc?'

The dismay and the scorn of Mr Verloc found vent in an attempt at
levity.

'Perfectly. But what of the Embassies? A series of attacks on the various Embassies,' he began; but he could not withstand the cold, watchful stare of the First Secretary.

'You can be facetious, I see,' the latter observed, carelessly. 'That's all right. It may enliven your oratory at socialistic congresses. But this room is no place for it. It would be infinitely safer for you to follow carefully what I am saying. As you are being called upon to furnish facts instead of cock-and-bull stories, you had better try to make your profit off what I am taking the trouble to explain to you. The sacrosanct fetish of today is science. Why don't you get some of your friends to go for that wooden-faced panjandrum – eh!

FUNERAL IN
BERLIN

LEN DEIGHTON

FUNERAL IN BERLIN

'Edmond Dorf' has been sent from London on a special mission to Berlin to negotiate for the defection of an important Russian scientist to the West. Johnnie Vulkan, the agent on the spot, has been detailed to give him every assistance.

The Berlin Defence is a classic defence by means of counter-attack.

Berlin, Sunday, October 6th

The parade ground of Europe has always been the vast area of scrub and lonely villages that stretches eastward from the Elbe – some say as far as the Urals. But halfway between the Elbe and the Oder, sitting at attention upon Brandenburg, is Prussia's major town – Berlin.

From two thousand feet the Soviet Army War Memorial in Treptower Park is the first thing you notice. It's in the Russian sector. In a space like a dozen football pitches a cast of a Red Army soldier makes the Statue of Liberty look like it's standing in a hole. Over Marx-Engels Platz the plane banked steeply south towards Tempelhof and the thin veins of water shone in the bright sunshine. The Spree flows through Berlin as a spilt pail of water flows through a building site. The river and its canals are lean and hungry and they slink furtively under roads that do not acknowledge them by even the smallest hump. Nowhere does a grand bridge and a wide flow of water divide the city into two halves. Instead it is bricked-up buildings and sections of breeze-block that bisect the city, ending suddenly and unpredictably like the lava flow of a cold-war Pompeii.

Johnnie Vulkan brought a friend and a black Cadillac to meet me at Tempelhof.

'Major Bailis, U.S. Army,' said Johnnie. I shook hands with a tall leathery American who was buttoned deep into a white Aquascutum trench coat. He offered me a cigar while the baggage was being checked.

'It's good to have you with us,' said the Major and Johnnie said the same.

'Thanks,' I said. 'This is a town where one needs friends.'

'We've put you into the Frühling,' the major said. 'It's small, comfortable, unobtrusive and very, very Berlin.'

'Fine,' I said; it sounded O.K.

185

Johnnie moved quickly through the traffic in the sleek Cadillac. Cutting across the city from west to east is a ten-lane highway that successive generations have named 'Unter den Linden' and 'Strasse des 17. Juni' and once was a gigantic path leading through the Brandenburger Tor to the royal palace.

'We just call it Big Street,' said the American as Johnnie moved into the fast lane. In the distance the statue on the Tor glinted gold in the afternoon sun, beyond it in the Soviet sector a flat concrete plain named Marx-Engels Platz stood where communist demolition teams had razed the Schloss Hohenzollern.

We turned towards the Hilton.

Just a little way down the street beyond the shell of the Gedächtniskirche with its slick modern tower – like a tricky sort of hi-fi speaker cabinet – apeing the old broken one is Kranzler's, a café that spreads itself across the Kurfürstendamm pavement. We ordered coffee and the U.S. army major sat on the far side of the table and spent ten minutes tying the laces of his shoes. Across in the 'Quick Café' two girls with silver hair were eating Bockwurst.

I looked at Johnnie Vulkan. Growing older seemed to agree with him. He didn't look a day over forty, his hair was like a tailored Brillo pad and his face tanned. He wore a well-cut Berlin suit in English pinhead worsted. He leaned back in his chair and pointed a finger lazily towards me. His hand was so sunburned that his nails seemed pale pink. He said, 'Before we start, let's get one thing clear. No one here needs help; you are superfluous to requirements as far as I am concerned. Just remember that; stay out of the way and everything will be O.K. Get in the way and . . .' He shrugged his shoulders. 'This is a dangerous town.' He kept his hand pointing into my face and gave a flash of a smile.

I looked at him for a moment. I looked at his smile and at his hand.

'Next time you point a finger at someone, Johnnie,' I said, 'remember that three of your fingers are pointing back at you.' He lowered his hand as though it had become heavy.

'Stok is our contact,' he said quietly.

I was surprised. Stok was a Red Army colonel in State Security.[1]

'It's official then?' I asked. 'An official exchange.'

Vulkan chuckled and glanced at the major.

'It's more what you might call extra-curricular. Official but extra-curricular,' he said again, loud enough for the American to hear. The

1. K.G.B.

American laughed and went back to his shoelace.

'The way we hear it, there is a lot of extra-curricular activity here in Berlin.'

'Dawlish been complaining?' Vulkan asked, captiously.

'Hinting.'

'Well, you tell him I'll have to have more than my present lousy two thousand a month if it's exclusive service he's after.'

'You tell him,' I said. 'He's on the phone.'

'Look,' said Vulkan, his solid gold wristwatch peeping out from the pristine cuff. 'Dawlish has no idea of the situation here. My contact with Stok is . . .' Vulkan made a movement with his cupped hand to indicate a superlative.

'Stok is one thousand times brighter than Dawlish and he runs *his* show from on the spot, not from an office desk hundreds of miles away. If I can bring Semitsa over the wire it will be because I personally know some important people in this town. People I can rely on and who can rely on me. All Dawlish has to do is collect the kudos and leave me alone.'

'What I think Dawlish needs to know,' I said, 'is what Colonel Stok will require in return if he delivers Semitsa – what you call – over the wire.'

'Almost certainly cash.'

'I had a premonition it would be.'

'Wait a minute, wait a minute,' said Vulkan, loud enough to bring the American out of his reverie. 'Major Bailis is the official U.S. Army observer for this transaction. I don't have to put up with dirty talk like that.'

The American took off his sun-glasses and said, 'Yes, siree. That's the size of it.' Then he put his glasses back on again.

I said, 'Just to make quite sure that you don't promise anything we wouldn't like: make sure I'm there at your next meeting with comrade Colonel Stok, eh?'

'Difficult,' said Johnnie.

'But you'll manage it,' I said, 'because that's what we pay you for.'

'Oh yes,' said Vulkan.

When a player offers a piece for exchange or sacrifice then surely he has in mind a subsequent manoeuvre which will end to his advantage.

Berlin, Monday, October 7th

Brassières and beer; whiskies and worsteds; great words carved out of coloured electricity and plastered along the walls of the Ku-damm. This was the theatre-in-the-round of western prosperity: a great, gobbling, yelling, laughing stage crowded with fat ladies and dwarfs, marionettes on strings, fire-eaters, strong men and lots of escapologists. 'Today I joined the cast,' I thought. 'Now they've got an illusionist.' Beneath me the city lay in huge patches of light and vast pools of darkness where rubble and grass fought gently for control of the universe.

Inside my room the phone rang. Vulkan's voice was calm and unhurried.

'Do you know the Warschau restaurant?'

'Stalin Allee,' I said; it was a well-known bourse for information peddlers.

'They call it Karl Marx Allee now,' said Vulkan sardonically. 'Have your car facing west in the car park across the Allee. Don't get out of your car, flash your lights. I'll be ready to go at 9.20. O.K.?'

'O.K.,' I said.

I followed the line of the canal from the Berlin Hilton to Hallesches Tor U-Bahnshation, then turned north on to Friedrichstrasse. The control point is a few blocks north. I flipped a passport to the American soldier and an insurance card to the West German policeman, then in bottom gear I moved across the tram tracks of Zimmerstrasse that bump you into a world where 'communist' is not a dirty word.

It was a warm evening and a couple of dozen transients sat under the blue neon light in the checkpoint hut; stacked neatly on tables were piles of booklets and leaflets with titles like 'Science of the G.D.R. in the service of Peace', 'Art for the People' and 'Historic Task of the G.D.R. and the future of Germany'.

'Herr Dorf.' A very young frontier policeman held my passport and riffed the corners. 'How much money are you carrying?'

I spread the few Westmarks and English pounds on the desk. He counted them and endorsed my papers.

'Cameras or transistor radio?'

At the other end of the corridor a boy in a leather jacket with 'Rhodesia' painted on it shouted, 'How much longer do we have to wait here?'

I heard a Grepo say to him, 'You'll have to take your turn, sir – we didn't send for you, you know.'

'Just the car radio,' I said.

The Grepo nodded.

He said, 'The only thing we don't allow is East German currency.' He gave me my passport,[1] smiled and saluted. I walked down the long hut. The Rhodesian was saying, 'I know my rights,' and rapping on the counter but everyone else was staring straight ahead.

I walked across to the parking bay. I drove around the concrete blocks, a Vopo gave a perfunctory glance at my passport and a soldier swung the red-and-white striped barrier skywards. I drove forward into East Berlin. There were crowds of people at Friedrichstrasse station. People coming home from work, going to work or just hanging around waiting for something to happen. I turned right at Unter den Linden – where the lime trees had been early victims of Nazidom; the old Bismarck Chancellery was a cobweb of rusty ruins facing the memorial building where two green-clad sentries with white gloves were goose-stepping like Bismarck was expected back. I drove around the white plain of Marx-Engels Platz and, at the large slab-sided department store at Alexanderplatz, took the road that leads to Karl Marx Allee.

I recognised the car park and pulled into it. Karl Marx Allee was still the same as when it had been Stalin Allee. Miles of workers' flats and state shops housed in seven-storey Russian-style architecture, thirty-foot-wide pavements and huge grassy spaces and cycle tracks like the M1.

In the open-air café across the road, lights winked under the trees and a few people danced between the striped parasols while a small combo walked their baby back home with lots of percussion. 'Warschau', the lights spelled out and under them I saw Vulkan get to his feet. He waited patiently until the traffic lights were in his favour before walking towards the car park. A careful man, Johnnie; this was no time to collect a jaywalking ticket. He got into a Wartburg, pulled away eastward down Karl Marx Allee. I followed keeping one or two cars between us.

Johnnie parked outside a large granite house in Köpenick. I edged past his car and parked under a gas lamp around the corner. It was not a pretty house but it had that mood of comfort and complacency that middle-class owners breathe into the structure of a house along with dinner-gong echoes and cigar smoke. There was a large garden at the back and here near the forests and the waters of Müggelsee the air smelled clean.

There was just one name-plate on the door. It was of neat black plastic: 'Professor Eberhard Lebowitz', engraved in ornate Gothic lettering. Johnnie rang and a maid let us into the hall.

'Herr Stok?' said Johnnie.

He gave her his card and she tiptoed away into the interior.

In the dimly lit hall there stood a vast hallstand with some tricky inlaid

---

1. To catch people with stolen passports, or people who spend nights in the East, the passports are often marked with a tiny pencil spot on some pre-arranged page.

ivory, two clothes-brushes and a Soviet officer's peaked hat. The ceiling was a complex pattern of intaglio leaves and the floral wallpaper looked prehensile.

The maid said, 'Will you please come this way?' and led us into Stok's drawing-room. The wallpaper was predominantly gold and silver but there were plenty of things hiding the wallpaper. There were aspidistras, fussy lace curtains, shelves full of antique Meissen and a cocktail cabinet like a small wooden version of the Kremlin. Stok looked up from the 21-inch baroque TV. He was a big-boned man, his hair was cropped to the skull and his complexion was like something the dog had been playing with. When he stood up to greet us his huge hands poked out of a bright red silk smoking-jacket with gold-braid frogging.

Vulkan said, 'Herr Stok; Herr Dorf,' and then he said, 'Herr Dorf; Herr Stok,' and we all nodded at each other, then Vulkan put a paper bag down on the coffee table and Stok drew an eight-ounce tin of Nescafé out of it, nodded, and put it back again.

'What will you drink?' Stok asked. He had a musical basso voice.

'Just before we move into the chat,' I said, 'can I see your identity card?'

Stok pulled his wallet out of a hip pocket, smiled archly at me and then peeled loose the stiff white card with a photo and two rubber stamps that Soviet citizens carry when abroad.

'It says that you are Captain Maylev here,' I protested as I laboriously pronounced the Cyrillic script.

The servant girl brought a tray of tiny glasses and a frosted bottle of vodka. She set the tray down. Stok paused while she withdrew.

'And your passport says that you are Edmond Dorf,' said Stok, 'but we are both victims of circumstance.'

Behind him the East German news commentator was saying in his usual slow voice, '. . . sentenced to three years for assisting in an attempt to move his family to the West.' Stok walked across to the set and clicked the switch to the West Berlin channel where a cast of fifty Teutonic minstrels sang 'See them shuffle along' in German. 'It's never a good night, Thursday,' Stok said apologetically. He switched the set off. He broke the wax on the fruit-flavoured vodka and Stok and Vulkan began discussing whether twenty-four bottles of Scotch whisky were worth a couple of cameras. I sat around and drank vodka until they had ironed out some sort of agreement. Then Stok said, 'Has Dorf got power to negotiate?' – just like I wasn't in the room.

'He's a big shot in London,' said Vulkan. 'Anything he promises will be honoured. I'll guarantee it.'

'I want lieutenant-colonel's pay,' Stok said, turning to me, 'for life.'
'Don't we all?' I said.

Vulkan was looking at the evening paper; he looked up and said, 'No, he means that he'd want the U.K. Government to pay him that as a salary if he comes over the wire. You could promise that, couldn't you?'

'I don't see why not,' I said. 'We'll say you've been in a few years, that's five pounds four shillings a day basic. Then there's ration allowance, six and eight a day, marriage allowance, one pound three and something a day, qualification pay five shillings a day if you get through Staff College, overseas pay fourteen and three and . . . you *would* want overseas pay?'

'You are not taking me seriously,' Stok said, a big smile across his white moon of a face. Vulkan was shifting about on his seat, tightening his tie against his Adam's apple and cracking his finger joints.

'All systems go,' I said.

'Colonel Stok puts up a very convincing case,' said Vulkan.

'So does the "find the lady" mob in Charing Cross Road,' I said, 'but they never come through with the Q.E.D.'

Stok threw back two vodkas in quick succession and stared at me earnestly. He said, 'Look, I don't favour the capitalist system. I don't ask you to believe that I do. In fact I hate your system.'

'Great,' I said. 'And you are in a job where you can really do something about it.'

Stok and Vulkan exchanged glances.

'I wish you would try to understand,' said Stok. 'I am really sincere about giving you my allegiance.'

'Go on,' I said. 'I bet you say that to all the great powers.'

Vulkan said, 'I've spent a lot of time and money in setting this up. If you are so damn clever why did you bother to come to Berlin?'

'O.K.,' I told them. 'Act out the charade. I'll be thinking of words.'

Stok and Vulkan looked at each other and we drank and then Stok gave me one of his gold-rimmed oval cigarettes and lit it with a nickel-silver sputnik.

'For a long time I have been thinking of moving west,' said Stok. 'It's not a matter of politics. I am just as avid a communist now as I have ever been, but a man gets old. He looks for comfort, for security in possessions.' Stok cupped his big boxing-glove hand and looked down at it 'A man wants to scoop up a handful of black dirt and know it's his own land, to live on, die on and give to his sons. We peasants are a weak insecure segment of socialism, Mr Dorf.' He smiled with his big brown teeth, trimmed here and there with an edge of gold. 'These comforts that you take for granted will not be a part of life in the East until long after I am dead.'

'Yes,' I said. 'We have decadence now – while we are young enough to enjoy it.'

'Semitsa,' said Stok. He waited to see what effect it would have on me. It had none.

'That's who you are really interested in. Not me. Semitsa.'

'Is he here in Berlin?' I asked.

'Slowly, Mr Dorf,' said Stok. 'Things move very slowly.'

'How do you know he wants to come west?' I asked.

'I know,' said Stok.

Vulkan interrupted, 'I told the colonel that Semitsa would be worth about forty thousand pounds to us.'

'Did you?' I said in as flat a monotone as I could manage.

Stok poured out his fruit vodka all round, downed his own and poured himself a replacement.

'It's been nice talking to you boys,' I said. 'I only wish you had something I could buy.'

'I understand you, Mr Dorf,' said Stok. 'In my country we have a saying, " a man who trades a horse for a promise ends up with tired feet".' He walked across to the eighteenth-century mahogany bureau.

I said, 'I don't want you to deviate from a course of loyalty and integrity to the Soviet Government to which I remain a friend and ally.'

Stok turned and smiled at me.

'You think I have live microphones planted here and that I might attempt to trick you.'

'You might,' I said. 'You are in the business.'

'I hope to persuade you otherwise,' said Stok. 'As to being in the business: when does a chef get ptomaine poisoning?'

'When he eats out,' I said.

Stok's laugh made the antique plates rattle. He groped around inside the big writing-desk and produced a flat metal box, brought a vast bunch of tiny keys from his pocket and from inside the box reached a thick black file. He handed it to me. It was typed in Cyrillic capitals and contained photostats and letters and transcripts of tapped phone calls.

Stok reached for another oval cigarette and tapped it unlit against the white page of typing. 'Mr Semitsa's passport westward,' he said putting a sarcastic emphasis on the 'mister'.

'Yes?' I said doubtfully.

Vulkan leaned forward to me. 'Colonel Stok is in charge of an investigation of the Minsk Biochemical labs.'

'Where Semitsa used to be,' I said. It was coming clear to me. 'This is Semitsa's file, then?'

'Yes,' said Stok, 'and everything that I need to get Semitsa a ten-year sentence.'

'Or have him do anything you say,' I said. Perhaps Stok and Vulkan were serious.

A bad bishop is one hampered by
his own pawns.

Berlin, Monday, October 7th

Going along the Unter den Linden wasn't the fastest way of getting to the checkpoint but I had to keep to the main roads in order to find my way about. I saw the 'S' signs on the Schnellstrasse and moved up to the legal 60 k.p.h. As I came level with the old Bismarck Chancellery, black and gutted in the bright velvet moonlight, a red disc was moving laterally across the road ahead. It was a police signal. I stopped. A Volkspolizei troop carrier was parked at the roadside. A young man in uniform tucked the signal baton into the top of his boot, walked slowly across to me and saluted.

'Your papers.'

I gave him the Dorf passport and hoped that the department had gone to the trouble of getting it made up by the Foreign Office and not been content with one of the rough old print jobs that the War Office did for us.

A Skoda passed by at speed without anyone waving it down. I began to feel I was being picked on. Around at the rear of the Taunus another Vopo shone a torch on the U.S. Army plates and probed the beam across the rear seat and floor. My passport was slapped closed and it came through the window accompanied by a neat bow and salute.

'Thank you, sir,' said the young one.

'Can I go?' I said.

'Just switch on your lights, sir.'

'They're on.'

'Main beams must be on here in East Berlin. That is the law.'

'I see.' I flicked the switch on. The troop carrier glowed in the fringe of the beam. It was just a traffic cop doing a job.

'Goodnight, sir.' I saw a movement among the dozen policemen on the big open bus. By now Johnnie Vulkan had also passed me. I turned left on to Friedrichstrasse and tried to catch up with him.

Johnnie Vulkan's Wartburg was some fifty yards ahead of me as I drove south on Friedrichstrasse. As I reached the red-striped barrier the sentry was handing Johnnie his passport and lifting the pole. The American sector was just a few feet away. He allowed the Wartburg through, then lowered the boom and walked round to me, hitching the automatic rifle over his shoulder, so that it clanged against his steel helmet. I had the passport handy. Beyond the barrier the low hardboard building that was the control post was a mass of red geraniums. In front of it two sentries exchanged words with Vulkan then they all laughed. The laughter was loud in the still night. A blue-uniformed Grenzpolizist clattered down the steps and ran across to my car.

'You are wanted inside,' he said to the sentry in his shrill Saxon accent. 'On the phone.' He turned to me. 'Won't keep you a moment, sir,' in English; 'I am sorry for the delay,' but he took the sentry's automatic rifle to hold just the same.

I lit a Gauloise for myself and the Grepo, and we smoked and stared across the hundred yards that separated us from that little walled island that is West Berlin and we thought our different thoughts or maybe the same ones.

It was less than two minutes before the Vopo returned. He said would I please get out of the car and leave the keys where they were. There were three soldiers with him. They all had automatic rifles, none of which were slung on anyone's shoulder. I got out of the car.

They walked me a few yards west on Leipziger where no one in the west sector could see us no matter how high on the ladder they were. There was a small green van parked there. On the door was a little badge and the words 'Traffic Police'. The motor was running. I sat between the German soldiers and one of them offered me a strange-tasting cigarette which I lit from the stub of my Gauloise. No one had searched me, put on handcuffs or made a formal statement. They had merely asked me to come along; no one was using coercion. I had agreed to go.

I watched the street through the rear windows. By the time we reached Alexanderplatz I had a pretty good idea of where we were headed. A couple of blocks away was Keibelstrasse: the Polizei Praesidium.

In the cobbled centre courtyard of the Praesidium I heard the sound of half a dozen marching men. Words of command were shouted and the rhythm of the boots varied. I was in a room on the first floor. It was thirty-three steps above the main entrance, where a guard in an armoured glass cubicle must press a small button to unlock the entrance gate. The aged wooden seat upon which I sat backed up against the cream-painted wall; there were two well-thumbed copies of *Neues Deutschland* lying on it. To my right a large window had the view divided into square spaces by solid-looking bars. Behind the desk was a middle-aged woman, her hair drawn tightly back into a bun. Every action on the desk brought the loud rattle of a large bunch of keys. I knew there must be a way out. None of those young fellows on late-night TV would find it any sort of dilemma.

The grey-haired woman looked up. 'Are you carrying any sort of knife or weapon?' Her eyes glinted clearly behind the thick circular lenses.

'No,' I said.

She nodded and wrote something on a sheet of paper.

'I mustn't be late back,' I said. Which didn't seem so hilarious a thing to say at that time.

The grey-haired woman locked each drawer of her desk and then left the room, carefully fixing the door wide open to preclude my taking a short walk around the filing cabinet. I sat there for five minutes, maybe ten. The whole situation was curiously simple and matter-of-fact, like waiting for a driving-licence renewal at County Hall. When the grey-haired woman came back she had my passport in her hand. She gave it to me. She didn't smile but it seemed friendly just the same.

'Come,' she said.

I went with her down the long cream corridor to a room at the extreme western wing of the building. The décor too was like County Hall. She tapped gently on a large door and without waiting for a reply motioned me through. It was dark inside the room with just enough light filtering through the window from the courtyard to see where the desk was. From behind the desk there was a sudden red glow like an infra-red flash-bulb. As my eyes grew accustomed to the dark I saw that the far side of the room was filled with a silvery sheen.

'Dorf,' said the voice of Stok. It boomed almost like an amplifier. There was a click from his desk; the yellow tungsten light came on. Stok was sitting behind his desk almost obscured by a dense cloud of cigar smoke. There was Scandinavian-style East German furniture in the room. On the table behind me there was a Hohner simple button-key accordion, piles of newspapers, and a chess-board with some of the pieces fallen over. There was a folding bed near the wall with two army blankets on it and high leather boots placed together at the head. Near the door was a tiny sink and a cupboard that might have held clothes.

'My dear Dorf,' said Stok. 'Have I caused you great inconvenience?'

He emerged from the cigar smoke in an ankle-length black leather overcoat.

'Not unless you count being scared half to death,' I said.

'Ha ha ha,' said Stok, then he exhaled another great billow of cigar smoke like a 4.6.2 pulling out of King's Cross.

'I wanted to contact you,' he spoke with the cigar held between tight lips, 'without Vulkan.'

'Another time,' I said, 'write.'

There was another tap at the door. Stok moved across the room like a wounded crow. The grey-haired one brought two lemon teas.

'There is no milk today I am afraid,' said Stok; he drew the overcoat around him.

'And so Russian tea was invented,' I said.

Stok laughed again in a perfunctory sort of way. I drank the scalding hot tea. It made me feel better, like digging your finger nails into your palm does.

'What is it?' I said.

Stok waited while the grey-haired one closed the door behind her. Then he said, 'Let's stop quarrelling, shall we?'

'You mean personally?' I said. 'Or are you speaking on behalf of the Soviet Union?'

'I mean it,' said Stok. 'We can do far better for ourselves if we cooperate than if we obstruct each other.' Stok paused and smiled with studied charm.

'This scientist Semitsa is not important to the Soviet Union. We have other younger men with newer and better ideas. Your people on the other hand will think you marvellous if you can deliver him to London.' Stok shrugged his shoulders at the idiocy of the world of politics.

'Caveat emptor?' I said.

'Not half,' said Stok in a skilful piece of idiom. 'Buyer watch out.' Stok rolled the cigar across his mouth and said, 'Buyer watch out,' a couple of times. I just drank the lemon tea and said nothing. Stok ambled across to the chess-board on the side-table, his leather coat creaking like a windjammer.

'Are you a chess player, English?' he said.

'I prefer games where there's a better chance to cheat,' I said.

'I agree with you,' said Stok. 'The preoccupation with rules doesn't sit well upon the creative mind.'

'Like communism?' I said.

Stok picked up a knight. 'But the pattern of chess is the pattern of your capitalist world. The world of bishops and castles, and kings and knights.'

'Don't look at me,' I said. 'I'm just a pawn. I'm here in the front rank.' Stok grinned and looked down at the board.

'I'm a good player,' he said. 'Your friend Vulkan is one of the few men in Berlin who can consistently beat me.'

'That's because he is part of the pattern of our capitalist world.'

'The pattern,' said Stok, 'has been revised. The knight is the most important piece on the board. Queens have been made . . . impotent. Can you say impotent of a queen?.

'On this side of the wall *you* can say what you like,' I said.

Stok nodded. 'The knights – the generals – run your western world. General Walker of the 24th Infantry Division lectured all his troops that the President of the U.S.A. was a communist.'

'You don't agree?' I asked.

'You are a fool,' boomed Stok in his Boris Godunov voice.

'I am trying to tell you that these people . . .' He waved the knight in my face. '. . . look after themselves.'

'And you are jealous?' I asked seriously.

'Perhaps I am,' said Stok. 'Perhaps that's it.' He put the knight back and he pulled the skirt of his overcoat together.

'So you are going to sell me Semitsa as a little bit of private enterprise of your own?' I said. 'If you'll forgive the workings of my bourgeois mind.'

'You live only once,' said Stok.

'I can make once do,' I said.

Stok heaped four spoonfuls of coarse sugar into his tea. He stirred it as though he was putting an extra rod into an atomic pile. 'All I want is to live the rest of my life in peace and quiet – I do not need a lot of money, just enough to buy a little tobacco and the simple peasant food that I was brought up on. I am a colonel and my conditions are excellent but I am a realist; this cannot last. Younger men in our security service look at my job with envy.' He looked at me and I nodded gently. 'With envy,' he repeated.

'You are in a key job,' I said.

'But the trouble with such jobs is that many others want them too. Some of my staff here are men with fine college diplomas, their minds are quick as mine once was; and they have the energy to work through the day and through the night too as once I had the energy to do.' He shrugged. 'This is why I decided to come to live the rest of my life in your world.'

He got up and opened one of the big wooden shutters. From the courtyard there was the beat of a heavy diesel engine and the sound of boots climbing over a tailboard. Stok thrust his hands deep in his overcoat pockets and flapped his wings.

I said, 'What about your wife and family, will you be able to persuade them?'

Stok continued to look down into the courtyard. 'My wife died in a

German air raid in 1941, my only son hasn't written to me for three and a half years. What would you do in my position, Mr Dorf? What would you do?'

I let the sound of the lorry rumble away down Keibelstrasse.

I said, 'I'd stop telling lies to old liars for a start, Stok. Do you really think I came here without dusting off your file? My newest assistant is trained better than you seem to think I am. I know everything about you from the cubic capacity of your Westinghouse refrigerator to the size your mistress takes in diaphragms.'

Stok picked up his tea and began to batter the lemon segment with the bowl of his spoon. He said, 'You've trained well.'

'Train hard, fight easy,' I said.

'You quote Marshal Suvarov.' He walked across to the chess-board and stared at it. 'In Russia we have a proverb, "Better a clever lie than the foolish truth".' He waved his teaspoon at me.

'There was nothing clever about that clumsy piece of wife-murder.'

'You're right,' said Stok cheerfully. 'You shall be my friend, English. We must trust each other.' He put his tea down on the desk top.

'I'll never need an enemy,' I said.

Stok smiled. It was like arguing with a speak-your-weight machine.

'Truthfully, English,' he said, 'I do not want to defect to the West but the offer of Semitsa is a genuine one.' He sucked the spoon.

'For money?' I asked.

'Yes,' said Stok. He tapped the fleshy palm of his left hand with the bowl of the spoon.

'Money here.' He closed his hand like a vault.

A CURIOUS EXPERIENCE

MARK TWAIN

A CURIOUS EXPERIENCE

This is the story which the Major told me, as nearly as I can recall it:

In the winter of 1862–3, I was commandant of Fort Trumbull, at New London, Conn. Maybe our life there was not so brisk as life at 'the front'; still it was brisk enough, in its way – one's brains didn't cake together there for lack of something to keep them stirring. For one thing, all the Northern atmosphere at that time was thick with mysterious rumours – rumours to the effect that rebel spies were flitting everywhere, and getting ready to blow up our Northern forts, burn our hotels, send infected clothing into our towns, and all that sort of thing. You remember it. All this had a tendency to keep us awake, and knock the traditional dullness out of a garrison life. Besides, ours was a recruiting station – which is the same as saying we hadn't any time to waste in dozing, or dreaming, or fooling around. Why, with all our watchfulness, fifty per cent of a day's recruits would leak out of our hands and give us the slip the same night. The bounties were so prodigious that a recruit could pay a sentinel three or four hundred dollars to let him escape, and still have enough of his bounty-money left to constitute a fortune for a poor man. Yes, as I said before, our life was not drowsy. Well, one day I was in my quarters alone, doing some writing, when a pale and ragged lad of fourteen or fifteen entered made a neat bow, and said:

'I believe recruits are received here?'

'Yes.'

'Will you please enlist me, sir?'

'Dear me no! You are too young, my boy, and too small.'

A disappointed look came into his face, and quickly deepened into an expression of despondency. He turned slowly away, as if to go; hesitated, then faced again, and said, in a tone which went to my heart:

'I have no home, and not a friend in the world. If you *could* only enlist me!'

But of course the thing was out of the question, and I said so as gently as I could. Then I told him to sit down by the stove and warm himself, and added:

'You shall have something to eat presently. You are hungry?'

He did not answer; he did not need to; the gratitude in his big soft eyes was more eloquent than any words could have been. He sat down by the stove, and I went on writing. Occasionally I took a furtive glance at him. I noticed that his clothes and shoes, although soiled and damaged, were of good style and material. This fact was suggestive. To it I added the facts that his voice was low and musical; his eyes deep and melancholy; his carriage and address gentlemanly; evidently the poor chap was in trouble. As a result, I was interested.

However, I became absorbed in my work by and by, and forgot all about the boy. I don't know how long this lasted; but, at length, I happened to look up. The boy's back was towards me, but his face was turned in such a way that I could see one of his cheeks – and down that cheek a rill of noiseless tears was flowing.

'God bless my soul!' I said to myself; 'I forgot the poor rat was starving.' Then I made amends for my brutality by saying to him, 'Come along, my lad; you shall dine with *me*; I am alone today.'

He gave me another of those grateful looks, and a happy light broke in his face. At the table he stood with his hand on his chair-back until I was seated, then seated himself. I took up my knife and fork and – well, I simply held them, and kept still; for the boy had inclined his head and was saying a silent grace. A thousand hallowed memories of home and my childhood poured in upon me, and I sighed to think how far I had drifted from religion and its balm for hurt minds, its comfort and solace and support.

As our meal progressed I observed that young Wicklow – Robert Wicklow was his full name – knew what to do with his napkin; and – well, in a word, I observed that he was a boy of good breeding; never mind the details. He had a simple frankness, too, which won upon me. We talked mainly about himself, and I had no difficulty in getting his history out of him. When he spoke of his having been born and reared in Louisiana, I warmed to him decidedly, for I had spent some time down there. I knew all the 'coast' region of the Mississippi, and loved it, and had not been long enough away from it for my interest in it to begin to pale. The very names that fell from his lips sounded good to me – so good that I steered the talk in directions that would bring them out. Baton Rouge, Plaquemine, Donaldsonville, Sixty-mile Point, Bonnet-Carre, the Stock-Landing, Carrollton, the Steamship Landing, the Steamboat Landing, New Orleans, Tchoupitoulas Street, the Esplanade, the Rue des Bons Enfants, the St Charles Hotel, the Tivoli Circle, the Shell Road, Lake Pontchartrain; and it was particularly delightful to me to hear once more of the '*R.E. Lee*', the '*Natchez*', the '*Eclipse*', the '*General Quitman*', the '*Duncan F. Kenner*', and other old familiar steamboats. It was almost as good as being back there, these names so vividly reproduced in my mind the look of the things they stood for. Briefly, this was little Wicklow's history:

When the war broke out, he and his invalid aunt and his father were living near Baton Rouge, on a great and rich plantation which had been in the family for fifty years. The father was a Union man. He was persecuted in all sorts of ways, but clung to his principles. At last, one night, masked men burned his mansion down, and the family had to fly for their lives. They were hunted from place to place, and learned all there was to know about poverty, hunger and, distress. The invalid aunt found relief at last: misery and exposure killed her; she died in an open field, like a tramp, the rain beating upon her and the thunder booming overhead. Not long afterwards the father was captured by an armed band; and while the son begged and pleaded, the victim was strung up before his face. (At this point a baleful light shone in the youth's eyes, and he said, with the manner of one who talks to himself: 'If I cannot be enlisted, no matter – I shall find a way – I shall find a way.') As soon as the father was pronounced dead the son was told that if he was not out of that region within twenty-four hours it would go hard with him. That night he crept to the riverside and hid himself near plantation landing. By and by the *'Duncan F. Kenner'* stopped there, and he swam out and concealed himself in the yawl that was dragging at her stern. Before daylight the boat reached the Stock-Landing, and he slipped ashore. He walked the three miles which lay between that point and the house of an uncle of his in Good-Children Street, in New Orleans, and then his troubles were over for the time being. But this uncle was a Union man too, and before very long he concluded that he had better leave the South. So he and young Wicklow slipped out of the country on board a sailing vessel, and in due time reached New York. They put up at the Astor House. Young Wicklow had a good time of it for a while, strolling up and down Broadway, and observing the strange Northern sights; but in the end a change came – and not for the better. The uncle had been cheerful at first, but now he began to look troubled and despondent; moreover, he became moody and irritable; talked of money giving out, and no way to get more – 'not enough left for one, let alone two.' Then, one morning, he was missing – did not come to breakfast. The boy inquired at the office, and was told that the uncle had paid his bill the night before and gone away – to Boston, the clerk believed, but was not certain.

The lad was alone and friendless. He did not know what to do, but concluded he had better try to follow and find his uncle. He went down to the steamboat landing; learned that the trifle of money in his pocket would not carry him to Boston; however, it would carry him to New

London; so he took passage for that port, resolving to trust to Providence to furnish him means to travel the rest of the way. He had now been wandering about the streets of New London three days and nights, getting a bite and a nap here and there for charity's sake. But he had given up at last; courage and hope were both gone. If he could enlist, nobody could be more thankful; if he could not get in as a soldier, couldn't he be a drummer-boy? Ah, he would work *so* hard to please, and would be so grateful!

Well, there's the history of young Wicklow, just as he told it to me, barring details. I said:

'My boy, you're among friends now – don't you be troubled any more.' How his eyes glistened! I called in Sergeant John Rayburn – he was from Hartford; lives in Hartford yet; maybe you know him – and said, 'Rayburn, quarter this boy with the musicians. I am going to enrol him as a drummer-boy, and I want you to look after him and see that he is well treated.'

Well, of course, intercourse between the commandant of the post and the drummer-boy came to an end, now; but the poor little friendless chap lay heavy on my heart, just the same. I kept on the look-out, hoping to see him brighten up and begin to be cheery and gay; but no, the days went by, and there was no change. He associated with nobody; he was always absent-minded, always thinking; his face was always sad. One morning Rayburn asked leave to speak to me privately. Said he:

'I hope I don't offend, sir; but the truth is, the musicians are in such a sweat it seems as if somebody's *got* to speak.'

'Why, what's the trouble?'

'It's the Wicklow boy, sir. The musicians are down on him to an extent you can't imagine.'

'Well, go on, go on. What has he been doing?'

'Prayin', sir.'

'Praying!'

'Yes, sir; the musicians haven't any peace of their life for that boy's prayin'. First thing in the morning he's at it; noons he's at it; and nights – well, *nights* he just lays into 'em like all possessed! Sleep! Bless you, they *can't* sleep: he's got the floor, as the sayin' is, and then when he once gets his supplication-mill agoin', there just simply ain't any let-up to him. He starts in with the bandmaster, and he prays for him; next he takes the head bugler, and he prays for him; next the bass drum, and he scoops *him* in; and so on right straight through the band, givin' them all a show, and takin' that amount of interest in it which would make you think he thought he warn't but a little while for this world, and believed he couldn't be happy in heaven without he had a brass band along, and wanted to pick 'em out for himself, so he could depend on 'em to do up the national tunes in a style suitin' to the place. Well sir, heavin' boots at him don't have no effect; it's dark in there; and, besides, he don't pray fair, anyway, but kneels down behind the big drum; so it don't make no difference if they *rain* boots at him, *he* don't give a dern – warbles right along, same as if it was applause. They sing out, 'Oh, dry up!' 'Give us a rest!' 'Shoot him!' 'Oh, take a walk!' and all sorts of such things. But what of it? It don't phaze him. *He* don't mind it.' After a pause: 'Kind of a good little fool, too; gits up in the mornin' and carts all that stock of boots back, and sorts 'em out and sets each man's pair where they belong. And they've been throwed at him so much now, that he knows every boot in the band – can sort'em out with his eyes shut.'

After another pause, which I forebore to interrupt—

'But the roughest thing about it is, that when he's done prayin' – when he ever *does* get done – he pipes up and begins to *sing*. Well, you know what a honey kind of a voice he's got when he talks; you know how it would persuade a cast-iron dog to come down off a doorstep and lick his hand. Now if you'll take my word for it, sir, it ain't a circumstance to his singin'. Flute music is harsh to that boy's singin'. Oh, he just gurgles it out so soft and sweet and low, there in the dark, that it makes you think you are in heaven.'

'What is there "rough" about that?'

'Ah, that's just it sir. You hear him sing

"Just as I am – poor, wretched, blind,"

– just you hear him sing that, once, and see if you don't melt all up and the water comes into your eyes! I don't care *what* he sings, it goes plumb straight home to you – goes deep down to where you *live* – and it fetches you every time! Just you hear him sing

"Child of sin and sorrow, filled with dismay,
Wait not till tomorrow, yield thee today;
Grieve not that love
Which, from above"

and so on. It makes a body feel like the wickedest, ungratefulest brute that walks. And when he sings them songs of his about home, and mother, and childhood, and old memories, and things that's vanished, and old friends dead and gone, it fetches everything before your face that you've ever loved and lost in all your life – and it's just beautiful, it's just divine to listen to, sir – but, Lord, Lord, the heartbreak of it! The band – well, they all cry – every rascal of them blubbers, and don't try to hide it, either; and first you know, that very gang that's been slammin' boots at that boy will skip out of their bunks all of a sudden, and rush over in the dark and hug him! Yes, they do – and slobber all over him, and call him pet names, and beg him to forgive them. And just at that time, if a regiment was to offer to hurt a hair of that cub's head, they'd go for that regiment, if it was a whole army corps!'

Another pause.

'Is that all?' said I.

'Yes sir.'

'Well, dear me, what is the complaint? What do they want done?'

'Done? Why bless you sir, they want you to stop him from *singing*.'

'What an idea! You said his music was divine.'

'That's just it. It's *too* divine. Mortal man can't stand it. It stirs a body up so; it turns a body inside out; it racks his feelin's all to rags; it makes him feel bad and wicked, and not fit for any place but perdition. It keeps a body in such an everlastin' state of repentin' that nothin' don't taste good and there ain't no comfort in life. And then the *cryin'*, you see – every mornin' they are ashamed to look one another in the face.'

'Well, this is an odd case, and a singular complaint. So they really want the singing stopped?'

'Yes, sir, that is the idea. They don't wish to ask too much; they would like powerful well to have the prayin' shut down on, or leastways trimmed off around the edges; but the main thing's the singin'. If they can only get the singin' choked off, they think they can stand the prayin', rough as it is to be bullyragged so much that way.'

I told the Sergeant I would take the matter under consideration. That night I crept into the musicians' quarters and listened. The Sergeant had not overstated the case. I heard the praying voice pleading in the dark; I heard the execrations of the harassed men; I heard the rain of boots whiz through the air, and bang and thump around the big drum. The thing touched me, but it amused me, too, By and by, after an impressive silence, came the singing. Lord, the pathos of it, the enchantment of it! Nothing in the world was ever so sweet, so gracious, so tender, so holy, so moving. I made my stay very brief; I was beginning to experience emotions of a sort not proper to the commandant of a fortress.

Next day I issued orders which stopped the praying and singing. Then followed three or four days which were so full of bounty-jumping excitements and irritations that I never once thought of my drummer-boy. But now comes Sergeant Rayburn, one morning, and says:

'That new boy acts mighty strange, sir.'

'How?'

'Well, sir, he's all the time writing.'

'Writing? What does he write – letters?'

'I don't know, sir; but whenever he's off duty, he is always poking and nosing around the fort, all by himself – blest if I think there's a hole or corner in it he hasn't been into – and every little while he outs with pencil and paper and scribbles something down.'

This gave me a most unpleasant sensation. I wanted to scoff at it, but it was not a time to scoff at *anything* that had the least suspicious tinge about it. Things were happening all around us, in the North, then, that warned us to be always on the alert, and always suspecting. I recalled to mind the suggestive fact that this boy was from the South – the extreme South, Louisiana – and the thought was not of a reassuring nature, under the circumstances. Nevertheless, it cost me a pang to give the orders which I now gave to Rayburn. I felt like a father who plots to expose his own child to shame and injury. I told Rayburn to keep quiet, bide his time, and get me some of those writings whenever he could manage it without the boy's finding it out. And I charged him not to do anything which might let the boy discover that he was being watched. I also ordered that he allow the lad his usual liberties, but that he be followed at a distance when he went out into the town.

During the next two days, Rayburn reported to me several times. No success. The boy was still writing, but he always pocketed his paper with a careless air whenever Rayburn appeared in his vicinity. He had gone twice to an old deserted stable in the town, remained a minute or two, and come out again. One could not pooh-pooh these things – they had an evil look. I was obliged to confess to myself that I was getting uneasy. I went into my private quarters and sent for my second in command – an officer of intelligence and judgement, son of General James Watson Webb. He was surprised and troubled. We had a long talk over the matter, and came to the conclusion that it would be worth while to institute a secret search. I determined to take charge of that myself. So I had myself called at two in the morning; and, pretty soon after, I was in the musicians's quarters, crawling along the floor on my stomach among the snorers. I reached my slumbering waif's bunk at last, without disturbing anybody, captured his clothes and kit, and crawled stealthily back again. When I got to my own quarters, I found Webb there, waiting and eager to know the result. We made search immediately. The clothes were a disappointment. In the pockets we found blank paper and a pencil; nothing else, except a jackknife and such queer odds and ends and useless trifles as boys hoard and value. We turned to the kit hopefully. Nothing there but a rebuke for us! – a little Bible with this written on the fly-leaf: 'Stranger, be kind to my boy, for his mother's sake.'

I looked at Webb – he dropped his eyes; he looked at me – I dropped mine. Neither spoke. I put the book reverently back in its place. Presently Webb got up and went away, without remark. After a little I nerved myself up to my unpalatable job, and took the plunder back to where it belonged, crawling on my stomach as before. It seemed the peculiarly appropriate attitude for the business I was in. I was most honestly glad when it was over and done with.

About noon next day when Rayburn came, as usual, to report, I cut him short. I said:

'Let his nonsense be dropped. We are making a bugaboo out of a poor little cub who has got no more harm in him than a hymn-book.'

The Sergeant looked surprised and said:

'Well, you know it was your orders, sir, and I've got some of the writing.'

'And what does it amount to? How did you get it?'

'I peeped through the key-hole, and see him writing. So when I judged he was about done, I made a sort of a little cough, and I see him crumple it up and throw it in the fire, and look all around to see if anybody was coming. Then he settled back as comfortable and careless as anything. Then I comes in, and passes the time of day pleasantly, and sends him on an errand. He never looked uneasy, but went right along. It was a coal-fire and new-built; the writing had gone over behind a chunk, out of sight; but I got it out; there it is; it ain't hardly scorched, you see.'

I glanced at the paper and took in a sentence or two. Then I dismissed the Sergeant and told him to send Webb to me. Here is the paper in full:

Fort Trumbull, the 8th.

'COLONEL, – I was mistaken as to the calibre of the three guns I ended my list with. They are 18-pounders; all the rest of the armament is as I stated. The garrison remains as before reported, except that the two light infantry companies that were to be detached for service at the front are to stay here for the present – can't find out for how long, just now, but will soon. We are satisfied that, all things considered, matters had better be postponed un—'

There it broke off – there is where Rayburn coughed and interrupted the writer. All my affection for the boy, all my respect for him and charity for his forlorn condition, withered in a moment under the blight of this revelation of cold-blooded baseness.

But never mind about that. Here was business – business that required profound and immediate attention, too. Webb and I turned the subject over and over, and examined it all around. Webb said:

'What a pity he was interrupted! Something is going to be postponed until – when? And what *is* the something? Possibly he would have mentioned it, the pious little reptile!'

'Yes,' I said, 'we have missed a trick. And who is '*me*', in the letter? Is it conspirators inside the fort or outside?'

That 'we' was uncomfortably suggestive. However, it was not worth while to be guessing around that, so we proceeded to matters more practical. In the first place, we decided to double the sentries and keep the strictest possible watch. Next, we thought of calling Wicklow in and making him divulge everything; but that did not seem wisest until other methods should fail. We must have some more of the writings; so we began to plan to that end. And now we had an idea: Wicklow never went to the post-office – perhaps the deserted stable was his post-office. We sent for my confidential clerk – a young German named Sterne, who was a sort of natural detective – and told him all about the case and ordered him to go to work on it. Within the hour we got word that Wicklow was writing again. Shortly afterwards, word came that he had asked leave to go out into the town. He was detained awhile, and meantime Sterne hurried off and concealed himself in the stable. By and by he saw Wicklow saunter in, look about him, then hide something under some rubbish in a corner, and take leisurely leave again. Sterne pounced upon the hidden article – a letter – and brought it to us. It had no superscription and no signature. It repeated what we had already read, and then went on to say:

'We think it best to postpone till the two companies are gone. I mean the four inside think so; have not communicated with the others – afraid of attracting attention. I say four because we have lost two; they had hardly enlisted and got inside when they were shipped off to the front. It will be absolutely necessary to have two in their places. The two that went were the brothers from Thirty-mile Point. I have something of the greatest importance to reveal, but must not trust it to this method of communication; will try the other.'

'The little scoundrel!' said Webb; 'who *could* have supposed he was a spy? However, never mind about that; let us add up our particulars, such as they are, and see how the case stands to date. First, we've got a rebel spy in our midst, whom we know; secondly, we've got three more in our midst whom we don't know; thirdly, these spies have been introduced among us through the simple and easy process of enlisting as soldiers in the Union army – and evidently two of them have got sold at it, and been shipped off to the front; fourthly, there are assistant spies 'outside' – number indefinite; fifthly, Wicklow has very important matter which he is afraid to communicate by the 'present method' – 'will try the other'. That is the case, as it now stands. Shall we collar Wicklow and make him confess? Or shall we catch the person who removes the letters from the stable and make *him* tell? Or shall we keep still and find out more?'

We decided upon the last course. We judged that we did not need to proceed to summary measures now, since it was evident that the conspirators were likely to wait till those two light infantry companies were out of the way. We fortified Sterne with pretty ample powers, and told him to use his best endeavours to find out Wicklow's 'other method' of communication. We meant to play a bold game; and to this end we proposed to keep the spies in an unsuspecting state as long as possible. So we ordered Sterne to return to the stable immediately, and, if he found the coast clear, to conceal Wicklow's letter where it was before, and leave it there for the conspirators to get.

The night closed down without further event. It was cold and dark and sleety, with a raw wind blowing; still I turned out of my warm bed several times during the night, and went the rounds in person, to see that all was right and that every sentry was on the alert. I always found them wide awake and watchful; evidently whispers of mysterious dangers had been floating about, and the doubling of the guards had been a kind of endorsement of those rumours. Once, towards morning, I encountered Webb, breasting his way against the bitter wind, and learned then that he, also, had been the rounds several times to see that all was going right.

Next day's events hurried things somewhat. Wicklow wrote another letter; Sterne preceded him to the stable and saw him deposit it; captured it as soon as Wicklow was out of the way, then slipped out and followed the little spy at a distance, with a detective in plain clothes at his own heels, for we thought it judicious to have the law's assistance handy in case of need. Wicklow went to the railway station, and waited around till the train from New York came in, then stood scanning the faces of the crowd as they poured out of the cars. Presently an aged gentleman, with green goggles and a cane, came limping along, stopped in Wicklow's neighbourhood and began to look about him expectantly. In an instant Wicklow darted forward, thrust an envelope into his hand, then glided away and disappeared in the throng. The next instant Sterne had snatched the letter; and as he hurried past the detective he said: 'Follow the old gentleman – don't lose sight of him.' Then Sterne scurried out with the crowd, and came straight to the fort.

We sat with closed doors, and instructed the guard outside to allow no interruption.

First we opened the letter captured at the stable. It read as follows:

'HOLY ALLIANCE, – Found in the usual gun, commands from the Master, left there last night, which set aside the instructions heretofore received from the subordinate quarter. Have left in the gun the usual indication that the commands reached the proper hand—'

Webb, interrupting: 'Isn't the boy under constant surveillance now?'

I said yes; he had been under strict surveillance ever since the capturing of his former letter.

'Then how could he put anything into a gun, or take anything out of it, and not get caught?'

'Well,' I said, 'I don't like the look of that very well.'

'I don't either,' said Webb. 'It simply means that there are conspirators among the very sentinels. Without their connivance in some way or other, the thing couldn't have been done.'

I sent for Rayburn, and ordered him to examine the batteries and see what he could find. The reading of the letter was then resumed:

'The new commands are peremptory, and require that the MMMM shall be FFFFF at 3 o'clock tomorrow morning. Two hundred will arrive, in small parties, by train and otherwise, from various directions and will be at appointed place at right time. I will distribute the sign today. Success is apparently sure, though something must have got out, for the sentries have been doubled, and the chiefs went the round last night several times. W. W. comes from the southerly today and will receive secret orders – by the other method. All six of you must be in 166 at sharp 2 A.M. You will find B.B. there, who will give you detailed instructions. Password same as last time, only reversed – put first syllable last and last syllable first. Remember XXXX. Do not forget. Be of good heart; before the next sun rises you will be heroes; your fame will be permanent, you will have added a deathless page to history. Amen.'

'Thunder and Mars,' said Webb, 'but we are getting into mighty hot quarters, as I look at it!'

I said there was no question but that things were beginning to wear a most serious aspect. Said I:

'A desperate enterprise is on foot, that is plain enough. Tonight is the time set for it – that, also, is plain. The exact nature of the enterprise – I mean the manner of it – is hidden away under those blind bunches of M's and F's, but the end and aim, I judge, is the surprise and capture of the post. We must move quick and sharp now. I think nothing can be gained by continuing our clandestine policy as regards Wicklow. We *must* know, and as soon as possible, too, where "166" is located, so that we can make a descent upon the gang there at 2 A.M.; and doubtless the quickest way to get that information will be to force it out of that boy. But first of all, and before we make any important move, I must lay the facts before the War Department, and ask for plenary powers.'

The dispatch was prepared in cipher to go over the wires; I read it, approved it, and sent it along.

We presently finished discussing the letter which was under consideration, and then opened the one which had been snatched from the lame gentleman. It contained nothing but a couple of perfectly blank sheets of note-paper! It was a chilly check to our hot eagerness and expectancy. We felt as blank as the paper, for a moment, and twice as foolish. But it was for a moment only; for, of course, we immediately afterwards thought of 'sympathetic ink'. We held the paper close to the fire and watched for the characters to come out, under the influence of the heat; but nothing appeared but some faint tracings, which we could make nothing of. We then called in the surgeon, and sent him off with orders to apply every test he was acquainted with till he got the right one, and report the contents of the letter to me the instant he brought them to the surface. This check was a confounded annoyance, and we naturally chafed under the delay; for we had fully expected to get out of that letter some of the most important secrets of the plot.

Now appeared Sergeant Rayburn, and drew from his pocket a piece of twine string about a foot long, with three knots tied in it, and held it up.

'I got it out of a gun on the water-front,' said he. 'I took the tompions out of all the guns and examined close; this string was the only thing that was in any gun.'

So this bit of string was Wicklow's 'sign' to signify that the 'Master's' commands had not miscarried. I ordered that every sentinel who had served near the gun during the past twenty-four hours be put in confinement at once and separately, and not allowed to communicate with anyone without my privity and consent.

A telegram now came from the Secretary of War. It read as follows:

'Suspend *habeas corpus*. Put town under martial law. Make necessary arrests. Act with vigour and promptness. Keep the Department informed.'

We were now in shape to go to work. I sent out and had the lame gentleman quietly arrested and as quietly brought into the fort; I placed him under guard, and forbade speech to him or from him. He was inclined to bluster at first, but he soon dropped that.

Next came word that Wicklow had been sent to give something to a couple of our new recruits; and that, as soon as his back was turned, these had been seized and confined. Upon each was found a small bit of paper bearing these words and signs in pencil:

EAGLE'S THIRD FLIGHT,
REMEMBER XXXX.
166.

In accordance with instructions, I telegraphed to the Department, in cipher, the progress made, and also described the above ticket. We seemed to be in a strong enough position now to venture to throw off the mask as regarded Wicklow; so I sent for him. I also sent for and received back the letter written in sympathetic ink, the surgeon accompanying it with the information that thus far it had resisted his tests, but that there were others he could apply when I should be ready for him to do so.

Presently Wicklow entered. He had a somewhat worn and anxious look, but he was composed and easy, and if he suspected anything it did not appear in his face or manner. I allowed him to stand there a moment or two, then I said pleasantly:

'My boy, why do you go to that old stable so much?'

He answered, with simple demeanour and without embarrassment:

'Well, I hardly know, sir. There isn't any particular reason, except that I like to be alone, and I amuse myself there.'

'You amuse yourself there, do you?'

'Yes, sir,' he replied, as innocently and simply as before.

'Is that all you do there?'

'Yes, sir,' he said, looking up with childlike wonderment in his big soft eyes.

'You are *sure*?'

'Yes, sir, sure.'

After a pause, I said:

'Wicklow, why do you write so much?'

'I? I do not write much, sir.'

'You don't?'

'No, sir. Oh, if you mean scribbling, I *do* scribble some, for amusement.'

'What do you do with your scribblings?'

'Nothing sir – throw them away.'

'Never send them to anybody?'

'No, sir.'

I suddenly thrust before him the letter to the 'Colonel'. He started slightly, but immediately composed himself. A slight tinge spread itself over his cheek.

'How came you to send *this* piece of scribbling, then?'

'I nev-never meant any harm, sir.'

'Never meant any harm! You betray the armament and condition of the post, and mean no harm by it?'

He hung his head and was silent.

'Come, speak up, and stop lying. Whom was this letter intended for?'

He showed signs of distress now; but quickly collected himself, and replied in a tone of deep earnestness:

'I will tell you the truth, sir – the whole truth. The letter was never intended for anybody at all. I wrote it only to amuse myself. I see the error and foolishness of it now – but it is the only offence, sir, upon my honour.'

'Ah, I am glad of that. It is dangerous to be writing such letters. I hope you are sure this is the only one you wrote?'

'Yes, sir, perfectly sure.'

His hardihood was stupefying. He told that lie with as sincere a countenance as any creature ever wore. I waited a moment to soothe down my rising temper, and then said:

'Wicklow, jog your memory now, and see if you can help me with two or three little matters which I wish to inquire about.'

'I will do my very best, sir.'

'Then, to begin with – who is "the Master"?'

It betrayed him into darting a startled glance at our faces; but that was all. He was serene again in a moment, and tranquilly answered:

'I do not know, sir.'

'You do not know?'

'I do not know.'

'You are *sure* you do not know?'

He tried hard to keep his eyes on mine, but the strain was too great; his chin sunk slowly towards his breast and he was silent; he stood there nervously fumbling with a button, an object to command one's pity, in spite of his base acts. Presently I broke the stillness with the question:

'Who are the "Holy Alliance"?'

His body shook visibly, and he made a slight random gesture with his hands, which to me was like the appeal of a despairing creature for compassion. But he made no sound. He continued to stand with his face bent towards the ground. As we sat gazing at him, waiting for him to speak, we saw the big tears begin to roll down his cheeks. But he ramained silent. After a little, I said:

'You must answer me, my boy, and you must tell me the truth. Who are the Holy Alliance?'

He wept on in silence. Presently I said, somewhat sharply:

'Answer the question!'

He struggled to get command of his voice; and then, looking up appealingly, forced the words out between his sobs:

'Oh, have pity on me, sir! I cannot answer it, for I do not know.'

'What!'

'Indeed, sir, I am telling the truth. I never have heard of the Holy Alliance till this moment. On my honour, sir, this is so.'

'Good heavens! Look at this second letter of yours; there do you see those words, "*Holy Alliance*"? What do you say now?'

He gazed up into my face with the hurt look of one upon whom a great wrong has been wrought, then said feelingly:

'This is some cruel joke, sir; and how could they play it upon me, who have tried all I could to do right, and have never done harm to anybody? Some one has counterfeited my hand; I never wrote a line of this; I have never seen this letter before!'

'Oh, you unspeakable liar! Here, what do you say to *this*?' – and I snatched the sympathetic-ink letter from my pocket and thrust it before his eyes.

His face turned white! – as white as a dead person's. He wavered slightly in his tracks, and put his hand against the wall to steady himself. After a moment he asked in so faint a voice that it was hardly audible:

'Have you – read it?'

Our faces must have answered the truth before my lips could get out the false 'yes', for I distinctly saw the courage come back into that boy's eyes. I waited for him to say something, but he kept silent. So at last I said:

'Well, what have you to say as to the revelations in this letter?'

He answered, with perfect composure:

'Nothing, except that they are entirely harmless and innocent; they can hurt nobody.'

I was in something of a corner now, as I couldn't disprove his assertion. I did not know exactly how to proceed. However, an idea came to my relief, and I said:

'You are sure you know nothing about the Master and the Holy Alliance, and did not write the letter which you say is a forgery?'

'Yes, sir – sure.'

I slowly drew out the knotted twine string and held it up without speaking. He gazed at it indifferently, then looked at me inquiringly. My patience was sorely taxed. However, I kept my temper down, and said in my usual voice:

'Wicklow, do you see this?'

'Yes, sir.'

'What is it?'

'It seems to be a piece of string.'

'*Seems?* It *is* a piece of string. Do you recognize it?'

'No, sir,' he replied, as calmly as the words could be uttered.

His coolness was perfectly wonderful! I paused now for several seconds, in order that the silence might add impressiveness to what I was about to say; then I rose and laid my hand on his shoulder, and said gravely:

'It will do you no good, poor boy, none in the world. This sign to the "Master", this knotted string, found in one of the guns on the water-front—'

'Found *in* the gun! Oh, no, no, no! do not say *in* the gun, but in a crack in the tompion! – it *must* have been in the crack!' and down he went on his knees and clasped his hands and lifted up a face that was pitiful to see, so ashy it was, and so wild with terror.

'No, it was *in* the gun.'

'Oh, something has gone wrong! My God, I am lost!' and he sprang up and darted this way and that, dodging the hands that were put out to catch him, and doing his best to escape from the place. But of course escape was impossible. Then he flung himself on his knees again, crying with all his might, and clasped me around the legs; and so he clung to me and begged and pleaded, saying, 'Oh, have pity on me! Oh, be merciful to me! Do not betray me; they would not spare my life a moment! Protect me, save me. I will confess everything!'

It took us some time to quiet him down and modify his fright, and get him into something like a rational frame of mind. Then I began to question him, he answering humbly, with downcast eyes, and from time to time swabbing away his constantly flowing tears.

'So you are at heart a rebel?'

'Yes, sir.'

'And a spy?'

'Yes, sir.'

'And have been acting under distinct orders from outside?'

'Yes, sir.'

'Willingly?'

'Yes, sir.'

'*Gladly*, perhaps?'

'Yes, sir; it would do no good to deny it. The South is my country; my heart is Southern, and it is all in her cause.'

'Then the tale you told me of your wrongs and the persecution of your family was made up for the occasion?'

'They – they told me to say it sir.'

'And you would betray and destroy those who pitied and sheltered you? Do you comprehend how base you are, you poor misguided thing?'

He replied with sobs only.

'Well, let that pass. To business. Who is the "Colonel", and where is he?'

He began to cry hard, and tried to beg off from answering. He said he would be killed if he told. I threatened to put him in the dark cell and lock him up if he did not come out with the information. At the same time I promised to protect him from all harm if he made a clean breast. For all answer, he closed his mouth firmly and put on a stubborn air, which I could not bring him out of. At last I started with him; but a single glance into the dark cell converted him. He broke into a passion of weeping and supplicating, and declared he would tell everything.

So I brought him back, and he named the 'Colonel', and described him particularly. Said he would be found at the principal hotel in the town, in citizen's dress. I had to threaten him again before he would describe and name the 'Master'. Said the Master would be found at No. 15 Bond Street, New York, passing under the name of R.F. Gaylord. I telegraphed name and description to the chief of police of the metropolis, and asked that Gaylord be arrested and held till I could send for him.

'Now,' said I, 'it seems that there are several of the conspirators "outside", presumably in New London. Name and describe them.'

He named and described three men and two women all stopping at the principal hotel. I sent out quietly, and had them and the 'Colonel' arrested and confined in the fort.

'Next, I want to know all about your three fellow-conspirators who are here in the fort.'

He was about to dodge me with a falsehood, I thought; but I produced the mysterious bits of paper which had been found upon two of them, and this had a salutary effect upon him. I said we had possession of two of the men, and he must point out the third. This frightened him badly, and he cried out:

'Oh, please don't make me; he would kill me on the spot!'

I said that was all nonsense; I would have somebody near by to protect him, and, besides, the men should be assembled without arms. I ordered all the raw recruits to be mustered, and then the poor trembling little wretch went out and stepped along down the line, trying to look as indifferent as possible. Finally he spoke a single word to one of the men, and before he had gone five steps the man was under arrest.

As soon as Wicklow was with us again I had those three men brought in. I made one of them stand forward, and said:

'Now, Wicklow, mind not a shade's divergence from the exact truth. Who is this man, and what do you know about him?'

Being 'in for it', he cast consequences aside, fastened his eyes on the man's face, and spoke straight along without hesitation – to the following effect:

'His real name is George Bristow. He is from New Orleans; was second mate of the coast-packet *Capitol* two years ago; it a desperate character, and has served two terms for manslaughter – one for killing a deckhand named Hyde with a capstan-bar, and one for killing a roustabout for refusing to heave the lead, which is no part of a roustabout's business. He is a spy and was sent here by the Colonel to act in that capacity. He was third mate of the *St. Nicholas* when she blew up in the neighbourhood of Memphis, in '58, and came near being lynched for robbing the dead and wounded while they were being taken ashore in an empty wood-boat.'

And so forth and so on – he gave the man's biography in full. When he had finished I said to the man:

'What have you to say about this?'

'Barring your presence, sir, it is the infernalest lie that ever was spoke!'

I sent him back into confinement, and called the others forward in turn. Same result. The boy gave a detailed history of each, without ever hesitating for a word or a fact; but all I could get out of either rascal was the indignant assertion that it was all a lie. They would confess nothing. I returned them to captivity, and brought out the rest of my prisoners one by one. Wicklow told all about them – what towns in the South they were from, and every detail of their connection with the conspiracy.

But they all denied his facts, and not one of them confessed a thing. The men raged, the women cried. According to their stories, they were all innocent people from out West, and loved the Union above all things in this world. I locked the gang up, in disgust, and fell to catechizing Wicklow once more.

'Where is No. 166, and who is B.B.?'

But *there* he was determined to draw the line. Neither coaxing nor threats had any effect upon him. Time was flying – it was necessary to institute sharp measures. So I tied him up on tiptoe by the thumbs. As the pain increased it wrung screams from him which were almost more than I could bear. But I held my ground, and pretty soon he shrieked out:

'Oh, *please* let me down, and I will tell!'

'No – you'll tell *before* I let you down.'

Every instant was agony to him now, so out it came:

'No. 166, Eagle Hotel!' – naming a wretched tavern down by the water, a resort of common labourers, long-shoremen, and less reputable folk.

So I released him, and then demanded to know the object of the conspiracy.

'To take the fort tonight,' said he, doggedly and sobbing.

'Have I got all the chiefs of the conspiracy?'

'No. You've got all except those that are to meet at 166.'

'What does "remember XXXX" mean?'

No reply.

'What is the password to No. 166?'

No reply.

'What do those bunches of letters mean – "FFFFF" and "MMMM"? Answer! or you will catch it again.'

'I never *will* answer! I will die first. Now do what you please.'

'Think what you are saying, Wicklow. Is it final?'

He answered steadily, and without a quiver in his voice:

'It is final. As sure as I love my wronged country and hate everything this Northern sun shines on I will die before I will reveal those things.'

I triced him up by the thumbs again. When the agony was full upon him, it was heart-breaking to hear the poor thing's shrieks, but we got nothing else out of him. To every question he screamed the same reply: 'I can die, and I *will* die; but I will never tell.'

Well, we had to give it up. We were convinced that he certainly would die rather than confess. So we took him down and imprisoned him, under strict guard.

Then for some hours we busied ourselves with sending telegrams to the War Department, and with making preparations for a descent upon No. 166.

It was stirring times, that black and bitter night. Things had leaked out, and the whole garrison was on the alert. The sentinels were trebled, and nobody could move outside or in, without being brought to a stand with a musket levelled at his head. However, Webb and I were less concerned now than we had previously been, because of the fact that the conspiracy must necessarily be in a pretty crippled condition since so many of its principals were in our clutches.

I determined to be at No. 166 in good season, capture and gag B.B., and be on hand for the rest when they arrived. At about a quarter past one in the morning I crept out of the fortress with half a dozen stalwarts and gamy U.S. regulars at my heels – and the boy Wicklow, with his hands tied behind him. I told him we were going to No. 166, and that if I found he had lied again and was misleading us, he would have to show us the right place or suffer the consequences.

We approached the tavern stealthily and reconnoitered. A light was burning in the small bar-room; the rest of the house was dark. I tried the front door; it yielded, and we softly entered, closing the door behind us. Then we removed our shoes, and I led the way to the bar-room. The German landlord sat there, asleep in his chair. I woke him gently and told him to take off his boots and precede us; warning him at the same time to utter no sound. He obeyed without a murmur, but evidently he was badly frightened. I ordered him to lead the way to 166. We ascended two or three flights of stairs as softly as a file of cats; and then, having arrived near the farther end of a long hall, we came to a door through the glazed transom of which we could discern the glow of a dim light from within. The landlord felt for me in the dark and whispered me that that was 166. I tried the door – it was locked on the inside. I whispered an order to one of my biggest soldiers; we set our ample shoulders to the door and with one heave we burst it from its hinges. I caught a half-glimpse of a figure in a bed – saw its head dart towards the candle; out went the light, and we were in pitch darkness. With one big bound I lit on that bed and pinned its occupant down with my knees. My prisoner struggled fiercely, but I got a grip on his throat with my left hand, and that was a good assistance to my knees in holding him down. Then straightway I snatched out my revolver, cocked it, and laid the cold barrel warningly against his cheek.

'Now somebody strike a light!' said I. 'I've got him safe.'

It was done. The flame of the match burst up. I looked at my captive, and, by George, it was a young woman!

I let go and got off the bed, feeling pretty sheepish. Everybody stared at his neighbour. Nobody had any wit or sense left, so sudden and overwhelming had been the surprise. The young woman began to cry and covered her face with the sheet. The landlord said, meekly:

'My daughter, she has been doing something that is not right, *nicht wahr?*'

'Your daughter? Is she your daughter?'

'Oh, yes, she is my daughter. She is just tonight come home from Cincinnati a little bit sick.'

'Confound it, that boy has lied again. This is not the right 166; this is not B.B. Now, Wicklow, you will find the correct 166 for us, or – hello!

where is that boy?'

Gone, as sure as guns! And, what is more, we failed to find a trace of him. Here was an awkward predicament. I cursed my stupidity in not tying him to one of the men; but it was of no use to bother about that now. What should I do in the present circumstances? – that was the question. That girl *might* be B.B. after all. I did not believe it, but still it would not answer to take unbelief for proof. So I finally put my men in a vacant room across the hall from 166, and told them to capture anybody and everybody that approached the girl's room, and to keep the landlord with them, and under strict watch, until further orders. Then I hurried back to the fort to see if all was right there yet.

Yes, all was right. And all remained right. I stayed up all night to make sure of that. Nothing happened. I was unspeakably glad to see the dawn come again, and be able to telegraph the Department that the Stars and Stripes still floated over Fort Trumbull.

An immense pressure was lifted from my breast. Still I did not relax vigilance, of course, nor effort either; the case was too grave for that. I had up my prisoners, one by one, and harried them by the hour, trying to get them to confess, but it was a failure. They only gnashed their teeth and tore their hair, and revealed nothing.

About noon came tidings of my missing boy. He had been seen on the road, tramping westward, some eight miles out, at six in the morning. I started a cavalry lieutenant and a private on his track at once. They came in sight of him twenty miles out. He had climbed a fence and was wearily dragging himself across a slushy field towards a large old-fashioned mansion on the edge of a village. They rode through a bit of woods, made a detour, and closed up on the house from the opposite side; then dismounted and scurried into the kitchen. Nobody there. They slipped into the next room, which was also unoccupied; the door from that room into the front- or sitting-room was open. They were about to step through it when they heard a low voice; it was somebody praying. So they halted reverently, and the Lieutenant put his head in and saw an old man and an old woman kneeling in a corner of that sitting-room. It was the old man that was praying, and just as he was finishing his prayer, the Wicklow boy opened the front door and stepped in, Both of those old people sprang at him and smothered him with embraces, shouting:

'Our boy! our darling! God be praised. The lost is found! He that was dead is alive again!'

Well, sir, what do you think! That young imp was born and reared on that homestead, and had never been five miles away from it in all his life, till the fortnight before he loafed into my quarters and gulled me with that maudlin yarn of his! It's as true as gospel. That old man was his father – a learned old retired clergyman; and that old lady was his mother.

Let me throw in a word or two of explanation concerning that boy and his performances. It turned out that he was a revenous devourer of dime novels and sensation-story papers – therefore, dark mysteries and gaudy heroisms were just in his line. Then he had read newspaper reports of the stealthy goings and comings of rebel spies in our midst, and of their lurid purposes and their two or three startling achievements, till his imagination was all aflame on that subject. His constant comrade for some months had been a Yankee youth of much tongue and lively fancy, who had served a couple of years as 'mud-clerk' (that is, subordinate purser) on certain of the packet-boats plying between New Orleans and points two or three hundred miles up the Mississippi – hence his easy facility in handling the names and other details pertaining to that region. Now I had spent two or three months in that part of the country before the war; and I knew just enough about it to be easily taken in by that boy, whereas a born Louisianian would probably have caught him tripping before he had talked fifteen minutes. Do you know the reason he said he would rather die than explain certain of his treasonable enigmas? Simply because he *couldn't* explain them! – they had no meaning; he had fired them out of his imagination without forethought or afterthought; and so, upon sudden call, he wasn't able to invent an explanation of them. For instance he couldn't reveal what was hidden in the 'sympathetic ink' letter, for the ample reason that there wasn't anything hidden in it; it was blank paper only. He hadn't put anything into a gun, and had never intended to – for his letters were all written to imaginary persons, and when he hid one in the stable he always removed the one he had put there the day before; so he was not acquainted with the knotted string, since he was seeing it for the first time when I showed it to him; but as soon as I had let him find out where it came from, he straightway adopted it, in his romantic fashion, and got some fine effects out of it. He invented Mr. 'Gaylord'; there wasn't any 15 Bond Street, just then – it had been pulled down three months before. He invented the 'Colonel'; he invented the glib histories of those unfortunates whom I captured and confronted with him; he invented 'B.B.'; he even invented No. 166, one may say, for he didn't know there *was* such a number in the Eagle Hotel until we went there. He stood ready to invent anybody or anything whenever it was wanted. If I called for 'outside' spies, he promptly described strangers whom he had seen at the hotel, and whose names he had happened to hear. Ah, he lived in a gorgeous, mysterious, romantic world during those few stirring days, and I think it was *real* to him, and that he enjoyed it clear down to the bottom of his heart.

But he made trouble enough for us, and just no end of humiliation. You see, on account of him we had fifteen or twenty people under arrest and confinement in the fort, sentinels before their doors. A lot of the captives were soldiers and such, and to them I didn't have to apologise; but the rest were first-class citizens, from all over the country, and no amount of apologies was sufficient to satisfy them. They just fumed and raged, and made no end of trouble. And those two ladies – one was an Ohio Congressman's wife, the other a Western bishop's sister – well, the scorn and ridicule and angry tears they poured out on me made up a keepsake that was likely to make me remember them for a considerable time – and I shall. That old lame gentleman with the goggles was a college president from Philadelphia, who had come up to attend his nephew's funeral. He had never seen young Wicklow before, of course. Well, he not only missed the funeral, and got jailed as a rebel spy, but Wicklow had stood up there in my quarters and coldly described him as a counterfeiter, nigger-trader, horse-thief, and fire-bug from the most notorious rascal-nest in Galveston; and this was a thing which that poor old gentleman couldn't seem to get over at all.

And the War Department! But, O my soul, let's draw the curtain over that part!

NOTE. – I showed my manuscript to the Major, and he said: 'Your unfamiliarity with military matters has betrayed you into some little mistakes. Still they are picturesque ones – let them go; military men will smile at them, the rest won't detect them. You have got the main facts of the history right, and have set them down just about as they occurred. M.T.

THE TRAITOR
OF ARNHEM

Lt.-Col. ORESTE PINTO

THE TRAITOR OF ARNHEM

Lt.-Col. Oreste Pinto was involved in intelligence and counter-intelligence work throughout the Second World War. In 1944, just before the battle of Arnhem, he was working as the head of the Netherlands Counter-Intelligence Mission.

The case I am now going to relate is certainly the most important that I ever experienced and is perhaps one of the most important spy cases in the whole history of espionage.

Let us consider the facts. If Field-Marshal Montgomery's daring bid for a spearhead attack across the Maas and Neder Rijn bridgeheads had succeeded and had the main forces linked up with the gallant paratroopers at Arnhem, a wedge of armour would have been thrust at the heart of Germany. Successful exploitation of the thrust would probably have ended the war in Europe before Christmas, 1944, six months sooner than was in fact the case. It is impossible to measure the saving in the lives of soldiers and civilians which would have resulted from such a shortening of the war. Hundreds of millions of pounds' worth of devastations of land and buildings would have been avoided. The British Government alone was spending some £16,000,000 per day in the war effort at that time. Had the European war been shortened by six months, it would have saved a gigantic sum in the neighbourhood of £2,900,000,000 for the Exchequer. When one considers what other governments, notably the United States, were jointly spending in prosecuting the war, the monies that might have been saved and later devoted to reconstruction for peace would amount to astronomical figures. More important still, had the Western Allies penetrated far into Germany and occupied all of Berlin and West Germany before the Russians arrived from the east, the whole sad story of Allied relations since 1945 might have been far different.

They are good grounds for claiming that the parachute landings at Arnhem, so boldly planned and daringly executed, might have been the turning point of the European war if they had succeeded. They did not succeed, as the whole world knows, but not for want of military skill and courage. In fact Arnhem is a bright flower of the British ability to fight on to the end against overwhelming odds. One man – and one man only – made the Arnhem landings a doomed venture from the start. He was a Dutchman named Christian Lindemans. Whether or not we can blame him for causing a six-months' prolongation of the European war with all its attendant sacrifices and tragedies, we can certainly charge him with the 7,000 casualties suffered by the gallant airborne forces during the ten days in which the trap they had dropped into slowly closed its jaws on them. Few spies turned traitors could claim responsibility for dealing such damage at one blow to their country's cause.

My job as head of the Netherlands Counter-Intelligence Mission attached to S.H.A.E.F. gave me the responsibility of organising in the area allotted to me the security arrangements behind the armies advancing through Flanders into Holland. This group of armies consisted of the British Second Army, the United States First and Third Armies and the Canadian First Army, a massive body of men and machines. As the tanks, the self-propelled guns and the infantry rolled forward, inevitably they left a trail of devastation and ruin behind them. Inevitably, many of the unfortunate civilians who lived in the path of the advancing armies were rendered homeless by shelling and bombing, particularly in those areas where the retreating Germans fought savage rearguard actions. Civil control was almost non-existent, since many members of the police forces and local authorities who had acted during the German occupation were either discredited or in hiding. Looting, famine, revolt were the grisly camp followers of the war. The Germans had not been slow to exploit these circumstances and had left behind them spies and saboteurs to continue the war from the rear of the Allied lines. Everything was in confusion and many civilians were making the most of their opportunity to pay off old scores and to indulge their wants free from police control.

Law and order had to be established promptly. Nothing would have pleased the German forces more than to cause Allied front-line troops to be taken out of the line for the task of restoring security in the rear areas. The methods we adopted therefore were rough and ready but at least effective. Big camps were set up by taking an open space and enclosing it in a solid ring of barbed wire. Machine-guns were erected around the perimeter and sighted to fire both inwards and outwards. Guards patrolled the wire and the one or two gates allowing entry or exit were manned continuously by sentries. All the homeless, the refugees, the suspected collaborators and spies were put into these camps and then gradually sorted out. As soon as the honest citizens could establish their innocence they were removed to more congenial quarters. Gradually, through this constant filtering, only the 'dregs' were left and they were interrogated, tried and punished according to their deserts. The method involved depriving the innocent of their liberty for several days, but in war unfortunately the guiltless often have to suffer for the good of the greater cause. We could not afford to make mistakes that might have seriously impeded the advance of the Allied Armies.

After Antwerp had been liberated, I had arranged for one of these large security camps to be erected in the neighbourhood. I happened to be passing near the main gate one day when I heard a commotion and went over to see what was happening. It was a surprising sight. Towering over the sentry on duty was a giant of a man. Well over six feet in height he was disproportionately broad, with a massive chest that strained and threatened to split his khaki shirt. His biceps bulging against the sleeves of his jacket seemed to be as big as an athlete's thigh. He must have weighed nearly eighteen stone but he was hard and solid all over, like a great monolith of a man. As if his physical appearance were not enough to make him stand out from the crowd, he was like a miniature mobile arsenal in the weapons he carried. In his leather belt were stuck two dark steel knives. A long-barrelled Luger pistol with marksman's sights graduated to one thousand metres was strapped to his right hip. A Schmeisser sub-machine-gun was slung across his huge chest and looked almost as innocuous as a water-pistol in contrast. His pockets had a sinister bulge that to my eye spelled out the presence of hand grenades.

This giant apparition had a smiling girl on each arm and was surrounded by a gaggle of admiring Dutch youths, obviously hero-worshipping him. The sentry who was barring his way was embarrassed and hesitant. As I approached the group from behind, I heard the giant rumble in a deep voice, '*Ach*, these two girls are good Dutch patriots. Tell your colonel that the great King Kong has vouched for them. They are to be released at once to drink wine with me.'

I had of course heard of this 'King Kong', the daring leader of the Dutch Resistance Forces who had been given the nickname for obvious reasons. His was a revered name in Occupied Europe for his brute strength, his fearlessness and the brilliant *coups* he had engineered against the Germans. But he had no right to come swaggering into the camp, to pick up a couple of girls and remove them before they had been screened by the proper authorities. Let him by all means be a hero in his own sphere but here he was trespassing.

I shouted out to him, 'Come here – you.'

He turned round, blinked and shrugged off the girls. He tapped his mighty chest with a forefinger that seemed to be as thick as my wrist. 'Were you talking to me?'

'Yes, you. Come here.'

He hesitated and then swaggered over to me, towering inches above me although I am of average height. Before he had a chance to speak I touched the three gold stars he wore on his sleeve.

'By what right do you wear those? Are you a captain and, if so, in what army?'

He expelled his breath in a growl. 'Now see here, I wear these three stars by authority of the Dutch Interior Forces – the Underground!'

'Really? And who are you?' I asked with mock naïveté.

'Me?' He was astounded that anyone could be so ignorant. He turned round to his loyal supporters and shrugged in dumb show as if to say that here was the eighth wonder of the world – a man who could not recognise the great 'King Kong' at first sight. 'Who am I? Why, Colonel, everyone knows who I am.' His voice bellowed out. 'I live at Castle Wittouck, headquarters of the Dutch Resistance.' He paused and swelled his mighty chest until I expected the buttons to burst off his shirt. 'I – I am King Kong!'

'The only King Kong I ever heard of,' I replied softly, 'was a big stuffed monkey.'

There was a titter from the sycophants behind him. He clenched his teeth and his fists so that for a moment he did actually resemble his cinematic namesake. My hand slid unobtrusively towards the Walthur automatic pistol I always carried in my shoulder-holster. If he managed to grasp me in those gigantic fists I realised he could break me in two as easily as one snaps a dry stick. But he merely glowered at me without making a move.

Sensing my advantage, I pressed on. 'As you do not hold the rank of captain in the Netherlands Army, you are not entitled to wear the insignia,' I said. I reached out and ripped off the cloth band with the three gold stars which he wore on his sleeve.

His Neanderthal jaw sagged and he changed colour. By now my hand was hovering over the pistol butt in case he attacked me in a sudden frenzy of wounded pride. But he stepped backwards instead of forwards. For a second the great King Kong looked sheepish, like a truant schoolboy. Then mustering his self-respect he shouted, 'I shall make a formal complaint of your treatment at Castle Wittouck without delay.' He strode away, leaving the two girls and his crowd of admirers gaping at his sudden departure.

So that was my first meeting with King Kong. In the ordinary way I should have been glad to greet him and pay my respects to the great resistance leader, the 'Scarlet Pimpernel' of Holland who had saved from the Gestapo dozens of refugees and Allied airmen shot down over Occupied Holland by conducting them along the secret escape-routes, who had fought daring skirmishes with the Nazi Sicherheitsdienst, the dreaded S.D. Security Police, and who had thumbed his nose at their efforts to trap him. Had he followed the formal courtesies of applying for permission to enter the camp, I should have welcomed him warmly and would have opened a bottle of wine in his honour at the mess. But as chief security officer of the camp, I was not prepared to have my authority flouted and a bad example given to the inmates and guards by allowing a civilian, however well-earned his fame, to break all the rules of military etiquette and ride roughshod over the regulations.

Musing on the encounter afterwards, I wondered whether I had perhaps treated my unexpected visitor too summarily. To deflate his arrogance so publicly might be an unwarranted piece of over-officiousness. He had behaved badly in the first place but possibly through sheer ignorance of military custom. Had I perhaps acted equally badly, if not worse, in treating him with undue severity?

And then a strange idea occurred to me, one of those flashes of intuition which often produce an unexpected train of thought. Why had he submitted so meekly to my brusque treatment? Any man with his outstanding record, even when consciously in the wrong, should surely have stood his ground and defended himself, especially when surrounded by hero-worshippers. Yet King Kong had suffered public humiliation without any more effective reply than a blustering threat and had retreated hastily at the earliest opportunity. Such conduct did not seem typical of the man and his reputation. Perhaps it needed investigating.

On my return to Intelligence Headquarters at S.H.A.E.F., I sent for my assistant. He was a remarkable fellow whose varied career had included being a sergeant in the French Foreign Legion and also a spy in Tangiers. He possessed an encyclopaedic memory which was the repository of odd facts and bits of information about the underground movements throughout Europe and the spies who worked on both sides of the 'fence'.

'Tell me, Wilhelm,' I asked, 'what do we know about the resistance leader nicknamed King Kong?'

He paused for a moment, screwed up his face in concentration and then rattled off the facts. 'Real name Christian Lindemans. Born in Rotterdam, the son of a garage owner. Ex-boxer and wrestler. Reported to have killed several men in tavern brawls. Dozens of girls listed as his intimate friends.' He grinned slyly.

'Would you like their names?'

I shook my head. 'Anything else?'

'Yes, sir. He's the eldest of four brothers – all Resistance men working on the escape-line.'

'Any been killed?' I asked.

Wilhelm's memory failed him for a moment. He went over to a filing cabinet and, riffling through the files, selected one. He turned over the sheets and then paused. 'No, none of them have been killed. One, the youngest brother, was captured by the Abwehr and so was a cabaret dancer named Veronica, who was a strong friend of Lindemans. They were both working on the escape-line.' He ran a finger down the typed page. 'Both were later released.'

'They were *what?*'

He shrugged his shoulders. 'That's what it says here – they were both released. Seems odd for the German Intelligence to release its prisoners, doesn't it? – but that's what the report says.'

'Anything else?' I asked. The tension in me was growing, and suspicions, from being a vague uneasiness, were beginning to crystalise.

'Yes, sir. Lindemans himself was captured by the Gestapo in a raid a few weeks later. He was shot through the lung, I see. His own Resistance group rescued him from prison hospital after a running gunfight.'

'Many killed?'

'Yes – one S.S. guard killed, two wouned. The Resistance men came off worse, though. Lindemans got away with three of them but the other forty-seven were all killed. Ambushed as they withdrew from the hospital.'

'Almost as if the Germans had known beforehand,' I said slowly.

Wilhelm stared at me, his eyes narrowed. He could guess the ideas passing through my mind. Then he nodded but said nothing.

'I'll borrow that dossier for two or three days,' I said, reaching out for the file that lay on the table between us. 'With any luck I may be able to add a page or two to it. I'll leave for Brussels in the morning.'

Once in Brussels, I found the problem was not so much locating men and women who had known Lindemans intimately but fobbing off the dozens who claimed intimate knowledge of him. A national hero in his native Holland, he was also a popular figure in Belgium and there were many who wished to bask in his reflected glory by posing as his closest friend. I could fill the pages of another book with the various stories, some with a germ of truth but mostly the wildest fiction, of his exploits which were told me by those who claimed his acquaintance. I was not looking for people who had once passed the time of day with King Kong and thereafter looked on themselves as his most trusted comrades-in-arms. I wanted men who had actually worked in the resistance with him and who could build up or refute the theory that was forming in my mind.

After a while I came on the track of one such man and arranged an appointment with him in the Café des Vedettes. We chatted amiably and before long I realised from his remarks that he really did know Lindemans and had worked with him.

'Were you one of the lucky ones who got away from that hospital raid?' I asked.

'No, unfortunately I missed that party. I got this little *souvenir de la guerre* about a month afterwards.' He pulled off his greasy black beret and proudly pointed to a bullet scar that ploughed a neat furrow across his scalp.

'A near thing,' I remarked.

He grinned. 'Yes, sir, quite close enough for my health's sake. I would have been most upset if it had arrived an inch or so lower.'

'How did it happen?'

'Well, sir, we were dynamiting a bridge. I was just bending down, fixing the fuses to the charges under the bridge stanchion when – just like that' – he snapped his fingers quickly once, twice, thrice – 'bullets began to crack all over the place. Somehow the Nazis had got wind of our plan and had planted an ambush. The sudden shock knocked me off the bridge into the river and luckily I had the presence of mind to stay under water until the current – it was very fast just there – pulled me out of sight of their guns. King Kong, our leader – he was magnificent! He got away right from under their noses. But the others—' He shrugged his shoulders.

'What were they shooting with?' I asked. 'Machine guns?'

The honest little Belgian patriot replaced his dirty black beret. 'Strangely enough, they weren't. You'd have expected machine-guns on a job like that but the odd thing was they all had sniper's rifles. They picked us off one after the other, like knocking tins off a wall. Every man hit – and there were eight of us – except King Kong. They couldn't hit him. What a man! He was born lucky, that one!'

'Strange,' I said quietly. 'The biggest target of all – and they couldn't hit him.'

'*Oui-dà!* Such a big target. But he was too smart for them was our great King Kong!'

A picture of sorts was beginning to take shape in my mind. Here was the famous Resistance leader on the one hand, the man whose daring, giant strength and romantic affairs had made him the darling of all patriotic Dutchmen and almost equally popular with his Belgian comrades. A born leader who had done the Nazis much damage and who had risked his life repeatedly for his country. On the debit side were four strange facts which did not yet add up to any conclusion. He had been strangely apprehensive when I had tackled him over wearing insignia of rank to which he was not entitled. He had not then behaved like an honest man who had nothing to fear. The Gestapo had released his brother and girl-friend from captivity. It was not like the Gestapo to lose the opportunity of revenging themselves, even indirectly, on one of their most hated enemies. The third and the fourth facts were that on at least two separate occasions, someone had obviously betrayed a Resistance raid to the Gestapo sufficiently far in advance for them to plant a careful ambush. In each case the only common factor who had escaped was the leader – King Kong. The evidence was by no means decisive but it was growing beyond the stage of coincidence.

I poured out some more red wine for the little Resistance man. 'They say that King Kong has an eye for the ladies,' I remarked casually.

'Oh yes, sir, there they speak the truth! He is *très galant* – not a girl who would not give anything to feel those big arms around her. I tell you, the pretty heiress who lives in the big château on the hill beyond Laeken – they say she gave all her jewellery, her family heirlooms, for his Resistance group war funds.' He smiled tolerantly. 'They also say he gave the sparklers away to other girls here in Brussels. But it is all rumours, rumours, where King Kong is concerned. There never was a great man who didn't have some dirty rumours spread about him by the envious.'

Shortly afterwards the interview ended. I drove off at once to the château near Laeken and found the lady of the castle at home. After the preliminary courtesies we began to discuss Lindemans. Yes, she had given him her family jewels but she was careful to stress that she had done so out of patriotic regard for the Resistance movement. He was a great man, indeed, but he had his weaknesses. She suspected that he had embezzled the jewels and not sold them for Resistance funds.

'What makes you thing that, Countess?' I asked.

'I do not like saying so, because after all he is such a brave man and has done such fine things for Belgium. But one day I saw a girl in the town wearing one of my emerald pendants. She was not a respectable girl, you understand? The pendant had belonged to my mother and I did not think it suitable that a girl of this kind should wear it. I thought perhaps the Resistance men had sold it locally to raise money, so I asked the girl if she would sell it to me, without telling her that it had once been mine. She said King Kong had given it to her and would strangle her if she sold it.'

'Did you find out her name?'

The Countess sighed. 'Ah, if there had only been the one girl. No, there were two – Mia Zeist was one and the other was called – let me see – ah, yes, Margaretha Delden. They were both notorious tavern girls here.'

Fortunately she did not glance up as she spoke for she would have seen a strange look on my face. Mia Zeist and Margaretha Delden were both listed on my security files as paid and highly valuable agents of the German Abwehr!

Terminating the interview as soon as I could without disturbing the conventions, I drove back to Brussels as fast as the camouflaged staff car would take me. There I put a telephone call through to Intelligence Headquarters at Antwerp. After some delay Wilhelm, my assistant, was brought to the telephone. Had he the addresses of Mia Zeist and Margaretha Delden? Yes, he could produce them, and after a few minutes did so. I borrowed a couple of security policemen from the Dutch Intelligence in Brussels and together we rushed to the first address.

We were too late. The flat was empty. Mia Zeist had fled – we learned later – to Vienna.

Jumping into the staff car, we drove to Margaretha Delden's apartment. The door was heavily bolted. We had no search warrant but there was no time to observe the niceties of etiquette. We smashed the door in. We burst into her room and found her lying on the bed. Normally she must have been a pretty girl but poison does not improve one's features. Her face was a mottled colour, like those marbled endpapers one sometimes comes across in old books and ledgers. Her lips were a ghastly magenta in colour and were stretched in a mirthless grin. She was still just breathing when we found her but she died in hospital that afternoon, without uttering a word.

So two vital witnesses in what I was already calling mentally the 'Lindemans Case' were to be written off the list. One had wisely fled in time. The other had killed herself and in dying had been faithful to the end to Lindemans. Although to him she had only been one of many. We recovered the Countess's emerald pendant but that was poor consolation.

I spent a further day and a night in Brussels, combing the back streets, the sordid cafés and the smoky cellars for more details of Lindeman's career. Gradually the jigsaw was being pieced together. Several independent witnesses confirmed that when his younger brother had been captured by the Abwehr, Lindemans was deeply in debt. In spite of his popularity various tradesmen and private citizens to whom he owed comparatively large sums were threatening to foreclose on him. I also learned that the cabaret dancer Veronica, who had been captured at the same time as the younger brother, had been King Kong's sweetheart from childhood. In spite of his countless amours and intrigues she had always been constant to him and he had always in the end come back to her. The Nazis must have known this and yet they had released both her and the younger brother without so much as breaking a leg or two or tearing out the odd fingernail as a memento of their enforced visit. It was not like the Nazis to show such clemency.

Other witnesses confirmed that, coinciding with the release of his sweetheart and his brother, Lindemans became suddenly affluent. Not only did he pay off all his debts but he lived even more riotously and expensively. He also grew increasingly reckless in his guerrilla battles with the Nazis. Each raid was more daring than the last and each suffered heavier casualties. Always the heroic leader escaped by the skin of his teeth, blazing away with his arsenal of weapons and using his giant strength to save himself. He would swear blood-curdling threats of vengeance on the Judas who must have betrayed the raid in advance but strangely enough the traitor was never discovered. And tragically there was never a lack of volunteers to accompany the redoubtable King Kong on his forays. It was considered an honour to risk almost certain death at his side.

It seemed strange to me that no breath of suspicion tarnished King Kong's own reputation. All the survivors whose stories I listened to were loud in their praises of his daring and resourcefulness. Surely, I thought, it should sooner or later have struck someone as a strange coincidence that King Kong himself always escaped. On reflection I realised that the very extent of his reputation could be a formidable cloak for treacherous activities. This swaggering giant of a man with his gallantry and lavish ways would appear almost superhuman, an indestructible being, to the little unknown men – the real heroes – who themselves hero-worshipped him and went gaily to their deaths for a smile and a pat on the back from one of his huge hands. And there was always the inescapable fact that he had himself been wounded, shot through the lung, and then captured by the German Security Police.

This idea made me pause. Was I being premature in condemning him as a spy, in spite of the evidence against him? Not even the fat Herr Strauch of the Nazi Intelligence in the Netherlands would thus risk the life of a valuable agent just to add circumstantial detail to the appearance of an arrest.

I pondered over this problem for several hours, chain-smoking one cigarette after another. It was the one piece that completely upset the jigsaw which I had painstakingly fitted together. On all other counts Lindemans was to be strongly suspected as a traitor. But this one inexplicable fact seemed to disprove his guilt. And then, accidentally, a possible explanation hit me. As was always my habit, I was mentally retesting all the links in the chain of evidence in the Lindemans Case to date. I had reached the point where the Countess had spoken about Mia Zeist and Margaretha Delden. To find out their addresses I had had to telephone all the way to Antwerp, although I was actually in Brussels, their home-town. The local Field Security had not known their addresses. Dutch Intelligence Headquarters in Brussels had not known. But S.H.A.E.F. Intelligence had known. We were all on the same side, fighting for the same general cause, but we had not pooled our information. There were always those petty rivalries and jealousies, the urge to keep the 'plums' of information to one's own headquarters, which tended to mar the co-operation between different services and different countries, all ostensibly on the same side for the same purpose.

Human nature being fairly constant the world over, it was reasonable to assume that a similar rivalry might exist between the three different branches of the German Intelligence – the Gestapo (the Security Police of the S.S.), the Abwehr (the Counter-Intelligence Service) and the Sicherheitsdienst (the German Field Security Police). If, as I suspected, Lindemans was a traitor in the pay of the Abwehr, since both his notorious girl-friends had belonged to it, the Gestapo and the S.D. Police might easily not have known this. Thinking of him only as one of the most redoubtable Resistance leaders, and of all men he was least able to disguise his bulk and appearance, they would probably shoot him on sight, only afterwards discovering that he was a valuable ally.

If this reasoning were true, what a blessing in disguise was this bullet wound to Lindemans! It was the perfect answer to anyone who might suspect that he was a traitor. And thanks to this ironic stroke of fortune he would have been able to go his way unscathed, betraying his comrades to sudden death, and condemning no one would know how many British and Belgian agents along the escape-route out of Occupied Europe to the torments of the Gestapo.

I decided that the circumstantial evidence against Lindemans was sufficiently strong to warrant my cross-examining him in person. I sent a message to the Headquarters of Dutch Intelligence at Castle Wittouck, where Lindemans was supposed to have reported me for my cavalier conduct in ripping off his badges a few days before. Needless to say, he had not acted on his threat. Instead I mentioned that I wanted the opportunity of a talk with him although I was careful not to reveal the main purpose behind my wish. Lindemans had many friends in high places, as was natural for so famous a Resistance leader, and I dared not risk the possibility of some casual remark or deliberate 'tip' forewarning him of my real purpose. So I merely left word that he was to report to me at eleven o'clock next morning at the Palace Hotel, Brussels, where S.H.A.E.F. officers were billeted.

The next morning I was punctual at the rendezvous. It was a warm, balmy morning in which only peace seemed possible in the sunshine. But the war itself was only a few miles away and everywhere, even in the lounge of this luxurious hotel, war had left its trademark. The military had moved in and businesslike folding tables and wooden chairs had replaced the luxurious armchairs where the social *élite* of Brussels had once gossiped over their coffee.

The chimes of eleven o'clock rang mellowly through the lounge but there was yet no sign of Lindemans. I was not perturbed. He could hardly avoid coming, since I had left specific instructions, but he could assert his native arrogance by arriving late. As I ran mentally through the questions to be asked, my right hand felt the rough comfort of the serrated grip of my Walthur automatic pistol which was loose in its holster. The action was cocked and there was a round in the breach. A slight pressure and it was ready for action. Lindemans might not yet realise that this was to be a life-or-death meeting for him but I did. Compared to his height and great strength, I was a little weakling and in unarmed combat would not have rated my life worth a minute once those massive hairy hands clamped down on me. But had not Damon Runyon, the scribe of Broadway, described the automatic pistol as 'the old equaliser'? Having it close to my hand cancelled out the physical difference between Lindeman and myself. I had some natural talent for shooting and hours of practice with my favourite Walthur had made me something of an expert. In any case, if King Kong objected too strongly to my questions, I could hardly miss the vast target he presented across the narrow width of a coffee-table.

The minutes went by and still there was no sign of him. I had expected him to be perhaps ten minutes or a quarter of an hour late, even half an hour if he wanted to gain some revenge for the humiliation he had suffered at the Antwerp Security Camp. But when it was after twelve o'clock and he had not arrived, I began to wonder whether I had perhaps misjudged his arrogance. Was he so confident in his reputation and the friendships he enjoyed with the politically powerful that he would deliberately disobey a specific order?

I had waited nearly two hours when I found the answer. Two young

Dutch captains strode smartly into the lounge of the hotel. From their bandbox appearance and the bright armbands they wore, I knew them as staff captains from the Netherlands General Headquarters staff. They marched over to my table and saluted in unison. One of them spoke. 'You are waiting for Lindemans, sir?'

'I am. And have been for nearly two hours.'

'We're sorry, sir, that you've been kept waiting. Lindemans cannot keep the appointment. He's had other orders.'

'Other orders? Whose orders?' I was growing angry but did not want these glossy young men to know it.

They drew themselves up even more erect and a tone of reverence crept into the spokesman's voice, like the hushed tone that the faithful use when they speak of God. 'Lindemans left this morning on a very special mission.'

My throat contracted so that I could hardly speak. I had hoped that following our meeting that would not now take place, Lindemans' treacherous activities would be curtailed even if I did not at once prove his guilt. And now he had not only eluded me but was probably this very moment leading brave men of the Resistance into a well-prepared trap.

'With the Interior Forces?' I asked.

The two staff captains hesitated and then assumed the importance that nearly all men show when they know a major secret of which their interrogator is ignorant. 'No, sir. He has been attached to the Canadians for special intelligence duties, but we are not permitted to tell you what those are, sir.'

(Later I learned what had happened. The Canadians required a really trustworthy local man who could secretly enter Eindhoven which was still in German hands and get in touch with the leader of the Resistance in that area. The messenger was to inform the Resistance leader that large Allied parachute landings were to take place north of Eindhoven the following Sunday morning, September 17th, and the Resistance leader was to prepare and concentrate his men to aid the paratroops and exploit the initial German confusion. The Canadians applied to Dutch Head-quarters who at once thought of Lindemans as the man for this special mission, little knowing that he might be a traitor and that I was on his track. One cannot blame them for not suspecting Lindemans, although it must be added that the facts about him, his reckless spending, his constant miraculous escapes from ambushes, had been known to them for months, and were so plain that it had only taken me a few days to collect them and tot them up. Sending Lindemans on such an errand was equivalent to broadcasting the news of the forthcoming Allied parachute landings on the B.B.C. news bulletins.)

But I did not know that the landings were about to take place. All I could then hope – a pious hope! – was that the special mission Lindemans was engaged on would not cost us too dear in casualties. All I could do was to carry out that last resort of those who have failed – to make out my official report and send it to S.H.A.E.F.

What happened three days later is too well known to the world to need more than the briefest of descriptions. At dawn on September 17th the largest airborne landing in the history of warfare took place. Nearly 10,000 men of the British 1st Airborne Division were dropped at Arnhem, while 20,000 American paratroops and 3,000 Poles were dropped at Grave and Nijmegen. Their task was to secure and hold bridgeheads over the Maas Canal, the Waal River and the Neder Rijn while armoured spearheads from the main forces plunged down the major road to join up with these outposts and force the water crossings in bulk. The operation under its code-name 'Operation Market-Garden' was like threading beads on to a necklace of armour and fire power. It was a daring plan and everything depended on the surprise effect to be obtained by dropping parachute troops well behind the enemy's front lines. If the Germans in the rear areas were taken entirely by surprise, it was estimated that several days must pass before they could regroup for an attack on the airborne bridgeheads. By this time the main forces would be well on their way and if the paratroops, reinforced with supplies of food and ammunition dropped by air, could hold out, a brilliant victory would result.

Everything seemed to be going according to plan. Air reconnaissance on the morning of September 16th showed that there was no abnormal German activity in the Arnhem area. But after dark that night the German Panzers rumbled quietly into position, taking up hull-down positions behind the hedgerows and ditches around the vital dropping area. At dawn the paratroops dropped out of the grey sky but not to find the enemy surprised and confused. From the start it was obvious that something had gone wrong but at the same time everyone thought that a lucky coincidence had caused the Germans to consolidate their armour and infantry in the one place where they were neither expected nor wanted.

Nine days later, nine days of gallant and hopeless fighting against an enemy that surrounded them on all sides, with food and ammunition running out and with their ring of defence drawn so tight that air-dropped supplies were more likely to land among the Germans than themselves, 2,400 survivors of the heroic 'Red Devils of Arnhem' struggled to safety back across the Waal River, leaving 7,000 casualties behind them. The daring *coup* had failed. Montgomery had suffered his first and only major defeat of the war. The war itself was to be continued for another eight months of killing and devastation. In the 'Black Winter' of wrecked dikes and trampled harvests that was to follow, nearly 200,000 Dutch men and women were to die through flood and famine. But still no one apart from myself seemed to suspect the real cause behind the failure of the operation. It was 'one of those things', 'the luck of the game' and so on. I was already fairly certain in my own mind that Lindemans was a traitor. Later, learning some hints of what his secret mission for the Canadians had entailed, I was all the more convinced.

THE SPY

JAMES FENIMORE COOPER

THE SPY

This extract is taken from one of the earliest spy
stories ever written, set during the American War of
Independence.

The commencement of the following year was passed, on the part of the
Americans, in making great preparations, in conjunction with their allies,
to bring the war to a close. In the south, Greene and Rawdon made a
bloody campaign, that was highly honourable to the troops of the latter,
but which, by terminating entirely to the advantage of the former, proved
him to be the better general of the two.

New York was the point that was threatened by the allied armies; and
Washington, by exciting a constant apprehension for the safety of that
city, prevented such reinforcements from being sent to Cornwallis as
would have enabled him to improve his success.

At length, as autumn approached, every indication was given that the
final moment had arrived.

The French forces drew near to the royal lines, passing through the
Neutral Ground, and threatened an attack in the direction of Kings-
bridge, while large bodies of the Americans were acting in concert. By
hovering around the British posts and drawing nigh in the Jerseys, they
seemed to threaten the royal forces from that quarter also. The
preparations partook of the nature of both a siege and a storm. But Sir
Henry Clinton, in the possession of intercepted letters from Washington,
rested securely within his lines, and cautiously disregarded the solici-
tations of Cornwallis for succour.

It was at the close of a stormy day in the month of September, that a
large assemblage of officers was collected near the door of a building that
was situated in the heart of the American troops, who held the Jerseys.
The age, the dress, and the dignity of deportment, of most of these
warriors indicated them to be of high rank; but to one in particular was
paid a deference and obedience that announced him to be of the highest.
His dress was plain, but it bore the usual military distinctions of
command. He was mounted on a noble animal of a deep bay; and a group
of young men, in gayer attire, evidently awaited his pleasure, and did his
bidding. Many a hat was lifted as its owner addressed this officer; and
when he spoke, a profound attention, exceeding the respect of mere
professional etiquette, was exhibited on every countenance. At length the
general raised his own hat, and bowed gravely to all around him. The

salute was returned, and the party dispersed, leaving the officer without a single attendant, except his body servants and one aid-de-camp. Dismounting, he stepped back a few paces, and for a moment viewed the condition of his horse with the eye of one who well understood the animal, and then casting a brief but expressive glance at his aid, he retired into the building, followed by that gentleman.

On entering an apartment that was apparently fitted for his reception, he took a seat, and continued for a long time in a thoughtful attitude, like one in the habit of communing much with himself. During this silence, the aid-de-camp stood in expectation of his orders. At length the general raised his eyes, and spoke in those low placid tones that seemed natural to him.

'Has the man whom I wished to see arrived, sir?'

'He waits the pleasure of your excellency.'

'I will receive him here, and alone, if you please.'

The aid bowed and withdrew. In a few minutes the door again opened, and a figure gliding into the apartment, stood modestly at a distance from the general, without speaking. His entrance was unheard by the officer, who sat gazing at the fire, still absorbed in his own meditations. Several minutes passed, when he spoke to himself in an under tone—

'To-morrow we must raise the curtain, and expose our plans. May heaven prosper them!'

A slight movement made by the stranger caught his ear, and he turned his head, and saw that he was not alone. He pointed silently to the fire, towards which the figure advanced, although the multitude of his garments, which seemed more calculated for disguise than comfort, rendered its warmth unnecessary. A second mild and courteous gesture motioned to a vacant chair, but the stranger refused it with a modest acknowledgment. Another pause followed, and continued for some time. At length the officer arose, and opening a desk that was laid upon the table near which he sat, took from it a small, but apparently heavy bag.

'Harvey Birch,' he said, turning to the stranger, 'the time has arrived when our connexion must cease; henceforth and for ever we must be strangers.'

The pedler dropped the folds of the great coat that concealed his features, and gazed for a moment earnestly at the face of the speaker; then dropping his head upon his bosom, he said meekly—

'If it be your excellency's pleasure.'

'It is necessary. Since I have filled the station which I now hold, it has become my duty to know many men, who, like yourself, have been my instruments in procuring intelligence. You have I trusted more than all; I early saw in you a regard to truth and principle that, I am pleased to say, has never deceived me – you alone know my secret agents in the city, and on your fidelity depend, not only their fortunes, but their lives.'

He paused, as if to reflect, in order that full justice might be done to the pedler, and then continued—

'I believe you are one of the very few that I have employed who have acted faithfully to our cause; and, while you have passed as a spy of the enemy, you have never given intelligence that you were not permitted to divulge. To me, and to me only of all the world, you seem to have acted with a strong attachment to the liberties of America.'

During this address, Harvey gradually raised his head from his bosom, until it reached the highest point of elevation; a faint tinge gathered in his cheeks, and, as the officer concluded, it was diffused over his whole countenance in a deep glow, while he stood proudly swelling with his emotions, but with eyes that modestly sought the feet of the speaker.

'It is now my duty to pay you for these services; hitherto you have postponed receiving your reward, and the debt has become a heavy one – I wish not to under-value your dangers; here are a hundred doubloons; you will remember the poverty of our country, and attribute to it the smallness of your pay.'

The pedler raised his eyes to the countenance of the speaker; but, as the other held forth the money, he moved back, as if refusing the bag.

'It is not much for your services and risks, I acknowledge,' continued the general, 'but it is all that I have to offer; at the end of the campaign, it may be in my power to increase it.'

'Does your excellency think that I have exposed my life, and blasted my character, for money?'

'If not for money, what then?'

'What has brought your excellency into the field? For what do you daily and hourly expose your precious life to battle and the halter? What is there about me to mourn, when such men as you risk their all for our country? No – no – no – not a dollar of your gold will I touch; poor America has need of it all!'

The bag dropped from the hand of the officer, and fell at the feet of the pedler, where it lay neglected during the remainder of the interview. The officer looked steadily at the face of his companion, and continued—

'There are many motives which might govern me, that to you are unknown. Our situations are different; I am known as the leader of armies – but you must descend into the grave with the reputation of a foe to your native land. Remember that the veil which conceals your true character cannot be raised in years – perhaps never.'

Birch again lowered his face, but there was no yielding of the soul in the movement.

'You will soon be old; the prime of your days is already past; what have you to subsist on?'

'These!' said the pedler, stretching forth his hands, that were already embrowned with toil.

'But those may fail you; take enough to secure a support to your age. Remember your risks and cares. I have told you that the characters of men who are much esteemed in life depend on your secrecy; what pledge can I give them of your fidelity?'

'Tell them,' said Birch, advancing, and unconsciously resting one foot on the bag, 'tell them that I would not take the gold!'

The composed features of the officer relaxed into a smile of benevolence, and he grasped the hand of the pedler firmly.

'Now, indeed, I know you; and although the same reasons which have hitherto compelled me to expose your valuable life will still exist, and prevent my openly asserting your character, in private I can always be your friend; fail not to apply to me when in want or suffering, and so long as God giveth to me, so long will I freely share with a man who feels so nobly and acts so well. If sickness or want should ever assail you, and peace once more smiles upon our efforts, seek the gate of him whom you have so often met as Harper, and he will not blush to acknowledge you in his true character.'

'It is little that I need in this life,' said Harvey; 'so long as God gives me health and honest industry, I can never want in this country; but to know that your excellency is my friend, is a blessing that I prize more than all the gold of England's treasury.'

The officer stood for a few moments in the attitude of intense thought. He then drew to him the desk, and wrote a few lines on a piece of paper, and gave it to the pedler.

'That Providence destines this country to some great and glorious fate I must believe, while I witness the patriotism that pervades the bosom of her lowest citizens,' he said. 'It must be dreadul to a mind like yours to descend into the grave, branded as a foe to liberty; but you already know the lives that would be sacrificed, should your real character be revealed. It is impossible to do you justice now, but I fearlessly entrust you with this certificate; should we never meet again, it may be serviceable to your children.'

'Children!' exclaimed the pedler, 'can I give to a family the infamy of my name!'

The officer gazed at the strong emotion he exhibited with pain, and he made a slight movement towards the gold; but it was arrested by the expression of his companion's face. Harvey saw the intention, and shook his head, as he continued more mildly—

'It is, indeed, a treasure that your excellency gives me; it is safe too. There are men living who could say that my life was nothing to me, compared to your secrets. The paper that I told you was lost I swallowed when taken last by the Virginians. It was the only time I ever deceived your excellency, and it shall be the last; yes, this is, indeed, a treasure to me; perhaps,' he continued, with a melancholy smile, 'it may be known after my death who was my friend; but if it should not, there are none to grieve for me.'

'Remember,' said the officer, with strong emotion, 'that in me you will always have a secret friend; but openly I cannot know you.'

'I know it, I know it,' said Birch; 'I knew it when I took the service. 'Tis probably the last time that I shall ever see your excellency. May God pour down his choicest blessings on your head!' He paused, and moved towards the door. The officer followed him with eyes that expressed deep interest. Once more the pedler turned, and seemed to gaze on the placid, but commanding features of the general with regret and reverence, and then, bowing low, he withdrew.

The armies of America and France were led by their illustrious commander against the enemy under Cornwallis, and terminated a campaign in triumph that had commenced in difficulties. Great Britain soon after became disgusted with the war; and the independence of the States was acknowledged.

As years rolled by, it became a subject of pride among the different actors in the war, and their descendants, to boast of their efforts in the cause which had confessedly heaped so many blessings upon their country; but the name of Harvey Birch died away among the multitude of agents, who were thought to have laboured in secret against the rights of their countrymen. His image, however, was often present to the mind of the powerful chief, who alone knew his true character; and several times did he cause secret enquiries to be made into the other's fate, one of which only resulted in any success. By this he learned that a pedler of a different name, but similar appearance, was toiling through the new settlements that were springing up in every direction, and that he was struggling with the advance of years and apparent poverty. Death prevented further enquiries on the part of the officer, and a long period passed before the pedler was again heard of.

ACKNOWLEDGEMENTS

Grateful acknowledgement is made to authors, publishers and literary agents for permission to include in this volume the works listed below.

TAYLOR'S RUN from *The Looking-Glass War* is reprinted by permission of John le Carré, William Heinemann Ltd and Coward, McCann & Geoghegan Inc. Copyright © 1965 by D. J. M. Cornwell.

Chapters one and two from *Shadow of Fu Manchu* by Sax Rohmer are reprinted by permission of the Society of Authors and Doubleday & Company, Inc. Copyright 1948 by Arthur Sarsfield Ward.

The extract from *The Human Factor* is reprinted by permission of Graham Greene, The Bodley Head and Simon & Schuster, a Division of Gulf & Western Corporation. Copyright © 1978 by Graham Greene.

The extract from *The Champagne Spy* is reprinted by permission of Wolfgang Lotz, Vallentine, Mitchell & Co Ltd and St Martin's Press, Inc.

The extract from *Strange Conflict* is reprinted by permission of the estate of Dennis Wheatley and Hutchinson Publishing Group Ltd.

The extract from *Funeral in Berlin* is reprinted by permission of Len Deighton, Jonathan Cape Ltd and G. P. Putnam's Sons. Copyright © 1964 by Len Deighton.

THE TRAITOR OF ARNHEM from *The Spycatcher Omnibus* by Lt.-Col. Oreste Pinto is reprinted by permission of Hodder & Stoughton Ltd and John Farquharson Ltd.